# The Wife's Choice

BOOKS BY EMMA DAVIES

*Lucy's Little Village Book Club*

*The Little Cottage on the Hill*
*Summer at the Little Cottage on the Hill*
*Return to the Little Cottage on the Hill*
*Christmas at the Little Cottage on the Hill*

*The House at Hope Corner*
*The Beekeeper's Cottage*
*The Little Shop on Silver Linings Street*

*My Husband's Lie*

*Letting in Light*
*Turn Towards the Sun*

*Merry Mistletoe*
*Spring Fever*
*Gooseberry Fool*
*Blackberry Way*

# The Wife's Choice

## EMMA DAVIES

Bookouture

Published by Bookouture in 2020

An imprint of Storyfire Ltd.
Carmelite House
50 Victoria Embankment
London EC4Y 0DZ

www.bookouture.com

ISBN: 978-1-83888-612-7
eBook ISBN: 978-1-83888-611-0

*For dreamers everywhere*

# PROLOGUE

There's a very fine line between secrets and lies.

Some would argue they're the same thing, but I'm not sure I'd go that far. One thing I do know is that one follows the other as sure as night follows day. But which is it? Does night follow day, or does day follow night? Do secrets lead to lies or do lies lead to secrets? Surely it's both, parasitic; each dependent on the other for their existence.

It's something I've come to ponder many a time over the last few months. How both these things have changed the course of my life for the last twenty-five years, irrevocably, and at times with a cost I thought was too hard to bear.

So, what defines us? Is it the lies we tell… Or the secrets we keep?

But maybe that's the wrong question. Maybe the question should be: which is worse?

# CHAPTER ONE

They catch me sometimes, thoughts of you.

Usually when I'm least expecting it. The way the light falls reminding me of the lane outside our house in the springtime. Some sound or colour, a smile from a stranger or the light in someone's eyes. My pupils dilate, my heart beats fiercely in my chest, and the pain of it sheer takes my breath away.

And the worst thing is that I know you're out there. Somewhere. That your life goes on, and yet I'm no longer a part of it. You chose that for me. And I know you had your reasons, but it still hurts.

It's at times like these that I wonder how you are. Does it still hurt? I'm guessing it must, it can't be easy. Most of all I wonder if you have someone to share any of that with, someone who helps you when it's tough, just by being there. Someone like I could have been.

The woman in front of me tuts, and her impatience breaks my train of thought, but not my line of sight. I can still see the man who is four ahead of me in the queue. The dark curl of his hair where it creeps over the edge of his collar that so reminds me of you. You skin was so soft beneath it. The place you always loved to be touched.

There are six in the line at the post office, all of us hunched and waiting, more or less unmoving beyond the odd shuffle, or impatient cluck. But I don't mind. There are worse places to be than standing here gazing at a complete stranger and remembering what it felt like when you were mine.

'Alys?'

I drag myself back to the present. 'Hi Angela,' I say, finding a smile. 'What a beautiful day.'

She looks at her watch. 'Is it? I only popped in for a couple of stamps, but it's so busy in here I don't think I'll bother. Anyway, I'm glad I've caught you. Is your phone not working again today? Only I've messaged you twice.'

'I'm not allowed my phone on the shop floor,' I reply mildly. I'm sure I've mentioned this before. 'Sorry if I missed you. Was it urgent?'

She frowns. 'I wouldn't have sent the message if it wasn't. But listen, I need to know about Scarlett's cake. Are you sure that Esme has everything in hand?'

'It's all under control,' I reassure her. 'I thought I told you that at the weekend.'

'Did you?' She pulls a face. 'Only I know how forgetful you are at times…'

I let her comment wash over me. 'Well, don't worry, I definitely did check with Esme, and I promise you the cake will be ready for the party.'

Angela nods.

'Your hair looks nice,' I add. 'Have you been to have it done?' It's Monday, so I already know the answer, but I ask the question anyway.

'Marco, bless him,' she replies, smoothing her hand over her lacquered and beautifully elegant chignon. 'What would I do without him?'

I take a step forward as the queue shortens by one. 'I know, let's just hope he never moves to another salon, wouldn't that be awful?'

Angela's eyes widen in astonishment. 'Heavens, Marco would never leave me in the lurch. You really should give him a call, you know. He could work wonders for you.' She eyes the end of my lifeless ponytail which is curling over the top of my shoulder. Even its bright-red colour seems faded these days.

I nod. 'Hmm… but he's a bit expensive really and I…' I trail off, tired of making my excuses. 'Anyway…' I gaze at the queue still ahead of me, the minutes of my lunch hour rapidly ticking away. 'Don't let me keep you, isn't it your book club meeting today?'

'I'm on my way there now as it happens.' She takes a deep breath. 'Right, well I'll be in touch later to see how things are going. I still haven't heard from Edward about what colour dress Natasha is wearing, so if you get the chance perhaps you could find out?' She glances at her watch once more and turns to go. 'Oh, and Alys? Don't forget to have Hugh's suit dry cleaned, will you?'

I'm about to reply, but my mother-in-law has already gone. I let out a breath, slow and cautious, and my eyes stray towards the counter. Damn, the man up ahead has gone. I've missed him, and now it's gone back to being just an ordinary day, in a queue at the post office and I probably won't have time to eat. Again.

I take out my phone.

*Morning Tash*, I text. *How did the dress-hunting go?*

A row of dots appears almost immediately as my sister-in-law starts typing her reply. *I'm dead.*

I smile at her response. *Well that will certainly solve the problem.*

*Not funny, Alys, what am I going to do? I only found two dresses I actually liked and they were both midnight blue. Angela will never speak to me again. Alys, help me pleeeaaase… Where else can I try?*

I think for a minute. There's only one possible solution. *Are you free tomorrow? Come round about seven and I'll see what I can do xx*

*Oh God, THANK YOU!! Are you sure you have the time?*

I don't really, but that's not the point. *Of course! See you then xx*

She blows a kiss in reply. And I inch another step closer to the counter.

It takes forever to get back to the shop and by then only a miserable six minutes remain of my lunch break, or rather four, if you count the two minutes it will take me to pop to the loo and walk back down to the sales floor. The sandwich that I hastily made this morning is now redundant and I stuff it back in my bag; I'll probably eat it later while I'm cooking tea. I eye my banana without enthusiasm, but it's going to have to suffice.

Hilary is already pacing the floor by the time I get back to the desk but, despite her beady eye and ever-present desire to make my life a misery, I'm on time and there's nothing she can say. I just hope she doesn't notice that my phone is jammed into the back of my waistband, hidden by my jacket over the top. It's on silent but there's no way I'm missing a message from Esme. Not today.

Her text doesn't arrive until gone four. Is that a good thing or a bad thing? Her interview was at three, so maybe they were late in starting… or it was a long interview… they could have shown her round and introduced her to everyone… or maybe it was awful and it's taken her this long to bring herself to tell me…

My mouth is suddenly dry as I walk behind the nearest row of shelves. Hilary is with a customer and they're looking at zips; as long as they have no sudden interest in voile I should be safe from her gaze. I only need a minute…

*Mum it went great!! And they were so lovely… Dear God,
please let me get this job…*

*You will! They'll have loved you, who wouldn't?* My fingers
are flying over the keys. *When will they let you know?*

*Tomorrow! Urgghh, I can't wait that long…*

*I'm so proud of you, sweetheart. And so glad it went well.
I have to go, but I'll speak to you soon and you can tell me
all about it. Love you xxx*

*Love you more xx*

I blink. And then several times more in rapid succession. My
girl. My Esme. How did you get to be so gorgeous?

A noise to my right makes me start, but it's just another customer and I clear my throat, jamming my phone into the back
of my skirt. There's only another hour until we close. I can make
it. I take down a bolt of fabric on my way back to the desk and
lay it flat, ready for cutting.

I've worked in Harringtons department store for twenty-five
years and eleven months. A lifetime. Almost. Or perhaps that's
just how it feels. It certainly wasn't meant to be that way. I had
my whole future planned out, all my dreams spread before me,
but then I met you, on the day I started with them, and my life
changed forever. It's how I can recall the number of years that have
passed with such accuracy – not that it helps of course, quite the
opposite in fact.

I haven't spent all that time here though, not in this branch.
I moved… afterwards… and I've been in this division of the
company ever since. I was even a manager for about ten years, but
then they closed soft furnishings and my job went with it. We've

hung onto dress fabrics, and the wool, which still does okay, along with a few bits and bobs – zips, buttons and the like – but we're tucked at the back of homeware and we don't need a manager; just Hilary, our supervisor, who was drafted in from bedding, and Elaine who works with me two days a week.

'Is that for personal use, Alys?'

'Yes, but I have the book here to record it,' I reply, tapping the cover of the red hardback notebook which records staff purchases and samples.

Her mouth settles into a thin line. 'Good, well make sure I sign it off. That's an expensive fabric.'

I nod and continue cutting. 'Hmm, and with any luck it might be the perfect material for Natasha. I think I mentioned there's a big family party next weekend, for my other sister-in-law, Scarlett. It's for her engagement and it's all a bit posh so we've got to be in best bib and tucker.'

One of Hilary's eyebrows raises a millimetre.

'Natasha has yet to buy a dress, so I think I'm going to be making one for her. After the disaster at Christmas she can't risk another faux pas.' I smile, folding up the fabric as I do so. Hilary's face is blank. 'You know, when Tash turned up at the swanky meal my mum-in-law had paid for wearing an almost identical dress to her?' I add, trying to jog her memory. I'm sure I told her about it. 'You wouldn't have thought it would matter that much, would you?'

But there's scarcely a change in Hilary's expression.

'Anyway…' I pull the red book towards me, opening the pages. 'I thought this would look so pretty on her. I'll see what she says.'

I don't know why I'm bothering to explain, really. Hilary has never been one for small talk and today she seems more uncommunicative than usual. I know I'm babbling, trying to fill the silence. It's the silence I hate most of all.

She pulls her face into a tight smile. 'Perhaps when you've done that you could sort out the knitting patterns for what remains of the day. They're in a dreadful muddle. I don't think they've been looked at for quite some time, and there are a few new ones to go out.'

I finish writing up the details of the sample I'm taking home and nod, handing Hilary the book before walking over to the knitting section, an area I tidied only the day before yesterday. It doesn't do to argue.

I've got very good at whiling away the time, finding jobs to do and keeping busy, but it's still a relief when I see Hilary cross to the storeroom to collect the blue folder. She'll place it by the till, ready to record the day's takings, and it's my signal that the end of the day has arrived. I wait a couple more minutes before joining her behind the desk. I never want to look too eager to leave, but in my head, at least, I'm already back home.

'It hasn't been too bad today,' I remark. 'The morning was busy.'

'*Busier*,' corrects Hilary. 'But only compared to this afternoon, which was even worse than yesterday.'

I purse my lips. 'That's why I wondered about running the craft classes, you see. We'd easily have time to do them. And I'm sure it would bring people in…' I trail off. 'Did you have a chance to look at the information I put together?'

Hilary regards me stonily for a moment. 'Not yet,' she says flatly, opening the folder, but then her expression softens a little. 'You can go now if you like. I can finish up here.'

I should argue, but I don't normally get let off my end-of-day duties and I'm desperate to get home to see Esme. Whatever the reason for Hilary's spontaneous act of generosity, I'm going to take full advantage of it.

'Thanks Hilary, if you're sure?'

She smiles. 'Didn't Esme have her interview today?'

I'd had no idea she was even paying attention when I'd told her, let alone that she would remember. I nod, careful not to mention that I've already heard from Esme. 'I'm desperate to hear how it's gone,' I reply. 'It will be such an amazing opportunity for her.' I look around one last time. 'Right then. Everything is tidy and ready for tomorrow, so I'll see you then.'

I'm three steps from the counter before Hilary stops me. 'Oh, Alys. Sorry, just before you go. There's a letter here for you.'

I stare at the white envelope in her hand, wondering where she's magicked it from. She's holding it out for me and there's something about the way she's standing and the borderline smug expression on her face that makes the penny drop with a dull clank. I ease the letter from her fingers with a forced smile.

'Thanks, Hilary.' There's no way I'm going to give her the satisfaction of opening it now. Not in front of her. 'See you tomorrow.'

Back in the staff room I stuff the letter inside my bag. I don't even need to read it to know what it says. My full name is typed on the front of the envelope. Not 'Alys'. Or 'Alys Robinson'. But 'Mrs A. M. Robinson. 305592. Haberdashery'. It's from Human Resources, and I'm not sure what I'm more upset about. The fact that I've just lost my job, or that my husband couldn't even be bothered to tell me himself.

# CHAPTER TWO

The kitchen is full of the most amazing smell when I get home. I got stuck in traffic, I'm late, hot, thirsty, tired and utterly fed up. But all that changes the moment I walk through the door.

Standing by the cooker in flip-flops, shorts and a baggy tee shirt, Esme is frying onions. Her long hair is tied up so that it snakes in a thick copper coil down her back.

'God, that smells amazing! What are we having?' I dump my bag on the table and cross the kitchen to have a better look.

'Just a curry,' Esme replies. But it won't be *just* a curry, not when she's cooking it. 'Sorry, I needed to keep busy…'

She turns to look at me and I can see the taut strings of tension on her face, the longing in her eyes. I open my arms for a hug. 'Never apologise for cooking tea,' I say. 'Especially not today.'

Esme surrenders for a few seconds, squeezing me breathless, but then pulls away. 'Why? Have you had a rotten day?' She can see it on my face too, I'm sure.

'No,' I reply, dismissing her question. 'I rather meant that I knew you'd be on tenterhooks. And this' – I point to the pan – 'has always been your way through everything. Why should today be any different?' I smile fondly, holding her look.

'Oh, Mum… I want this job so badly!' She holds her palms to her cheeks, blowing out air between her lips. 'You know how that feels. When you want something so much you think you might die if it doesn't work out.'

I did know how that felt. Once.

'Then it will absolutely happen,' I reply. 'The universe wouldn't dare deny you, Esme.' I grin. 'Well, it had better not, not if it knows what's good for it.' I cross to the kettle, lifting it to check the weight before flicking it on to boil. 'So, come on then. Tell me everything… What was it like? What were they like?'

Esme slides the pan of onions off the heat. 'Just perfect…' She sighs. 'Nancy was… just like you, so lovely, warm, funny… absolutely on it. In fact, even in the short time we were together she felt like she could be a bit like a second mum – does that make sense? Like she's going to look out for me, teach me everything I need to know, and not mind if I make mistakes, just encourage me all the same.' She stops suddenly. 'Well, maybe not me. Whoever gets the job.'

I smile. 'Go on…'

'And in the kitchen it's just her and her son, and me… whoever… so a really small team, tight-knit, really collaborative. Nancy has already said that everyone is an equal as far as ideas and suggestions go. How incredible is that? I mean, I'm straight from doing my diploma, I don't know anything, but that didn't seem to matter and… Sorry, I'm gabbling.'

'Would you like some tea?' I ask, eyebrows raised in amusement.

There's a swift nod. 'And Theo, that's the son, isn't really much younger than I am. A couple of years I'd say… long hair in a bun and a beard…'

'Oh?'

Esme blushes and I suddenly feel incredibly old.

'Mu-um… I'd be there to work, not lust after the staff. Besides, what would I want a boyfriend for? They only get in the way.' She gives me a stern look and sighs with longing. 'I'd learn so much, Mum, and just think… I'd be working at *The* Green Room. If nothing else that's going to look amazing on my CV.'

'I know. I still can't quite believe they've come to our little corner of the world. I would imagine that they'll find Norfolk a little different from the bright lights of the big city. Did they say why they're opening here?'

'Only that Nancy said she wants to step back a bit from what they're doing in London. The restaurant there has its own staff now and pretty much runs independently of her. Plus Norwich is already making a name for itself with vegan and vegetarian food, so it seemed a good fit. That's all she said really. Oh, and that as she's got older she has a hankering to live by the sea.'

I shrug. 'Fair enough. They seem as good reasons as any, and I guess we don't need to know why they're here, we can just be grateful to have them in the first place.'

Esme chews the side of her lip. 'I'm glad, actually. That it's not in London, I mean. This is… smaller, more me, to start with at least. And this Green Room isn't going to be like its counterpart. It's a completely new business and Nancy says she wants it to be different too, to make its own mark, have its own personality and that will be down to all of us.'

I can see how much Esme wants this. It's the most amazing opportunity for her, apart from anything else, but to have the chance to be in on something at its inception… It's the kind of thing I dreamed about once upon a time.

Her face falls a little. 'There is just one little problem…'

'Oh?'

'If I get the job, I might struggle with some of the evening shifts because of the bus timetable. So, I was wondering… whether you might be able to give me a lift? Just to start with until I can get something else sorted out.'

I smile. 'The something else being to learn how to drive? I think that's an excellent idea.' A little flicker of resolve stirs itself. 'And I know your dad isn't keen on the idea, but you have to learn sometime and now would seem to be that time, wouldn't it?'

Esme's eyes light up.

I pour water into our mugs, giving the teabags a good prod. 'In fact… I can help you learn too if you like. Have proper lessons as well, but any extra practice we fit in can only be good. I'll talk to Dad. I'm sure we can work something out.'

'Would you really, Mum? Are you sure?'

But I only have to look at her face to know how certain I am. And besides, if I needed any more persuading, I have a letter in my handbag which provides all the incentive I need.

'I'm not sure what time he'll be home this evening, but I'll make sure I talk to him tonight. Strike while the iron's hot and all that.'

She pulls me into a hug. 'Oh, Mum, thank you so much!'

I laugh. 'Don't be silly. It's the right thing to do. But I might just have a quick tidy up, you know how he hates mess.'

*

'I'm not saying I think it's a bad idea, Alys, just that there's no real need to rush into it. There's the cost to consider for one. Driving lessons are expensive and that won't be the end of it. Once Esme passes her test she'll want a car too no doubt.'

I pass Hugh a plate to dry. 'Quite possibly. But we can afford it, surely?' The expense has always been my husband's justification for saying no.

It's gone seven, our meal eaten, and Hugh and I are standing, as we have done nearly every evening of our married life, doing the washing up. It's his one contribution to the domestic side of our life together. I dip another plate into the foamy suds and smile. The wrongs I've attempted to put right over a bowl of hot water don't bear thinking about, but then twenty-three years is a long time.

I wrinkle my nose, wondering how to continue. 'Or do you mean it's going to be harder now that we'll just be on the one salary?' I pause. 'Although I wouldn't worry, I mean, my redundancy money will more than cover it.'

The cloth stills on the plate and I look across to study the side of Hugh's face with its receding hairline, greying hair now mixing with the dark.

'Ah,' he says, grimacing. 'I was going to talk to you about that.'

I listen for a moment, making sure that Esme is still safely up in her room. 'Good, because it comes to something when your husband is the manager of the company you've just been made redundant from, and you don't even know it's going to happen.'

'Alys, I'm sorry… I had no idea you were going to get the letter today, believe me. HR got the jump on me before I'd even had the chance to discuss it with you.'

'But you still could have told me, surely,' I reply. 'We both know these aren't spur-of-the-moment decisions. You must have known about this for weeks.'

He has the grace to look ashamed. 'About the redundancies, yes. The fact that you were on the list, no. HR decide all these things, Alys, you know that as well as I do, and the recommendation list only came out just over a week ago. And I did plan to tell you, it's just…' He looks across at me, concern etched on his face. 'Just that there never seemed to be the right moment. I didn't want to upset you…'

My eyes narrow, roving his face for any trace of misdirection. 'I'm glad to hear you were going to discuss it with me at least. Otherwise I might be tempted to think I wasn't even being afforded the same courtesies as regular members of staff – you know, those people who aren't married to the boss.' I raise my eyebrows, holding out another dripping plate.

He swallows. 'Which makes it even harder for me. Perhaps I should have let HR deal with it completely, that way you would have been notified before. But, given that we *are* married, I asked them not to. I thought it would be better coming from me. Besides, you know that things haven't been going as well as they could have. Retail is a tough market to be in just now and department stores are being hit hard. Even if I can't discuss the intricacies of the business with you, you were well aware that redundancies were being planned.'

'Yes, but I didn't think one of them was going to be me.'

Hugh eventually takes the plate, seemingly unaware that water has been dripping to the floor. 'Look…' He clears his throat and lowers his voice. 'Look, I can't be seen to be showing you any favouritism, Alys, for goodness' sake. What would it look like if I asked for you to be taken off the list? And your department is simply not making the money it should; the footfall doesn't justify three members of staff. This was purely a business decision. Besides, out of anybody in that department, you're the most… comfortable, shall we say.'

'That's hardly the point.'

'Isn't it? I should have thought that was entirely the point. I have a responsibility to all my staff, and if I can make a decision that accommodates several good outcomes instead of just one, then I have to take it. Hilary is on her own, as you know, and Elaine's family circumstances are… well, not like ours.' He scrubs crossly at the plate in his hand. 'I did think you might be grateful though. You can't tell me you actually enjoy your job, and now you've been set free from it.'

His face smiles up at mine and I bite back what I want to say. I know he thinks this is doing me a favour, it's just that…

'And at least now you'll be getting the opportunity to take things a little easier. Have more time to attend to things in the house, for example. You're always saying how pressured you feel.'

I've asked him to help out every once in a while; it's not quite the same thing. I fish out some errant cutlery from the bottom of the sink, wincing slightly at the words in my head. But I do need to say something.

'Sorry… I'm just a bit frustrated. No, I'm angry. Can you imagine how I felt today having Hilary hand me my letter, knowing full well what was inside? She couldn't decide whether to be sympathetic or smug, but you know how Hilary can be, so I was left feeling utterly stupid. I bet she laughed all the way home.'

'I don't suppose she did,' replies Hugh, looking contrite. 'But I am sorry, Alys. I can't apologise any more than I am doing. Eric is on holiday and so no one told me the letter was going out today. I didn't find out until after you'd gone home.'

I'm studying him as he speaks and his expression doesn't change. Hangdog, it's called, and Hugh wears it well. A burst of music sounds from upstairs reminding me why we started having this conversation in the first place.

'Well I'm certainly not going to let Esme lose out because of it. This could be a perfect opportunity for her to learn to drive. And have a little car.'

'I still think we need to think about it,' replies Hugh. 'It's a big step for her.'

'Hugh… Esme isn't a child anymore, it's about time she started taking big steps.' I try to soften my expression. 'We have to let her, Hugh. It's time for her to grow…'

His head drops. 'I know but…' He holds out a hand, which I take despite the soap bubbles on mine. 'She's still my little girl, Alys… It was bad enough when she was away doing her diploma, but now she's back home again I can't help thinking about the day when she leaves us for good. It's getting closer all the time.'

I swallow, giving his hand a squeeze. 'She had a job interview today…'

'You didn't tell me that,' he accuses.

'No, it all came about rather suddenly… But it's a good job, Hugh, amazing in fact, she—'

'Where is it? Who for?'

'The Green Room.' I hold his look, willing him to accept this the way he should.

'What, *The* Green Room? But that's in London, that's—'

'No, no, it's not. It's right here in town, opening soon. And yes, it is the same company, but they've decided to open a new restaurant here, and if Esme gets the job, she'll be right in there on day one, part of the team that launches it. Imagine how exciting that will be for her, Hugh. How incredible if they pick her over all the other candidates… and think what an opportunity like that could do for her career.'

Seconds tick by with no reply.

'Look, I know you don't like the idea of her working in catering but—'

'It's such a brutal job,' he argues. 'The money's rubbish, the hours are long and it's just stress as far as I can see. There'll be no time for her friends, for…'

'Hugh… It's what she wants to do. You can't change that, and you mustn't, just because…' I trail off. I'm not going to say it, and I know that Hugh won't either. 'Esme has had her heart set on this for a long time. Are you really going to be the one to spoil her dreams, just because they're not the same as yours?'

I lift my chin a little, meeting his gaze, and I can see the moment when he backs down, when he accedes that I'm right.

'I do understand how you feel,' I add, my fingers twisting with his.

'I know,' he sighs. 'I just find all this so hard…'

'Our little girl is growing up, but that's a *good* thing…' I remind him. 'And besides, if she does get this job then it's here, in town. She's going to be living at home for a while yet and—'

A loud thump sounds from upstairs, following by several more as heavy feet hit the stairs.

'Mum!'

I roll my eyes at Hugh. 'Let me guess… there's a wasp in her room…'

But it's not that at all. I can see straight away from the expression on Esme's face as she bursts into the room, the light in her eyes.

'Mum! I got the job!' She rushes forward, hurling herself into my arms. 'I can't believe it!'

I try to hug her but she dances wildly, unable to keep still, loud squeals punishing my eardrums.

'But I thought they weren't going to let you know until tomorrow…'

'I know! That's what they said… But Nancy just rang…' She stops, suddenly choked with tears. 'She said I was just what they were looking for and there was no point looking any further. She and Theo agreed… they want me on the team.' She sniffs, laughing and crying both, her eyes shining with pure unadulterated joy.

Hugh takes a step forward. Their eyes meet. And I send up a silent prayer.

But I needn't have worried. He opens his arms wide, his face split by a huge grin. 'Your mum's just been telling me all about it,' he says. 'I think it sounds perfect. Well done you!'

Esme pauses for just a fraction of a second but then she hugs him right back. 'Really, are you sure, Dad?'

'Of course! Oh, I'm so proud of you.' He holds her at arm's-length for a moment to get a better look at her, drinking in what he sees, before grinning even wider and pulling her in once more. I meet his eyes over the top of her head and nod, smiling in response to his.

'So, come on then, when do you start?' I ask.

Esme turns. 'They'd like me to go in tomorrow, just to have a bit more of a chat, but soon… I could even start the day after…'

There's a query in her eyes and I know what she needs me to say. 'Actually, your dad and I were just having a chat about the driving thing. You'll need to check out your shift times against the buses first, but any you can't get to, I can cover, for now at least. Everything else we can work out in a short while; once you're settled.'

Esme's eyes widen. 'But Mum, they could be early, or really late. And what about your own job?'

I flick a glance at Hugh. This is a subject I haven't finished discussing with him yet but now isn't the time to dampen the mood. 'I think my job can accommodate it,' I say lightly.

My heart swells at Esme's happiness. It's everything I want for her and more. She's just like I was at that age – so full of life, possibility everywhere you looked, with your whole future spread out in front of you – and I can remember it as if it were yesterday. Of course, things didn't turn out for me at all the way I wanted – they didn't for you either – but in Esme… maybe I get another chance to see how things could have been.

# CHAPTER THREE

'Can I just say thank you,' says Tash the following evening. 'If I haven't already said it a hundred times over. I know you're busy, but you really are saving my bacon.'

It's Hugh's evening for playing golf, so we're alone in the kitchen and it's fine to talk. 'Yes, well, don't thank me yet,' I reply. 'Wait until you see the dress first; you might regret asking me. But in any case I'm not going to be as busy as I have been.' I slide Tash's drink towards her. 'Hugh made me redundant yesterday.'

The glass is halfway to Tash's lips, but it stops mid-air. 'Oh… bit awkward…'

I sigh. 'Not altogether unexpected, now that I've had a chance to think about it. Harringtons has been hit just as hard as anywhere over recent years but it still came as a bit of a shock.'

'I bet. What are you going to do?' she asks, taking a slug of wine as originally intended.

'I don't know yet. Hugh thinks he's done me a huge favour. He rather likes the idea of me being at home.'

'Yeah, why is that?' asks Tash, correctly deducing my mood from the expression on my face. 'It's a bit of an old-fashioned view, isn't it?'

'I don't know really. I think it might just be that Hugh *is* old-fashioned. If he'd had his way in the past I would have had a houseful of children to look after and still be tied to the kitchen sink now.'

'Really? I didn't think it was that bad…'

I look at her concerned face and smile automatically. 'No, of course it isn't. Besides, there's nothing wrong with that, if it makes you happy. It just isn't for me, that's all.'

Tash pulls one of my pattern books toward her with her free hand. 'So, what *are* you going to do? Because I should have thought that was obvious.'

I shake my head. It's a conversation we've had on several occasions before. 'Stop it,' I reply. 'I'm far too old to go starting my own business now.' I watch her while she takes another swallow of wine, a cheeky grin on her face. 'Right, down to business. What kind of thing do you have in mind?' I ask. 'Demure, flirty, femme fatale?'

Tash could pull off any of those looks; she's gorgeous. Five-foot-nine, with a model figure, ice-blonde hair, baby-blue eyes and nearly fifteen years younger than me. But, even though on that basis I should hate her with a passion, I couldn't wish for a better sister-in-law.

She sighs. 'Do you know what I'd love?' she says. 'Something feminine… soft, floaty. Anything that's not made of Lycra.'

Tash is a personal trainer. Even now, of an evening, she's wearing skintight leggings and a vest top. I unhook my bag from the arm of one of the chairs. 'Well, in that case…' I pull out the sample of fabric I cut at work the day before. 'What do you think to this?'

I lay the sliver of silk on the table and watch her reaction. Her mouth drops open into a soft 'O' of surprise. 'It's perfect… so pretty.'

'And *not* midnight blue.' I grin. The material is cream silk, covered in pale pink cabbage roses; hideously expensive, but on Tash it will look amazing.

'I thought we might do something like this…' I pull the book back towards me and thumb through the pages, stopping at a very simple design. The dress is cut on the bias and will drape itself softly around Tash's curves, emphasising them without being clingy. A flippy hem adds to the romantic look.

'Oh God… It's so beautiful. Angela would hate that, she'd be green with envy…' A wicked gleam comes into her eye. 'I love it!'

I pick up my wine glass, holding it up to clink against hers. 'Then that's it, job done.'

'Just like that?'

'Just like that. I'll have to take some measurements from you and do a couple of fittings, but I've made this dress before – a long time ago, mind, when I could wear things like this – and it doesn't take long. I'll buy the material tomorrow while I can still get my staff discount and I'll have it made by the weekend. Which gives us next week to tinker with it if we need to.'

Tash is staring at me. 'What do you mean, when you could wear things like this? Oh, make another one for yourself, you have to!' She pauses. 'Maybe not exactly the same, otherwise we'd just be doing an Angela all over again, but a different fabric, something brighter… red, or… green. With your hair that would look amazing.'

'Tash, I really don't think—'

'Why not?'

I give an exasperated sigh. 'Well, for one thing, I'm an awful lot older than you and another… I don't exactly have your figure.'

She stares at me. 'What bloody rubbish! You have a great figure, if you didn't hide it all the time and, as for being older than me, that's just a number. If you look good, you look good.'

I pull a face. 'I don't think so, Tash. That's kind of you, but…'

'Hugh wouldn't like it?'

'He probably wouldn't… but, in any case, I don't think I'd be comfortable in something quite so… it's just not me,' I finish, lamely.

Tash takes a swallow of wine, watching me. 'I disagree,' she says. 'But okay, I can see I'm not going to convince you.'

I take a sip of my drink, wishing I could be more like her. 'Right, now I'm glad we've got that sorted.' I pause. 'We need to talk about far more important things. Which is why I'm glad I've got you on your own,' I say, leaning in towards her. 'How are things between Ed and Angela now, between the two of you…?'

Tash's face softens. 'I still can't quite believe Ed stood up to her, but things are certainly different.' She gives me a coy look. 'It's like we've fallen in love all over again.'

'It was a big thing he did for you,' I reply. 'Quite possibly the biggest declaration of his love for you he could make.'

'It certainly was.' She smiles. 'Utterly ridiculous of course… that he should have even had to. I mean, for goodness' sake we've been married for six years, you'd have thought that Angela would have got over it by now. But I guess I'm always going to be in Louise's shadow whatever I do. I have to accept that.'

'Don't put yourself down, Tash. Louise wasn't perfect by any means. But she died of cancer, unfortunately, and although I wouldn't wish it on my worst enemy, it put her on the highest pedestal on earth and you—'

'Will always be the second wife?'

'Yes, I'm afraid you will… But Ed loves you, for you, not because you're a replacement for Louise; he's just made that perfectly clear. Telling Angela that her behaviour towards you was unacceptable was long overdue, we all know that. You two couldn't have gone on the way you were. I'm sure it's caused a few… ripples having him ban her from your house, but that can't be all bad.' I catch Tash's eye and grin. Angela has never been as bossy or unpleasant with me as she has with Tash, but there've been many times when I wished Hugh would stand up for me.

'There is that,' she admits, smirking. 'And at least the ball is now in her court. I'm not about to change, I've told her that, so if she wants any kind of relationship with me, it's up to her.' She stops, fiddling with the stem of her wine glass. 'Problem is, Angela's not really talking to me at all at the moment and that isn't what I want either. I've just swapped feeling angry and hurt by her behaviour for feeling guilty that I've caused a rift between Ed and his mother.'

'*You* haven't caused a rift, Tash, Angela did that all by herself. And clearly that was a risk Ed was prepared to take. Things will settle down, I'm sure. And I for one am very glad that Ed's taken a stand, because I'm banking on you being a part of this family for a very long time to come. Louise was okay, we got on well enough, but she wasn't you, Tash, not by a long chalk.'

She smiles gratefully. 'I don't know what I'd do if I didn't have you to talk to,' she confides. 'You're just so... so, sensible and wise... Sorry, no offence, I didn't mean that the way it very probably sounded.'

'None taken,' I reply, amused. 'I am old, there's no getting away from it. Not necessarily wise, but definitely old.'

'You are not!'

'I'm nearly fifty, Tash... how on earth did that happen? One minute I was full of energy and hope and now I'm...' I trail off, suddenly choked by the enormity of what I am about to say. 'Now I'm a middle-aged married woman with a grown-up daughter. It's crept up on me rather.'

Tash sighs wistfully. 'Yes, but what an achievement. A long and happy marriage and a beautiful and talented daughter. That's a lot to be proud of.'

'It is, I know.' I look up at her, nodding, knowing she wants me to agree. 'Did I ever tell you I was married before?' The words are out of my mouth before I can stop them.

'No...' Tash looks genuinely shocked. 'I thought you and Hugh had been together since, well, forever.'

I smile, ignoring the voice in my head telling me, *No, it just feels like that.*

'How old were you?' she asks. 'You can only have been about fourteen.'

'Not quite. Early twenties,' I reply. 'Just one of those things... Been to uni, got my degree, had my life all planned out and then, bam... fell in love.'

Tash picks up the wine bottle and pours herself another half glass. 'So, come on then, tell me all about it.'

She's settling in for a good story, but I'm going to have to disappoint her. If I start talking about you now, who knows where it might end.

'There's not much to tell,' I reply. 'I met him in the canteen at work, the day I started at Harringtons. We only said half a dozen words to each other, but evidently that was enough. There was just something about the way he said my name, the way he looked at me, like he knew every part of me. And yet how could he...?' I break off, laughing. 'And yes, I am aware that sounds crazy. Anyway, we met one day and then he left the next. My first day, his last... But two weeks later I bumped into him again and it was like meeting my oldest friend. Or so I thought at the time anyway.'

Tash leans in. 'Oh my God, that's so romantic. So what happened?'

I dip my head a little. 'It didn't work out,' I say simply. 'We were not meant to be together, after all.'

'Oh, but the chances of you meeting at all in the first place. A day later and you would have missed one another. It's like fate, isn't it? Like you were destined to be together...'

It was. That's how it felt.

I laugh nervously. 'Obviously not, given what happened. And our meeting wasn't that surprising really. I'd got my job at Harringtons because a friend of mine from uni knew Hugh and recommended me to him. And Tom was a friend of Hugh's so I expect I would have bumped into him sooner or later even if we hadn't met at work—'

'Tom? Was that him...?'

I blush. I haven't said your name out loud for years. The shape of it feels strange on my lips.

'Yes, but anyway… that was it really. We had a stupidly whirlwind courtship, got married and then split up a year later. Hugh was just about to be promoted to the Norwich branch and, knowing that I could do with a change of scene, offered me a job, and the rest is history. We got together a while later, and then Esme came along and here we are, present day.' I roll my eyes at her.

'Aw, it's still a nice story. First love and all that, so sweet.' She eyes me cheekily. 'Do you still think about him?'

'God no,' I lie. 'Not in years. And I have no idea where he is. I lived in Cambridge back then – he could still be there for all I know.' I shake my head in amusement. 'Blimey, you know you're getting old when you start harping back to your youth, don't you? That's the trouble when your children grow up; you start living vicariously through them, reminiscing on what you did when you were their age.'

'Well, I can think of worse things,' replies Tash. 'Esme is a complete credit to you and Hugh. And just about to set sail on her own wonderfully exciting adventure; you must be so chuffed for her.'

'Oh, I am. Landing her first job since gaining her diploma and it's at The Green Room… It really doesn't get much better and will be the biggest feather in her cap. I don't think she's stopped smiling since she got the news.'

'I really hope it all works out for her,' says Tash. 'No one deserves it more than she does. And I'm sure things will be fine this time around, it's a completely different venture from the restaurant in London, isn't it?'

I'm about to reply when I suddenly realise what she's said. 'What do you mean, things will be fine this time around?'

Tash looks a little uncomfortable. 'Nothing… Really, I didn't mean there was anything wrong…' Her mouth makes a little moue of apology. 'Sorry, Alys, I don't know the details, only that there was some funny business down in London. I shouldn't have said anything.'

'No, I'm glad you have. If there's anything not right about this job, I'd rather know now, for Esme's sake. What do you mean by funny business? Fraud? Breaking hygiene regulations? Cooking horse meat…?'

Tash smiles, shaking her head. 'I don't think it was anything serious. I mean, if it was, they wouldn't still be in business, would they?' She breaks off and bites her lip. 'Alys, I don't actually know what happened… it was just something that Hugh said. He—'

'Hugh?'

She frowns. 'Yes, Hugh. He popped in earlier to see Ed…' She studies my face. 'Oh, you didn't know. And now I've put my foot in it.'

I lay a hand on her arm. 'Tash, don't look so worried, you haven't done anything wrong. Hugh goes to see Ed all the time, they are brothers, it's allowed… I'm just surprised that he would be discussing something like this with Ed so soon after finding out Esme got the job. It was only yesterday.'

'I just got the impression he was a bit concerned, that's all. But then, maybe that's just Hugh being Hugh. He always has had a tendency to wrap Esme in cotton wool, hasn't he?'

I wrinkle my nose. 'He has.'

'And I'm sure it absolutely is the most perfect opportunity, it certainly sounds it. I should just ask Hugh about it if you're worried but, like I said, I doubt it's anything serious.'

# CHAPTER FOUR

'But what if I'm completely useless?' wails Esme the next morning as I pull into the small parking area at the rear of The Green Room.

'What if you're not?' I counter, smiling fondly at her. I reach across and stroke her hair. 'Okay, so this being your first day in a new job, I feel duly obliged to offer the statutory mother-to-daughter words of advice… whether you want to hear them or not.'

Esme smiles. 'Who are you trying to make feel better, you or me?'

'Hah!' I reply, caught out. 'But you're quite right. I'm terrified too. I won't be able to settle all day until I know it's gone well.'

'At least you didn't say *if* it goes well.' She groans, but she's grinning. 'Go on then, let's hear your pearls of wisdom.'

'Okay, well firstly, and very obviously, just do your best. No one can ask any more of you.'

Esme nods. 'Yep, got that.'

'Secondly, always be yourself, and lastly, remember that no question is ever stupid. We've all had first days and better to ask than pretend you know.'

There's an expectant look. 'That's it?' she says after a moment. 'After all these years, that's the sum total of your motherly advice?' She laughs. 'Thanks, Mum.'

'You're very welcome,' I say. 'Now go and be extraordinary.'

She takes a very deep breath, one hand on the door handle. 'God, I'm nervous.'

'I know. But that's a good thing. The most important things in life always make us nervous. That's how we know how much they mean to us.' I grin. 'You can have that one for free.'

'Right, I'm going,' she replies, leaning across to kiss my cheek. 'I'll see you later. Thanks, Mum.'

And just like that, she's gone.

I watch her as she walks to the restaurant door, poised despite her nerves. 'You'll be just fine, sweetheart,' I murmur under my breath, feeling suddenly emotional. It hardly seems a day ago that she was holding my hand for balance as she learned to walk, and now look at her. Vivacious, daring, full of joy and spirit; all the things I was, once. I start the engine quickly before I begin to cry.

*

Hilary doesn't make me feel any better. She's always had a tendency towards condescension but I'm not really sure I can cope with it today.

'I know you're not going to be with us for much longer, Alys, but we still have plenty to be getting on with.' I'm carrying several bolts of fabric when she says it; it's hardly called for. 'And I've asked Elaine to call in later too. I know she doesn't normally work today, but I thought you could show her the stock system.'

I've already walked past her, only one ear listening, but I slowly turn. 'The stock system?'

'Yes.' Hilary's face registers surprise. 'Maintaining that will fall to Elaine once you're gone, she'll need to learn how to use it.'

'I see,' I say quietly. 'And you'd like me to teach her, would you?'

'Yes please.' Hilary is growing bored of the conversation. 'And, let's see how we go, but I've made a list of the other duties that are specific to you and, if we have time today, we can pick off another couple and have a go at those too.'

I stare at her, feeling a slow bloom of anger rise within me. Anger I've got so used to quashing that I automatically force a smile before I even know what I'm doing.

Hilary checks her watch before glancing around the department as if expecting hordes of people to miraculously appear once the store is open. She's not looking at me and, as I stand letting the seconds tick by, I realise it's as if I'm not even here. I can't believe she is being so insensitive. Asking me to train up my replacement when I've only just been made redundant.

'Couldn't you at least wait until I've gone?' I mutter.

Two pink spots appear on Hilary's cheeks. *Oh God, did she hear me?*

'Well, I…'

An image of Esme from this morning floats into my consciousness, her enthusiasm, her self-assurance despite her nerves. How has my life come to this? I lift my head a little, trying to find some dignity.

'You see, the thing is, Hilary, I've worked at Harringtons since I was twenty-two. And maybe it wasn't the career path I originally wanted but I've worked hard, and when I was the manager here we were successful too. But you know what happened next. Staff got redeployed, the sales area shrank, they no longer needed a manager… But I've never complained. Or been uncooperative. I've simply got on with my job, serving and advising customers and trying to make what we have here the best it can be. So please don't ask me to end my time teaching someone else my job. I appreciate it has to be done, but with all due respect, Hilary, erm… I wondered if you might be the best person to do it.'

Dear God, did I really just say all that? Even though I didn't tell her what I really felt. I find a smile from somewhere. 'Sorry, Hilary. This isn't personal at all, I just feel it's a bit… insensitive.' I swallow.

Her cheeks are now flaming. 'I see,' she says, her voice barely under control. 'Well I think you've made yourself perfectly clear,

Alys. Although I must say I'm surprised. If you didn't want to be in the position you are now then you should have said something, instead of taking it out on me just because you've changed your mind.'

I shake my head, flustered. 'Changed my mind about what?'

'Oh, come on, don't act so innocent, not when you've just given your little speech. The redundancy of course. You can't have it both ways, Alys. Either you want to go, or you don't.'

'But I *don't* want to go... I had no idea I was even being considered for it.' I'm trying to recall the conversation Hugh and I had at the kitchen sink. And as far as I can remember I've never really discussed the redundancies with him, other than offering sympathy when I heard that he was having to consider it. But that was purely in my role as a supportive wife, not as an employee.

'And I'm expected to believe that, am I? Just like we're all led to believe that you don't get special treatment because your husband's the boss. That's a little hard to take seriously when you somehow get your wish, even though there weren't any voluntary redundancies being offered, and walk away with a very tidy lump sum. No, no special treatment at all.'

'No, it's not like that, I...'

I feel physically sick, struggling to make sense of her words. Because everything she's just described doesn't fit with the way things have happened at all. If they did, then that would mean... My thoughts come to a sudden stop. And in their absence a wave of embarrassment rolls over me. I've been made a laughing stock. Worse, I've been manipulated and humiliated. It's all I can do to remain standing and not run for the staff room.

I stare at her a few seconds more before turning and walking away, leaving her with her mouth hanging open in shock. She's clearly just worked out that I genuinely had no idea what she was talking about and, if anything, that makes it worse. Now I have her pity too. I dump the bolts of fabric I'm holding before taking down another from the display and proceeding to measure out and cut a length of it. I take it back over to where she's standing.

'I'd like to purchase this with my staff discount please,' I say, handing her the material I need to make Tash's dress. 'And then I'm going home. I'm sorry, Hilary, but I'm not feeling at all well.'

Her eyes narrow suspiciously. 'Really, what's the matter with you?'

'I… I probably shouldn't have come in actually. I haven't felt right since I got up this morning,' I reply, thinking on my feet. 'Perhaps that's what's made me… testy,' I reply. 'Sorry.'

I'm not even sure why I'm apologising when it's me who has been made to feel bad.

'But what about the department?'

'I thought you said Elaine was coming in?' I reply. 'With the two of you I'm sure you'll manage. It hasn't been that busy, after all.'

'Oh, for goodness' sake,' she splutters. 'You can't go, not just like that.' I look at her face, see everything she thinks of me reflected in her eyes, and know exactly who I have to thank for it.

I grit my teeth. No one else is going to stand up for me. 'Maybe I shouldn't,' I reply. 'But I'm going anyway.'

*

I don't go straight home. I don't think I can face having to stare what I've just done square in the face. I'm not sure who I'm most angry with – Hugh for letting people think that I wanted this redundancy, in fact that I might have even asked for it, or me for being so pathetic as to stay there in the first place. Instead, I wander through the outdoor market, marvelling as I always do at the variety of wonderful smells from the street-food vendors. It's something I usually enjoy, the bustle of folk going about their days, the bright-coloured canopies of the stalls lifting my spirits. Today, though, I feel so far removed from it all that instead I trace the streets to walk along the river.

I swing the bag I'm carrying onto my other shoulder. A couple of books, a water bottle, some papers, my lunchbox and some pens; all the contents of my locker. Not much to show for over two decades of work. Because I'm not going back. How can I? And Hugh will get his wish, after all. The stupid thing is he almost certainly thinks he's done me a favour. I'm furious with him, but it won't have been done deliberately, just without thought. Careless.

I come to rest on one of the bridges, pausing for a moment to feel the warm summer sun on my face. A soft breeze ripples the water beneath me as I gaze down at it, my distorted reflection staring back at me. The image is hazy, much like I've become. Not overweight exactly, but a little softer in places than I'd like. Ill-defined. A wife. A mother. But what else? I don't even have a job now.

And the money didn't even occur to me. How disgraceful is that? When other people have to count every penny. And yet I can lose my job and not even consider it a problem, not really. There was a settlement statement with my redundancy notice, but I scarcely glanced at it before shoving the letter back into its envelope, eyes widening as I took in the amount of money. So am I guilty of complacency? Or did I know, all those years ago, that my marriage to Hugh was a safe bet? I turn my thoughts aside and carry on walking. *Don't go there, Alys.*

My mobile goes off just as I'm climbing into my car, but I don't need to look at it to know who it's from. Hilary would have wasted no time in raising a hue and cry once I'd left, but I don't want to talk to my husband just now. So I ignore it and drive home. I can use the extra time I've suddenly found to make a start on Tash's dress. Which is exactly what Hugh finds me doing a few hours later.

I'm bent over the kitchen table with a mouthful of pins when he arrives, cutting out the pattern from the fabric I bought this morning. He eyes me a little warily. No doubt noticing that I've made no comment about his early return from work.

'What are you making?' he asks, frowning a little.

'A dress, for Scarlett's engagement party.'

He peers a little closer. 'Oh, well done. Yes, it's probably time to have something new.'

I turn over the piece of fabric I've been cutting so that he can see it better, running my hand along its silky length. 'Isn't it beautiful?'

He studies it for a second before flicking his eyes to my face and back down again. Classic Hugh.

'What?'

'Nothing… it's just a slightly unusual choice of material.'

I cock my head. 'Hmm, I just fancied something a bit different. Don't you like it?'

'No, I do… I just wonder if it isn't a little… gaudy.'

'Gaudy?' I stroke the material again. 'Oh… not romantic, or feminine even? That's what I was hoping for.'

'Maybe gaudy's not the right word… perhaps frivolous might be better, or…' Hugh stops. 'Oh dear, I'm not making this any better, am I? I really like it, Alys, it's just that I prefer you in slightly plainer things. I think they suit you better.'

I bite my lip. 'Oh. Well, maybe you're right, especially about the frivolous bit. Even with my staff discount it was pretty expensive. It's silk, you see.' I sigh.

'Is it?'

'Although of course, a dress like this in the shops would easily cost four times as much,' I add hastily.

'It will look lovely, I'm sure.' Hugh smiles. 'And you deserve to have something new.' He turns away, having settled the matter, and loosens his tie, dumping his bag on the side. 'Anyway, how are you feeling?' he asks. 'A bit better perhaps? I had a message to say you weren't well.'

I look up. 'And who would that have been from, I wonder?'

'I don't actually know,' he says carefully, catching the change in my tone. 'Monica took the message.'

That would be Monica, his secretary, who is good friends with Hilary. 'I see,' I reply. 'And did you speak to her?'

'Monica?'

'Hugh, stop being obtuse. You know perfectly well I mean Hilary.'

'I didn't, no,' he admits. 'She was busy on the shop floor, but I did get the gist of what happened.'

'Did you? And while she was explaining that to you, did she also tell you what she told me? That I'd been made redundant because I asked to be? That's what she'd heard – that despite the fact that there were no voluntary redundancies on offer, I somehow got my way, bagging myself a nice lump sum into the bargain. Although, of course, it had nothing to do with the fact that I'm married to you.'

I raise my head to glare at him. 'I've never been so humiliated, Hugh. They're all sneering at me behind my back – which is bad enough – but what I want to know is why they thought I'd asked to be made redundant in the first place? It had to come from somewhere.'

Hugh raises both hands. 'Well, don't look at me. Why would I say something like that? Besides, what you're suggesting wouldn't be the slightest bit ethical.'

'No, it wouldn't, would it? It would also be a lie. But it does make me wonder whether certain conversations you've had haven't turned out to be quite as confidential as you'd like. You are aware, I suppose, that Monica and Hilary are good friends?'

'For Chrissakes, Alys, I know you're cross about all of this, but you can't go around accusing Monica of having a big mouth.'

'I'm not just accusing her of having a big mouth, Hugh. I'm accusing you of repeating things I'm supposed to have said that I have simply haven't. Those ideas had to come from somewhere and how else would Monica have been able to pass on the juicy details?'

Hugh glares at me. 'Oh, that's just ridiculous! What on earth's got into you, Alys? This is nothing more than silly tittle-tattle; gossip spread by jealous employees.'

'It might be,' I agree. 'Although I'm not sure what they've got to be jealous of, Hugh. Because I certainly don't receive any other benefits at Harringtons for being married to you. Quite the opposite, in fact.'

He's watching me closely. 'So you don't actually feel unwell then?'

I hold his look. 'Other than a severe case of humiliation, no, I'm perfectly fine.'

He strides around the kitchen, jaw working, as he searches for what to say. 'Alys, you can't just walk out of your job… if that's what you've done. How do you think that looks? This could be extremely embarrassing for me.'

'Hugh, I don't care how it looks. I've been at Harringtons all my working life and, despite being careful and never raising my head above the parapet because I'm married to the boss, I finally understand that it's done me no good at all. So, yes, I think I have just walked out of my job. And, as you've managed to fix everything else, you can surely fix this. I don't care what you tell them, Hugh, but I shall be taking the remainder of my notice period as sick leave. Invent some hideous disease. Tell HR I'm suffering from stress, or that I've broken my leg in four places and the bones are being held in place with pins, I really don't care.'

I grind to a halt, trying to catch my breath. 'And that's another thing. This is just so typical of you. You're far more worried about how this is going to go down at work than the fact that I'm furious with you over things you've clearly said. Things you haven't denied, I notice.'

The seconds tick by.

'I don't need to deny them, Alys,' says Hugh quietly. 'Because I know they're not true. Just as I know that I would never do anything to hurt you. Now I don't know what's got into you today, but perhaps you *aren't* feeling well because you're certainly not your usual self. That being the case I'll overlook your hurtful comments, but you might want to think about what you've said.'

Hugh's voice is calm and reasoned. It's impossible to have an argument with him, he just refuses to get riled. It infuriates me, but it also leaves me with nowhere to go.

My shoulders sag. 'Maybe it's just a midlife crisis.'

'Isn't it me who's supposed to have one of those?'

I glare at him.

'Sorry, I wasn't trying to make light of it. What were you going to say?'

'I don't know,' I reply, shrugging. 'Except perhaps that it was seeing Esme this morning. She was nervous, yet so confident at the same time. And happy – on the threshold of a new and exciting part of her life. It made me realise how much she's growing up. That she isn't going to need me any more, and I'm wondering where that leaves me. No job, my role as a mum if not diminishing then at least undergoing massive change. Where did my life go, Hugh? Esme is just starting to live her dreams, but when did I live mine?'

He doesn't know what to say. Because he knows I'm right, and somehow that makes it worse. He regards me for a moment, obviously still smarting from my comments, and I'm sure he knows he should probably offer up some comfort. But he doesn't. Instead he paces back across the kitchen once more, a distracted look on his face.

'Yes, well, let's hope Esme's dream turns out to be just that and doesn't suddenly become a nightmare.'

'Oh, for heaven's sake, Hugh, why on earth would it do that?' I narrow my eyes. 'I see. You've got something to say about that too as well, haven't you? Tash mentioned that you'd been talking to Ed about The Green Room when she was here yesterday. So, what is it you don't like? I can't see how you can possibly have an opinion on it yet when Esme has only just started there. Or why everything has to be a problem.'

He rolls his eyes. 'I'm not saying it is. But forewarned is forearmed and it doesn't hurt to check these things out. I mean, what do we really know about these people? Beyond all the glitzy stuff we've seen in the papers. Nothing. And yet we're allowing our daughter into their care and—'

'We're not allowing her, Hugh. Esme has made the decision herself, something she's perfectly capable of doing. And it is her decision. You know, maybe it's you who's having the midlife crisis, after all. You just can't let her grow up, can you? I hate it too, the feeling that she's slipping away from us, but at least I try to let her have her wings, instead of clipping them.'

And for the first time I see anger flicking in Hugh's eyes. 'That's wholly unfair, Alys, and you know it. I only want the best for her and if that means checking out a few things, then so be it. I'm not meddling or interfering in her decision at all but she is still living under our roof and, as her father, I think it's only prudent to have a broader picture of her employer. Just as we did with her schooling, college and the university she went to. In fact, all the important things in her life, and that was simply to ensure her happiness. So please don't suggest I'm doing anything untoward here. Besides, you might be interested to hear what I've found out.'

'And what's that supposed to mean?' I hate myself for asking. I've taken the bait, yet again.

'Only that we've all seen photos of the owner, that rather garish woman with the ridiculous haircut, heard all about her business acumen and vision for the company, but did you know that there's a *Mr* Green Room too? And he's an altogether different kettle of fish.'

'Go on…' I intone.

'Reclusive on the one hand, shuns publicity, and yet when he is around, he's moody, aggressive, physically violent at times too. One of their former staff members gave an exposé last year, detailing how awful it was to work there.'

'Oh, honestly. It sounds like sour grapes to me – a disgruntled employee who thought he or she would cash in on The Green Room's popularity with a kiss-and-tell story. Hardly original. Besides, as far as I'm aware, the only people running this new venture are Nancy, the woman you think is garish, and her son. No mention has been made of anyone else.'

'Let's hope that's the case then because this man doesn't sound like someone we should be encouraging Esme to mix with.'

A noise sounds from the conservatory behind me. It's open to the garden against the heat of the day and standing there is Esme, an extraordinarily good-looking young man beside her.

There's a moment of agonised silence before the man's face splits into a wide grin.

'I'm Theo, it's lovely to meet you,' he says, stepping forward, his hand outstretched. 'And you're quite right. I think my dad's a complete arse too.'

# CHAPTER FIVE

If ever there was a time I wanted the ground to swallow me up, this is it. But Theo, to his enormous credit, keeps a smile on his face, seemingly unperturbed by Hugh's comment.

'Just dropping Esme home as promised,' he says, turning to her. 'We've had such a great day, haven't we?'

Esme manages to nod, but her face is scarlet and you don't have to be a genius to work out how she's feeling.

'That's incredibly kind, Theo, thank you,' I say. 'I'm Alys, by the way. And this is my husband, Hugh. Would you like to come in for a drink? Something cool, or…' But he's already shaking his head.

'Could I make it another time?' he says easily. 'Only I'm just on my way to meet a supplier for dinner and had better not be late.' He smiles again. 'Are you okay for transport in the morning, Esme? I can swing by this way and pick you up if necessary.'

Esme's expression is clear. I reply on her behalf, 'No, I can't let you do that. It's really no problem for me to drop her off. But thank you, Theo, it's very kind of you to offer.'

He looks almost as if he's about to bow and, with one final glance at Esme, still smiling, he holds up a hand in farewell. 'See you tomorrow,' he says, and then he's gone, retracing his steps out of the conservatory and back down the garden path with a jaunty gait as if he hasn't a care in the world.

No one says a word, conscious that, this time, Theo needs to be out of earshot before anyone speaks.

'What a charming young man,' I say, brightly. 'And good-looking too.' With his long dark hair tied up in a bun and neat beard, there is something very appealing about him.

'Yes,' replies Esme. 'He is.' She stares at Hugh, challenging him to contradict her. 'In fact, he's so nice he was determined to come in to say hello and introduce himself just now. He didn't have to, he could have just dropped me outside and driven off. And given what he heard when he arrived, I rather wish he had. But there you go, Dad, always thinking the worst, trying to invent a problem where there is none. Except that today I'm not going to let you spoil things for me, not when the rest of it has been so brilliant.'

She comes over to me and gives me a kiss. 'Hi, Mum,' she says. 'Would you like a hand with dinner?'

I shake my head. 'You must be exhausted,' I reply. 'So no, love, you go and chill for a bit, no more cooking for you. I'm glad you've had such a good day though.'

She smiles, running a hand through the coil of her ponytail. 'I might have a shower, actually, if that's okay?'

'Of course. Food will be a while yet.'

I watch as she drops her bag over the back of the chair where I've been sitting before and takes out her water bottle. An expectant hush falls over the kitchen as she leaves the room and there are so many things I could say at this point, but I don't. Just a look at Hugh is enough to make my feelings known.

He clears his throat gently. 'Right, well… I'll make a cup of tea, shall I?'

*

Hugh and I never did finish our discussion last night, if you could call it that. Esme barely spoke two words to him the entire evening and I can't say I blame her. I didn't do much better myself, not quite yet prepared to swallow his justifications. He's left for work now, but not before he had one last shot at trying to convince me I ought to go to work myself, even promising to have a word with Hilary so that there was no awkwardness. I think my glare was sufficient to deter him from saying anything further. I have no idea what I'm going to do now I'm not working but, for today at least, I'm going to enjoy my freedom.

I sip my cup of tea, relishing a more relaxed start to the day, before swinging my legs over the side of the bed, and standing up to finish my drink. I shall be dropping Esme off at work again this morning and I don't want to make her late; she's feeling bad enough as it is, for obvious reasons. I did offer to come inside with her and speak to Theo in order to apologise for the things Hugh said last night, but Esme gave me a pained look that was code for *don't be ridiculous, you'll only make things worse*, and so I just smiled and nodded. She's probably right. It's bad enough one parent putting their foot in it; two would be unforgivable.

An hour later, she grabs her bag from the footwell and hastens from the car, flashing me a cheery smile. If she's feeling nervous this morning, she doesn't show it.

'Thanks, Mum,' she says, before rushing across the car park, eager to be inside doing what she loves. I watch her as she goes, the stark contrast between her day and mine occupying my thoughts. I'm about to reluctantly head for home when a bright-red sports car darts into the parking space beside me.

Before I've even had a chance to pull forward, there's a friendly wave in acknowledgement and, almost immediately, the woman driver is out of the car and hurrying towards me. I wind down the window.

'Hi!' The smile that greets me is broad, the face animated with laughter lines and bright-red lipstick. 'You must be Esme's mum.' She slaps her forehead. 'Don't tell me… Alys?' A hand is thrust towards me, which I shake despite the awkward angle.

'Nancy?' Her hair is even shorter than I've seen in recent photographs, but it's definitely her. She'd be striking anywhere.

She nods several times. 'It's very good of you to drop Esme off,' she says. 'Especially as it's so early. I'm sorry about that.'

'No, it's fine, honestly. I'm an early bird anyway.'

We smile at one another. 'That must be where Esme gets it from then,' she replies. 'I'll see if I can get Theo to drop her home again tonight, save you having to come back. As long as you don't mind, of course. It makes much more sense to try to do this between us, doesn't it?'

'I'm hoping that Esme can learn to drive soon… But yes, in the meantime, that would be great.'

'Good. That's settled then.' Nancy beams. 'Well, it's lovely to meet you… In fact, would you like to come in for a drink? The kettle will be on.'

I pause, uncertain. 'I'd better not, but thank you anyway. I'm not sure that Esme would appreciate it.'

'Oh God, yes, good point. Parents, how embarrassing… What are we like? Another time then?'

I nod. 'Yes, I'll let her get a bit settled first.'

Nancy withdraws herself from the window. 'Right, well I'd better get on, crack the whip and all that.' She suddenly checks herself. 'I don't mean that at all…' And she holds my look. 'I'll take good care of Esme today, don't worry…' She gives a little wave, her bright-red lips pulled into a wide smile. 'Bye for now.'

I'm touched by her words; that was such a lovely thing to say. And, as Hugh's words from the previous evening come back to me, I realise that I don't want to let how he feels sour this new working relationship for Esme. Nancy's not garish at all, far from it. And if I'm going to say anything I need to say it now. 'Um, actually…'

Nancy turns.

'Would you mind if I spoke to you about something, just quickly…?'

'Not at all,' she replies, coming back to the window. 'But don't let's do it in the car park… I tell you what, I'll get Theo to take

Esme on a tour of our suppliers. It's one of the things we were planning to do over the next few days, so if it's today, that won't hurt at all.' She grins. 'And we can have that cup of coffee, after all.'

I climb from the car and follow her to the door. Christ, I feel old. And drab.


So I've read about it. I've seen photos. But I've never actually been inside The Green Room in London, and nothing could have prepared me for what it feels like to walk inside now. It's alive, literally… Hanging from the stained-glass ceiling, clinging to the walls and standing anywhere there's a space are plants of every shape and variety. Two enormous monsteras flank the entrance, towering above as you walk into the room but, for all that, the space is huge, airy, and full of the most amazing light. And smells. It's not unlike walking into a botanical garden.

'Esme said it was beautiful but… I've never seen anything like this.'

'Good,' says Nancy, a delighted look on her face. 'That's the idea. We want people to be blown away before they even eat the food. Which, we hope, is equally impressive of course.'

'I'm sure it will be. This is incredible and it looks as if you're ready to open.'

'A couple more weeks,' Nancy replies. 'We still have some last-minute deliveries of equipment to be made, as well as a few decisions to make. We want to get everything embedded too: all our menus, our suppliers, everything we do and how we're going to do it. I don't want anything to go wrong. Mainly for our diners' sakes, obviously, but also for ours. I want us to be able to enjoy this, not just on the first night, but every night, and stress brought about by needless irritations is not only preventable but soul-destroying too.'

She indicates that I should take a seat at one of the tables just as a peal of laughter echoes from what I take to be the kitchen.

'That'll be Theo,' she says. 'He's altogether far too cheerful in the morning, but it gets us all going. Let me grab some coffee and then I can despatch him and Esme on their way and she won't even know you're here.'

I sit down gratefully, head about ready to explode from all the sudden thoughts that have rushed in during the last five minutes. Not just how this place looks, but Nancy herself, so different from what I'd expected. I'm thrown. I wasn't sure what I would feel coming here, but I'm mortified and hugely embarrassed that Hugh, by taking the stance he has, might have made things awkward for Esme. Her employers have already shown themselves to be caring on so many levels and his overbearing attitude is the last thing she needs. I look around me, mildly panicked; I haven't a clue what to say to Nancy.

And she's back, much earlier than I expected, bearing a fully loaded tray which includes a plate of biscotti.

'Now you have to try one of these,' she says, placing the tray on the table. 'Or even several. They're a new recipe, and Theo thinks they're divine, but then he would. I'm not sure myself.'

'Oh.' I stare at the biscuits. 'I'm afraid I'm not much of a connoisseur. In fact, I don't really ever eat those.'

'Too crunchy?' asks Nancy, nodding. 'The trick is in the dunking. You see, the Italians do it with gusto, only in hot wine actually, not coffee, but we Brits are just too reserved. We think it's altogether too common, I expect, so we just flirt with the coffee when what's required is a really good wallow.' She stops to look at me. 'I never asked, sorry… Do you even like coffee?'

I laugh. Nancy looks positively distraught. 'Yes, don't worry… and I will dunk, I promise.'

She picks up the jug and begins to pour our drinks, the appetising rich aroma of coffee filling the air. She looks at me for a moment, appraising something.

'I probably should come clean,' she says. 'Because I suspect you're already feeling awkward and I think I know why you're here.' She gives me an apologetic smile. 'Theo mentioned something,' she says.

'Yes… I rather wondered if he would. And I feel awful, I really must apologise.'

'You don't need to.'

I look at her in surprise.

'Firstly, because on the basis of what your husband has probably heard, he has a point, and secondly, because if your husband said something out of turn, shouldn't he be the one apologising?' She pushes a cup of coffee towards me. 'Of course, there's a third point here as well, which is that, unless you share your husband's opinion, I'm here talking to you, not him, and so anything he said has no bearing on how *we're* going to get along.'

'Oh…' I reply, feeling suddenly overwhelmed. *That's just the sort of thing you would say.* 'I hadn't really thought about it like that.'

'No. We're not supposed to, are we?' continues Nancy. 'We get so used to apologising for other people's behaviour we just can't help ourselves.'

I grin. 'I still feel like I need to apologise.'

Nancy picks up a biscotti. 'You can recount what he said if you like, explain the context, but I shan't let you say you're sorry.' She waves the biscuit at me. 'But first… dunk.'

She pauses while I follow suit, nodding slightly with every second that passes until we hit five. 'Now, eat.'

I bite as instructed, mouth filling with flavour as I chew. Not tough at all.

She's watching me like a hawk. 'What do you think? What flavours are you getting?'

'Umm… well almond, obviously, the coffee… but, something else, not the cherries…' I nibble a little more. 'Cinnamon?'

Nancy gives a triumphant smile. 'Yes… and do you like it?'

'I do…'

'But?'

I screw up my face. 'I think I'm just a bit old-fashioned,' I say. 'But I like my biscuits sweeter than this. It's lovely though.'

'Hah!' replies Nancy. 'I said they should be sweeter. Thank you, Alys, you've just made my day.' She leans forward. 'A little mother-son rivalry,' she adds. 'Occupational hazard. But I've interrupted you. You were about to explain?'

I take another mouthful of the delicious coffee and clear my throat. 'Hugh is a little… protective of Esme,' I begin. 'She's an only child and he finds it difficult to understand that she's an adult now and can make her own decisions. So I don't think he was being deliberately provocative, but he sees "doing his homework", as he calls it, part of his duty as her father. Everyone else sees it as downright annoying.'

I smile. 'So what Theo heard, taken out of context, was the end of Hugh's attempt at providing me with some background to your company. He mentioned an interview he'd read, given by a former staff member of yours, that wasn't exactly complimentary and that therefore Theo's dad wasn't someone we should encourage Esme to mix with. That's when she and Theo walked in.'

These were hard words to say but I was determined to say them. Nancy has already shown herself to be entirely open and honest and I'd like to start as I mean to go on.

To my surprise she laughs. 'Oh, that's priceless,' she says. 'And Theo agreed, I gather. Although I bet you wanted the ground to swallow you up.'

'Just a little…'

'Well then, I should let you know that it was a fair comment,' she says. 'And that the bones of what was reported in the article are also true. But of course, not the whole story. It never is, is it?' She smiles. 'How much do you know about us, Alys?'

'Not a lot, I'm afraid.'

'Don't apologise,' she admonishes, grinning. 'So, The Green Room is me and my husband, Sam. Actually, he's my ex-husband, but I still can't quite get used to that.' She gives a wistful smile. 'Not because we shouldn't be divorced, that was absolutely the right thing to do, but because we're still very close. Although we've been divorced for several years now, it's only recently been made public, partly for Theo's sake. Sam is the brains behind the business. His idea, concept, marketing, and a whole heap of other stuff besides, while I cook. I'm also the public face of the company, because Sam is categorically not. In fact, he rarely steps foot inside the restaurant.'

She pauses to drink, watching me over the rim of her cup. 'The interview your husband referred to was given by a young man who worked with us in London for a number of months. To start with we had a good relationship but sadly, over time, he took advantage of the fact that Sam was absent from the restaurant to throw his weight around. He made the mistake of thinking that because Sam wasn't physically there, he didn't know what was going on. And when Sam spoke to him about it, he didn't take it well.'

She pauses again. 'My husband has a disability and… when he's in a lot of pain, he can be very… sharp with people. He occasionally loses his temper when things are very bad. So yes, he did shout – although to be fair most of it was at me – but it was overheard just the same. We all accept it wasn't the way to behave but Sam was disappointed and upset – disappointed because he felt let down by someone he respected taking advantage of a situation, and also upset by the knowledge that he'd been taken as a fool. Too often people see only the feebleness of his body and think his mind is the same. They don't see the Sam I know – the brilliant entrepreneur, someone who is kind and thoughtful, and yet who also sits and cries with pain some nights. Someone who takes the snide comments and shocked looks in his stride, burying away the hurt.' She gives a tight smile. 'It's a bit of a bugbear of his.'

'I can imagine.'

'So I hope you won't think too badly of us.'

'I don't think badly of you at all. You didn't have to share any of that, Nancy, but I do appreciate it.'

'I've already explained the set-up to Esme and, although Sam is still involved in the running of things in London, we both agreed that this new restaurant was to be a solo venture. In any case it's time for Theo to take on more responsibility, and although Sam may pop in from time to time, that's the extent of it. I hope that reassures you that nothing untoward will happen here.'

'It does, although now I feel even worse about the things Hugh said. You've gone out of your way to make Esme feel welcome.'

'Hugh is a father and Esme's his little girl. It's really quite all right. Theo finds his father frustrating as well and theirs is definitely what you'd call a love-hate relationship. But I've also heard from Esme how well the two of you get on so, unless there's anything else you feel you should say, I think we should talk about something far more exciting. A little dickie bird told me that your sister-in-law has just got engaged to Rupert Freedman…'

I put my cup down, astonished. 'Do you know him?'

'Oh yes, one of our very good customers.' Nancy seems to be enjoying herself.

'Is he? What's he like? I don't know much about him.'

She gives a wicked laugh. 'Utterly gorgeous… we've all been chasing him for years. I was devastated to learn he'd been caught.'

'Well that might explain why my mother-in-law has gone into total meltdown over the engagement.'

'It certainly would. But listen, I'm going to be totally open about this, and you can tell me to take a running jump, but Esme mentioned she's making the cake for their party and so I've offered her the use of the kitchen here. It makes perfect sense. But, apart from that, I wondered whether we might be able to provide anything else for the party. As our gift… and the opportunity to bag some truly wonderful publicity of course.' She's grinning from ear to ear.

I can't help but laugh. A sudden vivid image of Angela having an apoplectic fit leaps into my head. She will hate it if I get involved, especially if it's providing food from somewhere like The Green Room.

'I have no real idea what the arrangements are,' I say. 'But I'd be delighted to find out. I'm sure we can think of something… to our mutual benefit.'

Nancy raises her mug as if to make a toast. 'Oh I'm so glad you came in this morning, Alys. I've a feeling this is all going to work out wonderfully well.'

# CHAPTER SIX

Hugh surveys himself in the full-length mirror in our bedroom, doing up his cufflinks before slipping on his jacket. It's a new suit, expensive, and beautifully cut. Even if it doesn't quite hide the softness of his rounded stomach. He has a wardrobe full of suits but Scarlett's high-profile engagement has obviously necessitated the purchase of a new one. Besides, his brother, Ed, has bought one too and Hugh would never let that go unchallenged.

'It looks good,' I say, handing him his tie.

'I would hope so,' he grumbles. 'It cost enough. But we mustn't let the side down.' He glances at me before turning back to perfect a full Windsor knot. 'What happened to the dress you were making?'

'Oh, I decided not to wear it.'

Hugh's still looking in the mirror but his gaze travels the length of my body. 'Well, I'm sorry to have to say it, Alys, but I did wonder what had come over you. It really wouldn't have been your thing at all. No, what you have on is far more suitable.'

'But I've worn this dress countless times before.'

'I admit that perhaps it would have been nice to have something new, but that suits you, Alys, it always has. You look lovely.'

'Well I feel like a dumpy middle-aged woman.' I meet his look. 'And yes, Hugh, I'm well aware that's what I am.'

He frowns. 'I didn't say that. I don't know why you need to be so defensive, I said you looked nice and you do. Besides, that dress is far more appropriate. It's less revealing for a start, and far more elegant than some showy number.' He pauses. 'Are you going to wear your hair up?'

'I might do. I haven't decided yet.'

Hugh checks his watch. 'We shall need to leave in fifteen minutes and no later.'

I'm well aware of the time, and I've been ready for ages; it really doesn't take long these days. I narrow my eyes, squinting at my reflection. 'What do you think? I've time to do it either way.'

He makes a show of considering my question. 'Down, I think. Up can be a little… messy, and I'm not sure today is going to be that sort of occasion. Besides, your hair is such a beautiful colour – you know how I like to see it hanging down your back in a glossy sheet.'

I cross the room and flick on my straighteners.

*

I must admit I was surprised, albeit reassured, by Scarlett and Rupert's choice of venue for their engagement party and, now that we're here, incredibly grateful. There are quite a number of posh cars in the car park and I think, were it in some swanky London hotel, I would feel even more uncomfortable. As it is, The Grainger is a modest size, slightly shabby, but comfortable, with a variety of reception rooms which, although linked, still allow plenty of places to hide.

I'm standing in one of them now, almost an anteroom. It's no bigger than ten-foot-square, but its windows overlook the front courtyard and that's why I'm here, waiting for Esme to appear. She's bringing the cake straight from The Green Room and Nancy is driving her over in their liveried van. I've seen photos of the cake so I know it's amazing, but for Esme's sake I can't help but feel an extra glow of pride that she's going to arrive and have everyone know that she works for such a prestigious restaurant.

A roar of laughter from the other room catches my attention and I look over to see Ed and Tash standing in the centre with Rupert and another man called Ollie, who's going to be Rupert's best man. I have no idea what they're talking about but it's Tash who catches my attention. She looks stunning. As tall as Ed in her heels, the dress I made her fits like a glove, softly draping around her shoulders with a little nipped-in waist and a floaty skirt. The colour of the roses on the fabric perfectly brings out the hint of pink in her cheeks and makes her hair glow. It's elegant and sexy at the same time and, with her hair piled into a messy updo, her exposed neck will make most men in the room want to caress it with their fingers.

She and Ed arrived before we did and I saw Hugh's eyes widen at the sight of her dress as we walked into the hotel to say hello, but he didn't say anything. Of course not. Not there in front of everyone. But he will. Later.

The sound of tyres on gravel draws my gaze back outside to see Nancy and Esme arriving. It's a little past noon and the formal part of the day is scheduled for one, although in truth the party began yesterday, on Friday afternoon. A handful of Rupert and Scarlett's friends from London all arrived for a weekend-long celebration, which so far has seen a boating trip and an extended dinner with dancing into the small hours. It's only the family that have been restricted to today's festivities but, even so, things won't wrap up until tonight. There's a formal lunch with a toast for the happy couple and the cake, of course, and then tonight guests will be treated to a buffet, courtesy of Nancy.

I hurry into the foyer to open the doors, grateful that there are no steps up into the hotel. I had horrible visions of Esme proudly carrying her creation, missing her footing, and splattering an enormous quantity of sticky icing over the walls and floor. But even now I can see Nancy opening the rear doors of the van to pull out some folding contraption that magically becomes a trolley. Of course; nothing would be left to chance.

Nancy sees me and gives a little wave just as Esme climbs from her own seat. She still manages to take my breath away. Her bright-red dress should clash horribly with her hair, but it doesn't. She looks incredible. A cascade of corkscrew curls hangs down her back, those at the front held away from her face by invisible clips. It's how I used to wear my hair, back when… I chase the thought away. She flashes me a nervous smile, but then Nancy is beside her, saying something that makes her laugh, and I see what she has become in just a few short days; part of a team.

Esme collects her cake from the back of the van and slides it expertly onto the trolley before standing back, deferring to her employer to bring the cake inside. But instead I'm touched to see Nancy take a step backward and wave Esme on. I watch as she slowly wheels her creation toward me, grinning like a Cheshire cat as Nancy looks on, clearly proud of her protégée. It brings a lump to my throat for some reason.

'Hey Mum,' says Esme, as she reaches me, a little shy now. 'What do you think?'

But my words are stuck, held fast by my emotion. All I can do is gaze in awe at the stunning two-tiered cake and nod with tears in my eyes.

Esme looks heavenward, grinning. 'Oh, Mum…' she says, pretending to be exasperated but I know she's pleased by my response. 'Just pray for me. If it's too hot in there it'll all melt.'

The cake itself is formed from two circles of simple but exquisite ruffle-iced layers, one on top of the other. They're decorated with a handful of sugar-paste rosebuds, no more, but surrounding the whole thing is a delicate covering spun from caramel, gossamer threads dotted with tiny balls that catch the light like dew drops on a web. I'm no baker but even I know that this can only be done at the last minute; the fragile shell is prone to breaking and, as Esme fears, to softening and collapsing.

I watch as she slowly pushes the decorated trolley forward, towards the stand at the rear of the main room where the cake will be displayed until it's ready to eat. The crowds of people part like the Red Sea as she moves among them and, by the time she is not even halfway, tentative claps have given way to a rousing round of applause.

'She did good,' says Nancy, the biggest smile on her face.

'Oh, she did *very* good,' I reply.

Nancy's arm reaches around my shoulders, pulling me in as my emotions threaten to get the better of me. 'You'd better get used to this,' she says. 'That girl is going to go far. There's just something about her.'

Scarlett comes running across the room, exclaiming in delight at the wondrous thing Esme has created before pulling her into a hug. Rupert is close behind, not yet familiar enough with Esme to go for the full-blown family embrace, but he kisses both cheeks, quite enough to make her blush like crazy. They chat for a couple of minutes before I see Esme gesturing towards us and, as I watch, all three begin to walk in our direction.

'Ey, up,' mutters Nancy. 'Best gracious smile on…' She steps forward. 'Rupert!' she exclaims, offering each cheek for the ubiquitous air kiss. 'It's so lovely to see you again.'

'Ah, Nancy… and here you are still looking as young and gorgeous as ever, I see.' He creates a little more space to allow Scarlett to stand by his side, a solicitous arm in the small of her back. 'And I can't tell you how excited I was to hear about your new venture. Having just bought a place in this neck of the woods, the thought of schlepping back to London for some decent food wasn't altogether appealing, but now…' He leans in a little closer. 'And of course I'll be sure to tell all my friends,' he whispers, giving a conspiratorial wink. 'Especially since you've given us such a generous gift to help celebrate our impending nuptials.'

'Would you?' gushes Nancy. 'Oh, you are a dear. And it's my absolute pleasure.'

She turns slightly toward me, rolling her eyes, an expression that only I can see. 'And you must be Scarlett,' she says, turning back and holding out her hand. 'It's so lovely to meet you. Even though I'm insanely jealous of course. Most of London has been chasing Rupert for years.'

Scarlett giggles. 'And a few of them caught him, I believe.'

'Well, I'm heartbroken, obviously, but many congratulations on your engagement.'

Scarlett catches at Rupert's arm. 'Well, it's lovely to meet you too, and Rupert's told me all about The Green Room,' she says. 'I can't wait to come and give it a try.'

'You must,' replies Nancy. 'As soon as we're open. And on the house, of course… Now, I do hope the hotel wasn't too put out over our muscling-in on their buffet?'

'Not at all,' replies Rupert. 'Once I'd explained the situation, they were only too happy to oblige.' Which I guess means that Rupert is probably still paying them anyway but no one's going to mention it. It's obviously very much a you-scratch-my-back-and-I'll-scratch-yours kind of situation, but maybe that's just how it goes in the circles they move in.

'And you have an amazing cake too. Isn't Esme talented? I'm going to have to watch myself with her around.'

I feel a touch on my arm as Hugh materialises beside me. 'That's my girl,' he says, beaming at Nancy.

'Oh, my husband, Hugh,' I say.

Nancy takes his proffered hand. 'You should be very proud,' she says, laughing as Esme squirms with embarrassment. 'And I'm immensely pleased to have her on board. It's almost as if she's one of the family.'

I force down the smile that's trying to flit across my face at Nancy's words. I'm sure it's an oblique reference to Hugh's criticism of her family, but Hugh would have a fit if he thought anyone was making fun of him.

'And just in case you were wondering,' adds Nancy, looking at Rupert and Scarlett. 'I had absolutely no hand at all in the making of your cake. It was all down to Esme; the original idea, the planning, and the execution. All I did was mop her fevered brow.'

Rupert checks his watch. 'We'll be sitting down to eat shortly, Nancy, but you'd be very welcome to join us. Or have a drink perhaps, at the very least?'

She smiles but shakes her head. 'I should get back,' she says. 'Otherwise I fear my promise to deliver you with a buffet this evening will come unstuck. But that's extraordinarily kind of you.' She holds out her arms to Esme. 'I shall see you later but for now go and enjoy the party, you deserve it.'

They hug and goodbyes are said. I don't know why but I walk Nancy to the door. 'Thank you,' I say. And we both know it's for more than just helping Esme to deliver her cake.

'I hope you enjoy the party too,' she says. She knows I haven't been looking forward to it. 'And that your mother-in-law isn't too put out that we've taken over the buffet arrangements.' She gives me a cheeky grin.

I turn, seeking Angela out from among the gathered people. 'That's her,' I say. 'In the midnight-blue dress.' Amusingly she's standing talking to Tash, who is probably finding it screamingly funny that she's actually managed to end up not wearing the same colour dress.

Nancy nods. 'And who's the tall woman beside her? Wow, what a figure.'

'That's Natasha, my sister-in-law.'

'She looks stunning. I love her dress. It wouldn't suit me, more's the pity, I'm too short, but it's lovely. You have such an attractive family.'

*All except me*, I want to say. Impulsively I give her another hug. 'Thanks, Nancy, I'll see you later.'

I wait in the doorway until the van has reversed and pulled away. I know I'm stalling for time – Hugh is waiting for me inside, and I can practically guess what he's going to say.

'Come back and join the party, Alys, we've hardly seen you.'

I smile. 'I know. I guess I was just a little nervous, for Esme, you know. I wanted to make sure that everything was all right.'

'Which it is. She's outdone herself, and you can see for yourself what the reaction is.'

I can. Esme is still surrounded by a crowd of people, no doubt eager for all the details. 'I'm just so pleased for her. I know it's early days, but she seems to have really fallen on her feet.'

'So then relax,' replies Hugh. 'Nancy does indeed seem lovely and is obviously well thought of by those who know her. She had Rupert practically eating out of her hand.'

I flick him a glance, but there doesn't seem to be any undercurrent to his remark. He smooths the knot of his tie. 'I had no idea that caterers could be so well known.'

I raise my eyebrows. 'I don't think you'd really call them caterers, Hugh. Nancy is a first-class chef who runs a first-class restaurant. I know we don't move in the same circles as Rupert's friends clearly do, but in London The Green Room has something of a celebrity status. They have some very high-profile customers. She *is* providing a buffet this evening, but that's as a favour to Rupert. It isn't something she would normally do.' I register the change in his expression. 'And I know what you're thinking, but that isn't Nancy's intention for this new restaurant. It's a lot more low-key, so you needn't worry about Esme.'

'I just don't want her to get into something that's way over her head.'

I lay a hand on his arm. 'She won't, Hugh. She has her head very firmly on her shoulders. Look… I know this isn't your first choice of career for her,' I say gently. 'But some day our daughter would like to run her own restaurant and I'm afraid you're going to have to get used to the idea. I don't think it's about to change any time soon.'

'Which is fine for you...'

I stare at him, his face slightly puffy from the heat. 'No one suggested that she become a chef, Hugh, she just decided all by herself... And honestly, if she's going to do this thing, then I'd much rather she do it in a company with Nancy at the helm. She's being taken good care of.'

He looks as if he's about to say something else, but instead nods, motioning towards the place where Nancy was parked just a moment ago. 'I hadn't realised you two had become so friendly.'

I give him a sideways look. He doesn't know that I've had coffee with her practically every morning this last week. 'She's that sort of person,' I reply. 'It's hard not to be.'

His lips are slightly pursed. 'Yes, well, I perhaps wouldn't get too friendly, Alys. She is Esme's employer at the end of the day, and I'd hate there to be any awkwardness if something went wrong.'

I feel a flicker of irritation. Why does Hugh's concern always have to cross the line into something far more negative? 'What on earth could go wrong?'

But he has no reply.

I take his arm, smiling. 'Come on, they'll be serving lunch soon and, as you quite rightly pointed out, I've hardly said hello to anyone yet.'

I try my best but by late afternoon I've sunk into a despondent gloom. Esme and Tash, my usual defenders at family occasions, have got chatting to a couple of Rupert's nephews and I can't say I blame them. The men are young, good-looking, incredibly well dressed and have an air of success about them that you can almost smell. By contrast, having tried to mingle with a few of

Scarlett's friends, I realised pretty quickly that they're people I will never have much in common with.

Scarlett loves to tell people she was actually christened Charlotte, but later changed her name by deed poll, and it gives a good indication of the group she mixes with. In fact, I'm surprised she didn't pick Rebellion as her middle name while she was at it, she's practically made it into an art form. Consequently, despite us being roughly the same age, her friends, while polite, don't really want to spend too long with a middle-aged housewife and mother who must seem incredibly boring. So instead I've been saddled with Angela for the last hour and I've almost had enough.

I look up as Hugh comes back towards me, carrying a cup of tea. A glass of wine would be lovely but, as usual, I'm the designated driver. I don't really mind but it's not much fun watching everyone else get merrier and merrier while you're stone-cold sober.

'There you go,' he says as he sits down. 'That should perk you up a bit.'

I bite my tongue. 'Thanks, Hugh. I'm thirsty, it's really hot in here.'

Like most people he's taken off his jacket, although his tie is still firmly in place. 'Not a bad do though,' he comments, taking a swig from his glass of beer. 'The free bar helps. And Rupert's bunch seem a lively crowd.'

I nod. 'Bright young things,' I say, smiling. 'But yes, Scarlett and he seem well suited. They're having a whale of a time. Good luck to them, I say.'

Hugh is studying me. 'Is everything okay?' he asks, voice low as his eyes dart sideways towards his mother.

'Yes, fine. Sorry, Hugh, I'm just not much in the mood for a party today. Tired, I think.'

'I thought you seemed a bit glum.'

I breathe in deeply and pull a smile onto my face. 'A bit out of sorts, but I'll be fine.'

He nods, looking out across the room to where a group of people are still sitting at the dining tables as serving staff clear around them. 'Why didn't you tell me that you were making that dress for Natasha?' he asks.

My smile freezes. 'Oh, I don't know. Maybe I just wanted to know what you really thought about it.'

He looks puzzled. 'But I would have told you honestly what I thought, whether the dress was for you or her. I don't see what the difference is.'

'No difference, Hugh, but that's rather my point. You obviously didn't think the dress was right for me and yet today, wearing it, everyone has commented on how amazing Tash looks. Including you.'

'Yes, well. It suits her, I will admit, but Tash is very different from you, she's…'

'Younger?'

'Well of course she is, but I still don't—'

'Hugh, I'm forty-eight. But right now, I feel as if I'm eighty-eight. When did forty-eight get to be so old?'

He shakes his head. 'I really don't see what you're getting at, Alys. You and Tash are completely different and it's ridiculous to try to compare yourself to her.'

'I wasn't actually. All I was saying is that at forty-eight you'd think I'd still be able to wear a dress like that and look good.'

'I didn't say that you wouldn't, Alys… if you like that sort of thing… which I don't. I still don't think it's all that suitable.'

I sigh. 'You know, Hugh, just once I wanted to feel like a woman, to have eyes on me in the room. Like I was more than just a wife and mother.'

There's a hint of alarm in Hugh's eyes. 'Yes, but I like you in what you have on. You've always looked nice in that and what would have been the point in encouraging you to wear a dress like Tash's when I knew it wouldn't be right for you? I couldn't bear it if people were laughing at you, and more to the point neither could you.'

'Laughing at me?'

'All right, not laughing. But you know what I mean. When people try too hard, wear things that aren't suited to their age or shape. Mutton dressed as lamb, that kind of thing.'

'I see…'

'I was only trying to help.' He pats my hand helplessly.

My throat suddenly constricts and I'm surprised to find the feeling familiar.

I drink my tea and excuse myself after a few more minutes, claiming I need the bathroom and a bit of fresh air after the stuffiness of the room. The cloakroom is empty, cool and calm after the noise outside and I stand for a few moments, breathing deeply.

I wash my hands slowly, savouring the feel of the silky soap on my skin, and then rinse them, staring into the huge mirror that covers one wall. My pale, clear skin is a little flushed, but still unlined except for the crinkles around my eyes when I smile. My hair is beginning to rebel against the straighteners, trying to find its natural curl, and it might have faded a little in comparison with Esme's copper tresses but I still haven't had to resort to colouring it. My nose is unremarkable, my cheekbones high and my lips generous. I stare, assessing what I see, details of a face I see every day, a collection of features which, added together, I've always thought are okay, pleasing even, on a good day. But it's the eyes I don't want to look at – almond-shaped, olive-green in colour, and ringed by mascaraed lashes. But they're not mine. They're the eyes of someone who's dying inside.

What on earth has got into me? I turn off the tap, holding my still wet hands against my cheeks for a moment before pulling out several paper towels from the dispenser. I pat my face, willing myself calm, and straighten my dress. It must be the menopause, I think. Rampant hormones that are doing me no good at all. I need some fresh air; I wasn't lying about feeling hot.

So instead of rejoining the party I slip out of the door on the other side of the hallway and into the gardens. It's still warm and sunny, but there's a breeze blowing and I gulp in fresh air as if I've been drowning. I'm going to have to find myself something to do, I realise. I know I've been having morning coffee with Nancy but, even so, I'm still home by ten a.m. and there's only so much that needs doing in the house, or that I want to do. Being at home all the time is clearly not right for me. I'm sure that's why I've been feeling so low; as if I've lost my identity, become irrelevant. But for heaven's sake I was a shop assistant, a job I didn't even like much, that can't be the only reason why I feel the way I do.

I've been wandering along a path that bisects the lawns surrounding the hotel, but now I've reached a gate that gives access onto the road and the rear car park. I'll have to cross over if I want to carry on. My hand is already on the latch as a bright-green van passes me, the company logo clear on the side doors. I check my watch, realising it must be time for Nancy and Theo to bring the food over for this evening's buffet. Without even thinking about it, my steps quicken as I pass through the gate and follow the van down the road.

It isn't quite as grand here in the service car park, but it's a sizeable space and The Green Room's van has drawn up on one side of it. By the time I reach it, Theo has already hopped out and opened the rear doors, pulling several stacked trays towards him.

'Theo!' I wave. 'Hello.'

He straightens. 'Hi, Alys,' he says, grinning. 'Erm, shouldn't you be in there, having a wonderful time?'

I grin back, aware that Esme has probably told him plenty about our family dynamics. 'I should… but I popped out for some fresh air and somehow I seem to have stayed out. Can I give you a hand?'

He eyes my dress. 'I wouldn't, if I were you. You'll end up with all kinds of stuff down you.'

I grimace. 'But perhaps a small price to pay for doing something useful.' The cab door has opened on the other side of the van and I can hear footsteps approaching from the front. I look past Theo, readying a smile to greet Nancy.

Except it isn't Nancy.

It's you.

And my world turns upside down.

# CHAPTER SEVEN

I've thought about this moment so many times. Relived each second over and over, every time slightly different from the last. What would I say? What would I do when faced with you, returned, as if from the dead? But now that you're here, I don't know what to do, or say. The breath has gone from my body, the words have dried in my throat.

You're older, of course you are, it has been over twenty years since I last saw you and time has wreaked its change on us all. Your hair is grey at the temples, and there are lines on your face. On the one side. It's hard to tell on the other, the skin thickened and twisted from the tangle of scars that run from your cheek right the way down your neck. You stand with a stoop, leaning your weight on a stick, and even the shock on your face can't hide the discomfort you're in. But you're alive. And up until this moment I hadn't even known if there was still air in your lungs.

'Oh God, I'm sorry,' says Theo. 'You two haven't met, have you? Alys, this is my dad, Sam... Dad, this is Esme's mum...'

Sam? So you have a new name now too. It wasn't enough that you just disappeared, that I've never seen you or spoken to you since you said goodbye. You had to create a new identity for yourself as well. Did you really not want me so much that you couldn't bear to be found? Or was it the other way around? That you didn't want to even hear your old name and be reminded of a life you once had? One that had me in it. And yet, here we both are. You have a wife and son, and I have a husband and daughter. Standing in a car park, staring at each other, knowing we have to say something.

'Hi,' I say, holding out my hand. 'It's lovely to meet you.' Your eyes are on my hair and my face. Are you disappointed?

And then your hand is in mine, fingers burning into my skin. 'Alys,' you say, as if it's the first time you've ever heard the word. 'It's good to meet you too. Nancy has nothing but praises to sing about Esme.'

Our skin detaches. There's nothing else to say. Nothing that really matters anyway. 'Thank you,' I reply. 'And for giving her the opportunity, she's really loving it.' I look at Theo. 'I'll go and fetch her, shall I? She can give you a hand.'

'Yes, okay. I've just sent her a text actually, told her I'd meet her in the kitchen.' He points to a blue door on the left of the building. 'Through there.'

'I'll go and find her, make sure she's not lost.'

'Mum will be here in a minute. She's bringing the car separately,' he says. 'Only I'm staying with Dad this weekend.'

I nod as if it's all perfectly natural and then I smile at you, knowing I'm about to flee, wondering why every time I had imagined our meeting in my head, it never ended with my leaving. I guess it's true what they say – that we never know how we're going to react to something until we're faced with it.

I focus my sight on the blue door and draw my body towards it, one step after the other until I'm safely through.

*

I wander through the next few days like a ghost in my own skin. Scarcely seeing, scarcely hearing, everything at a distance from me, seemingly impossible to reach. But I know I can't go on like this. Hugh isn't the most perceptive of men but even he has noticed. I've pleaded a migraine. It isn't an outright lie

– my head is full of pain, just not the sort that any painkillers will touch.

The worst thing is that I have absolutely nothing to occupy me. I drop Esme off at work and then I have the whole day to fill, adrift and utterly without purpose. I may not have found my job at Harringtons all that rewarding, but it at least required my presence. Now, I have nowhere to be and no one to talk to, and I can't bear another day of mindlessly watching the TV to pass the time, or walking aimlessly, letting thoughts churn in my head with no resolution.

So, this morning, I'm going to clean; good old-fashioned manual labour to eradicate the pesky thoughts in my head that have no right to be there. And I'm going to start with the oven.

I probably should have read the instructions on the can of cleaner, especially the bit about using in a well-ventilated room. The kitchen window is open but I'm still spluttering at the over-powering smell and have to throw open the back door. There's a man standing by my car. And the furious pounding in my chest that has seemed ever-present the last few days notches up a gear.

'Tom…?' Your name barely makes it out of my mouth.

He looks up. 'Sam,' he corrects.

The seconds click by. 'I can't call you that. It's not your name.'

'But it has been, for a long time, Alys.' His voice is gentle as he comes towards me, his pronounced limp excruciating to watch.

I ignore his comment and stand away from the door, letting him into the kitchen.

'Is Hugh—?'

'No. He's at work.'

His face visibly relaxes and he steps over the threshold.

'I'm sorry, it stinks in here,' I say. 'I've been cleaning the oven.'

He nods, looking around him, his eyes flicking over the small details of our family life.

'How do you even know where I live?' I ask.

His eyes are full of apology. 'Your daughter works for Nancy so her details are on file…'

I nod. 'Yes, of course. Sorry… I wasn't accusing you…' I trail off and clear my throat.

'You look well—'

'How have you been?'

Our words collide, a sudden noise in the quiet space.

He fidgets, adjusting his weight on his stick. 'Sorry,' he says. 'You first.'

'Do you need to sit down?' It comes out more bluntly than I'd intended, and he winces slightly at my words.

Despite the appearance of the rest of his body, his eyes haven't changed one single bit. Still hazel, flecked with gold and grey, so that one minute they dance and another they're soft like seal fur. 'Thank you. That might be wise. I have a feeling this could be more than a two-minute conversation.'

I motion to the hallway. 'We'll go in the other room. I don't think I can stand the smell in here.' I take us through, conscious of the family photos on the wall as we pass, the wedding portrait on the mantelpiece in the living room. Pictures of the life I've led without you.

He pauses, trying to figure out which chair to sit in. Not the big squishy sofa, which some days I struggle to be free from. Or the battered leather armchair which sits low to the ground. So instead he's left with the wingback; upright, easier to get up from, but unmistakably Hugh's. I should have thought. How can our meeting be so full of things to trip us up, when all I've ever done is picture how perfect our reunion will be?

I wait until he's settled before I take a seat in the corner of the sofa. 'You look well,' I say, repeating my comment from earlier.

'Do I?' He seems to find my compliment funny. 'Well, I guess I do compared with the last time you saw me; in a hospital bed, covered in tubes and wires. But then again it's hard for me to judge when every day of my life is an endless collection of things which hurt or things which don't work.' He drops his head, sighing. 'Sorry,' he says. 'That wasn't necessary.'

I take a deep breath. I can't let us fight. Not after all this time. 'I'm sorry too,' I say. 'I know it can't be easy, and how you are is probably the last thing you want to talk about. It's just… this is all such a shock. I didn't even know if you were alive.' I pause. 'After the divorce came through I tried to find you several times, but you'd disappeared. It was as if you never even existed. Now, of course, I understand. But why did you change your name?'

There's raw agony on his face and he doesn't reply. So I'm to draw my own conclusions. I see. 'So… well, you… you're walking though. That's an improvement on what the doctors first thought.'

His face softens. 'I can tell you what's happened, Alys. If you want me to?'

I nod, fumbling up my sleeve for a tissue. 'Should we get a drink or something?'

'If you'd like,' he replies. 'Yes, maybe that might help.'

I get up, suddenly needing some space. I'm not yet ready to hear Tom's story, to learn about the blanks in my life. 'Do you still drink coffee?' He used to take two sugars. I wonder if he still does.

'I do, but not so often these days. Actually, just water would be fine, if that's okay?'

I nod and head back into the kitchen, shutting the oven door on my way through. I fill a glass with water from the tap and make Tom wait while I make myself a coffee. I stare at it for a few minutes, willing myself to pick up the mug, but a sudden wave of emotion hits me and instead I rush through the conservatory and into the garden, where I stand, gulping in air. Seeing you again has brought back all those feelings from the day of your accident.

I stare at the bright colours of the potted flowers surrounding the conservatory, conscious of the amount of time that's passing. But it's a few moments more before I'm able to take one final cleansing breath and retrace my steps. I pick up the drinks and return to the living room, handing Tom his glass of water.

'Yes,' I say simply. 'I'd like to know.'

He takes a sip as he searches for a place to start. 'So some of it you're already aware of,' he begins. 'The broken leg, the smashed pelvis, cracked vertebrae... all of which healed, eventually.' He turns his head slightly. 'The scarring... was more severe than I ever thought it would be. I guess it was simply a matter of priorities. At the time of the accident, keeping me alive was more important than what I was going to look like *if* I survived. That, and whether I would ever be able to walk again. This is a vast improvement actually, on what it used to be. I've lost count of the number of operations I've had. I've been offered more but... sometimes you just have to know when to stop.'

I swallow. 'Does it hurt?'

His eyes close. 'Yes. At times unbearably so. Painful, itchy, like fire ants walking over my skin. But it's got better with time.' He gives a rueful shrug. 'Age is the ultimate irony; some things get better, some things get worse... But the walking is an improvement. I'm told I bucked the odds, but even so I still spent several years in a wheelchair. More operations; legs and back filled with metal rods, repairs to the nerves, and an awful lot of blood, sweat and tears. Learning to walk again is one of the hardest things I've ever had to do.'

He gives a tight smile. 'It's a damned good job babies never know quite how hard it is or I don't think they'd bother. So yes, I'm mobile, up to a point. Can't walk too far before exhaustion hits me like a freight train, but better than I did before. The rest of me... everything else you see is just the passage of time.'

I don't know what to say.

His eyes are clear and steady. 'And yet, none of that answers your question, does it? The only question you really have. The question to end all questions. Sure, you've asked the rest out of politeness, but it doesn't really matter how I am. I'm alive, I'm sitting in the same room as you. For goodness' sake it's perfectly obvious how I am. So, shall I answer the big one?'

My eyes burn into his. 'Don't mock me, Tom. What do you want me to say? I haven't seen you in over twenty years, and the last time I did I was married to you.'

His gaze sinks to the floor. 'I know, I'm sorry.'

I shake my head. The teeniest of movements. The biggest of hurts.

'What for? For sending me away, or for never contacting me?' Anger fuels my words. 'I thought you were dead, Tom. You probably should have been. I thought it was the worst day of my life when the police came to see me. To tell me you'd been in a car accident. And when I saw you, lying there, so broken, the only thing I cared about was that you were still alive. Nothing else mattered while there was a tiny glimmer of hope. And I prayed and prayed that they would be able to keep you that way, that none of the things the doctors feared would happen, and eventually you would get to come home and I wouldn't have to live my life without you. I even started carrying out random acts of kindness, anything to tip the scales in my favour. If I was a good, kind person, then surely nothing bad could happen. And at the end of it all, *you* were supposed to be my reward.'

There's a patch of stubble on your chin where the hairs are slightly longer than the rest. Maybe you missed them when you were shaving. I stare at them, transfixed, anything so I don't have to meet your eyes.

'But instead, just when you were beginning to recover; at the end, which I thought would be a beginning, you sent me away. Told me our marriage was over. And because I thought I understood what you were going through, and that you needed time to come to terms with things, I did as you asked. I never thought you meant it, not until the day you disappeared. *That* was the worst day of my life. Not one word, Tom, not one visit, in all that time. Not even to see if I was okay.' I lift my eyes to his. 'Did you not even care, Tom, is that it?'

He pauses before answering, dropping his words into the room, each one a ticking grenade. 'No, I cared too much.'

I stare at him, a maddening anger rising within me. 'What the hell is that supposed to mean? If you cared, you had a very funny way of showing it. Do you know how much I would have given to see you, to speak to you? How much I told myself that all I had to do was wait and one day you would come back to me. If you truly cared, you would have done, not stayed away.'

'I have my reasons,' he says, bitterly.

'Well, they must have been good ones, for you to have been gone all this time.'

'They were… At the time, they were.' His jaw clenches and unclenches, eyelids flickering as he struggles for what to say. His eyes rove the room, resting for a moment on a book that's sitting on the coffee table, before moving to the mantelpiece.

'So you and Hugh married,' he says. 'How long is it now? Twenty-odd years?'

I pause. 'Twenty-three.' His eyes narrow and I hold his look. Don't you dare tell me it was so soon after us. I know it was.

'And Esme? Yes, you have a beautiful daughter too, talented as well. A beautiful home. A life.'

'For God's sake, Tom, why are we even talking about any of this? My marriage, Esme… What's the point?'

Tom shakes his head sadly. 'No, you see, that is very much the point, Alys. That's how we got to be here; because life *does* go on. Your life went on. And so did mine. Despite those times when things happen that we swear we will never forget, that we will never be able to move on from, that feeling lessens. We pick up our feet and we take a step forward. And after a while more time passes and the past becomes something we leave behind. Even you, Alys. Despite what you've just said, you have a life now.'

'I would have had a life with you.'

Tom shakes his head. 'Perhaps. But it would have been a very different life from the one I wanted for you. And if you're honest with yourself, not the one you wanted either.'

'But you had no right, Tom, that was never your decision to make…'

'Do you know why I married Nancy?' he asks suddenly.

I raise my eyebrows. 'I would imagine because you loved her.'

'Yes, because I loved her. But also because she wasn't you. And that made it so much easier. So, if you want to know why I sent you away, that's why. Because Nancy never knew the old me, she never knew Tom, and so I never had to wonder what she was really thinking. And although I knew it hurt her to see me in pain, to watch me struggle, I never had to worry about what she really thought of me – whether she secretly longed for her old husband back – whether she stayed out of pity, or because she just didn't have the courage to leave.' He shrugs. 'And yet, in the end, she left me anyway.'

'She still loves you,' I say.

He smiles. 'I know. We probably get on better now than we've ever done, simply because we're two separate people. She can be her and I can be me, and there's space between us to breathe. But our marriage… became damaged. And in the end there was too much to repair.'

I nod, sadly. 'I guess I can understand that. Despite our best intentions, things don't always work out the way we want them to. But I like Nancy. We've got quite friendly over the last week or so and I can imagine that she's been good for you.'

'She doesn't let me get away with much, that's true. Or pull any punches. Nancy can be one of the kindest, most generous people I know, but she also has no qualms about letting you know if she considers your behaviour to be out of line. And in my case, she takes the greatest delight in doing so. I think it's become a point of pride.' A slight trace of a smile lifts the corners of his mouth. 'I can't tell you how funny I thought it when she told me what Hugh had said about me.'

'He said it about the owner of The Green Room, Tom. It wasn't personal.'

'It wouldn't have mattered if it was. Nancy warned me not to rock the boat and to stay out of his way. She doesn't want there to be any unpleasantness. But neither do I, so don't worry, I'll take the greatest care to stay out of his way.'

'But there's no need, really, I—'

'There's every need, Alys. There are some things from my past life I've no wish to revisit, and my friendship with Hugh is one of them.'

'I see,' I say steadily. 'So why *are* you here, Tom? If it's not to rekindle your friendship with Hugh? I'm not deluded enough to think that you've suddenly decided to beg my forgiveness after all these years.'

He's studying me quite intently. 'How have you been?' he asks, instead of answering my question. It throws me for a minute. I wasn't expecting it and I have no idea how to answer.

'You must be incredibly proud of Esme,' he adds. 'She's beautiful, intelligent and it's not hard to see where she gets her creative spirit from. What are you doing now? Did you get to be the conservationist you always dreamed of?'

'Tom, what are you doing? Why are we even talking about this? Will it help assuage your guilt knowing that my life turned out exactly the way I wanted it to? Or do you think it will make *me* feel better? Confirmation that I've achieved all these things without you, after all.'

He looks as if I've just slapped him. 'You're angry, still. I get that… And yes, maybe guilt is one of the reasons why I'm here.

But I couldn't have us meet the way we did the other day and not come and speak to you. That would have been inexcusable.' He runs a hand across his chin. 'And if it's any consolation, Alys, it's taken me three bloody days to get here. I had no idea what I was going to say to you… In fact, I wasn't sure if you would even let me in. I'm also very well aware that the way I treated you was appalling and, even if I had good reason, it isn't that I haven't thought about it through the years, of course I have.'

'Then I'll repeat the question… Why are you here, Tom? What on earth do you think it's going to achieve?'

He leans forward in his chair, hand scrabbling for his stick. 'I don't know, okay? I guess I just thought I owed you some sort of an explanation.'

'Which you've provided.'

He glares at me. 'Alys, I'm trying to do the right thing here and you're determined not to let me, aren't you?'

'What did you expect, Tom? That we'd just pick up where we left off all those years ago?'

'No, I didn't expect that, of course not. But I did think we might be able to come together as rational adults and discuss it. I don't know, find some closure from it even.'

I shudder. I hate that word, closure. Like that's the end of it. And everything is fine now. How can it be fine when I don't want to forget you? I never have.

I get to my feet. 'I think you'd better go now,' I say.

His eyes bore into mine until I can bear it no longer and I look away as he struggles to stand. I remember the look in his eyes when he told me our marriage was over, and it's not much different now.

He limps after me to the door where we stand in the hallway, a lifetime of hurt and pain forming a chasm between us.

'You've straightened your hair,' he says more gently. And I really wish he hadn't.

'I've been straightening it for years, Tom. I'm not a curly-haired sort of girl any more.'

The look on his face is hard to define as his jaw tightens.

'Then you need to call me Sam,' he replies. 'I'm not Tom any more. I haven't been for a very long time.'

# CHAPTER EIGHT

I stalk back into the kitchen, heart pounding, cheeks flushed. If I had something in my hand, I would hurl it somewhere, watch it smash into smithereens, the broken pieces of my hurt littering the floor where I might crush them underfoot till no trace remained.

How dare Sam ask me about my life now? As if he has any right to know. His name jars in my head, alien and strange. I don't know anyone called Sam and yet Tom is as familiar to me as breathing. Or at least he once was. But even as I try to push aside this new name from my head, I realise that I can't because the Tom I knew doesn't exist any more.

My anger is fading fast and I pick up the can of oven cleaner, shaking it ferociously, trying to stave off the inevitable. I'm going to have the cleanest oven on the bloody planet if it kills me. Except that no amount of activity is going to stop the wall of emotion that's building, and within seconds I've sunk into one of the chairs at the table, letting it break and tears stream down my face.

Well done, Alys. I hope you're proud of yourself. You couldn't have made that any worse if you'd tried. Yes, you had questions and things you needed to say. Things that were long overdue, even things that you have been bottling up for years. But the very last thing you should have done was said them today, bundled them all up in a tight, hard little ball, and thrown it at Sam with all the force you could muster. So whatever you get now, you well and truly deserve it.

I'm not sure how long I sit there, shouting at the little voice in my head to shut up, to stop telling me things I already know which are only making me feel worse. I know I've behaved badly, I don't need reminding that I have pretty much ensured that I won't ever see Sam again. My irritation is rising once more. I shouldn't want to, for goodness' sake. I have a husband, a daughter, a… I gaze around my bright, sunlit kitchen… a lovely home… a life. And I've had a perfectly good one without Sam for the last twenty-odd years. I'm about to berate myself some more when my mobile phone lights up with a message.

*Are you busy today? Only if you're at a loose end, I have a proposition for you. Feel free to come over anytime. The usual cake and coffee applies. Nancy x*

It's not until I'm halfway to The Green Room that I realise seeing Nancy might not be such a good idea. I haven't seen her since the party and, although in some respects I would love to be able to speak to her, what would I say? *I'm sorry if I'm not my usual self, only I've discovered that your ex-husband is also mine.* But I've already told her to expect me and, besides, I'm nothing if not intrigued by her suggestion of a proposition.

I pull up in the car park and sit for a minute to gather my thoughts before checking my face in the mirror. My hasty attempts to repair the damage that a bout of ugly crying has reaped would appear to be holding up. Even if I do look a little pale, I doubt that Nancy will be able to tell the difference.

The kitchen is full of the most amazing smell as I enter, tentatively pushing open the door despite already having been told to just walk right in. Nancy jumps up as soon as she sees me, leaving Theo and Esme sitting at the table. They're poring over pages and pages of what look like handwritten notes, as well as photographs, Theo in charge of a large notebook in front of him.

'Come in, come in,' says Nancy, beckoning me forward. 'You've come at just the right time.'

'Have I?'

Esme looks up, smiling. Whether she knew in advance that Nancy had asked me over, I have no idea, but I'm pleased to see she doesn't look too put out by my presence.

'Hi, Mum. We're going through Nancy's enormous stash of recipes, trying to decide on a shortlist, but it's driving us mad.'

'So, I'm going to retire from the process and leave these two to see what they come up with,' says Nancy. 'Having three people all voicing their opinions really isn't getting us anywhere.' She looks over to the cooker. 'Now, there's some soup on the go if you'd like some, or I can find a slab of beetroot and chocolate cake. It sounds revolting but is anything but, I promise.'

'Could I have the soup if it's not too much trouble?' The thought of a warming bowlful of savoury loveliness is hugely comforting. 'I probably ought to at least try to stop eating cake.'

'Why?' asks Nancy, genuinely interested.

How do I explain that, at the moment, once I start on the sugary stuff, I probably won't stop.

'Oh, for heaven's sake,' says Esme, rolling her eyes. 'She's just doing that mum thing. You know… *Oh, I couldn't possibly have anything nice…* Mum, life's too short, eat the cake.'

'Easy for you to say,' I reply. 'When you have a gorgeous figure.' I stick out my tongue at her. 'And for your information, I just fancy the soup, that's all.'

Theo laughs. 'Esme's just jealous because she made the cake and I made the soup,' he says, elbowing her gently. 'And I can see where Esme gets her figure from,' he adds chivalrously. 'But one bowl of soup coming up. Would you like a chunk of granary bread to go with it?'

'Yes, please.'

Theo smiles at his mum. 'You go, I'll bring them through,' he says.

I follow Nancy down into the main restaurant. 'You have him well trained,' I comment.

Nancy smiles as she turns to speak. 'He didn't need much training actually. I'm incredibly lucky.' She lowers her voice. 'Don't tell him I said this, but Theo is such a sweetie. Fortunately, he's picked up on some of his father's more endearing qualities while leaving the others behind.'

The mention of Sam sends a pulse of electricity rippling through me and I'm suddenly very conscious of where I'm standing. Coming here was such a bad idea, but I can hardly excuse myself now. Nancy is still leading the way, pausing by the table we usually sit at but instead walking on past.

'Let's sit a bit further down today,' she says. 'The outlook here is so much nicer, plus the light is a little better.' She smiles mysteriously. 'I want to show you something,' she adds.

Intrigued, I follow her, taking a seat while she doubles back to collect something. It's a plain buff-coloured folder which she lays on the table. She taps the top of it lightly as she sits down.

'Now, before I show you this, I want to ask you a question,' she says, a mischievous look on her face. 'And don't look so worried.'

I am worried. I haven't a clue what she's going to say.

'When we were at Scarlett's party the other day, I commented on your other sister-in-law's dress as I was leaving. She is quite beautiful, but it was the dress that caught my attention. You know the one – pale silk with big roses all over it.'

Unease begins to unfurl itself within me. I nod cautiously.

'But when I mentioned it, giving you the perfect opportunity to say that you had made it, you didn't. You just agreed that you liked it.' She cocks her head to one side. 'I'm just wondering why that was.'

I stare at her. 'Did you know I had made it when you commented?'

'No, of course not, Esme told me afterwards, but that's beside the point. I would have commented whether I knew or not. The dress was stunning.'

'Yes, well my sister-in-law would look gorgeous wearing a bin bag. Fortunately, I love her to bits, otherwise I think I'd hate her with a passion.'

Nancy smiles. 'You have a very photogenic family,' she says. 'But you still haven't answered my question.'

'No, because I don't know how to answer it,' I reply, truthfully. 'It wasn't a deliberate omission on my part, more that it didn't occur to me *to* say anything.'

Nancy is studying me quite intently. 'Hmm… I thought that might be the case.' She pauses as Theo approaches carrying a tray and waits while he puts it down. 'Thanks, love. Now you two come up with some blistering menus, I'm counting on you.'

Theo grins at me with an amused expression on his face that clearly says, *see what I have to put up with?*

'You're just like a lot of women our age, hiding their light under a bushel…' She laughs. 'I can see you're wondering what I'm talking about because I'm not like that at all. And you're right, I'm not, but I was once. So, if I were to ask you again why you didn't say anything, what would you say now? Have a think, and I'm not being critical, I'm just interested. You'll understand why in a minute.' She unloads the bowls of soup from the tray and slides one towards me, together with a spoon. A plate of bread soon follows which she places between us.

'Okay…' I say slowly. 'I guess I just don't feel comfortable bragging about the things I've done. That's the first thing. The second is that yes, whilst I'm capable of making a dress, so are a lot of other people. I don't consider what I did to be especially remarkable.'

Nancy leans forward. 'Lots of people run restaurants, Alys, and yet I'm convinced that ours is special. In fact, I go out of my way to tell everyone it is.'

'Well then, I don't know why I find it so hard. Perhaps we're just different.'

'Perhaps… But I should probably explain why I asked you all that,' she says. 'It's something I've been musing over, that and other things… You see, I've been asked to speak at a conference for women in business, and I would normally turn that sort of thing down. But then I thought, actually I do have something to say, and if there are people willing to listen, maybe I should say those things, after all. So I've been trying to pull together some ideas for what to speak about. And when you dismissed your glowing talent the other day, I was interested to know why.'

I make a face. 'Yes, I'm not really an empowered sort of person, I've always shied away from that sort of thing. I find it a little… overwhelming sometimes.'

'Or perhaps it's that the people who advocate it are overwhelming?'

I grin. 'Something like that. Support is great, but evangelism isn't really my cup of tea. Not everyone wants to be changed. And there's nothing wrong with that either.'

'That's a very good point,' says Nancy. 'I shall bear that in mind…' She takes another mouthful of soup. 'Is that the way I come across?'

'No, not at all,' I reply. 'But I think it's very easy to assume that all women want the same things. That having fought, quite rightly, to put things on a more equal footing with our male counterparts that now women must somehow all want their lives to be different. Many don't. If they do, then great, those opportunities should be there. But if not, then that's okay too. Change isn't always a good thing, or for everyone.'

'No that's true, although I do think sometimes that it's fear that holds us back. I think we're actually scared of changing. Because change takes us away from the comfortable and the familiar and heaven knows what might happen then.'

I hold her look, spoon poised in mid-air. 'Indeed…'

Nancy smiles. 'Anyway, apart from anything else, what I also wanted to say is that I did absolutely love your sister-in-law's dress and, contrary to what you think, I know my way around clothes enough to know that you do have a great talent for dressmaking. To which end I would very much like it if you could make me an outfit too. One to wear when I'm giving my speech. How's that for empowerment?'

She falters at the look on my face. 'I've offended you… Alys, forgive me, I hadn't intended—'

'No, you haven't offended me,' I interrupt, sighing. 'You've quite accurately deduced that I'm a woman of a certain age who faces the prospect of the life ahead of her with abject loathing.' I smile. 'Forgive me, I'm not feeling myself at the moment, whatever that is… and I've had somewhat of a trying morning. One that reminded me of the bright, shiny young thing I once was, while obviously leaving in its wake the polar opposite.'

'Maybe you should have gone for the cake after all…' There's a glimmer of a smile. 'I can still get you a slice?'

I look up. 'No, honestly, this is perfect.' I tear off a hunk of the bread and dip it in the soup. 'And I'd be delighted to make something for you,' I add, looking to change the subject. Nancy is so easy to talk to; I'm in very grave danger of letting my mouth run away with me. The next thing I know I'll be discussing her ex-husband with her, and that's definitely not something I should be doing. 'Do you have an idea for an outfit in mind?' I ask.

Nancy leans forward, grinning. 'Well, as it happens, I do.' She wrinkles her nose. 'But… I'm not sure whether it's a good idea or not. It might also be…' She opens the folder and takes out a picture, and then another and another, laying all three facing me on the table.

For a moment neither of us says anything. Nancy bites her lip. 'It's a ridiculous idea, isn't it?' she says.

I pull one of the photos a little closer. It's been torn from the pages of a magazine.

'No, actually… I'm surprised – it's not at all what I thought you might have in mind and…' I study her, as a dressmaker would, taking in her shape and colouring. Her tiny frame, slender figure, good bust, strong enough shoulders to hold up the structure of the jacket. And her short white hair, standing in peaks, wide mouth, big smile. Oh, it would be perfect. And in fact, she's already wearing chef's whites so it's not such a great leap of imagination. 'There are very few women who could pull this off… but you'd look amazing!'

Nancy's whole face lights up. 'Do you really think so? I wasn't sure, with my hair…?'

'No, that's what makes it so perfect… And you're sure you want all these… spangles?' I look at the expression on her face. 'Yes, of course you do.' I put down my spoon. 'Wow, I've never made a tuxedo before, let alone one that Elvis wouldn't look out of place wearing, but… well, I guess there's a first time for everything.'

'This event I'm going to, it's being run by the chamber of commerce, a very male environment. In fact, I bet it's killing them to even put on an event of this sort, and there's a terribly devilish streak in me that wants to take them by the scruff of the neck. I'm supposedly speaking about the growing number of successful businesswomen and I've a horrible suspicion that what they'd really like me to say is that of course it's all down to my husband… It wasn't their idea that my speech be about empowerment, I just thought that it was too good an opportunity to miss and, that being the case, I should at least dress the part.'

Her expression is so earnest it makes me laugh. 'So, sticking the middle finger up at the patriarchy?'

'Something like that.' She pauses. 'It's about saying who you really are, isn't it? Being proud of it – *this is me, take it or leave it, but I'm making no apologies.* It's taken me quite a lot of my adult years to realise this unfortunately, but now that I have... well, there are quite a few things in my life that have changed just recently, and...' She grins at me triumphantly. 'It feels good.'

'Really?' I shake my head. 'Sorry, I don't mean that it doesn't feel good, just that I'm surprised to hear you say that. You don't come across as someone who has ever had any trouble with their identity.'

Nancy pulls a face. 'Don't let the red lipstick fool you,' she says. 'I've got good at putting on a certain face for the punters... and the cameras. But inside my own four walls, very different story.' She grins suddenly and I get the feeling that this is where the confidences end. For now, at least. 'So, what do you reckon then? Tuxedo, or something a little less bling?'

'Oh no, tuxedo definitely. You should one hundred per cent give a speech wearing that. You'll have all the women there eating out of your hand before you even open your mouth.'

'Hah, I wish,' she replies. 'But then at least if my speech is rubbish, they'll have something else to ask about. Now, how do we go about this? Are you sure you're happy to make something like this? I haven't exactly gone for the easy option.'

I flex my fingers. 'No, it's absolutely fine. It's ages since I've got my teeth into something more complicated, I'm rather looking forward to it. When do you need it for?'

'Yes, that's the tricky bit. In a couple of weeks' time, I'm afraid. It's really short notice and I've no idea how long something like this takes to make. I've probably made it impossible, haven't I? You must have loads of other commitments.'

I make a show of thinking for a few seconds. 'Well... as long as you don't count a husband and daughter, none at all. In fact, now that I don't even have my job to go to, I'm all yours.'

She looks confused. 'But I thought...' She breaks off. 'Sorry I thought... assumed, you had your own business, as a dressmaker. I'm sure Esme mentioned something... And your sister-in-law's dress...'

'Done as a favour, no more. No, up until a week ago I worked in the textile and haberdashery department in Harringtons, that's all. I probably should have said something before but after nearly twenty-six years of sterling service, I've just been made redundant. It's all still a bit raw.'

'Oh…'

'Yes, it's a bit of a bugger, especially seeing as it's my own husband who made me so. He's the manager there,' I explain. 'He has this idea in his head that all I've ever dreamed of is being a housewife, or "having some time to myself", as he puts it.' I grimace. 'It's my reward, apparently, for twenty-odd years of sterling service to him.'

Nancy smiles, looking at me quite intently for a moment. 'And I can see that's not going down too well… Twenty plus years is a long time to work somewhere.'

I stare at the soup in my bowl. 'It's an incredibly long time to work somewhere… And do you know what's even more incredible? That it was only ever meant to be a stopgap after leaving uni. Something to tide me over until…'

Nancy raises her eyebrows.

'Well, I was going to say until I got my dream job. But that just sounds faintly ridiculous.' I look around the room as if I've only just realised where I am. 'Where have the last two decades gone, Nancy? Where has my life gone? I've stayed in a job I've tolerated at best for all that time… never done anything else. How on earth could I have been so complacent?'

'Happy, maybe…?' she replies. 'I think we've all been there. The years go by and we're quite content with our lot. It isn't until something changes that we're forced to re-evaluate. And in my experience, that's when the cracks begin to show.'

'Cracks? Yawning chasms more like…'

'Well, so now this could be the opportunity you've been waiting for,' says Nancy. 'Make my tuxedo for me and not only will I pay you for it, obviously, but if my outfit attracts the kind of attention I'm hoping it will, then it'll be great publicity for you.'

'Publicity?' I frown. 'Sorry, I'm not sure I follow you.'

'Just think about it. The women at this event will all be aspiring businesswomen. They could well be in need of a new outfit for the next opportunity to be seen; the next dinner, or charity event… launch of their own business, all kinds of things. And word of mouth is the best advertisement there is. You could find yourself with quite a bit of business coming your way. And before you know it, you have orders lined up and you're a self-employed designer. Maybe you'll get your dream, after all.'

I shake my head. 'But that's just it,' I say. 'I never wanted to be a designer. I started making clothes because I couldn't afford to buy any, that's all.'

My head is suddenly full of thoughts, thoughts I've not had for a very long time.

Nancy grins. 'Ooh, come on, you've got to tell me now. What was it you always wanted to do?'

But I spoon up the last of my soup instead of answering. It's something that belongs to another part of my life. 'Do you know, I'm not even sure I can remember.'

# CHAPTER NINE

Sorry, Hugh, what did you say?' I look up from where I'm sitting at the kitchen table, my laptop in front of me, momentarily distracted by what's on my screen. Hugh is standing nearby holding an armful of books.

'I wondered if we really needed to keep these any more,' he says. 'We've had them for years, and all they do is sit on the shelves and gather dust. Do you even look at them now?'

I drag my eyes away from the screen, forcing myself to concentrate. I hate it when Hugh's in one of these moods – his getting-things-done mode – because invariably it involves asking me so many questions that I end up getting his things done too, even if I'm trying to do something else at the time. I peer at the titles in his arms.

'What are you doing?' I ask, as I realise the significance of his question. 'Yes, I look at them, and no, we can't get rid of them.'

Hugh looks as if I've just burst his balloon. 'Oh,' he says. 'It's just without that bookcase, we'd have an awful lot more room.'

The email that just appeared in my inbox is still desperately trying to claim my attention. I close the laptop lid, biting back the sigh of frustration that I'd love to give vent to.

'Okay, you've lost me,' I say, getting to my feet. 'Why do we need to move the bookcase?'

He smiles. 'Come with me.'

I follow him upstairs and into the larger of the two spare bedrooms. Even so, it's still a space only a little over ten-foot square. With the bed taking up the lion's share of the room, there's very little left for anything else. Except the bookcase, and its collection of my art and history books which I have guarded zealously over the years. The shelves are missing some of their 'teeth' and I unload the books from Hugh's arms, sliding the volumes back where they belong. He indicates another pile on the carpet.

'What about those then?' he asks. 'Some of them are mine, and I'm happy to pass those on.'

There's a stack of a dozen or so books. 'But what difference will it make?' I ask. 'Even if we took away half of all the books here, we'd still need a bookcase. I can't see what we'd gain from it.'

Hugh takes my shoulders and gently angles my body until I'm facing back into the room. He points to the small area of recessed wall behind the door. 'I thought that if I put up some shelves there, we could rehome the books, do away with this bit of furniture entirely and then, by freeing up this whole wall, have a workbench along here and into the corner.' He grins proudly at his suggestion.

'A workbench?'

'Yes,' he replies. Triumphant. 'You've been working on your laptop all morning, perched at the kitchen table, and I thought it might be nice for you to have a proper place to work from. I mean, I have my study, so in a way it's only fair. We could make this room really nice – not necessarily decorate it, but make it more cosy so it doesn't look like a guest bedroom. Maybe even take the bed out, have a sofa perhaps…'

'I'm only looking at patterns online,' I reply. 'I don't really need a room for that.'

'Yes, but what about when you're actually making something? Like you did for Tash's dress the other week. Then you had to leave everything all over the kitchen table.'

I scrutinise his expression, trying to work out his motive, wondering if that's what the problem is: that I'm messing up the kitchen.

'That's not a problem,' he says. 'Just… well, I thought you might prefer to have somewhere where you don't have to keep constantly tidying everything away. I know how you like things to be in their place.'

I don't actually, Hugh, I think to myself, that's you. I hate to tell him, but if we did turn this room into a workspace for me, it would mostly look like a bomb had exploded.

'And you could get really busy if what Nancy says is true. Then what will you do? If you're going to set up a small business, we might as well do it properly.'

I take a moment. I need to be careful how I phrase this. 'I think Nancy was just trying to be kind,' I reply. 'Trying to flatter me in case I needed any more persuading to help her out. I don't suppose for one minute that I'll have a queue of people at the door. Dressmakers are ten a penny for one thing but, more importantly, most people who want something special don't like to take too much of a chance; they'll go for what they know and trust. They'll go somewhere like Harringtons.'

Hugh smiles at the truth of my statement. 'Possibly,' he agrees, willing to concede only so far. 'But it wouldn't hurt to be prepared, would it? Too late to think about how you're going to run a business once you're swamped with orders. You need to put things into place beforehand.'

There's nothing for it, I'm going to have to spell it out. 'Hugh, I'm sorry, but I don't really want to turn my dressmaking into a business.'

'Oh, don't you? I just thought… you keep saying how you need to find something to do, that you don't want to be stuck at home all day. And I thought this could be perfect.'

'But I'd still be stuck at home all day.'

'Would you? I would have thought you'd be going out to see clients.'

'Sometimes… But the reality is that wouldn't be very often. Most of the time I'd just be here, sewing all day, by myself.'

He nods. 'Well, yes, when the work was being done.' He stares at the room and the changes he's made, sloshing around in the cold water I've just poured all over it.

I soften my expression. 'Hugh, it's a lovely idea, really, but… can I just think about it for a bit, before we go ahead with all this? I'm only really making this outfit for Nancy as a favour. And I am quite excited about it, but I think that's more to do with wanting to get it right for her than any opportunities that might come my way as a result. I haven't tackled the making of anything more complicated for a while, and I'll admit, I *have* been bored this last week or so. I'm looking forward to the challenge and having something to focus on for a while, but I'm not sure I want to wholeheartedly go down that route. Not just yet anyway.'

Hugh takes another look around the room. 'Yes, I can see that. But you know, I think we should go ahead and do it anyway. What would it hurt? We have the space and once we've made the alterations the room is always there. Ready and available whenever you need it.'

I look at my husband's face, at how pleased he is with his decision. How can I possibly refuse him when he's gone to so much trouble? But once the room is done, I'll feel obliged to use it – silly to be cramped in the kitchen when I have a space designed just for me. I tell myself to stop being so ungrateful, but I can't shake off the feeling that, yet again, Hugh has made up his mind how I'm to live my life and it's all so sensible and logical that it's what I'll end up doing because I can't think of a good enough reason not to.

But I'm also aware of a new sensation. One that I push back with all my might. It's rough, scratchy, and more than a little unnerving; a rope against my neck, a noose tightening…

'Right. Well, I think I've got some old bits of wood in the garage. I'll have a look and we can take it from there.'

He goes back downstairs and I watch him, my hand trailing across my books on the shelf. He's right, I don't look at these any more, I haven't for a long time. But they're a piece of me from way back when, and I can't get rid of them, it would be like cutting me off at the roots.

It's another twenty minutes before I can safely get back to my laptop and the email that had claimed my attention before. I've made a cup of tea and Hugh is busy hunting for materials for the room makeover. Now I can puzzle over the thing that struck me as odd without having to explain myself.

Of course the email is more than likely a scam; some hideous virus-laden message which will have my bank account details isolated before you can say, *sell to the highest bidder.* It's just that there are words contained in the link that sits on the page which are of real interest. I stare at the message again, but there's really not much to decipher.

*I saw this and thought of you…*

And then the link.

No, 'Dear Alys,' no greeting at all in fact. No signature either. And the email address is not one I recognise – mouzel@gmail. com. I click on it to expand the details, but there's nothing else. No tell-tale string of letters and numbers that makes me think it's being bounced halfway across the world.

So, I'm back to the link again and the words that jump out at me as if they're written in bold. Textile… Conservator… Hidden among a collection of queries within a search string. I eye the kitchen door as if mistiming my opening of the link might cause a minor explosion with disastrous consequences. But the coast is clear and so, screwing up my eyes, I click.

I'm surprised when what actually opens is not a dodgy link to buy Viagra, but a page on the IIC website – the International Institute for Conservation of Historic and Artistic Works. A bit of a mouthful by anybody's standards, but, most importantly, the industry standard. The job I'm looking at has me glancing up nervously once more as if Hugh will somehow be able to catch me out, to see through walls and know what I'm looking at.

I skim-read the contents. They're fascinating. In fact, so much so that a bloom of heat travels up from my toes and out onto my cheeks. But, just for a moment, the job description can wait. Something else is claiming my attention. I narrow my eyes, trying to catch the thought that's flitting through my head, some flicker of memory that won't sit still. Just when I think I've got it, it laughs and skips away, teasing. But there is something there, and when I trap it, pin it down and stare at it, I'm amazed I didn't see it straight away. The email address… such a giveaway.

I hit the reply button, thinking. I could make this long or short, but there really is only one question I need answering.

*Why…?*

Then I hit send and consign my message to the ether.

I clear my throat, sit up a little straighter, and navigate back to the internet tabs I have open and the pages of patterns I've been browsing. My concentration is shot to pieces, but now I need to do something to keep myself occupied. The one thing I won't do just yet is look at the job advert that Sam sent to me.

Within seconds a reply comes pinging back, sending another little shock wave through my system.

*I just came across it. It seemed… timely.*

Bullshit. Did it ever.

And how dare he think he knows what's right for me?

He is right, of course. A job like this was all I ever dreamed of, so it would be perfectly natural for Sam to assume that I was working in this field. But that's utterly beside the point.

*You didn't just come across this… you went looking.*

*Okay, so I went looking…*

Well at least he has the decency to admit it. Although that rather begs the question why he did it in the first place. He doesn't know anything about my circumstances. And if he does, who told him? More to the point…

I start typing again.

*Again, why? And who gave you my email address?*

I flick back to my internet search. I will not stare at the screen waiting for a message to arrive. I will not.

The seconds click by as I scroll from image to image, staring at the details of patterns for Nancy's tuxedo without seeing any of them. But still I keep scrolling. What is he doing? Is he sitting there, picturing me in my kitchen, in the lounge perhaps, wondering what to say, how best to explain? Maybe he's gone to get himself a cup of tea…

I shake my head. For God's sake, Alys, you're pathetic.

A sudden ping.

*Can I see you?*

*Yes.*

# CHAPTER TEN

I'm early. I'm always early for everything and it drives me mad. I would so love to be one of those people who just arrive for things, casually, in a relaxed manner, on time and with no fuss whatsoever. Instead, I fret and double-check details, triple-check them actually, and then arrive with so much time to spare that I can really go to town torturing myself over what I'm wearing, what I'm going to be doing and all the possible things that could go wrong.

And the more important the meeting, the earlier I am. So it's a full twenty minutes before I see Sam making his way slowly across the car park towards me. I doubt he's spotted me – I'm perched on the end of a bench alongside the river, partially shaded by one of the willow trees that line its course through the city. And, after a tortured never-ending weekend, when my mind conjured Sam into some mythical, almost super-human being, who had the power to bring about massive disaster, it's a relief to see that he's just a man after all. One wearing jeans and a tee shirt, and walking with a pronounced limp. Not a threat to my life at all.

I wouldn't say that Sam was ever good-looking, not in the traditional sense, but there was always something about the way his features arranged themselves that was pleasing to the eye. They carried the sense of who he was right out there for all the world to see. Except that now, of course, one half of his face has been given a different personality, scarred by the accident that punched a hole through his life. And mine. It's a stark reminder, should any be needed, of what Sam has been through over the last two decades; it isn't just my life that has been so different from what I imagined.

I stand up as he approaches so that he'll see me easily. Today is rife with opportunities for things to go wrong and I don't want anything to be awkward, not even our greeting. He raises a hand when he spots me, his face creasing into a grin.

'Hi,' he says easily.

And I stand there, squinting into the sunlight at the man who used to be my husband.

'Am I late?' he adds. 'I wasn't expecting the traffic.'

I shake my head. 'I was expecting more. I got here early.'

There's silence for a moment as each of us tries to work out what to say next. I don't want to compliment him on the way he looks, because that might imply that he's dressed up for the occasion, and give entirely the wrong message. But he does look well. Far more relaxed than when I saw him last and he seems comfortable in his skin, even though he won't be. And I don't want to say something banal about the weather either.

'Sorry, I've just realised I don't even know where you live,' I say. 'Have you come from far?'

'Today no, I'm staying with Nancy at the moment.' He smiles at the sudden alarm in my eyes. 'I've told her I'm meeting someone I used to know way back when from work,' he adds. 'Which is perfectly true. Don't worry, Alys, this isn't going to cause any problems; I know you two have become friends.'

I smile my gratitude. 'It's good that you and she still get on well,' I say.

He hesitates for a moment, as if weighing something up, but then his face clears. 'Yes. Well there's Theo to consider of course and…' Sam gives a little snort of amusement. 'Although he thinks I'm an arsehole actually. Still, I don't suppose I'm the first parent whose kid thinks that. I'll be up here for several weeks, that's all, just to give Nancy a hand with a few things until The Green

Room opens, then it will be just her running the show and I'll disappear back home.'

'Which is where?'

A gentle smile creeps over his face. 'I have a flat in London, but for the most part – well as much as I can manage anyway – I have a house in Cornwall.' He's regarding me with amusement and the penny suddenly drops. I should have realised.

I slap a hand against my forehead. 'Mousehole, of course…' I pronounce the word Mouzel, just like the locals do.

He grins. 'I did wonder whether you would work out who sent the email, but it didn't take you long. I'm impressed.'

'Well, you always did dream of living there.'

He watches me for a second before his gaze drops. It was my dream too.

'And is *The Little Country* still your favourite book?' I ask quickly, moving on.

He smiles. 'One of them. I'm a little more well-read these days, but it will always have a place in my affections. And yes, it's lived up to my expectations and now that the business pretty much takes care of itself, I'm happy to say I'm able to spend more and more time there.'

'That's good.'

The conversation is in danger of coming to a halt once more and it's a relief when Sam looks at his watch.

'Right,' he says. 'Well, shall we?'

I look at him quizzically. 'Yes, we'd better. Did you have anything in mind? There are some good places to eat locally, or…' I trail off. I'd been about to suggest we simply walk along the river, but I'm not sure how easy that will be for Sam.

He looks a little apologetic. 'Actually, I've made some arrangements. I hope that's okay?' When I don't reply, he continues. 'I just thought it might be easier if we had something specific to do… so… come back to the car and I'll explain. We need to drive, but it's not far from here.'

'Okay…' I say slowly. 'Sounds intriguing.'

The conversation falls away as we make our way through the car park. I hadn't intended it to, but I can't think of a single thing to say and now I'm conscious of every step we take.

'We may be out for a few hours,' says Sam after a minute or two. 'Is that okay? I'm not sure how long you can park here.'

'It's all day,' I reassure him. 'That's why I suggested it. I used to park here for work, before I was made redundant.'

He nods. 'Hmm, Esme mentioned that,' he replies. 'I offered to pick her up one morning on my way into the restaurant but she thought you might rather do it. That you were at a loose end…' he adds, explaining.

'Which is why you sent me the job advert…' It's all beginning to make a little more sense.

He looks at me sideways. 'One of the reasons. Still, not much fun though, I don't suppose. Where did you work?'

That surprises me. I thought he knew. 'Harringtons,' I reply.

He stops dead, eyes wide. 'You're still working at Harringtons? Were still working…?' I can see his thought processes join up the dots. 'So… what, *Hugh* made you redundant. Oh my God, that's priceless!' A bark of laughter escapes before he can stop it. 'Sorry,' he says. 'I shouldn't laugh.'

'No, you bloody shouldn't.' I can see he wants to say something else, but he holds his tongue and we walk in silence the rest of the way. As soon as we're settled in the car, however, he turns to me.

'Sending you that job advertisement was really insensitive of me, Alys. I'm sorry, I really should have thought. I just assumed…'

'What? That I was working as a conservator already, not still stuck in my sales assistant job, the one that was just temporary until I found something better?'

A slight flush colours his cheeks. 'Shit,' he says succinctly. 'Well done, Sam. I really couldn't have got that more wrong if I'd tried, could I? And worse, I have a horrible feeling that you're going to hate today.'

'Oh?'

He sighs. 'I've arranged for us to go and see the textile conservation studio at the National Trust. They're having an open day, you see, and I thought… I don't know whether you've ever been, but I thought that at least if you hated me then the day wouldn't be all bad… I don't want you to hate me.'

'I don't hate you, Sam. I don't know you.'

'No,' he says quietly.

'I did hate you. With a passion. And I've been through all the other emotions too over the years. I guess you have as well.'

His hand is still on the car key, poised in the ignition switch. He doesn't know if we're going yet.

'But sending me the job details and thinking I would like the open day are both incredibly kind thoughts, Sam, whatever you did or didn't know. And I've never been to the studio. They don't have open days very often. In fact, I think it's only once a year, but I've either been working or talked myself out of going before now… It always felt a little like rubbing salt in the wound… But today, I think I should like to go very much indeed.'

Sam dips his head a little and starts the engine, but neither of us says a word as he navigates out of the car park and into the traffic. It isn't until we reach a stretch of road that's a little less busy that the conversation resumes.

'So, I think I know where I'm going,' says Sam. 'But you're the local. Please shout if I start heading in the wrong direction.'

'It isn't far,' I reply. 'About half an hour or so. Just follow the signs for Cromer and the Blickling Estate. The studio is almost next door.'

The car falls silent. I try every which way to start a conversation but, somehow, every opening feels wrong. Today is fraught with danger. There are too many things that need saying, and similarly too many that must remain unsaid. There's no way I can afford to loosen my grip on the lasso that's holding my thoughts corralled. God forbid any of them should jump the fence. So I sit back and try to enjoy the luxury of the car we're travelling in and the scenery passing by me on a day when, remarkably, I'm not rushing from one place to the next.

Eventually I manage to ask a few questions about how much of Norfolk Sam has seen, if any. Does he like it? Is he happy that Nancy and Theo are now living here? I learn that Nancy's parents have a bungalow on the coast and suddenly The Green Room coming to Norwich makes a lot more sense.

The heat is finally beginning to leave my face as we draw up into the car park for the conservation studio. I wasn't lying when I made the comment, I am genuinely excited to get a glimpse inside. And whether that sparks some yearning deep inside of me, I don't care, not today anyway. I can deal with that another time. I lean down into the footwell to pick up my handbag and my hand is already on the door handle when Sam's voice comes from beside me.

'So, Alys Robinson. If you're not a curly-haired kind of girl any more, what kind are you?'

I'd forgotten how he could take the legs out from under a perfectly straightforward conversation, and my carefully rehearsed speech goes straight out the window. 'Sam, don't do this.'

'Do what?'

I smile. 'Be like you used to be…' I can't think of anything else to say.

He laughs, throwing his hands up in the air, because he knows exactly what I mean. But then he adopts a more serious expression. 'Don't worry, Alys, I'm not how I used to be at all. In fact, I'm a shadow of my former self.' He's holding my look with the frank expression that I remember of old. 'But I promise that I'm no threat to you. I'm not here to cause trouble.'

He's watching me as he talks and, despite what he's just said, he's as direct as he always was. It was one of the things that I admired about him, actually; how he never used to shy away from talking about the things that really mattered. The things that even us adults, with all the supposed wisdom of our years, find too difficult to discuss. And he's right of course, we should talk about it.

'So, what is today all about then, Sam?'

His reply is immediate. 'I just didn't like the way we parted the other day. It didn't seem right, not when we once loved one another, were married. Even now that's no longer the case, it seems wrong not to acknowledge it and try to pretend it never happened, however much we might wish it hadn't. Our past has brought us both to where we are today and the intervening years haven't left either of us unscathed.'

He gives me a sad smile. 'I know you have things you need to say, Alys. Just as I know you probably would like to see me dipped in a vat of boiling oil at the very least. I'd be a fool if I didn't acknowledge that you'd have every right to say and do those things. I'm just not sure what good it would do.'

'Actually I wanted you cut into tiny pieces and dipped into a vat of boiling oil,' I reply. 'But you're not stupid, Sam, I know everything that I might want to say has been in your head for years, same as in mine. I know you will have thought up replies to all the questions and counter questions I'd ask, just as I've thought endlessly about what to ask you. What I would say to you if I ever met you again. And now, when faced with the prospect, it's bizarre how little of it matters.' I'd removed my arm from the door handle but I place it back there now, leaning my body to the side as if about to get out of the car. His hand catches my arm.

'The only thing you need to know is that I never meant you any harm, Alys, quite the opposite, in fact. And the same is true now. But for all that you meant to me back then, I can't just pretend that I'm not curious about you now, and what your life has become.

That would be like pretending you don't exist.' He pulls a face. 'So, tell me, Alys, what kind of woman are you now? Your hair is not the only thing about you that's changed.'

I climb from the car, drawing in a deep breath that's meant to calm the flutters in my stomach. I wait until he's levered himself out too.

'What kind of woman am I?' I say, staring out across the car park for a second, before flicking my gaze back to him. 'I have absolutely no idea.' I push the car door closed. 'Let's go inside, shall we?' I add, as a cloud crosses the sun.

He's right about what he said. And up to a point I'm just as curious as he is. The only difference is that I can't see what good indulging this curiosity would do. Aside from possibly making small talk at the restaurant on the odd occasion over the next couple of weeks, it's unlikely that I'll ever see him again. Once The Green Room opens, he'll go back to his life and so will I. Besides, I really don't want to describe my life to Sam; it's bad enough that I have to think about how little I've achieved without telling him too.

But, as soon as we enter the conservation room, I realise how clever Sam has been in bringing me here today. And I can't help the smile that lights up my whole face. Laid out across a vast table in the centre of the room is a carpet, of the kind that once upon a time I would have given my eye teeth to work on. It's probably a hundred and fifty years old, almost certainly Axminster, but the chenille wool facing has all but gone in vast areas and it breaks my heart to see it so forlorn. The colours would have been so beautiful when it was new.

There are only half a dozen or so people in the room, the central space in a huge converted barn, one wall bare brick and the rest whitewashed, allowing light from the huge arched window to flood the area. A mezzanine level sits to the rear, while to the left and right are smaller workrooms. We were handed a booklet of information by a member of staff at the door but this is no museum space; it's an actual working environment and there are people here going about their business as if the handful of visitors are mere ghosts from the past.

I give Sam a tentative look, but he smiles, waving a hand in the direction of the carpet. 'Go,' he says. 'Don't worry about me. I'll just… mooch.'

But he won't because Sam always had a deep and genuine interest in the people and things around him, and I don't suppose that's changed over the years. Still, I'm pleased he isn't expecting me to stay glued to his side. I make for the central table before turning slightly to watch as he makes his way to one of the smaller rooms. When we entered I'd caught the slight surprise on the face of the person who greeted us, the sight of Sam's scars unexpected. She recovered herself well, but it was still there, and I can't help but wonder if Sam even notices now, or whether he's so used to this reaction from people that he's long since stopped seeing it. Not for the first time I think about what kind of life he must have had.

I've come to rest beside a young woman and perhaps she can sense my longing, or maybe it's just concern that my fingers might stray onto the wool beside her, but she looks up as I hover. Her face is welcoming.

'You can touch them if you'd like,' she says, indicating the skeins of coloured wool.

'They're such beautiful colours,' I reply. 'So delicate.'

She nods. 'They're dyed specifically for the project,' she says. 'Even down to colour matching areas where the original has faded.' She points to the part she's working on. 'See…' She lifts a hank of wool. 'This shade is lighter so that it matches where the wear and tear has lifted the colour. If all the wool we used for our repairs was the same as the original colour, it would look out of place, rather than a sympathetic restoration which is what we're aiming for.'

I nod. 'Even down to the wefts, that's incredible.' My hair has fallen over my face and I tuck it back behind my ears to get a better

look, laying a finger gently on an area of the carpet immediately
to the woman's right. 'It really doesn't look like it's been repaired
at all and yet when you compare it to an area that hasn't been
touched yet, it's obvious.' I sigh with pleasure.

The woman looks up, surprised. 'I'm impressed. Most people
would think that patch still needed attending to.'

'Would they?' I smile nervously. 'Perhaps it's just my age. I'm
old enough to know how a carpet like this should look.'

She laughs, but she's studying me more closely. 'Have you ever
thought about becoming a conservator?' she jokes.

The breath catches in my throat. 'Oh, I wish…' I break off,
eyeing the carpet again, tracing the intricacies of the pattern. 'Once
upon a time maybe, but not now, I think I might be a bit past it…'

'Nonsense…' She looks up at me, a smile of encouragement
on her face. 'You should go and talk to Becky if you're interested.
Seriously, she looks after our volunteers and we need all the help
we can get.' She indicates the enormous area of carpet still in front
of her. 'There are all kinds of things you could get involved with.
Not all of it as skilled as this.'

'Oh, I don't know. It sounds lovely, but I haven't worked with
anything in years. I'd be terrified I'd get it wrong.'

'So you have some experience?'

'A little, and I do mean a little, but it was from ages ago, when
I was at uni. A work-placement thing.'

'In restoration?' She puts down the thread she's holding. 'What
did you study?'

'Textiles,' I reply, a little sheepishly. 'Followed by an MPhil in
textile conservation.'

She lets out a long slow whistle. 'Then I should definitely go
and talk to Becky.' She points to the mezzanine level. 'She's hiding
up there, but tell her I sent you. My name's Lucy.'

'Then thank you, Lucy, I will.' I move my finger to touch
one of the skeins of wool, as a warm glow begins to blossom

somewhere deep inside. 'You've been really helpful. And this is beautiful, just stunning.'

I'm amazed how much time has passed by the time I find myself back in the main room again. I haven't seen Sam on my way round so I guess I've probably just missed him, but it isn't until I'm standing looking around me that I realise he's not here at all. I'm about to double back to check the smaller rooms again when I spot the member of staff from reception heading towards me.

'Are you looking for the man you came in with?' she asks. 'Only he gave me a message to say there's no rush at all, but he'll be waiting in the tea room next door, whenever you're ready.'

I check my watch again. 'Oh God, when was this?'

She waggles her head from side to side. 'Hmm. About an hour ago… but he did say to tell you not to worry about the time.'

I thank her and head for the door. I really had no idea I'd be this long, and Sam must be bored out of his tree. Despite my rush, however, and the spots of rain that are falling, I can't help but stop when I get outside to take one final look at the building behind me. My visit here has been quite an eye-opener.

I find Sam nursing a pot of tea, his head deep in a book.

'Listen to this,' he says, before I can even apologise for my lateness. He begins to read. '"We all want quiet. We all want beauty… We all need space. Unless we have it, we cannot reach that sense of quiet in which whispers of better things come to us gently." How incredible is that? It was written by the co-founder of the National Trust, Octavia Hill…' He consults the book again. 'Back in 1883.'

There's a second cup on the table and he begins to fill it with tea. 'Don't worry, it's a fresh pot, it will still be hot.' Once it's full he pushes the cup towards me. 'I'm always stunned when I come across someone who thinks the same things I do, even now. It reminds me I'm not the only one.'

I falter, teaspoon clinking against the cup as I stir in the milk. It's what he used to say to me because I *did* think the same things he did. 'Well, that just goes to show that some things never change. Do you still read poetry?'

'Of course,' he says grinning. 'I'm still breathing, aren't I? Have you found any gems lately?'

I carefully lay the spoon in the saucer as I answer. 'I don't really read poetry any more. In fact, I don't really read…'

Sam looks as if I've just personally insulted him. 'What? Why the hell not? No, I don't believe it. Alys, the one I always joked was born with a book in her hand.' He's regarding me intently.

'What?' I ask, irritated.

He shakes his head. 'Nothing, it doesn't matter.'

But I know what he was going to say. *You straighten your hair, you don't read poetry, you gave up following the career of your dreams. Where is the Alys I once knew?*

I drink my tea and the silence stretches out.

'Okay,' he says gently when neither of us can bear it any longer. 'I'm not making any judgement here, Alys, I'm actually interested to know why you didn't pursue the things I always thought you wanted. It's obvious how interested you still are, I only had to look at your face in the studio to see that. So what happened to the dreams you once had?'

I want to say, *you did*, but I don't. 'I guess my life just got in the way. It's pretty much as simple as that.'

And I can't say any more. How can I when I don't even know how it happened myself? Sam looks disappointed but he nods, knowing I'm not going to elucidate.

'But what about you?' I ask. 'You obviously got your wish to be a top-class chef, but I can't believe I didn't know you were behind The Green Room.' He's silent for a moment, eyes still on mine as he acknowledges my challenge. 'But then, why would I?' I add. 'Why did you change your name, Sam?'

For a minute I think he's not going to answer, but then I realise he's just trying to find a way to put it into words.

'I had my reasons,' he begins. 'But basically, I didn't much like the person I was before. Or the life I had. I thought that if I became someone else, it would help.'

'And did it?'

He smiles, wistful and brief. 'In part.'

I've thought about how it must have been for Sam so many times. His life transformed by an accident – a young man with his whole life ahead of him, newly married, and in love – all gone in the blink of an eye. And there were times when I thought I wanted nothing more than to erase my memory. How lovely it would be to simply live my life without thoughts of my past hunting me down, sometimes when I least expected it. But then I realised that it would mean a life lived without the joyous, wondrous spark that was you, and I couldn't bear it. That I might never have known what it felt like to be with you. And so I settled for the pain, however much it hurt, because the alternative was unthinkable. Why should Sam be any different?

I nod, knowing it's as much about what I don't say as what I do. And that sometimes there's just altogether too much water passed under the bridge. I check my watch.

'It's getting late,' I say. 'Maybe we should think about getting back.'

'At least finish your tea,' replies Sam. 'There's no rush, is there?'

The drive home seems to take no time at all and we both know that a threshold has been crossed. The conversation seems lighter somehow, even though there's a poignant undercurrent that isn't sadness, but something close to it. Recognition perhaps – that we've both reached the place we were aiming for, even if we didn't really want to be there at all.

'I'm glad we did this,' I say, as Sam pulls back into the car park. It seems an age since I was last here. 'It's been lovely and the conservation studio was an inspired choice, so thank you.'

He dips his head in acknowledgement. 'I wasn't sure if you would come, but I'm glad you did. It's helped, I think…' He looks tired, I realise, his face a little drawn.

'Take care of yourself, won't you?' I pause, feeling the need to say more, but not sure what. 'I hope the visit wasn't too much, all that hanging around. I had no idea I'd taken so long.'

'A small price to pay. And I hope, good timing, if it's given you a little food for thought.'

I nod. 'Maybe… Anyway, thanks again, Sam.' I push open the car door and am halfway out before his voice comes again.

'Alys?'

I turn back.

'I did a terrible thing… and I've held onto my guilt for a very long time, so I want to thank you too. Perhaps now we can both stop torturing ourselves.'

I smile and nod, seeing the relief in his eyes. And then I walk away without looking back. I did a terrible thing too, Sam. If only you knew.

# CHAPTER ELEVEN

I sit for an inordinately long time the next morning staring at my laptop. First there is the email that's taken me nearly an hour to compose, all of half a dozen lines, and secondly there's the job advertisement that Sam sent to me, the request for more information link glowing like a neon sign. And lastly, of course, I can't stop thinking about yesterday. And Sam.

The email is to Becky Wilson, the lady I met at the studio, the one who gave me her card and told me I should definitely get in touch if I ever wanted to do any volunteering. And I still don't know whether to send it, just as I don't know whether to request an application pack for the textile conservator job. It wouldn't hurt, I know, but let's be honest here, I don't stand a hope of getting it. I don't have any experience, so all it will be is simply finding out a little more about it. And getting my hopes up unnecessarily, there is that.

The doorbell interrupts my thoughts and I get up to answer it, suddenly realising that I haven't even washed up the breakfast things yet. I smile in relief when I see who it is.

'Tash!' I welcome her in with a hug.

She wrinkles her nose. 'I might be a bit sweaty, sorry. I've just come from a new client around the corner and now I've got an hour-and-a-half wait until my next one.'

'So, you thought you'd come and bum a coffee?'

She grins in reply. 'Is that okay? There didn't seem much point in going home.'

'Of course it's okay. Excuse the mess though, I've had a bit of a slow morning.'

I realise belatedly that Tash is still staring at me. 'Is that natural?' she asks, holding up a hand to catch a tendril of my hair.

Her question confuses me for a moment until I realise that my hair has long since dried from coming out of the shower and I've been so lost in contemplation that I haven't yet put on any make-up or bothered to pull my hair straight from its wild corkscrews.

'Oh my God…' she says slowly, eyes raking my head. 'How did I not know you have curly hair?'

'You must have…'

She's shaking her head. 'No, I really didn't… It looks incredible.'

I frown, tucking it back behind my ears. 'Now you know where Esme gets her waves from. Although hers are obviously far more restrained than mine.'

Tash peers at me. 'And freckles too…' She stands back. 'You look about ten years younger.'

I walk ahead of her into the kitchen, laughing. 'You're obviously badly dehydrated,' I say. 'Come and sit down and I'll get that coffee on.'

'It's true,' she protests, audibly tutting. 'And I am not dehydrated. Why don't you believe me?'

I busy myself with the kettle. 'How are you anyway?' I ask. 'Recovered?' I haven't seen her since Scarlett's party when she was undeniably worse for wear. She pulls a face.

'Oh, I'm all right *now*,' she replies. 'At the beginning of the week, not so good.' She sits down pulling a face. 'You always say you'll never do it again, don't you? Drink, I mean. And then…' She sighs. 'I'm getting too old for this partying lark and Rupert's friends are far too good at consuming large quantities of alcohol… Have you got any biscuits?'

I place the tin on the table, smiling at Tash's ability to eat whatever she likes.

'They seemed a nice crowd though,' I say.

Tash nods vigorously through a mouthful of chocolate chip cookie crumbs. 'I'm just so happy for Scarlett,' she says. 'You know how controlling Angela can be. But, after years of trying to stand up for herself, I think Scarlett might just have found her happy ever after.'

I finish making the coffee and hand her a cup. 'I hope so. I don't think Angela's ever forgiven Scarlett for changing her name. Now she'll be utterly furious that she'll no longer be able to dictate to her.'

'Well there you could well be right. Charlotte to Scarlett must grate on Angela's nerves every time she hears it.' Tash giggles as I take a seat beside her. 'I shouldn't say it, but that makes me rather happy. Oh dear, Angela is having a hard time of it, isn't she? First she has Ed standing up for me and taking her to task over her behaviour and now Scarlett is finding her feet too.' Tash swigs a mouthful of coffee. 'Makes you wonder when it's going to be your turn to surprise us, doesn't it?'

'Oh, I don't think there's any danger of that. Hugh and I have always toed the line…' I break off, biting my lip. It would be good to talk to Tash, but the trouble is I know what she'd say and I'm not sure I want to be convinced.

'Now, there's a face,' she says, cutting into my thoughts. 'Why do I get the feeling that the worm is about to turn?' She studies me for a moment. 'I'm right, aren't I?'

I sigh. 'Let's just say that the worm is thinking about it,' I reply. 'Not that it's anything serious, there's just something I'm mulling over, that's all.'

Tash looks at her watch. 'Oooh, that sounds exciting. Go on… I've got a little while yet.'

I angle the laptop towards her, still showing the page for the job advertisement. 'Not really exciting. Just that I've been thinking about what to do with my time. Contrary to what Hugh believes,

I can't spend my days stuck inside the house and I've come across a couple of things that have always interested me but… well, I'm worried they're a bit desperate.'

'Desperate?' She peers at the screen. 'Textile conservation…' She looks back at me. 'Er, how is that desperate? It's hardly risqué. I thought you were going to say you wanted to become a lap dancer or something.'

'Tash…'

'What?' She grins. 'I've always said that underneath all the square clothes you wear is a body desperately trying to get out. But seriously though, conservation is not something I would have necessarily pegged you for being interested in. I get the textiles bit, I mean what with the dressmaking and everything.'

'Yes, you see, that's just it. I left uni with a degree in textiles and then did a further qualification in materials conservation, that's all I wanted to do. Except that… well, you know the rest. Hugh, Esme, Harringtons, blah, blah, blah. And a part of me would love to pick it back up again, but I'm worried I'm just kidding myself. Kidding myself that it isn't just a desperate attempt by a middle-aged woman to reclaim some of her youth. Jeez… midlife crisis or what?'

Tash doesn't say a word, simply stares at me for so long I begin to feel very uncomfortable. Her brow furrows. 'How did I not know any of this about you?'

'I don't know… it just never really seemed… important. It's so long ago now, and I haven't really thought about it in years and—'

'You should do it,' says Tash, firmly. 'Definitely, absolutely, without a doubt, do it. What have you got to lose?'

I shrug. 'The last remaining shred of self-confidence I have?'

'But it could also give you a very much needed boost.' She pouts at me. 'Don't put yourself down, Alys, you're as bad as some of my clients. And if you carry on, I shall be forced to send you on a cross-country run, or worse…' She pulls my laptop towards her, running her eyes over the information as she finishes her coffee. 'Have you even sent for the details yet?'

'No,' I admit. 'Because I'm honestly not sure that Hugh would approve.'

'Well, why the hell not? He wants you to be happy, doesn't he?'

Her question surprises me. I've never actually considered that Hugh gives it any thought.

'Tash, Hugh made me redundant because he thinks I want to be a housewife. He'd see my applying for another job as some sort of… betrayal. You know how old-fashioned he can be.'

'But presumably you've told him you don't want to stay at home?'

'Yes, but he has this curious knack of being so bloody reasonable that I end up thinking my idea was rubbish and agreeing with him.'

She smiles. 'Alys, this isn't about what Hugh wants, it's about what you want, surely. It's your life, after all. So, Hugh aside, what's stopping you?'

And, of course, I know exactly what's stopping me. It's the same thing that's had me dithering about all morning, even if I don't want to admit to it. I take a deep breath. *Come on, Alys, get it out in the open and then you can stop worrying about it.*

'Actually there is something else. Something a bit… unexpected. You see, I had help finding this vacancy, and I'm wondering if this is giving me a prejudiced view of it, making me think of it as overly positive.' I fiddle with the handle on my mug. 'There's no easy way to say this so I'm just going to come out with it… Do you remember when you came for your dress-fitting and I told you about my first husband? I bumped into him the other day, at Scarlett's party. He's the husband, well ex-husband, of the woman that Esme is working for.'

Tash's eyes are two round saucers. 'No way!' she exclaims. 'Blimey, I bet that was awkward.'

I grin, nervously. 'Just a little. He's changed his name, so I had no idea who he was, but turns out he's the whole brains behind The Green Room.'

'The mysterious recluse that Hugh's been so worried about?'

'One and the same.' I tuck my hair back behind my ears. 'But there's something else you should know. The reason why we split up all those years ago is because the man I called Tom was involved in a horrific car accident. He came so close to dying, Tash, it was the worst time of my entire life. He wasn't expected to walk again and had burns all down one side of his face and neck. I'll spare you the gory details, but his recovery was slow and painful and, just at the point when I began to hope that things might be okay, he sent me away, refusing to see me. He said that he couldn't bear for my life to be ruined because of him and so he was setting me free.'

'Oh, but that's so romantic! Sorry, it is if you think about it. It's like something from a film.'

I give her a sideways glance. 'Maybe, but the reality was more like a horror story. So, anyway, that was it, and Sam, as he is known now, got better. He's walking now, albeit with a stick, but he met Nancy shortly after we split up and together they set up The Green Room, with him literally hiding in the shadows because of his injuries.'

I let my words settle in the room for a moment as Tash tries to get to grips with them. But I know she has a good memory, and she'll realise why I'm so worried any minute now. I see the moment when she does. Her head jerks up and she leans towards me.

'But you said that when you met he and Hugh were friends… Oh, shit…'

'Exactly. You have to promise me that you won't say anything to Hugh, or anyone else for that matter, not for the moment anyway. Until I can find a way of telling Hugh. I'm pretty certain that Nancy doesn't know, but imagine how horrendous all this could be for Esme. She'll never forgive me if this ruins her dream job.'

'But there's no reason why it should. Is there...? Alys?'

'No,' I say quickly. 'Sam and I are ancient history. I can't pretend it hasn't been the most enormous shock, but we're grown adults and this isn't a fairy tale. We met up yesterday, because as you might imagine there were one or two things we had to say to each other. And for Esme's sake neither of us wanted things to be awkward.'

'Christ, I bet...' She slides a hand over my arm. 'What did you do? Was it okay?'

I nod. 'Civilised. Water under the bridge and all that. A line drawn underneath things. And I'm glad actually. Over the years I think I'd built Sam up in my mind... he could well have been the romantic hero from the film you were talking about. You know, because he was my first love and we were destined to be together. I'd got this idealised notion of him in my head, when actually the reality of it is that we're just two people who used to be together and now we're not. It's a bit like the monster under the bed. You always think it's there and yet in reality it never is.'

'Yes, I get all of that but what I'm not clear about is what this has to do with you applying for a job.'

'Only because it was Sam who sent the details of it to me. Before he knew who I was he'd heard Esme mention that I'd been made redundant, and once he did know he was looking for a way to make contact with me. Not unreasonable to assume I was working in the industry I'd always intended to, and so he found it and sent it on. It was a friendly gesture to break the ice, but now of course he's got my interest well and truly piqued. Trouble is, I can't tell whether it's because I'm just clutching at straws, secretly still paying attention to my inner soppy romantic notions, or relishing the prospect of really pissing Hugh off.'

'Ah,' replies Tash succinctly. 'There is that...' And then she laughs. 'I just reckon you're overthinking it, Alys. You're out of work for probably the first time since you were on maternity leave, bored at home, Esme isn't so dependent on you, and so for a million and one reasons it's actually the perfect time to be looking at what you want from your future. Apply for the job, find out about it at least, but only for the reason that it interests you. You don't even have to tell Hugh how you came across the advert. He's not to know Sam sent it to you, unless you tell him, and why would you need to do that?' She tips her head to one side. 'Are you likely to see Sam again?' she asks.

'God, no. He's only up here for a few weeks until the restaurant's open, then he's leaving Nancy and her crew to get on with it and heading back to Cornwall where he lives.'

Tash pushes the laptop back towards me. 'I rest my case,' she says. 'So there's really no problem. I won't mention anything to anyone and then you can pick your moment to have a chat to Hugh. Put him in the picture and then there's no misunderstanding and everything can carry on exactly as it is. The only difference is that now you'll have an opportunity to pursue something you've always longed to do. If nothing else you can enjoy the way that makes you feel.'

I think about her words, knowing that I've been in grave danger of making something very simple become exceedingly difficult. 'Thanks, Tash, you have a real knack of sorting out my muddle of a brain.'

She reaches for the biscuit tin. 'I know,' she says, eyes twinkling in amusement. 'And my services are so cheap. All it takes is a few bickies.' She plucks out a couple more, popping one of them into her mouth virtually whole as she gets to her feet. 'Right, I must be off.' She checks her watch again. 'Thanks for the coffee, Alys. And stop being so damn sensible, you've done enough of that over the years. It's time to follow your heart.'

I see her to the door, wandering back into the hallway after she's gone, where I stare at myself in the mirror for quite some time. Tash might be a little heavy-handed at times, known for blundering in where others fear to tread, but she's nothing if not honest. If she said she loves my hair, then I really do think she means it. And as for looking younger… I narrow my eyes at my reflection.

I have one foot on the bottom stair tread all set to go and remedy both my hair and my make-up, when I stop. Maybe I'll ask Esme what she thinks first. I could leave them as they are, just for today. What would it hurt?

*

If I was nervous before Hugh arrived home, then his look at my wayward hair as he comes in through the door is enough to send my spirits crashing through the floor. His reaction is all too predictable.

'Oh dear, have your straighteners broken?' he asks as he kisses me on the cheek. He puts his briefcase down on the floor.

'No,' I reply. 'But Tash popped in this morning between clients. I hadn't got around to straightening it by the time she came and… Actually, she'd never seen it this way before and said she really liked it. I thought I might leave it for a change.'

'Oh, bless her, she's such a sweetheart, isn't she?'

'I don't think she was being kind, Hugh. I think she really meant it.'

He studies me. 'Possibly, but don't forget that Tash is in her thirties, Alys. She likes… well, the way she dresses for a start – perfectly fine – but a little on the trashy side.'

'I don't think she dresses trashily,' I reply, cross that I should need to defend Tash of all people. 'She has a gorgeous figure, why shouldn't she show it off a little?'

Hugh opens his mouth to reply but then closes it again, rethinking what he was going to say. 'We're sidetracking some-what… All I meant is that Tash quite possibly does like your hair and that's perfectly fine. But she isn't you. And she doesn't know what you like, does she? You're an independent woman, Alys, and you can make up your own mind about things. You don't need to follow what Tash thinks if you don't want to.'

*But what if I do want to?* I'm not in the slightest bit surprised that these words don't actually make it out of my mouth. I really don't need to be getting into a disagreement about this, I have far more contentious subjects to deal with this evening. And so I push my words back into the little corner of my mind, the one which holds all the others I don't say.

I hold out my hand for his jacket. 'Would you like a drink?' I ask, even though I filled the coffee pot just before he arrived.

'What's for dinner?' he asks on cue.

'Salmon,' I reply.

'And green beans?'

I nod.

'Then, yes, a coffee would be lovely now, and some wine perhaps with dinner.'

I busy myself in the kitchen. I know I should have told Hugh yesterday that I'd seen Sam. I thought I might have been able to start one of those 'guess who I bumped into today' kind of conversations, but I didn't. I couldn't find the words. Or was it that something told me it would be a really bad idea? Now though, too much time has passed. It isn't the kind of thing you can just drop into conversation and it's even harder to bring up the subject in such a way as to make it sound innocent – what am I thinking, it *is* innocent – but I'm going to have to say something soon. A little lie, obviously, but that can't be helped, and Theo will be dropping Esme home in about an hour. I'd like it out of the way before then.

I'm telling myself this means that I won't need to say anything to her either, but what I'm really thinking is that having Esme come home in the middle of a 'discussion' might also be the perfect excuse to curtail it. Just as I'm also thinking that whatever I might have said to Tash about Sam isn't strictly true. We *are* just two people who used to be a couple and now we're not, but when we were sitting having a cup of tea together yesterday, that didn't stop me from feeling more alive than I have in years.

I pour the coffee and carry it through to where Hugh has settled himself. The shine from the leather on the back of his chair curiously matches the one on the top of his head. I've never noticed that before.

'Have you had a good day?' I ask, handing him his drink.

'Routine,' he replies. 'Did you pick up my suit from the dry cleaners?'

I stare at him in horror. 'Damn, I knew there was something I'd forgotten!' I roll my eyes. 'Sorry, I'll do it tomorrow. It's not really surprising though, given the shock I had this morning. I nearly rang you in fact, but then I thought you'd probably be busy and the last thing you'd need is me blabbering on.'

Hugh fixes me with a direct look. 'What happened, Alys?'

'God, it was so embarrassing. I nearly had the fright of my life and poor Nancy…'

I cross to the other chair and perch on the edge. I can't do this when I'm towering over Hugh. Besides, I need something solid beneath me.

'I dropped Esme off today as usual and then remembered we were almost out of milk. So I popped to that little shop just up past the restaurant. I was only in there a minute, and was coming out when I met Nancy coming in, holding the door open for a man walking with a stick. I said hello to her, obviously, smiling at the other person… and Christ, Hugh, it was Tom.'

'Tom?'

'Yes, Tom… from before, my…' I'm really not sure how to put this. But Hugh doesn't need any more information.

'Tom Walker?' He puts his drink down on the coaster that sits on the small table beside him, a very measured, precise movement. 'Tom Walker, as in the cowardly bastard who dumped you the minute the going got tough.'

I baulk at his words. Whatever Tom did, that's hardly a fair explanation of what happened. But I nod.

'And did he recognise you?'

Another nod. 'And poor Nancy just stood there the whole time we were speaking, doing this double-take thing, backward and forward between the two of us, looking more and more confused. God, I wanted the ground to swallow me up. It was bad enough seeing him but then Nancy introduced us and…'

I lay a palm against each cheek. 'I thought to start with that he must simply be someone she knew in the restaurant business maybe. But he isn't, she introduced him as her ex-husband. God, this is so weird… He isn't called Tom any more, Hugh, he's changed his name and calls himself Sam now.'

Hugh's mouth drops open slightly as he stares at the wall behind me. 'Wait a minute. Let me get this straight… So what you're telling me is that Tom Walker is actually the mysterious co-founder of The Green Room?'

I want to laugh. 'Ridiculous, isn't it? I mean, why would he need to change his name?'

'I have no idea. Except that no normal person would, that I do know.'

'And to think he's been living in London, running an enormously successful restaurant, when he could have been dead for all we knew. I still can't believe it. The only thing I can think of is that it had something to do with the accident. He was walking, with a stick admittedly, but…' I falter, meeting Hugh's eyes. 'He was horribly scarred… all down one side of his face and neck. Do you think that was why?'

Hugh considers my words. 'Almost certainly,' he replies. 'The accident became the root of everything that man did, the way he behaved.' He softens his expression a little but even so he doesn't quite manage to take away the cold light from his eyes. 'I'm not saying it wasn't a terrible thing to happen, we both know it was.

It was horrific and must have been terribly hard to bear but, I'm sorry, you know how I feel. Tom used what happened to him as an excuse to treat you appallingly and it sounds to me as if his whole life has been an attempt to run away from his situation instead of facing up to it. Changing your name doesn't make you into a different person. Or a better one.'

He's looking for me to agree with him and I manage a small nod.

'And I sincerely hope he doesn't think he can come sniffing back around you. He caused you enough trouble the first time around.' A look of pain crosses his face. 'I dread to think what would have happened to you if I hadn't come along to take care of you. Nor can I believe how much it still hurts me knowing that you met because of me. If only I'd kept my mouth shut then…' Another thought dawns and he shudders. 'Except Esme… Now he's her boss, for goodness' sake.'

'No,' I say quickly. 'No, he's not. He's simply Nancy's husband. Ex-husband,' I add, reminding myself. 'Sam will have nothing to do with this new restaurant, it's very much Nancy's baby; she told me that herself, remember? He'll be here for a couple of weeks to support her with a few things for the opening and then he'll be going back to wherever it is he came from. There's no reason to think that any of us need ever see him again.'

Hugh is searching my face for any clue that I'm not telling the truth. 'So, if that's the case then I think we should keep Sam's real identity from Esme, don't you? As far as she's aware he's Theo's dad, Nancy's husband, and that's the end of it. I don't like the thought of lying to her, although it isn't really lying as such, but I can't see why she would need to know that you and he were… Well, you know…'

'But what if Nancy…?'

'Then put her in the picture,' he replies. 'But only her. She's supposedly an intelligent woman, I'm sure she'll understand perfectly.'

*

It isn't until later when we've been in bed at least ten minutes that Hugh's voice murmurs against my shoulder. 'You weren't thinking about going to see Sam at all, we're you?' he asks.

The room is dark, not totally, but enough that Hugh won't be aware that my eyes are still staring out into the night.

'Of course not,' I reply. 'Why would I want to see Sam?' I let out my breath tiny bit by tiny bit.

'Good,' says Hugh. 'Because you know I'd never let anything hurt you.'

His tone is light, his voice casual. And the arm that lies across my shoulder feels like it's pinning me to the bed.

# CHAPTER TWELVE

'Mum, come on, you know I want to get there early today.'

We're running late the next morning and it's making me clumsy. I never have any trouble pinning up my hair but today I'm all fingers and thumbs. Or perhaps it's not the fact that we're rushing that's making me nervous.

Esme doubles back to where I'm standing before the mirror in the hallway.

'Won't be a sec,' I say, through a mouthful of hair grips.

She stares at me for a moment, before tutting in the exasperated way that children reserve only for their parents. 'Just leave it down,' she says, studying me. 'Actually, do leave it down, it looks great.'

'Really?'

I grin as I see her eyes raise heavenward. 'Okay, okay, I'll leave it down. Right, I'm ready, we can go.'

'I don't know why you don't believe me,' she says. 'It isn't as if I've never told you before. I've always preferred your hair curly and I don't know why you straighten it, just because Dad says so.'

'That isn't why, I just… It was easier for work, that's all.'

'Yes, but you're not at work now, are you?' she replies.

'No, I'm not. Good point.'

Despite the early hour, Theo is already waiting in the car park when we arrive at The Green Room. He hurries over to the car.

'Oh, thank God,' he says as Esme opens her door. He ducks his head down to wave at me. 'Morning, Mrs Robinson.'

'Alys!' I correct.

He grins, ducking back out. 'I was hoping you were going to be in early today. Mum isn't going to be in until later and she's left me a list of things to do as long as your arm.' He pulls a face. 'Which ordinarily would be fine except that I met up with a few mates last night and it turned into a bit of a session. My coordination is shot to pieces, look.' He holds his hand out as if to prove that they're shaking. They're not, they're rock steady. 'I need help…' he pleads. 'Besides, I've forgotten my bloody keys.'

Esme grins but then her face falls. 'Oh, I'm supposed to have my first driving lesson this afternoon. I can cancel it though, I didn't know—'

'No, you won't, I'm just being pathetic. Anyway, Mum hasn't forgotten and she won't be long. She'll be back way before you have your lesson.'

'Come on then,' Esme replies, fishing her keys out of her bag and jingling them at him. 'Let's go and get some coffee on. I've got some paracetamol in my bag too if you need some.' She turns back to wave. 'Bye, Mum, see you later.'

'Good luck with your lesson,' I call, smiling as I pull away, anxious not to take too much more time. I know exactly why Nancy won't be at work until later, because she's meeting me. And that's what's making me nervous.

She arrives at the house about ten minutes after I do, giving the front door a jolly series of knocks. Nancy always looks full of energy and, despite the early hour, it's almost brimming over this morning as she stands on the threshold grinning at me.

'Oh, this is so exciting,' she says, coming forward to kiss both my cheeks. 'I've never had a dress-fitting before. Well, tuxedo-fitting…'

I've spent the last few minutes frantically trying to clear the kitchen of all the clutter that has mysteriously appeared overnight. But if Nancy notices the mess she shows no sign of it.

'Have a seat,' I say, pointing to the table where my patterns are already laid out, along with a tape measure, notebook and my laptop. 'I've had a few ideas, but it will be great to see what you think. Can I get you a coffee before we start?'

'Please… and if you can make it so that the spoon stands up in it, so much the better. I did not want to get up this morning.'

Blimey, if that's the case then I'd hate to see how she looks when she's not tired. But I know how she feels. A fizzing ball of anxiety in my stomach has kept me awake for most of the night and it isn't because I'm worried about Nancy's outfit.

She plonks down her handbag on the table and rummages in it for a second before pulling out a paper bag.

'Elevenses,' she says, looking at her watch pointedly. It's only half past eight. 'Or breakfast, if that's more appropriate. I wasn't sure what you'd prefer, so I brought plain ones, chocolate ones and almond.' She grins as she hands over the bag. 'Although they're only little, so you could have one of each.'

I peer inside, releasing the most mouth-watering aroma. Croissants, and freshly baked ones too. My heart sinks a little. Nancy is so lovely and I feel awful knowing that I'm probably about to ruin her day. But I smile, inhaling deeply to show my appreciation.

'I don't think I need an occasion to eat these,' I reply. 'In fact, I don't think I'll even bother with a plate, they're not going to last long.'

Nancy sighs as she sits down. 'You have such a beautiful house, Alys,' she says, looking around the sunny space. 'I'm renting at the moment, which is… okay. But I can't relax, not properly anyway. I am so looking forward to finding a place of my own once The Green Room is up and running and life calms down a little. Somewhere like this would be perfect; a cottage tucked down a little lane, but not too far away from everything you need.' She gazes out through the patio doors. 'And a big garden too. I don't get huge amounts of time, but I do love to grow things, don't you? Big fat tomatoes, herbs…'

'I would imagine in your line of work it's almost a necessity,' I say. 'But we do love it here. We moved a few years after we were married and I can't imagine being anywhere else. That might seem odd to some people but…'

Nancy shakes her head. 'No, that's the way to do it, isn't it? Get the mortgage paid off and then retirement isn't quite so scary.' She checks herself. 'Although you're far too young for that yet, of course.'

I nod and smile, simultaneously trying to add up the number of years we've been here in my head. Nancy's just made a very good point, and I make a mental note to check something.

'I'd love to feel that this move will be my last,' she continues. 'Time to finally put down some roots. Sam and I moved around a fair bit when we were younger, out of necessity mostly, trying to build up various businesses. It wasn't until The Green Room was born that things began to settle, but I don't like London. Neither does he ironically, he splits his time between there and Cornwall now.'

*I know.* And I almost say it, stopping myself at the last moment and instead painting on an interested expression. I really wish she hadn't mentioned his name. 'Well, I'm sure you'll find somewhere that will suit you perfectly. It's a lovely part of the country and I'm certainly happy to have my brains picked for information once you start looking.'

'Deal,' says Nancy, firmly, turning her attention to the things on the table.

I finish making the coffee and bring the pot over to the table along with the bag of croissants which I rip open. I'm rather enjoying the lack of formality.

'Right then, shall we have a look?' I begin. 'We probably need to decide on a design for your suit first of all, and then we can talk about fabric and embellishments, that kind of thing. I'll take a few measurements too, if that's okay?'

It doesn't take long. Nancy is one of the most decisive people I've met and within an alarmingly short amount of time she has not only chosen the style of jacket she wants but the material too. Even the type and quantity of bling that she'd like stitched to it. It rather takes the wind out of my sails – I'd banked on a little more time to work up to things, but now, there is still half a pot of coffee left, some croissants and a torturous conversation to have.

Nancy plonks her mug down, raising a hand. 'Ah,' she says. 'Before I forget, I must give you this.' She fishes in her bag once more, this time pulling out a lime-green envelope. A lush vine trails its way across one corner. 'Tah-dah!' she exclaims, handing it to me. 'And I jolly well hope you're going to come.'

'Oh, is this what I think it is?' I ask, sliding out a thick piece of card. 'Esme mentioned that the invitations were on their way.'

'Our grand opening is only a week away, can you believe it?' Her face lights up. 'I am so damned excited about this. So please tell me you can come because Esme is going to shine like the brightest of stars, and you have to be there to see it. You and Hugh.'

A sudden welling of emotion hits me and all I can do is nod. Nancy lays her hand on my arm. 'She's going to make you very proud.'

'I already am,' I manage, seeing my own thoughts reflected back in Nancy's eyes. 'And for you too. This is your baby, Nancy, and having Theo with you too, it must be very special.'

'It is,' she affirms. 'For all sorts of reasons. It's taken a while to get to this point, but now that we're all here, I couldn't ask for more and Sam is being an absolute darling. It's a big thing for us, you know… with all that's gone on. A new beginning. *My* new beginning. But he's genuinely happy for me, I can't begin to tell you how much that means.'

His name chokes in my throat. 'I can imagine.' I'm struggling to say any more, very conscious that Nancy is so close to me.

'He'll be at the opening too, loitering in the background somewhere. He doesn't like the whole party thing… with his scars and everything…'

I nod.

'But I should introduce the two of you anyway. He doesn't bite, honestly.'

I smile, but I feel like a rabbit caught in the headlights. I have to say something.

Nancy is watching me. 'Is everything okay, Alys? You look a bit… anxious.'

Her sentence dangles in the air between us, a line that I'm wriggling on the end of.

'It's just that I've already met Sam,' I blurt out. 'I bumped into him at Scarlett's wedding and Theo introduced us.'

'Oh, well then that's okay.' She narrows her eyes. 'What…? It's not okay?'

'No it is, it's fine. But… well, that wasn't the first time I've met Sam. I knew him years ago, actually. Hugh and he… they were friends from uni originally, and I haven't seen him since, at least not in a very long time. I had no idea he was your husband, you see, because back then his name was Tom…' It's as vague as I can make it, but then I remember what it is I really need to say. 'Actually, Nancy, I—'

But her expression is changing, her eyes widening, the struggle for clarity of thought writing itself large across her face. 'Oh my God…' she says slowly. 'You're The One.'

She sits back in her chair, staring at me. 'Of course you are. Oh, I knew it would be someone lovely like you. I don't believe it, after all this time.'

'Nancy, I don't know what to say, it's—'

But before I can say anything further she leans forward again and pulls me into a warm embrace. 'Oh, my poor darling,' she says. 'This is horrible for you. Are you okay?'

I let myself be hugged, stunned by Nancy's reaction. Of all the things I'd imagined her saying, that certainly didn't feature. The One? What on earth does she mean by that?

She pulls away. 'I can't imagine how you must be feeling,' she says. 'It must have been an incredible shock… You've seen him since though, haven't you? The accident, I mean. You knew how he looked…'

I nod weakly, wondering if Nancy is playing some sort of horrible game with me, but she isn't, her face is full of sympathy.

'Sort of,' I reply. 'Although there were bandages and… he wasn't expected to walk.'

She pours me out another mug of coffee. 'Tell me,' she says. 'Or shall I tell you? I can see how confused you are. That's my trouble, you see, I tend to just open my mouth and jump in… I'm sorry.'

And from nowhere my eyes fill with tears, brought on by the warmth flowing from this woman, a woman who also used to be married to Sam.

'Could you?' I reply, not sure I can do as she asks.

Her hand reaches across to give mine a squeeze. 'Perhaps I ought to tell you a little about my marriage to Sam,' she says. 'That might be a good place to start. You see, it hasn't always been what you might call conventional. We began as friends, funnily enough when he ran over my foot with his wheelchair. It wasn't the most auspicious of starts – after I'd given him a mouthful of abuse, he retaliated with a self-pitying comment about being in a wheelchair, to which I replied that just because he was in a wheelchair it didn't mean he wasn't an arsehole.' She looks at me and grins sheepishly. 'I know, he caught me on a really bad day… Anyway, much to my surprise we both burst out laughing and that was the start of it.'

I can't help but smile; Nancy paints a very vivid picture.

'We went for a coffee and he told me how godawful his life was and I told him how godawful mine was too but, by the end of it, we were both more than a little surprised to discover that we felt better. A year and a very large number of medical appointments later, we got married. He changed his name just before, saying that his old life was over – although that's never really the case, is it? You think it is. You might hope that it is. But things never properly laid to rest have an annoying habit of popping back up… Usually when you least expect it.'

She absently breaks off a piece of croissant and pops it in her mouth, chewing thoughtfully.

'And I knew there'd been someone else. I always knew. Sam wouldn't speak about it as such, he wouldn't talk directly about anything to do with his accident, but some of the things he said when we first got together – they could only be said by someone who'd had their heart broken. And the guilt… oh, by the bucketload. But even though I knew all this, I still married him. We were quite open about it, I even used to tease him, saying that one day I would meet her and then what would we do?'

I don't know what to say. She's speaking in such a matter-of-fact way, but her words are heavy with meaning. And, as yet, I have no idea how this makes me feel.

She smiles then, as if she knows what I'm thinking. 'But you mustn't be sad about it. We always loved one another and we had a good marriage, it's just that we both knew that it also gave us a place to hide – from the outside world, but from ourselves too. Just as we knew that there would come a time when that arrangement would no longer serve its purpose. For me I guess that's come a little earlier than it has for Sam.' She stops for a moment, looking at me, not with anger, but with something I can't quite define. 'That was you, wasn't it? The one who broke his heart.'

I shake my head. 'No,' I whisper. 'He broke mine.'

And even though I'm sitting in my kitchen with Sam's wife, in a house I share with Hugh, the trappings of our life together all around me, I can remember it like it was yesterday.

'He was Hugh's friend,' I say. 'And I almost didn't meet him at all. I'd started work at Harringtons and I met him, not surprisingly, in the canteen.' I smile at the memory. 'He told me not to have the fish because the colleague who had cooked it had no finesse. Said I should have his pie instead because it would warm my soul. The next day he went to work in a small restaurant that had just opened. My first day, his last, and that, as they say, would have been the end of it, had I not bumped into him a couple of weeks later. Our courtship was swift and… intense. We married soon after and I truly thought my life couldn't get any better. Until, of course, his accident changed all that.'

'I don't even know what happened,' says Nancy. 'Only that he was involved in a car crash.'

'No one really knows. It was New Year's Eve and Sam had been working. The restaurant where he worked was late in closing and he was driving home afterwards. Either he or someone else ran a red light at a crossroads. A lorry ploughed into him and his car was crushed against a wall.' I pause to clear my throat. 'He wasn't expected to live.'

The image of a face floats in front of me. Even now my memory of it is so clear; the young policeman whose duty it had been to come and tell me the news. He must have cut himself shaving that morning and during the day a small spot of blood had dried on his face. I remember telling myself to stop staring at it and concentrate on what he was saying, but I couldn't, I was transfixed. It was the shock; I know that now.

'It was days before we even knew that Sam would live but, in my stupidity, I thought knowing he was going to make it would be the end of everything. Instead, it was just the beginning. I think Sam knew what was ahead of him. I'm sure the doctors had spelled it out and Sam, being Sam, decided that he couldn't bear to put me through what was coming. So he chose not to, sending me away…'

'And he broke your heart,' says Nancy quietly.

'Yes, he broke my heart. I didn't understand it at the time. I thought love could conquer everything… but now…' I look up at Nancy's soft expression. 'Now, I think I might understand.'

I look down at the table as a silence stretches out between us. The bag of croissants, the mugs of coffee, my notebook and pen – it all seems so ordinary, and yet the day has turned into anything but.

'You must hate me,' says Nancy.

I look up in horror at her words. 'No! How could I hate you? Not when it was you that helped Sam through it all. I always hoped there would be someone, even if it couldn't be me.' I take her hand as a tear trickles down my cheek. I don't even know where it has come from. 'I thought you might hate *me*.'

Nancy looks confused. 'But you've done nothing wrong. And all this must have come as a horrible shock; meeting him under such circumstances.'

The breath catches in my throat. 'It did rather, for both of us, I think, and—'

'Have you spoken to him yet?' she asks, but then almost immediately she nods. 'Ah yes… Sam met up with an old work friend the other day. That was you, wasn't it?'

'I probably should have told you, I'm sorry.' I pause, struggling for a way to explain. 'But there was nothing clandestine about it, Nancy. I think Sam was just trying to be circumspect and I… well, I wasn't really sure what *to* say to you. It's rather a hard subject to broach.'

'Perhaps… But I suspect that's more down to how you feel about it than anything.' She smiles. 'I'm not Sam's keeper, Alys, and if I ever was I'm certainly not now. Besides, I'd be a fool if

I couldn't see that you two have things you need to talk about, *should* talk about actually, for both your sakes.'

I nod. 'Which we did, and it helped, I think. Laid a few ghosts to rest, that kind of thing.' Stirred up a few too, but I'm not going to mention that.

'So how have you left things between you?'

Her question surprises me. 'I don't really know. I mean, it's not as if we—'

Nancy reaches out a hand. 'Would it help you to know that I'm with someone new?' she says, a slight smile on her face. 'With Sam's blessing, I might add.'

'Oh.'

I stop to think. Does it make a difference? It shouldn't really… Although perhaps the question I should be asking myself is to what does it make a difference?

It's hard to know how to answer her question, but I clear my throat, as much to marshal my thoughts as anything.

'I think it's like you said the other day,' I begin. 'About fear and being scared of changing… I was in a bad way when Sam and I split up. I already knew Hugh as a friend and when things began to develop between us, I realised I needed him, and I needed the comfort, safety and security that I knew marriage to him would bring. But I guess now I can see that the trade-off for my marriage to Hugh has been the loss of me – the things that make me who I am. I've become a certain person over the years, but not necessarily the one I thought I was going to become. Does that make any sense?'

I wait for her to nod before continuing. 'And I think meeting Sam again has reminded me of the person I was before, that's all. He sent me some information too, about a job that I've always wanted to do, and if I decide to go after it, then I don't think I'm going to stay the same. I find that a little…disconcerting. But really, that's all there's been to meeting Sam again; setting in motion something that I wasn't expecting and, who knows, it might turn out to be a very good thing indeed. But whatever I decide to do, Sam will be going back home soon and I'll be getting on with my life too. And that's exactly the way it should be.'

'Don't have any regrets, Alys, not when you have the chance to change your future.'

'No, not regrets as such. Just a slight worry about the repercussions of things changing.' I pause. 'But actually, it's Esme that I'm more concerned about now…'

Nancy looks up, startled.

'I'm worried that this might be a little awkward for her. Not because I want to hide my past history with Sam as such, just that… well, you know how kids view their parents. She's going to think this is *weird*…'

'I hadn't thought about that,' agrees Nancy. 'But you're right. She'll think it's *very* weird. I mean, God forbid a parent should have had a life before they came along. Or be a person in their own right, other than just their mum.'

She picks up her mug again and swallows its contents. 'No, I think that as far as your relationship with Sam is concerned, for now at least, there's no need for Esme or Theo to know anything beyond the fact that you've just met him – in his role as my ex-husband, Theo's dad and one half of The Green Room. It doesn't have to be any more difficult than that, does it? In fact, it's all very simple really.'

'Absolutely,' I agree, nodding eagerly and mightily relieved that Nancy is so astute. 'Perfectly simple.'

# CHAPTER THIRTEEN

I can't remember the last time I went shopping, not for something like this anyway. A sparkly, expensive show-stopper of a dress that will cost far too much money and I will probably hate when I get home. But that's not the point. I am not going to The Green Room's opening in the same bloody thing I've been wearing for every special occasion, including Scarlett's engagement party.

And I haven't even mentioned it to Hugh. Not just the circumstance of buying such a frivolous outfit but the opening either. If he's been paying attention, he'll know when it's taking place – Esme has mentioned it enough times. But whether or not he's actually taken in that this is an event which means a great deal to his daughter is another thing entirely. I'll speak to him about it later of course, but first I want to see how I get on today because, ironically, Harringtons has always been the place to go to buy anything like what I'm after, but now is the last place I'm going to look.

I stood in front of the full-length mirror in our bedroom last night for quite some time, staring at my reflection. The wardrobe door was open, its contents all saying the same thing – *we're old, we're plain, and we're nearly all the same colour*. But the loudest message of all, the one being shouted by nearly everything I own was, *we're boring*, and I could hear it clear as a bell. I wasn't deluded enough to think that I could ever wear anything that Esme would favour, but I did sneak into her room for just a second to retrieve the stunning red dress she had recently worn and hold it up against me for a moment. I'd had a dress like this once. Before.

I didn't try it on. I wouldn't, not without asking Esme first, but in any case I doubt it would have fitted. But just the feel of the soft slippery fabric, the colour of it and the way it lit my face was enough for me to remember what it had felt like all those years ago. Because, more than anything, that's how I wanted to feel.

I'm now standing peering into the window of a shop I've never been in before. It has that slightly intimidating look about it, the one that says you can't just drop in here nonchalantly in your lunch hour, with scruffy shoes on and wearing an ill-fitting uniform. If you come in here, you should at the very least attempt to look gorgeous first. So I'm really not sure whether I'm going in now, but there is the most amazing green dress in the window that I know I may live to regret not buying if I walk on by. I'm just at the point where I've convinced myself to stop having foolish ideas when I catch the eye of an immaculately made-up woman inside who gives me such a dazzling smile I can't turn away. I push open the door and try to remember that I am free to leave at any time.

Except that I don't, not for at least three quarters of an hour, and when I do I'm clutching a bag containing a dress that actually made me flinch when I was told the price of it. And then I remembered the lump sum that will soon be winging its way to me, courtesy of my redundancy, and something rather wicked came over me.

The whole process has taken far less time than I imagined it would and I'm now in something of a quandary. I could go straight home, but somehow the thought of returning sooner than planned doesn't appeal. I'm already walking, heading back up towards the marketplace automatically, but I stop and look around me, as if seeing the possibilities of my freedom for the first time. And, as I do so, I catch a flash of sunlight on glass and I know I'm going to do something I haven't done in a very long time.

The library isn't particularly busy, but then its great glass edifices have always given it a feeling of space, its layout allowing customers plenty of room to browse. I pause for a moment to stare up at the sky through the intricate ceiling dome, feeling a little thrill of excitement ripple over me. All these books, all this knowledge, stories and facts at my fingertips. Where on earth do I start?

I know where I'm going to end up, but I want to savour my journey there, to take my time and explore. So many things I've missed over the years and I chide myself for being so foolish. How could you do this to yourself, Alys? Be so neglectful of a part of you that you should have tended and allowed to bloom, but instead have let wither and die. No, I remind myself, it's not dead, not completely extinguished of life, merely dormant, waiting for the right conditions to allow its rebirth.

Once upon a time I would have known what I was looking for. I would have recognised the authors' names, their titles, but the sea of novels in front of me now is uncharted water and I have no idea where to begin. A display pulls me forward and within minutes I'm lost, drinking in words greedily as if I've been wandering in the desert for days without water. I smile inwardly at my sudden appetite, knowing that I can't possibly eat all that I want to. I catch the eye of a man standing opposite who already has an armful of books.

'I tell myself that just one more won't hurt,' he says with a smile. 'And then I wonder why my arms feel twice as long by the time I've carried them all home.'

'I haven't even got a clue where to start,' I reply. 'I've got out of the habit of reading lately, and when I say lately, I mean years and years. And now, looking at all these books, I'm wondering how I could ever have let that happen. Silly, isn't it?'

He gives me a sympathetic look. 'But you're here now, that's the main thing. And the books don't seem to mind. I've promised so many that I'll get to them one day, and they're still waiting, but so far none of the words have wandered off to find a reader who's more reliable than me. Believe me, it's never too late,' he says, looking fondly at a table of novels. 'But if you need a recommendation, this blew my mind.' He pushes a navy-blue book towards me, embellished with a golden starburst on the cover. 'And we're talking serious book hangover…'

I pick up the book, laughing. 'Thank you,' I say. 'That's exactly what I need.'

He gives a small bow. 'And when you've read that, come back and I'll recommend another fix. We'll have you addicted again in no time.'

I frown at him quizzically before he moves the pile of books he's holding slightly to one side revealing a small white pin badge.

'Oh…' I reply, light dawning. 'You work here.'

There's another bow. 'At your service,' he says. 'And I'm here every day so there's no excuse. My name's Max.'

'Alys,' I reply, momentarily taken aback by the charm of the young man in front of me. 'And thank you. I will – come back, that is.'

He leans forward. 'And tell me, Alys. Are you a member of the library…? I'm just wondering, as you said you hadn't been reading recently.'

'Oh…' I hadn't even thought. I put down my things, pulling my handbag around so that I can rummage in it. 'I would have been, years ago, but…' I pull out my purse, turning to the stuffed section in the back that houses my collection of things I keep just in case. And eventually I find it; a little dirty, battered, and almost certainly out of date, but my old library card.

Max holds out his hand, giving me an amused look. 'I tell you what. You carry on browsing, take as long as you like, and when you're done, pop to the front desk over there, and ask for me. I'll have a new card ready and waiting for you and we can get all your details up to date. How's that?'

'Amazing,' I reply, grinning. 'Max, I shall be forever in your debt. There's just one last thing you could help me with…' I lean towards him and whisper something across the space between us.

He grins. 'Well now,' he says. 'You and I are going to get along like a house on fire. Up the stairs,' he adds, pointing. 'And away to your left… We've a lovely new Robert Frost anthology if that takes your fancy.'

'How did you know I was a fan?' I ask.

Max gives me a pointed look. A very knowing look. But then simply smiles, raises my old library card in salute and walks away, still carrying his bundle of books.

I pick up the blue-bound title that he recommended and head to the second floor, feeling almost light-headed with pleasure at the thought of so much to explore. I haven't felt this way for a very long time, not since…

I thrust the thought from my head and turn resolutely to the left as I reach the top of the stairs. That was then and this is now, but I'm still determined to enjoy myself.

I have no idea how much time has passed when a hand enters my field of vision to the right. It's holding a slim volume out towards me.

'You should definitely read this,' says the voice, and I can hear warm amusement in its tone.

I turn to see Sam's eyes ablaze with light, the little flecks of gold within them dancing in the sun.

'Hello,' I say.

He smiles, but he looks tired. 'Why, Alys, you wouldn't be looking at poetry now would you?'

I'm holding several books, their distinctive Faber and Faber bindings a giveaway. 'I might be,' I say, grinning. 'What are you doing?'

Sam looks around him as if wondering where he is, and I groan inwardly at the stupidity of my question. 'Um…' he replies, not wanting to state the obvious. 'Although actually what I have been doing more recently is sitting at that table over there watching you. Were you aware that you still smile while you're reading? I'd forgotten you do that.'

I lift a hand to touch the corner of my mouth. 'Me too,' I reply. 'But then I'd also forgotten how much I enjoyed doing it.'

'I can tell,' he says. 'You look more… relaxed. Happier.'

'Do I?'

Sam nods. 'More like your curly-haired self.'

There's a moment of uncomfortable silence when I wonder whether he is going to say anything further. But he doesn't. Neither of us is going to comment on the spirals of hair that spill across my shoulders and down my back. I'm wondering how to reply when Sam shifts his weight audibly from one side to the other, passing his stick between hands.

'Listen, we don't have to go straight away – I'm quite happy to sit and wait – but if you're done here, would you like to go and grab a coffee?'

I know what the answer should be, but it isn't the one I give. 'Actually, that would be lovely,' I reply. 'And it probably is time to leave. I think I've got more than enough books to keep me going. For the time being at least.'

Sam glances at all the titles I've already collected. 'Well, the good thing about libraries,' he says, 'is that you're not just limited to the one visit. You can always come back.' His eyes are twinkling in amusement.

'Oh, I'm definitely going to do that,' I say. 'I haven't even started on the history of art books.'

Max is true to his word and ten minutes later, books checked out with my new library card, Sam and I are sitting on one of the picnic tables at the back of the market square. It's safer this way, being out in plain view of the public instead of tucked away in a coffee shop somewhere, less intimate somehow. Besides, there is a stall here that does the most amazing cakes and biscuits.

I leave Sam to settle himself comfortably while I go and buy our coffees. The market is busy; it's always bustling, and in the summertime there's often nowhere to sit. Except that when I return I can see that Sam still has the whole table to himself. I slow as I approach, watching a young mother with her daughter looking for a place to stop. The child is fractious, carrying a carton of fruit juice, but even so, after a glance in Sam's direction, the woman continues walking. And I wonder if Sam even sees this any more; this subconscious decision-making that goes on around him all the time. And my heart goes out to him. He deserves so much better than this.

I lay our drinks down on the table, dropping the paper bag that contains our enormous cookies. 'I wasn't sure what you'd like,' I say. 'But then I remembered that you always had a passion for Toffee Crisps so I hope that's still the case.' I push the bag towards him. 'These can almost give you diabetes just by looking at them. But every once in a while, just so good.'

Sam grins. 'Diabetes,' he says. 'The one condition I don't have. Excellent. I shall enjoy it no end.'

I take my seat beside him, pulling out my own cookie, which is studded with chunks of Snickers bars. 'I decided to apply for that job,' I say. 'Or at least, not quite apply, but I've been looking on their website and they offer volunteer placements too. So that's what I'm going to do. For the time being, anyway, and then who knows? Once I have some experience, and have brushed up on my knowledge and skills, maybe one day there will be a job at the end of it. But I'm never going back to work in Harringtons, or any other shop, and I am not going to sit at home watching my life pass me by.'

Sam's mouth has dropped open and my own eyes widen in response to what I've just said. Up until that moment I hadn't even been sure that I'd made up my mind, but I clearly have, and with a conviction I didn't even know I possessed.

'Sorry,' I say. 'That all came out a little more… forcefully, than I intended. I think I might have been bottling it up rather.'

But Sam merely raises his eyebrows. 'I'm glad,' is all he says, before taking a huge bite of his cookie. He chews for a moment, a look of pleasure growing on his face. 'And yes, I do still have a passion for Toffee Crisps.' He drops his gaze to the floor where my bag sits tucked into the side of his legs. 'I have a confession to make,' he says, looking back up at me with a mischievous smile. 'I had a tiny peek at what you've bought. A new dress… Is that for the grand opening?'

'It's green,' I reply. 'I thought it would be appropriate. But now that I think of it… probably everybody will be wearing green.'

'Well I won't be if that's any consolation.'

I catch the look in his eye. 'Not really,' I say. 'And I can't believe how much money it cost me. I've never spent that amount on a dress before. Never spent that amount on *anything* before come to think of it. I don't know how I'm going to explain it to Hugh.'

'Don't.'

I shake my head. 'No, I have to. I've never been very good at hiding things, and I'll only fret about it if I don't.'

'Ah, Alys… You always were so honest.'

I lower my biscuit. 'What's that supposed to mean?' I ask. I can't fathom the expression on his face.

'Nothing,' he says lightly. 'Just an observation. Not everyone is as truthful as you.'

A sudden heat floods my face, and I shove in a mouthful of biscuit to hide my feelings. That's not true at all.

But if Sam has noticed he makes no show of it. 'Well, whether you tell Hugh or not I'm sure you'll look lovely.' He pauses a moment, studying his coffee cup. 'You know, after Friday, Alys, I'll be heading home… not straight away, but a day or so afterwards.

Nancy doesn't really need me here, it's just for moral support really, although I'm not sure she even needs that. But, once they're open, there's no more real reason to stay.'

'No,' I reply. It's a small, quiet noise that sits in the space between us. 'But I'm sure she has appreciated you being here.' I can't believe I'm going to say this. I thought at one time that I would have got down on my knees and begged if it would have made Sam stay. 'And it's probably for the best.'

'Probably.' Sam holds my look for a moment, his eyes clear and bright in the sunlight. 'But it's been good to see you again, Alys. To know that you're okay, settled.'

'And that you didn't ruin my life after all?' But I smile; it's not meant as a rebuke. 'I should thank you actually,' I say. 'I think you've given me just the kick up the bum I needed. You've made me realise how complacent I've become and that maybe now *is* the time to make a few changes.'

'Well now you're just being kind,' replies Sam. 'I don't think I had anything to do with it at all.'

But he has, I know he has.

I dip my head. 'We may have to agree to disagree but, either way, it's been good to see you too. To know that you're okay… Settled.'

He smiles at my repetition of his words. There doesn't seem much else left to say. He picks up his cup of coffee and drinks half. 'It's weird, isn't it? One minute you're twenty with your whole life ahead of you and the next you're fifty, looking backward, and knowing that, whatever happens, just the passage of time inevitably means that your best years have already gone by.'

'Ah yes, but some of us have made more of those years than others,' I say. 'I mean, look at you and all that you've had to contend with. And yet you're incredibly successful. You put The Green Room on the map and there aren't many people who can say that about their lives. I think I always had ambition, just not at that level. But who knows, maybe I'm a late bloomer.'

'Or maybe your life is just too small for you now,' replies Sam. 'That happens. It's a bastard when it does but…' He fingers a crumb of his biscuit. 'We grow out of things, Alys. We grow out of people too.'

He isn't looking at me, and I can't tell from the expression on his face who he's referring to. Is it him doing the growing, or is it me? And if it's me, it begs the question just who I've grown out *of*…

I stare out across the marketplace, at all the people going about their daily lives, and I can't help but wonder if any of them feel the way I do now. I check my watch and pick up my paper cup to finish my coffee. I think it's probably time to go before one of us says something dangerous, or thinks it. But I haven't banked on the way that Sam never dodges difficult conversations.

'Will we see each other again?' he asks.

His voice is light and his face, when I look at it, open and relaxed. But there is still an ambiguity to his question, and I need to be sure I answer it the right way.

'Well, I would imagine it's inevitable, from time to time. I don't know exactly how Esme sees her future but I think she's planning on being with The Green Room for quite a while. I'm sure there'll be occasions when you're needed here. Or you're simply just around, as Theo's dad… and Nancy's ex-husband.' My words dry up. This isn't what he meant and we both know it.

Sam smiles. He could always tell when I was being evasive. 'Perhaps I should rephrase my question,' he says. 'Do you *want* to see me again?' He pauses for just a second. 'That's not an invitation by the way, I'm just interested to know. Because I think at least one of us needs to admit that it would probably be a very, very bad idea.'

He sighs. 'I'm not doing this very well, Alys, but what I'm trying to say is that I can't ignore what you meant to me all those years ago, just as I suppose the same to be true for you. That doesn't mean that we should do anything about it. For our families' sakes, for Hugh, for Theo and Esme… for us too.'

'I agree. For heaven's sake, Sam, apart from anything else we're not the young kids we were when we got married. We're different people now, with a lifetime of experiences and hopefully wisdom between us. And don't worry, I don't feel slighted, what I feel is grateful. I won't pretend that seeing you again hasn't been a shock, but what it has done is settle all those "what if" questions that I've been carrying around for years.'

He smiles a little sadly.

'I think it's human nature, isn't it?' I continue. 'To hang onto issues from our past we think are unresolved, to carry them with us and harbour little hopes and dreams of a life that could have been so different. The trouble is in doing so we lose sight of the life we actually have. I think I understand that now.'

Sam nods, squinting into the sun. He's staring past me, looking at something in the distance, whether real or in his head I can't tell, but as I watch him, a smile turns up the corners of his mouth.

'I feel I should offer a toast,' he says, picking up his coffee cup once more. 'To the future?'

'Yes, to the future, and all who sail in her.' I lean forward to collect my bag from Sam's feet. 'I should get going,' I say. 'I've got books to read, if nothing else.'

'You have,' he replies, reaching for his stick. He pushes himself up from the table, taking a moment to centre his balance, and then draws in a breath, looking around him as if noticing the beautiful day for the first time.

'What are you going to do now?' I ask.

'I wasn't sure,' he replies. 'But you know, I think I might go and have a look around the cathedral. I promised myself I would before I went home.'

'Oh, you should. It's the most complete Norman cathedral in England, did you know? And the gardens are beautiful too. There's a stillness there that is so…' I trail off, trying to find the right word.

'Still?'

I laugh. 'Yes, absolutely. They're very still.'

Sam takes a step forward. 'Then I shall do just that.' He pauses a moment. 'Thanks for the coffee and the diabetes,' he says. 'And I'll see you on Friday at the opening.'

I nod.

'Wearing your green dress?'

'Quite possibly,' I reply.

I watch as he moves away, his slow rocking walk almost painful to watch. I turn to collect our empty cups and the paper bag that held our biscuits and I'm just about to pop them in the nearest bin when I hear my name.

'If you've got nowhere you need to be,' asks Sam. 'I don't suppose you'd like to accompany me to the cathedral? One last heated debate about architecture for old times' sake?'

*

'Is Tom going to be there?'

My dress lies on the bed, its cost momentarily forgotten as Hugh refocuses his attention.

'His name's Sam, Hugh, you can't go around referring to him as Tom. In fact, you mustn't, for Theo's sake as much as anything. For all I know he has no idea his dad ever went by any other name.'

Hugh tuts. 'Yes, well whatever his name is, is he going to be there?'

'I really don't know,' I reply. Not a lie as such. 'I can't just pointedly come out and ask, that would look odd. But, given the occasion, yes, I would say there's every chance Sam will be there.'

Hugh thinks for a moment, scuffing his toe against the carpet. 'Then if you don't mind I'll give the party a miss.'

'You can't do that,' I hiss, furious. 'This is Esme's big night. For goodness' sake, Hugh. I don't especially want to see Sam again but all you have to do is be civil to him. Just a polite hello, there's no need to say any more.'

I narrow my eyes in confusion, wondering if I've missed something. 'You know you're pouting like a six-year-old,' I say, suddenly remembering something from a few days ago. 'And I got the impression that Sam wasn't very keen about meeting you either. In fact, that he had no intention of rekindling your friendship. Did something happen between you?'

'Well, I should have thought that was obvious,' says Hugh. '*You* did. You're the thing that happened between us.' But then he stops dead. 'Hang on a minute, when did Sam tell you this?'

Too late I realise I've let slip something I shouldn't have. But there's also something not right about what Hugh just said either. My head is spinning. 'Hugh, how can *I* be the thing that happened between you and Sam, when you and I came after we'd split up?'

But he's not about to be sidetracked. 'No, no you don't. Don't try to deflect this back onto me. Answer my question, Alys. When exactly did Sam mention that he wasn't keen on meeting me again?'

I swallow. There's no point trying to lie when Hugh will never let this drop. I'm going to have to tell him. 'When he came to see me a few days after I bumped into him at the shop. He came to apologise for his behaviour. To do the decent thing, Hugh. It would have been rude just to ignore the fact that we'd met, however briefly it was, and so he came to say he was sorry, for all the hurt and the upset he had caused, and to try to explain why.'

'I didn't realise you'd seen him again,' Hugh replies, coldly, completely ignoring the facts of what I've just said.

'No, and I didn't tell you because I knew you'd react like this.'

His eyes are blazing. 'So when did you meet? My God, Alys, did you let him into our home?'

'So what if I did?'

'After what he did to you.' He shakes his head. 'I can't believe you would do that.'

I let out a sigh of frustration. 'For goodness' sake. You're making him out to be something of a monster.'

'He is a monster, Alys. He ruined your life.'

'No, he didn't, Hugh. You made sure of that.'

His eyes grow wider as I see my barb strike home. And my heart sinks. I really shouldn't have said that.

'And what's that supposed to mean? What are you trying to tell me now? That you'd rather I hadn't come to your rescue?'

I stare at him. 'No, of course not, don't be so silly…' I trail off, as I realise what it is about his words that's irritating me. 'Is that how you really see it; that you came to my rescue? I thought we'd fallen in love, Hugh, or is that not what happened at all? Did you plan to rescue me all along?'

'Oh, and who's being silly now?'

'Am I? I don't think so. I'm just wondering why you're having such trouble accepting that Sam and I simply bumped into one another and, whether you like it or not, neither of us can change that fact. Neither can we ignore it. Sam tried to do the right thing and now you have a problem with that too. It isn't as if it actually changes anything, but at least he bothered to try to explain.'

Hugh looks as if he's going to argue further, but he won't; criticising Sam at this point would only make him look bad. But he hasn't finished.

'And so once he'd finished explaining, what did you say to him?' he asks.

'Simply that I accepted his apology. What else could I do? And yes, I told him that he'd hurt me, and that over the years I've thought of a million and one things I could say if we ever met. But do you know what, Hugh? In the end none of it matters, so *that's* what I told Sam. I thanked him for coming to see me and I wished him well in the future, knowing that once the restaurant is open it's unlikely we'll ever need to see one another again.'

I raise my eyebrows. A challenge. 'So, that being the case, do you think that you could try to do the decent thing, for Esme's sake, and come to the restaurant opening, be polite to Sam if you meet him, and draw a line under this like I have?'

Hugh's eyes flick across to the bed. 'And you're wearing that dress, are you? Even though it cost a ridiculous amount of money.'

'Yes I am,' I reply. 'I haven't bought myself anything in a long time. I even had to attend your sister's engagement party wearing something the whole family has seen on at least ten different occasions. Not that *you* did, I might add. How much did your suit cost, Hugh? So this time, for Esme, and for me actually, I thought I deserved to treat myself. And don't tell me we can't afford it. Not when I earned every penny of my redundancy from Harringtons.'

There's something unfathomable in the depths of Hugh's eyes, but then he stalks from the room without saying another word. And it isn't until afterwards that I realise he never answered my question about how I came between his friendship with Sam.

# CHAPTER FOURTEEN

Esme looks as though she doesn't know whether she wants to jump up and down with excitement or run and hide. One single mistake is all it would take. A dish over-seasoned, a sauce burned, a plate of food dropped and The Green Room's opening night will be a disaster.

The press are due to arrive at any moment, and the rest of the guests in half an hour, so for now there are just the five of us standing in the kitchen. Where Sam is, I have no idea.

Nancy looks amazing – confident and assured – but then she's the only one out of all of us who is used to events like these. Used to working a room with press and reporters, columnists and fellow chefs, even the odd celebrity. It's not going to be quite as high-profile an event as it would be for The Green Room in London, but for Esme and Theo it may as well be. It's their first taste of being under the spotlight.

'And whatever else happens,' says Nancy, 'I want everyone to enjoy themselves.'

'Easy for you to say,' remarks Theo, sliding a look at Esme, who rolls her eyes.

'Well of course it is,' she counters. 'We all know what we're doing. And I have the best team there is: professional, committed and, above all, extremely talented. There's nothing to go wrong.' She winks. 'Besides, tonight is a showcase event, so we're well ahead of the game. And, as you know, preparation is everything and we are *very* well prepared.'

My eye is drawn to the counter tops where rows and rows of plates are laid out. The guests are all being served the same set course so everything that can be done in advance has been and the menu has been specifically chosen with this in mind.

Nancy checks her watch. 'Right, I must go through, ready to meet and greet.' She straightens her dress, breathing deeply. 'Do I look all right?'

'Gorgeous,' answers Esme, turning to me. 'And so do you, Mum.' Her face is alight with happiness and my heart swells a little more. If only Hugh shared her sentiment. He's only just stopped sulking, but he's here and, as I glance at his smiling face, at least prepared to make an effort.

He looks around the kitchen. It's the first time he's even been to the restaurant. 'So, you're all prepared then,' he says. 'Everything under control?'

Esme nods, biting her lip a little now that Nancy has gone. 'As we'll ever be,' she says. 'Although maybe you should ask me that in half an hour...' Her eyes flick to the huge clock on the wall. 'Actually...'

I nod. 'Yes, we should let you get on,' I say. 'You can't begin to get yourselves organised if we're hanging around.' I touch a hand to Hugh's sleeve. 'Come on, let's go and get a drink and leave them to it.'

Hugh follows me out into the main restaurant where there are already quite a few people gathered. I'd asked Nancy to seat us unobtrusively at the back but, even though our table is tucked away, it still affords a wonderful view of the room. We've no sooner reached it when a young woman materialises in front of us. She's wearing white from head to toe.

'May I get you something?' she asks, smiling. 'Some champagne perhaps?'

'Just something soft for me, please. An orange juice if you have it.'

She smiles her assent, nodding at Hugh in turn.

'I'll have the champagne,' he replies, but before he can sit down, the waitress indicates that he should wait a moment. She slides the chairs away from the table, offering a seat first to me and then to Hugh before melting away.

Hugh holds my look, raising his eyebrows. 'Very slick,' he comments before looking around the room. 'So who's coming to this shindig anyway?' he asks.

'I really have no idea,' I reply. 'I haven't asked, but in any case, even if I knew the names I doubt I'd be any wiser. I'm guessing they'll be local dignitaries plus a few friends. I know Nancy has also drummed up a bit of publicity by running a competition, giving six couples a chance to be the first to dine here.'

The waitress reappears carrying a silver tray which holds our two drinks. She places them on the table before retreating once more, only to reappear seconds later with a jug of water and a platter filled with little morsels that smell divine. 'For the table,' she informs us.

Hugh stares at the plate of food as if he's never eaten before. 'God, I'm starving,' he says. 'But heaven only knows what this is.'

'They're lemon and garlic artichoke crostini,' I inform him. Which he would know if he'd been listening to what Esme had been saying at the dinner table the night before.

He pops one in his mouth, chewing slowly, before nodding. But it's such a grudging gesture it makes me want to slap him. In fact everything about Hugh is irritating me tonight, I don't know why. I take a sip of my orange juice before standing up, keen to do something which will break my mood.

'I'll be back in a second,' I say. 'I forgot, but I'd promised Esme I'd take some photos of the big day for her.' I pick up my phone and head back to the kitchen.

I can't tell at first whether Esme is laughing or crying but, as I enter the room, Theo pulls her into a hug. They cling together for a moment or two and something about the relaxed way they fit together catches my eye. But then they pull apart, laughing, a little embarrassed, and I realise that all I've seen is the easy familiarity of people who work together day in day out. At least that's what I tell myself it is.

Esme pulls a face. 'Bit of a wobble,' she squeaks, flapping at her pink cheeks. 'But I'm okay now. It suddenly hit me what's happening tonight.'

Theo smiles. 'Yes, a room full of people are going to have a wonderful meal,' he says and Esme flashes him a grateful look.

'Yes, they are,' she agrees, firmly.

I wave my phone. 'Come on then, let's get some photos for posterity,' I say. 'The two of you.'

I'm about to wave my hands to signal that they should move closer together, when Theo's arm goes around her shoulders, pulling her in. It's an entirely natural pose as they both smile, relaxed for the camera, but I can feel my fingers tighten around the edge of my phone and a little flicker of anxiety gnaws at my stomach. Why didn't I see this before?

I think back to all the times I've seen them together, the occasions when Esme has mentioned Theo's name. Is there anything more between them than just a good working relationship? No, I'm certain there isn't. Esme would have mentioned something… wouldn't she? I snap another shot.

'Right, Mum, your turn. Let's have some pictures of you. After all you look amazing in that dress. Just like Grace Kelly.'

Theo comes forward. 'You and Esme,' he says. 'I'll take them.'

And so I stand and pose and smile and try not to think about all the horrible things that could go wrong.

There's no sign of Hugh at our table when I return, but then I catch sight of him standing with a group of people who have obviously just arrived. The waitresses are hovering with drinks and there's an awful lot of air kissing going on. The mayoress is among them, together with a couple of other men I recognise but can't put names to. As I watch, Hugh shakes hands with one of them and I realise that despite his reticence about coming here tonight, he's actually in his element. He'd obviously had no idea that Nancy would be quite so well connected with the local business community, and his position as manager of Harringtons makes him a perfect fit.

Nancy is walking towards the group accompanied by a young man with a camera around his neck and, as he automatically takes charge of the group, arranging them for the official photos, I see Nancy look around. She waves as she spots me and comes hurrying over.

'No excuses,' she says, grinning. 'Over you come. I want you standing next to me. As mum to one of my fabulous chefs you deserve to be in the limelight. Plus, I want everyone to see how amazing you look.'

I pull at her arm. 'But Nancy I don't know anyone. They're all bigwigs and I'm—'

'Don't you dare say it! You're not *just* anything… Now, smile, because the sooner we do this the sooner we can all eat. We were so busy earlier I missed lunch and now I'm so hungry I'm terrified my stomach is going to make the most horrendous growling noise.'

True to her word, Nancy positions me next to her as she stands poised and assured, smiling broadly for the camera. In a matter of moments we're done and she rushes off to the kitchen to collect Esme and Theo to repeat the process. I'm left standing adrift beside an elegantly dressed man, who looks to be about the same age as me. He's slim, silver-haired and has piercing blue eyes.

'I'm Mark Lawrence,' he says, holding out his hand, and there's something about the way he says it that catches at my memory. His manner is direct although his voice softly spoken.

I take his hand, frowning slightly. 'I feel as if I should know you,' I say. 'Except that…' I tap my head. 'Nothing's forthcoming.'

He places a hand over his heart. 'I'm devastated…'

It's a corny line and I'm just wondering whether he's flirting when his smile broadens. 'Although to be fair, I've changed quite a bit, whereas you look just the same as you always did…'

I squint at him, desperately trying to work out where I should know him from.

'Of course, I'm here in my official capacity this evening as a writer for *Olive* magazine. Given the occasion and the prominence of The Green Room, I'd have been here to cover the opening anyway. The fact that Sam and I went to uni together just makes this all the more agreeable.'

And it comes to me. The memory rushing in, leaving my heart pounding. Because the last time I saw Mark was on the day I married Sam. The smile is still on my face. Does he know, I wonder, what came after the wedding? He must do… He's stayed in touch with Sam, after all. He must know how things are now… I just pray that he doesn't mention it.

'Mark… Of course! Oh my God, but you're…' I break off, a hand over my mouth.

'Half the size I was,' he finishes for me, eyes twinkling.

'Well, yes. Sorry… that was an awful thing to say.'

'Not at all. A statement of fact. I was a big fat blob when you knew me and now I'm not. But, if you remember, I was also somewhat of an environmental activist and when I left uni and started work, got my own place, I decided to become a vegetarian. Giving up my fry-ups had an immediate effect on my waistline and I've never looked back.'

I grin. 'So I see. You look great! But you were studying politics, I seem to remember – what happened to that?'

'I decided I was never going to make PM so a career in politics seemed somewhat irrelevant when I graduated. You might also remember I read English Literature alongside and that seemed the much easier option. I went into journalism and I've been with *Olive* since its inception. And how about you? What are you doing these days, Alys?'

It's on the tip of my tongue to reply 'nothing much', or that 'I'm a housewife', but then I realise that I don't have to. I'm standing here, at the opening of a prestigious restaurant, wearing a gorgeous dress. I can be anything I want to be. In fact, it's safer if I am.

'I'm actually just about to do some retraining,' I reply. 'I've spent most of my life working with textiles in one way or another but now I'm refocusing on conservation rather than production.' It isn't a complete lie, I mean dressmaking and selling haberdashery are product based… sort of. And I don't need to mention Harringtons; Mark will assume I moved on from there years ago. 'Maybe it's my age but I've always loved history, and the older I get the more relevant it feels.'

'Then that sounds perfect.'

We smile at one another, both wondering what else to say. But I can see that now Mark's initial surprise at seeing me is over, he's beginning to think a little more about the circumstances of the evening. If he's here to cover The Green Room's opening, then he'll obviously know that this is Nancy's endeavour, just as he'll know why this new venture doesn't include Sam. All of which must make him wonder why I'm here. Hugh is still standing a little way from me. I have no idea whether they've met, introduced themselves perhaps, or even recognised one another. But the chances of that are slender, surely? As far as I'm aware the two men have met only once and that was a very long time ago. There's an outside chance Mark might think he looks vaguely familiar but that should be all… Unless of course, Sam has filled in the blanks for him.

But I can't just walk away, it would be rude. 'So, are you here to write a nice piece for Nancy?' I ask, directing the conversation back onto what I hope is safer ground. 'I hope you're not one of those writers who pens damning critiques because I can't wait to see what's in store for us tonight.'

Mark smiles and I'm relieved that he's happy to follow the conversation. 'Not at all. It will be all good. I've long been a fan of The Green Room's cuisine, so this will be very much a celebratory article.' He glances over to where Theo and Esme have been posing for the photographer. It looks as if they're just about finished. 'In fact, I should probably go and get some background information, make sure I've got my facts straight and all that. Enjoy your evening, won't you? It's been lovely to see you again.'

It might be my imagination but I'm sure his gaze settles on Hugh for just a moment before turning back to me. There's a second or two where I think he's going to say something, but then he checks himself.

'It's been lovely to see you too, Mark,' I reply. 'I'll look forward to reading your article.'

I scuttle back to our table, relieved to be tucked safely out of the way, and pop one of the little crostini in my mouth, willing myself to relax. Hugh joins me after a few minutes and I see that most people are now taking their seats. They look happy, ready to enjoy the food, and I offer up a prayer for Esme that all will run smoothly.

I needn't have worried. If there are any panics in the kitchen, it certainly doesn't show to those of us in the dining room. Plateful after plateful of exquisite food is brought out, from the porcini mushrooms with truffle oil to the robust white bean, parsnip and apple sausages, mustard mash with a heavenly cider jus; the food is delicious and the presentation nothing less than perfection.

'Well, that was all rather good,' says Hugh, wiping his mouth. 'As you know, I'm not much of one when it comes to food like this, I'd rather just have a good steak, but yes, I enjoyed that.'

It's on the tip of my tongue to argue but there's little point, I will never succeed in changing Hugh's mind. And it would only spoil the evening.

'Just wait until you taste the dessert,' I reply. 'I had a little sample the other day and it was utterly gorgeous.'

Hugh straightens his knife and fork. 'I hadn't realised you'd been here quite as much as you have.' His voice is cool.

'I do have to drop Esme at work every day,' I reply evenly. 'And Nancy's very friendly, she invites me in for coffee sometimes, as you know. That's how we got talking about the dress I made for Tash,' I remind him. 'And why she asked me to make her tuxedo. It's nice actually. Being included. Especially as this is such a big thing for Esme.'

'Well, Nancy's very gregarious,' replies Hugh. 'I will say that.' He looks around the room, to where she's circulating among the tables, stopping to chat every now and again, although her eagle eye is missing nothing. 'But I'm pleased to see she's on her own this evening. No Sam in tow. She clearly doesn't need him.'

It's astonishing how Hugh can put his own unique slant on any situation and I can't help but wonder why I haven't noticed this before.

'I don't think tonight has anything to do with Nancy needing Sam or otherwise. They've had an incredibly successful partnership, don't forget, and that's what it was, a partnership. This is a different venture, that's all, and Sam is just as keen to see it succeed as Nancy is.'

Hugh scowls. 'I don't know why you're so keen to defend him all the time.'

'I don't know why you're so keen to put him down the whole time.' I study his face. 'You used to be friends, Hugh, what happened?'

He's saved from having to reply by the reappearance of the waitress who clears our plates. She's followed by another moments later who lays down two plates, each filled with a generous portion of the heavenly panna cotta I was so lucky to sample earlier.

Hugh picks up his spoon and with one last look at me proceeds to demolish his dessert. The discussion, if you can call it that, is over.

I have no idea how many times the glasses have been topped up, but it isn't until Hugh swigs back his remaining champagne that I realise how pink his cheeks have got. I stare at the jug of water on the table and pour myself a large measure, grateful to be keeping a clear head.

The conversation around the room has continued at a steady hum throughout the meal, convivial and relaxed, but I'm suddenly aware that it's dying away. No sooner do I realise that than a spontaneous round of applause starts up and I see Nancy walking back into the room with Theo and Esme in tow.

I pick up the napkin from my lap, dropping it onto the table before standing and adding my own enthusiastic clapping to the mix. Esme looks a little like the proverbial rabbit caught in the headlights, but her face is split by a broad grin as Nancy leads her forward. She reaches behind her, catching hold of Theo's hand to pull him forward, and I see their fingers entwine just for a second or two. I'm overjoyed that everything has gone so well for them all. Esme has fought so hard to get to this point, her single-minded determination getting her through, even when it looked as if Hugh wouldn't budge and would try to push her into the career he had chosen for her instead of allowing her to study what she wanted. The fact that she's now basking in everyone's well-deserved praise makes me feel even more happy for her.

Hugh is also on his feet, a smile on his face as he looks around a room full of people intent on showing their appreciation for the wonderful food they've just eaten. But I can't help but wonder whether he is genuinely pleased for Esme or whether he's just happy to bask in the reflected glory of being her father. I shake my head. I know I need to get rid of such thoughts, but they're there and even banishing them won't make me forget them.

Nancy makes a brief speech, thanking everyone for coming, before asking for another show of appreciation for the chefs. There's no need to say too much – she's spoken to each and every person here individually – but it's a signal as much as anything that the evening is winding to an end. Coffee will be served shortly and I guess after that people will begin to drift away. Some will be here for a while yet, wine and conversation still flowing, but, all too soon, Theo and Esme head back to the kitchen. There is still much to do. Opening night is just the start of things – from tomorrow the restaurant will be open six days out of seven and aside from clearing up there is much to prepare in order to leave everything in readiness for another working day. But I can't wait until Esme eventually gets home to see her and so I slip from the table.

Laughter sounds from the kitchen threshold and I don't even think why as I enter the room. It hadn't occurred to me that Sam would be here now, this late in proceedings, but as I spot him I realise that it makes perfect sense. He would never appear when there was a chance of being seen publicly.

He's standing talking to Esme and Theo, his arm gripping his son's shoulders as he offers his congratulations. He looks over and I see his eyes widen slightly as he takes in my dress, the slight nod he gives me causing a wave of heat to travel over my cheeks. But I'm pleased by his reaction. That's all it takes – a moment's appreciation – and I wish that Hugh could have put aside his petty jealousy to show me that instead of making me feel as if I've done something wrong.

Nancy is there too, radiating excitement into the room, and she waves when she spies me, beckoning me forward.

'Come and say hello, Alys.' Her smile is warm and I realise she's trying to make this easy for me, trying to show me that she really is okay with me meeting Sam.

'Well, what did you think?'

'Oh, Nancy, as if you have to ask,' I reply. 'It was amazing. All of it. The food, obviously…' I break off to beam at Esme. 'And the restaurant too, which looks incredible, but what also struck me is how much people were enjoying themselves, how relaxed they looked. That type of atmosphere is something you really can't manufacture, but you have it here, there's no doubt about that.'

Nancy nods, thinking about what I've just said, and I realise she wasn't just looking for an easy compliment, she's genuinely interested in hearing my opinion.

'I think it's all the plants,' she says. 'Seriously. We've always said that. I think they put people in a good mood.'

'You may well be right,' I reply. 'But whatever it is, it's working.'

Esme comes rushing forward. 'Mum!' she exclaims, before throwing her arms around me, squeezing me in a tight hug. 'Oh my God,' she adds breathlessly, but she can't say anything else, she's completely overcome.

I rub her arm as we pull apart. 'You've done amazingly,' I reply. 'I'm so proud of you.'

Nancy comes forward and places an arm around Esme's shoulders too. 'Time for one last victory tour then, I think,' she says, beckoning to Theo. 'Go on you two, go and bask in the limelight a little; people will be drifting off soon and they'll want to say goodbye.' She shepherds them towards the restaurant like a mother hen, shooing them away before turning to me with a warm smile and a meaningful look. I know that she's done this so that meeting Sam here is a little less awkward and I'm touched by the kindness of her gesture.

And then he's walking towards me, his face lit up. 'Aren't they brilliant?' he says, his eyes dancing in the bright light. 'Hello again.'

He looms towards me, his fingers touching the bare flesh of my arm. I'm being pulled towards him. It's a social kiss, no more, cheek gently against cheek, one on each side…

And that's okay until a voice from behind startles me, its harsh sound cutting through the room.

'Hello, *Sam*…'

# CHAPTER FIFTEEN

The atmosphere in the room changes in an instant, as if a blast of cold air is moving past me.

'Hello, Hugh,' replies Sam, stepping out to one side. He stares at my husband, silent and motionless, as I look between them helplessly.

Hugh's greeting was loud, meant to be assertive, but I can see now how uncomfortable he looks. I suddenly realise that this must be the first time he's seen Sam since his accident, seen the damage that has been wrought. And I have no idea what he's thinking.

Sam lifts his chin a little. 'Well now, how do you like what you see, eh, Hugh? What's that look for? Surprised? Horrified? Or just plain annoyed that I'm here at all?'

I'm acutely aware of Nancy standing a matter of feet away, a look of horror on her face. My own thoughts are in disarray. Why is Sam being this way? I understand that it must be a shock meeting Hugh again, but rubbing Hugh's nose in the way he looks isn't fair, surely? It's almost as if he wants him to feel bad about it.

I look at Nancy mutely. I don't know how to stop this. It's already gone too far. There is something happening here that goes way beyond the meeting of two people who haven't seen each other in twenty-odd years.

I take a step back towards Hugh, beseeching him to keep quiet, but his face is flushed from too much champagne and I can see that he's not going to back away from Sam's goading.

'Just stay away from my wife, okay?'

A cold slither of unease snakes its way down my back.

Sam raises a hand in the air, a placatory gesture, although his other hand, the one that clutches his stick, is white at the knuckle.

'Well, fancy that,' he says. 'After all these years your message hasn't changed one iota.'

I stare at him. What on earth does he mean?

'Given the number of years that have gone by since we last met, I'd have hoped you could have come up with something a little more considered, more nuanced than just a bald threat. But it would seem not. Don't worry though, Alys and I have said all that we need to, and the status quo remains. At least I think it does…'

There's a mocking expression on his face that I don't like the look of, but it changes to one of sympathy as he looks at me. 'I'm so sorry, Alys, Nancy… I'll go. I've no wish to make things awkward.' He grimaces. 'Any *more* awkward.'

Nancy is desperately trying to keep her composure but I can see how shocked she is and my anger flares in an instant. This isn't Sam's fault, the only one to blame here is Hugh.

'No, you won't Sam, you stay right where you are. It's us that's leaving. You stay here and enjoy your time with your family.'

I can count the times on one hand that I've argued with Hugh, but right now I could cheerfully kill him. I close the distance between us.

'Don't say another word,' I hiss into his face, my eyes burning into his. I grab hold of his arm and pull him towards the back door. Hugh is considerably taller than me and infinitely more powerful – he could easily resist my action if he wanted to, so I know it's only the shock of my behaviour that's allowing me to manoeuvre him in this way. My handbag is still hanging on the back of the door where I left it for safekeeping and I snatch it up before yanking open the door and pushing Hugh out into the night. I have the advantage for now, but it won't last long.

My hand is on my car keys. 'Get in.' It's taking every ounce of willpower I possess to stand my ground and for one moment I think Hugh is going to fight back, maybe even hit me. He looms over me, his jaw working, brain trying to keep up with what's happening, but for once in my life I'm not backing down. If looks could kill he'd be stone-cold dead by now, and he knows it.

He strides away from me in the last instant before my resolve cracks, leaving me shaking, standing in the car park wondering what on earth I'm going to do next. Or rather *how* I'm going to do it.

There is a stunned silence as I walk back inside the kitchen. Nancy is holding Sam's arm, while he looks as if someone has kicked him repeatedly. His eyes are ablaze.

'Oh, Nancy,' I say. 'I'm so sorry, I don't know what to say. Hugh…' But I trail off, I can't finish the sentence. 'I don't know what on earth's got into him, I should get him home, I…' Tears are filling my eyes, and they spill over at a touch on my arm. 'Your special day…' And the tears fall faster.

She shakes her head. 'Go,' she says, softly. 'I'll take care of it. Everything will be all right.'

'Esme…'

'I know,' she says soothingly. 'Don't worry. I'll think of something.' She's shaking her head and I realise that she will make our excuses, smoothing things over to take care of her family, and that includes Esme. Her eyes reach mine extending trust and friendship, nothing more, and I kiss her goodbye, whispering my thanks.

I walk back out to the car, slamming the door after me as I climb into the driver's seat. Hugh sits sullenly, the import of what he's just done finally beginning to sink in. I turn and stare at him for a moment, the artificial light from the car park throwing dark shadows across his face, but he remains resolutely facing forward.

'How could you?' I say in disgust and then I drive us home in silence.

Once we're there Hugh stalks into the kitchen and flicks on the kettle. It's an automatic reaction as much as any desire to have a drink, although perhaps a coffee *would* be a good idea; it might sober him up a little bit.

There are so many thoughts crowding my head it's becoming almost unbearable. Mostly they're centred around Nancy and Sam and how awful they must be feeling. Nancy's special night, the culmination of all her determination and hard work, ruined by Hugh's insensitive behaviour. And everything had gone so well, the celebrations should be continuing long into the night, and yet all she's been left with is a nasty taste in her mouth. It doesn't even begin to cover how embarrassed she must be.

But of course Hugh's behaviour wasn't just insensitive, it was thoughtless at best, selfish, and born out of stupid jealousy. But that isn't the worst of it. It was provocative too. His comment to Sam was peculiarly barbed and directed at a man he hasn't seen in years, a man who, as far as I know, has never caused him any harm. In fact, quite the reverse. And I simply can't work it out. Hugh is sometimes a little excitable when he's had too much to drink, belligerent even, but not malicious.

I move past him, collecting two mugs from the cupboard. He's loosened his tie and pulled his shirt out from his trousers, trying to look relaxed. But I know Hugh, and his attempt at appearing affable doesn't mean a thing; he'll still be determined to make his point and have things his own way. But that isn't going to work tonight.

'Are you going to tell me what that was all about?' I ask, turning around.

'I should have thought that was perfectly obvious,' he says, deliberately mild. 'Sam kissed you... or did you kiss him?'

'And you really think that's a good enough reason for totally ruining the evening, do you? Yes, I kissed Sam, but then I also kissed Theo and Nancy, and Esme... and you for that matter. It was the type of kiss you reserve for social occasions, Hugh, not a full-on snog, and I didn't see you holding back with our lady mayoress. Or is that somehow different because it was you and not me?'

'I don't recall ever being married to the lady mayoress…'

I hold his look. 'This is boring, Hugh. We've already had this conversation and I explained perfectly well what the situation is with Sam. I didn't hide the fact that I'd met him again. You, on the other hand, haven't seen him in over twenty years. You can see what he's been through, and you also know that he owns a very successful restaurant. And yet, knowing all these things, without an ounce of compassion, or thought, or tact for that matter, the only thing you can manage to say to the man is *stay away from my wife*? For goodness' sake, Hugh, have you any idea what you sounded like?'

'Have you any idea what you looked like?' His eyes flash with indignation.

'And what's that supposed to mean? Don't you dare put this on me, when you're the one in the wrong here.'

'And yet there you are dressed up to the nines…'

I stare at him, anger growing with every second. 'So that's what this is really all about, is it? The fact that I'm wearing a dress you don't like… At least I hope that's all it is, because as pathetic as it may be, if it's not that it would sound suspiciously like you're accusing me of something here, maybe even of having an affair…? And that really would be ridiculous.'

Hugh doesn't answer.

'So then, back to the dress… Just what exactly is it you don't like, Hugh? The fact that it cost a lot of money? Money I earned, I might add. Or the fact that I bought it without your consent, your knowledge even…?' I'm watching the expression on his face. 'Could it even be because, God forbid, I look *nice*?'

'You look ridiculous. Like mutton dressed as lamb. Like one of those women who go out and buy expensive things just because they can, with more money than taste.'

'No, Hugh. I don't. Everyone else has told me how great I look. Everyone but you. I just don't think you can stand it, can you? Knowing that other people might be looking at me with admiration.'

As soon as I say it, I realise I've walked right into his trap.

'And which other people would that be, Alys? Sam? Is that who you were dressing up for?'

I can hear the kitchen clock ticking, marking the beats of silence as I glare at him. But I'm not about to respond to his jibe; I've spent far too much of my life doing what Hugh wants. There's a point to be made here, one that has been bothering me for quite some time and which I'm only just beginning to understand. And it has nothing to do with Sam, and everything to do with me.

'You like to look good, Hugh, don't you? You like to be seen wearing nice clothes – nice shoes, gold cufflinks, an expensive watch. I didn't see you hiding any of that this evening as you hobnobbed with the mayoress and the chair of commerce and his cronies. So why is it that it's okay for you to look the part, but the one time I thought I might like to be appreciated, as a woman in my own right and not just as your wife, you find fault with everything?'

He eyes me steadily. 'You didn't answer my question.'

'Do I really need to, Hugh? I've already explained about my meeting with Sam and how it came about. I had no more idea who ran The Green Room than you when Esme got the job. I certainly didn't imagine for one minute that it would mean seeing him again. But now that I have, I can't just ignore it. What I *can* do, however, is accept that Sam belonged to a part of my life that has long since gone. And, as far as I'm concerned, that's where it will stay. So, to answer your question, no, my dress was not for Sam's benefit, or any other man's for that matter. In fact, it wasn't even for yours. I've had enough of passing all my decisions through your filter first, Hugh.' I bang the mugs down onto the kitchen counter. 'And you'd better get used to that fact.'

He pulls at the knot of his tie and slides it from his neck, his expression unreadable. 'I really don't know what's got into you lately.'

'No? Maybe it's just that I've remembered I'm a person too. Instead of just a wife and mother. I've felt alive the last few days, actually alive, instead of sleepwalking through my life. Do you know how that makes me feel? Wondering what I could have achieved if I'd have set my mind to it. Wondering who I might be if I hadn't allowed you to decide for me.'

'Oh, don't be so ridiculous, you're obviously hormonal, Alys. I don't even know why we're having this conversation, and—'

'Don't you? Well, shall I tell you? You insulted me tonight, Hugh. Everything I am and everything I do. The sad thing is, though, that I don't even care about that, because in trying to make your stupid point to Sam, not only did you make things incredibly awkward, but you were also extremely rude to Nancy, whose guest you were. You might as well have thrown her hospitality back in her face. But even that's not the worst thing you did… Because can you imagine what might have happened if Esme had heard what you'd said, or if she finds out? Not only would you have utterly ruined the biggest night of her career, but you'd have made it impossible to keep my past relationship with Sam under wraps. Jesus, Hugh, you couldn't have shone a bigger light on the situation if you'd tried. Did you even stop to think about that?'

And for the first time this evening he actually looks a little disconcerted.

'Maybe it's for the best if she knows…'

'No, Hugh, it isn't. How can it be? She's waited so long for an opportunity like this despite everything you've done to stop her following the career she wanted and—'

'I have never stopped her!' he exclaims. 'I've asked her to consider her future, and to think carefully about what she wants to do. But any parent would do that.'

'Would they? Because I sometimes wonder whether you have another reason for not wanting Esme to be a chef, Hugh. One that has nothing to do with its suitability as a career.'

He stares at me. He knows exactly what I'm talking about, but he's not going to say anything. He can't, because he won't want to admit that I'm right, or quite how precarious he's made this situation.

'But whatever your reasons,' I add. 'You had better start thinking about what you're going to say to Nancy, because you have the biggest apology to make. And you're on your own with this one. I am not bailing you out like I usually do, not this time.'

I cross the kitchen to the doorway. 'And while you're at it, don't think I've forgotten the way Sam reacted to seeing you, or what he said, so you might like to have a think about explaining that to me too. Oh, and if you want a coffee, make it your bloody self, I'm going to bed.'

I stand in front of the bedroom mirror for quite some time after I leave Hugh, looking at my reflection. I'm still angry but my rage is birthing a new feeling too; something I haven't felt in a long time. I'm not exactly sure what you'd call it – a resurgence of my inner confidence, pride almost, as if I've woken from a sleep, energy filling me with purpose. Because I'd felt good tonight. For once I'd liked how I looked. I smile to myself. What was it Sam said? More like my curly-haired self, and he's right. It's exactly how I used to feel, all the time. In fact, I never even had to question it.

I undress and then, padding through to the bathroom, I slowly take off my make-up, rubbing cream into my skin and relishing its cool silkiness. Hugh won't appear for ages yet. He's always been a night owl, but I'm expecting him to give me a wide berth tonight and I'm looking forward to having the bed to myself for a bit; the clear calm space is just what I need. I climb beneath the covers and lie flat on my back, arms folded loosely over my chest. Closing my eyes, I try to quieten my breathing and, once I feel my anxiety begin to loosen its grip, I let my thoughts drift.

Much to my surprise I realise I must have fallen asleep, as my eyes flick open, suddenly alert. The bed shifts a little beside me as Hugh stirs, but I don't think it's this that has disturbed me. His breathing is deep and even and he looks to have been that way for some time. A crack of light suddenly appears under the door and I realise then what's woken me. Esme is home.

With a backward glance I slide from the bed and out the room, pulling the door gently closed behind me. Once Hugh is asleep it's unlikely anything will wake him, but I'd rather that didn't happen. I meet Esme on the landing. Her smile is tired but happy.

'Hi,' I say softly.

She's already changed out of her chef's whites and is wearing pyjama bottoms and a tee shirt, her long hair let down from its band, flowing over her shoulders. She looks very grown-up, as if suddenly wise beyond her years.

I open my arms and she slips inside, wiping away the passage of time. Neither of us speaks as I stroke her head. After a few moments she pulls away.

'We did it, Mum,' she says.

'Yes, you did,' I reply. 'But you look tired now.'

'I'm knackered,' she replies, grinning and catching hold of my hand. 'Come downstairs,' she whispers.

The kitchen is dim as we enter, lit only by the lights along the skirting, and I'm shocked to see from the glowing clock on the cooker that it's nearly one in the morning. Esme is already at the cupboard, pulling out the packet of chocolate biscuits that are her go-to when she needs a boost. She offers me one first.

'This is a bit of a let-down,' I say. 'After the meal we've just had. Did I tell you how amazing you were?'

She bites into her biscuit, tucking her hair behind the ears. Her face looks ghostly in the half-light and she's obviously exhausted.

'That's what Nancy said,' she replies. 'You two are so alike at times.'

'Me and Nancy? Well, I shall take that as a compliment,' I add. 'But I don't think so. Nancy is vivacious and outgoing, successful, determined…' I trail off. 'Oh dear, I'm not doing myself any favours here.'

'I think you have all those traits, actually, you just don't wear them on your sleeve like Nancy does. But you *are* alike in many ways… wise, caring, and she always acts as the go-between as well. The buffer between Theo and Sam just like you do with Dad. What was wrong with him tonight, did he have too much to drink?' she asks.

'Something like that,' I say. 'I don't think he noticed until we were on our feet again. I thought it wise to get him home but I hope our running off didn't spoil the end of the evening for you.'

A dreamy expression comes over her face. 'No… not even Dad could do that. It was so good, Mum. I've never felt anything like it.'

'Then I'm glad.'

She pops the last of her biscuit in her mouth. 'Okay,' she says, coming forward to give me another hug. 'I'm going to bed now, Mum, I'm wiped out.'

'I'm not surprised,' I reply. 'You've cooked your little heart out today. I'm so proud of you.'

'I'm proud of you too, Mum,' she says. 'And you did look amazing tonight.'

I just hope that she will go on being proud of me. 'You go up, love,' I say, smiling. 'I'm just going to get myself a drink.'

She hands me the packet of biscuits. 'Night, Mum.'

I watch her leave, listening for her footsteps on the stairs as I collect a glass from the cupboard. I fill it with water and hold it against my cheek for a moment. I don't really want a drink but it gives me an excuse to wait downstairs for a few minutes. A thought had come to me earlier when I'd been talking to Hugh about my dress. Something about the expression on his face hadn't seemed quite right. I set the glass back down on the side and open the cupboard under the stairs where I keep the bag I used for work. It's sat there ever since I left Harringtons and inside it is the letter I received from the HR department informing me about my redundancy. There's a detail I want to check.

# CHAPTER SIXTEEN

Despite my lack of sleep, I'm wide awake again at six the next morning. It's Hugh's weekend to work so he'll be getting up soon, but I'm really not in the mood for conversation this early, and especially not with Hugh. So I snuggle back into my pillows as best I can and pretend. I don't suppose Hugh is particularly looking forward to having to apologise to Esme for leaving so early last night; predictably, he makes no attempt to wake me, and leaves even earlier than usual.

By half past seven I'm alone with my thoughts once more. I've tried not to overthink last night, but more and more of its detail is coming back to me, and almost all of it centres on Sam. Was Hugh right? Did I dress up for him? Because as much as I tell myself that I really hadn't known for definite that Sam would be at the opening, I'd known there was every chance he would be. So whatever excuses I'm making for myself, I probably need to look at my motives a little more closely. It's just that having someone's eyes light up when they see you provokes a very powerful response, whether you want it to or not.

I haven't felt that in a very long time and I'm struggling to get Sam's words out of my head. *Is* my life too small for me now? *Have* I grown out of something? Or someone? And if so, why? Why now, when nothing has really changed? Except that something has changed, and I can feel it within me from my toes right up to the top of my curly-haired head.

Sam isn't the only thing I've been thinking about, however. There's also the small matter of my redundancy money. I push aside the bedclothes and head back downstairs, retracing my steps of the night before.

I hadn't really looked at the letter from HR since I'd received it. I hadn't wanted to. It was life-changing money, money that I needed to think about very carefully. But it wasn't the amount I had wanted to check again last night, but the date on which it should have been paid.

I get myself a glass of water, drinking half before setting it down on the table and opening the understairs cupboard once more. I flick on the light and take out the letter, rereading the details, slowly, making sure that in my anger last night I hadn't misunderstood what it said.

My heart is beating hard as I refold the piece of paper and stow it back in my bag. I finish my drink and collect a biscuit, trying not to jump to conclusions. I'm sure there's a perfectly logical explanation for it. I pause in the hallway for a moment to listen out for Esme, but there are no sounds of life from above and I imagine she'll be sleeping for a while yet. I hope so. Then I push open the study door and slip inside.

I rarely come in here, unless it's at Hugh's behest. It's always been made very clear that this is his domain and I kick myself for not having taken an interest in our financial matters before. I guess, just like so many other things, I was content to let Hugh take charge of them. After all, hasn't he always made it clear he is very happy to do so? But now that I *am* here, I'm determined to find what I'm looking for. You see, payday was a few days ago, at the end of the month, and, according to HR, in their very bland and badly worded standard letter, my redundancy payment should have been made together with my final salary. And my salary had already been paid into my bank account, but I certainly would have noticed the appearance of an extra thirty thousand pounds. So, did this money simply never arrive… or, has it gone somewhere else?

I've always assumed we are like most couples. But, actually, I really have no idea how other husbands and wives manage their financial affairs. Hugh and I have our own accounts, into which our salaries are paid, and then we each transfer an amount into a joint one which pays for all the household bills. Obviously Hugh earns considerably more than I do – or rather, did – so he pays a greater share, but I never check this account. The bills are paid by direct debit and anything else we need – our groceries, petrol, that kind of thing – I simply pay for on my chip and pin card. There have never been any problems with this account and Hugh has made it clear that he keeps a careful eye on it so we never overspend. I trusted him, why wouldn't I?

The files are easily found. Hugh keeps everything in apple-pie order and I know that the latest bank statements have arrived, they came the other day. And I did what I always did, which was to leave them on the side for Hugh to file. I pull the folder with our joint account details towards me and turn to the most recent page, my sense of foreboding growing stronger all the while. Because I already know what I'm going to find and, sure enough, as I scan the page, I see an amount leap out. All thirty thousand pounds of my redundancy money. But what is it doing here in our joint bank account when it should have been paid into my personal account, just like my salary has been every month? There's only one person who could have changed the instruction for the payments, and that's Hugh.

I stare at the blank wall in front of me, fury rising. Anger at Hugh and disgust with myself for being so… unaware. Was I simply a trusting, faithful wife? Or complacent and naive? And the answer to both those questions scares me. I don't have any idea what's been going on. It's bad enough that Hugh would even think to redirect my redundancy money into another account, but the even more disturbing question is why…

I slide the file back onto the shelf, my unease growing as I take out another from the shelf below. I shouldn't even be thinking the things I am, but now my thoughts are jumping all over the place and I suddenly remember something Nancy said about having your mortgage paid off and being safe and comfortable. Because Hugh and I have lived in this house since we got married, twenty-three years ago, which should mean that in two years' time it will be paid off. All of a sudden it seems very important that I check.

And the figures can't lie, it's all there in black and white. Whereas we should only have one or two years left to repay our mortgage in full, instead we still owe a considerable sum of money. I flip back through the pages of statements until I find a letter from nearly twelve years ago which explains what happened. While I was busy juggling working at Harringtons, bringing up Esme and looking after the running of our home, Hugh had remortgaged our house to the tune of eighty thousand pounds.

I lift my head, staring across the room as thoughts tumble through my mind. Questions about my redundancy, but now, more importantly perhaps, questions about why my husband needed to raise such a large sum of money twelve years ago. What was it for? And where did the money go?

A glance at the clock on the wall confirms that it's still early and I wander back into the kitchen, my thoughts scattered. The realisation that Hugh has been keeping secrets from me for so long is taking up a huge space inside my head, and suddenly my well-ordered, albeit boring and staid, life is beginning to feel as if it's in freefall. Esme is still sleeping overhead, no doubt dreaming blissfully, and I'm terrified of what the repercussions of all this might be for her. I never wanted to keep things from her, to hide away the truth and live the lie that Hugh wanted us to. But it seems as if over the years my husband has become an expert at lying, and I realise how ill-prepared I am for what must surely be coming.

I make a quick coffee and grab another couple of biscuits. I don't want to linger over breakfast and run the risk of Esme finding me taking the study apart. Because there is one thing I'm certain of, which is that forewarned is forearmed. My notebook is still on the side, full of the measurements I wrote down for Nancy's tuxedo. But although I do need to make a start on it, that's not what I want the paper for. I pick it up and head back to the study.

I've been systematically making notes for about half an hour when I suddenly realise that the faint noise I've been hearing is actually my mobile phone ringing from the kitchen. It doesn't sound for long before switching to the answerphone so I make a mad dash for it, snatching it up at the last minute. It's a local area code number but not one I recognise and my heart is in my mouth as I quickly slide my finger across the screen to answer the call. The woman's voice is not one I recognise.

'Alys Robinson?'

'Hi, yes, hello.'

'This is Becky, from the National Trust. I'm really sorry to call you at the weekend—'

'Not at all, it's fine, don't worry,' I reply, hoping I didn't sound too flustered when I answered the call.

'I'm just ringing about the application you sent in for the vacancy we're advertising, but I noticed that you've also written to me about volunteering opportunities.'

'Yes, I…' My heart, which had taken a sudden upward leap, now sinks back down again.

'You see, the thing is,' continues Becky. 'I'm unexpectedly in the office today. I know it's very short notice, and a Saturday, but I wondered if you might be free to come and have a chat sometime this morning?'

I stare at the window in front of me, trying to see my reflection and mentally assessing how long it will take me to make myself look presentable.

'I'd be very happy to,' I reply. 'I can be with you in about an hour.'

There's a pause. 'Yes, that would suit me very well. So I'll see you about half past ten then? You know where to find us, don't you?'

'Yes, I do. I came to your open day, so that's great. Thank you. I'll see you then.' I end the call, heart beating wildly, and with another glance at the clock dash upstairs to get changed.

I don't really remember the drive over to Blickling Hall but it seems in no time at all I'm pulling into the car park where I sat with Sam only a week or so ago. And although I don't want to admit it, I really wish he was here with me now. My good-luck charm. Plus, of course, his ridiculous sense of humour would've kept me from feeling nervous. As it is I can barely speak.

Job interviews, even if they have been downgraded to a simple chat, are not something I'm familiar with, and my experience of them extends to one single solitary occasion when I applied for my job at Harringtons. I've had a few internal interviews for posts there, of course, but those were different. The setting was known to me, the people too, but this, this is not something I do.

The conservation centre isn't open to the public today, but my hesitant knock at the door is answered immediately and, within minutes, I'm sitting up on the mezzanine level where I first met Becky, a glass of water on the table by my side. Becky's greeting is warm and friendly but there's an efficient briskness to her actions that is somewhat scary. I don't think she's going to waste much time before getting down to business.

'Right, well, I won't beat about the bush, but I'm not sure whether you're aware that this is the second time we've advertised this job. The third, actually, in the last six months, and I'm not very hopeful about finding a suitable candidate this time around either.'

'Oh… I see. No, I didn't know that.' My heart falls even further. It's obviously not going to be me then. 'I only just saw the advertisement actually… A friend sent it to me.' I smile, for what it's worth. 'And I'm aware that my application is something of a long shot. My degree is almost as old as the textiles I'd be working on.'

Becky smiles, giving me a sheepish look. 'I'm sorry, that came out completely wrong. I hate interviews,' she admits, and I realise that what I'd taken as briskness is actually nerves. She's almost as bad as I am. 'I didn't mean that your application was useless, which is how *I* made it sound, but rather that, like all these things, there's a required level of experience and qualifications that I'm supposed to adhere to. And I'm afraid on that basis that, whilst your degree is sound, it was rather a long time ago and not backed up by recent practical experience.'

I nod.

'I can see that you're a dressmaker too, which is useful but…'

'Um, it's just… I think I was trying to show that my interest in textiles has remained throughout my life, even if my career hasn't really supported it.'

She gives me a sympathetic look. 'Which it did,' she says. 'There wasn't anything wrong with your application…' She pauses. 'Maybe wrong is not quite the right word. Perhaps I mean irrelevant?' She looks at me quizzically. 'Which is to say that what you've been doing is relevant and you were right to include it in your letter, but I'm sorry, it still doesn't meet the minimum criteria for the role. So… you're probably wondering why I've asked you here.'

Poor girl, she looks so uncomfortable that I can't help but warm to her. She's doing her level best to let me down gently and I put on my best grateful expression.

'You see, the thing that interested me most about your application was that you also sent in a separate request to become a volunteer. I hoped you would when we met the other week.'

So she did remember me; I hadn't been entirely sure. I smile nervously. 'I know, I've just shot myself in the foot, haven't I?'

Becky pulls a face. 'Not necessarily…' She fidgets a little in her seat. 'I'll be perfectly honest with you, Alys, I've had a few people sitting where you are now, and when I mention the "V" word they look at me like I've grown an extra head. So when I saw that you're happy to undertake voluntary work too, I got a little bit excited. I can't offer you the conservator job, well not right now anyway, but I'm hoping that I might be able to work something out for the future. Even if that means being a little bit… creative with the vacancy.'

She leans forward as if she's worried someone might overhear her. 'I had a chat with Lucy – she's the other woman you met when you were here before – and if you came and volunteered with us for a few months she'd be very happy to take charge of some training for you whilst you're here. She'd oversee the work you do, but she'd also get you up to the required standard. We reckon that if I pull the vacancy now, in a few months' time you could reapply and, well…'

I stare at her. 'Sorry, are you saying that you think I can get the job?'

She pulls at her lip. 'I can't *promise* but, given the field of applicants we've had recently, and with the experience we could give you, I'd be pretty certain you'd get it, yes. I'm only sorry I can't offer you anything now. I'm afraid the next few months would have to be on a purely voluntary basis.'

'No, no, I understand. I don't know what to say.'

'But you'd be interested?'

I don't have to think about it for very long. 'When can I start?' I say.


If I was preoccupied on my drive to Blickling Hall, it's nothing compared with the drive home. My head is full of more thoughts than ever, but now in among the mix is one tiny gleaming ray of hope for the future. It sounds daft, but my future is the one thing I've never really thought about. I don't think you do when you have children. You think about *their* future, all the time, but yours seems something that you can only attend to after everything else has been settled. But today, so far, has been a stark reminder of how suddenly everything can change.

The house is quiet when I enter, my note to Esme still on the side where I left it. Only the sound of the shower running overhead lets me know that she's up and about again; getting herself ready for the restaurant's first night of actual business. This is the real start to her new beginning. I crumple up the note and throw it away. No point complicating things just yet.

I make a quick cup of tea and carry it through into the conservatory, throwing open the doors to the garden. It's normally far too hot to sit in here during the summer, but today is a little overcast and, with the doors open, it's perfect. Birdsong floods in. I sink back into the cushions of my favourite squishy chair, wrap my fingers around my mug for comfort, and let myself drift.

I never intend to spend time thinking about you, it's just something that happens every now and again. When my subconscious knows that thoughts of you are just what I need to get me through the day. And it helps, it reminds me that once upon a time there was something different in my life, something better. And if I've had it in the past, surely I can find it again in the future.

Maybe that's why I feel so weird now. Because the last few days have felt like a return to the past. The place where I could be me, comfortable in my skin, happy, with the things I desired within reach. And I've tried so hard to push aside thoughts of this other time, but it still exists, I've seen a glimpse of it now, and however much I try to resist, its lure is strong. Perhaps that's why it scares me so much.

Because in the here and now I feel like a fish out of water and entirely misplaced. As if this is somewhere I'm no longer supposed to be. I feel as if I'm growing too fast, like a green shoot being pulled towards the sun, but bending in the wrong direction, towards somewhere I want to be, somewhere I think I need to be, but somewhere my head is telling me I absolutely shouldn't be.

The sadness of this hits me hard. I'm crying before I even draw another breath and I cannot help but wonder if you feel the same way too. And even though I know it's wrong, I'm hoping that you do…

I sit up straighter, dashing away my tears as my heart beats faster. *I'm hoping that you do… I'm hoping that you do…* There, I finally admitted it and I know I can't keep living a lie. I don't understand why any of this is happening, but for all that I understand of the way the universe works, I cannot imagine that it's happening for no reason. And that being the case, is it wrong to let it unfold…? It's a question I have no answer for.

I check the time. There's still a little while before I have to take Esme to work and I need to finish what I started this morning. If I have any chance of changing things, then I need to be prepared.

# CHAPTER SEVENTEEN

I've never been reckless, but surely there can be no other word for what I'm about to do. I've thought about it so much my head hurts. I've cried, grown angry, been wracked with guilt and overwhelmed with love for my family, all in the space of a few hours. But, at the end of it all, I had to make a decision. And I have no way of telling if it's the right one. I guess time will be the judge of that.

It isn't even that I don't love Hugh, I do. I don't know what I would've done without him in the early days, the first few months after Sam sent me away. I was overwhelmed with grief, and alone in a new town where I knew no one. He was my rock, my saviour and, to start with, nothing more than my friend. I honestly don't think I could have got through it if he hadn't been there.

And then Esme came along and I was totally unprepared for motherhood. For the searing bond of love that obliterated everything, but which came at such a price. The sleepless nights, the feeling of utter helplessness as I struggled to cope with her needs, and the terror that my life would never be the same again. But, gradually, we learned to properly love one another, unconditionally, and those early years with her became the best of my life.

I don't really know when my marriage first began to go wrong. How could I when I didn't even see that it had? But now I wonder whether gratitude had just replaced love and I didn't even notice. And if it wasn't gratitude then it was guilt – for even daring to find fault with someone who had done so much for us. But now it would seem that my gratitude is no longer enough, nor my guilt, and so perhaps if I can cast both these things aside, Hugh and I can get back to where we need to be. And in order to do this, I have to lay some ghosts to rest.

I'd suggested that Sam and I meet by the river again. I'm feeling hemmed in enough by my thoughts as it is, I don't want to feel constrained by my surroundings too. Besides, the afternoon has brightened and out here in the open there's less risk of us being overheard. I'd planned on getting here early so that I could sit quietly and let the flow of water soothe my nerves, but it seems as if Sam has had the same idea. I can already see him as I approach the bench, sitting in that slightly lopsided way of his which accommodates his bad leg. The sight of him ties my stomach into an even tighter knot.

I join the path a little upriver so that I can walk towards him and not approach from behind. But even so he doesn't see me until I'm almost upon him. I guess he's lost in his own thoughts.

'Hi, Sam.'

His face lights up as he automatically moves his leg underneath him to stand.

I put out a hand. 'No, it's okay, don't get up. I'll sit.' And it's as much because I know that he'll kiss me if he stands as it is that I don't want him to struggle. It makes me even more nervous when I see that he's worked this out too, and I perch uncomfortably beside him on the edge of the bench.

His look is candid and challenging, even though he smiles. 'Afternoon, Alys,' he says. 'This is a surprise. I didn't think I would hear from you again after the other night.'

And I have absolutely no idea what to say. How to even begin this conversation. 'I just wanted to say goodbye… Before you go.'

'Okay…' He frowns a little. 'Except I think your husband did that for you. Right when he accused me of… well, I'm not sure exactly what, but fraternising at the very least.'

'Sam, don't. Please don't make this any harder than it already is. I'm sorry, okay. Hugh was being a complete arse, and I still don't understand why, but—'

'Don't you?'

I stare at him. 'No… Other than he's always been the jealous type. There's no excuse for his behaviour, but I'm not actually here to apologise for him.'

'Good,' replies Sam. 'Because I think you'll find that's his responsibility.'

His words catch at my heart. 'Do you know that Nancy said something very similar to me almost the first time I met her?'

'Did she? I'm not surprised. Nancy is a very good judge of character and we obviously share the same opinion of your husband.'

I look away, staring out across the river. I should never have come.

There's a long sigh from beside me. 'Alys, I'm sorry. Please, just ignore me. I've got far too good at being belligerent these last few years. I can see you're really struggling with this and I've no desire to make it any harder for you. Neither am I particularly offended by what Hugh said the other night. I really didn't expect anything better from him.'

'You see, that's just it,' I groan. 'Honestly, what is it with you two? And don't give me some cock-and-bull story this time, I've already had that from Hugh.'

'Why, what did he say?' asks Sam, a cautious note creeping into his voice.

'That he doesn't like you because of what you did to me, which doesn't really make any sense. I mean, it sort of does, but not really. It would make more sense if he was glad you behaved the way you did.'

A flash of pain crosses Sam's face for an instant, forcing his eyes shut. His jaw clenches.

I put out a hand. 'Are you okay?' I ask, looking around, wondering if I might need to call on someone for assistance.

There's a brief nod. 'Then if that's what Hugh said, who am I to argue?' he replies.

'That doesn't answer my question.'

'No? Then I guess you'd better go back to your husband and ask him again.' He holds my look for a second before dropping his head. 'Sorry,' he says for the second time.

'For God's sake, this is getting us nowhere, Sam. I didn't come here today to talk about Hugh...' I trail off, frustrated with myself. 'Well in a way I did, but more my marriage than Hugh himself. I thought it might help you to understand if you knew how I felt.'

I swallow. No, that doesn't sound right either. I'm trying to get my thoughts in order but the more I try to think what to say to make it right, the more they skitter away from me. A sudden movement from my side pulls me back. Sam has pushed himself up from the bench so violently he's almost overbalanced. He takes a couple of steps, leaning heavily on his stick, until his movements are under control.

'Alys, I didn't come here to listen to you talk about Hugh either... or your marriage. I'm leaving for home tomorrow and the last thing I want is to have you justify Hugh's behaviour and then tell me that it's okay because he loves you, and you love him. I know I messed up, Alys. I know I behaved badly and I've had enough years to think about the consequences, so please don't make it any worse by—'

'She's yours, Sam...' I blurt out, wanting to snatch back my words the moment they leave my mouth. This isn't how I wanted to tell him. The news shouldn't be borne on the back of Hugh's name, like an afterthought, like a...

For a moment I think Sam might be about to vomit. His hand is over his mouth, he's hunching forward, the colour draining from his face.

'Esme,' I say. 'She's…'

And he's nodding, fumbling with his stick, stumbling to the bench where he sags like a half-empty bag of potatoes.

'Esme…' he repeats. 'Esme… Oh my God… All these years. I couldn't, but…' He's shaking his head, his body almost rocking with the motion. 'I never knew…' He looks at me then, eyes dark hollows against his pale skin, rimmed with red, a trace of spittle clinging to his open mouth. 'I never knew…'

I clutch at his hands. 'Sam, I'm so sorry. So sorry… I couldn't tell you. I wanted to. Dear God, I wanted to… When she was born, all I wanted was for you…' I break off, the memory of those emotions assailing me. The anguish and pain of childbirth, the fear bringing an almost overwhelming grief for you. The desire to have you with me so strong that it was all I could do not to send Hugh away. I remember it now and the breath catches in my throat. It could have been yesterday, the feeling is so strong. My eyes fill with tears.

Sam looks at me in horror. 'What have I done to you?' he says, raising a hand to lay it softly against my cheek. 'Either way, a life sentence…'

His fingers burn my skin, but I don't want him to take his hand away; I've waited so long to feel his touch. And yet it's wrong, I know that. Sam made his decision a long time ago and in doing so he made mine for me. I shake my head. No, I made my own decision. No one forced me to go with Hugh, to move away with him and start a new life. I went willingly and I have no one else to blame for that decision, least of all Sam.

It's killing me to move away, but I catch his fingers, gently pulling them so I can hold his hand in mine. I linger a second, two seconds, wanting more but still I release him. A tear spills down my cheek.

Sam's eyes search my face, his own a mixture of so many emotions. And then he suddenly smiles, sniffing. 'I have a daughter… Esme. She's beautiful.'

'I know,' I whisper.

'Tell me,' he urges. 'What was she like?'

'Hard work,' I say, smiling wistfully. 'Feisty, but always ready to laugh too. And bright-copper hair from the moment she was born. She'd get this look on her face sometimes and you knew there'd be no stopping her until she'd done what she set out to. Walking, riding a bike, learning to read. Always the same expression on her face. And eating olives by the time she was four…'

Hugh hated that of course, the fact that Esme would eat anything I put in front of her with gusto; always wanting to try new things. He used to say she was contrary, but I know he fought against loving that side of her because it was Sam all over and nothing he did could change it. Of course it's why he tried so hard to stop her from training as a chef. And equally why I battled so hard to make it happen. Kidding ourselves that Sam had nothing to do with it.

He grins at that. 'And you still hate them?'

'With a passion.'

He turns slightly, leaning his weight against the back of the bench, his face turned upwards to the sun. His eyes close for a second or two and then reopen, gazing out across the river.

'I don't know what to feel,' he says. 'I can't take it all in. That she's been here all this time and I never knew.'

'I wanted to tell you. I tried, but…'

'I'd made it impossible.' He nods, knowing that his actions were to blame.

'I didn't even realise I was pregnant straight away. I put the tiredness and the nausea down to grief, I… But by the time I did know, you'd gone away. And I'd moved too.'

I lick my lips, trying to draw some moisture back into my mouth. 'When the divorce papers came through, I tried again, to see if I could find you through your solicitor but, of course, he wouldn't tell me where you were. After that, well Esme was growing and Hugh forbade me. I had to stop looking, Sam. What could I do? Hugh had taken us in. He was my husband and now Esme's father. I couldn't do that to him, I just couldn't.'

'No, I gave you no choice, did I?'

'You did what you thought was right, Sam. I understand that. It's taken me a long time to realise it, but I know you did it with my best interests at heart. It hasn't been easy for you either, I'm aware of that.'

He doesn't answer, but his expression lets me know that he's thinking about the truth of my words. I take another deep breath, screwing up my courage, because there's one thing I want to ask him, a question that has haunted me for years. And I almost can't bear to ask it for fear of the answer. But I have to know, one way or the other.

'Sam…? Would things have been different if you'd known about Esme? Would you still have sent me away?'

His face looks agonised now and I realise that this is the first time he's had to consider this question. 'Alys, that's not fair, I…' But then he stops. 'Yes,' he says, decisively. 'Yes, at the time I would have. If anything, that would have made me more determined. To make sure that you both could have a better life. That's all I ever wanted.'

I nod, a small smile touching my lips. However much it hurts, it was the best possible answer he could have given me, and I know without a shadow of a doubt how much Sam loved me. How much he wanted to set me free. But what now? Now that I've returned? We sit in silence for a few moments and I'm agonisingly aware of how close our hands are to touching. If I were to reach out with my fingers and curl them around his, what then? I push the thought away.

'Who else knows about this?' asks Sam, suddenly.

'No one,' I reply. 'Well, Hugh, of course, but no one else.'

Sam gives a bitter laugh. 'Christ, I bet he's loved this, hasn't he? Properly got one over on me this time. Not content with simply having you.' His eyes are wild, staring. 'I can't imagine him ever giving her up, not without a fight anyway. I don't stand a chance, do I? I never did.'

My eyes narrow in confusion and I sit up straight, facing him. 'You have to tell me what happened, Sam. Please. I need to know.'

But he shakes his head violently. 'No, I can't be the one who tells you, Alys. Hugh can hang himself, I want no part of it.' His eyes are locked on mine and I can see he isn't going to back down.

I heave an exasperated sigh. 'Sam, Hugh doesn't even know I'm here. He forbade me to tell you about Esme, actually, but it isn't his decision to make, not solely anyway. I couldn't let you leave without telling you.'

He pauses to wait for a young mother to walk past, pushing a pram. It seems to crystallise his thoughts. 'So why *are* you telling me now? Because I'm just about to go and I can disappear and do the decent thing – stay out of your lives?'

'No!' My denial is quick. 'I'm telling you because I think you have a right to know… And I didn't want you to leave and risk never seeing you again… For Esme's sake…' I swallow. I'd give anything to add *and mine*…

Sam nods, his face turned slightly away from me. He repositions himself on the bench, wincing slightly as he shifts his hip. 'What do *you* want, Alys?' he asks eventually. 'Do you want me to be a part of Esme's life?'

I let out a breath. 'That's not my decision to make either,' I say. 'Esme doesn't know about this yet, Sam. I wanted you to know first, but I will tell her, soon, I have to. She has just as much right to know. And when she does, then I guess how much you see one another, if at all, will be up to her. And you and your family. I haven't forgotten how much this will impact on them either.'

'But you won't stop her?'

'No, I won't. But Hugh might. He'll try, anyway.'

Sam nods. 'And where does this leave you?' he asks gently.

I brush lightly at a greenfly that has landed on my arm. 'Well I would hope that Nancy and Theo will be understanding,' I say, smiling bravely. 'I think they will be from what I know of them and, although it might be a little… difficult to start with, maybe in time a different sort of relationship can be forged between you all. Different, but still good. I have high hopes of that happening. As for Hugh? He'll just have to get used to it. And he will, he won't have much choice. Life will go on.'

'I hope so too, Alys. That's a nice thought. But when I asked about you, that wasn't really what I meant.' His eyes are soft on mine.

'No, I know…' The last of my courage is failing, but I have to do the right thing. That's what all this has always been about. 'Sam, Hugh's my husband. We've been together for twenty-three years. I can't…' My throat closes. I can't even bring myself to finish the sentence.

His fingers close over mine. 'I understand,' he says. 'And thank you, Alys. For letting me know.' Barely more than a whisper. His hand moves away, the warmth from his body gone. And there's nothing else left to say.

I get to my feet, managing one last smile before I turn away, tears already running down my cheeks as my heart breaks open.

I can't bring myself to say goodbye.

# CHAPTER EIGHTEEN

I take the last remaining pin from my mouth before standing back slightly to get a better look at the fit of Nancy's jacket. I survey it critically, nodding in confirmation at what I see.

'That ought to do it,' I say. 'How does that feel?'

Nancy gives an experimental wriggle. 'Plenty of room,' she replies. 'It feels great.'

'Not too tight under the arms?'

She raises them gently above her head, conscious of the pins down each side. 'No… Perfect.' She holds out a leg for inspection. 'And the trousers feel great too.'

'I think we've got the leg length right now. With the shoes you're wearing they sit perfectly. Just got to bling it up now and we're sorted, I think.' I take another look. 'Just stand up straight for me again.'

She does as I ask, and I take a couple of steps backward, moving left to right to check the overall fit once more. It's only when I check back to Nancy's face that I realise she's been watching me closely.

'Are you sure you're okay?' she asks. 'You're not still worried about the other night, are you?'

Nancy has this way of looking at you that instantly makes you want to divulge your deepest secrets. But I mustn't, it really wouldn't be fair on either Sam or Esme and I'm feeling guilty enough as it is. Sam left yesterday and I still haven't found the right opportunity to speak to Esme and my parental skills, or rather the lack of them, are preying heavily on my mind. I should have told her long before now. I should have listened to my instinct and ignored Hugh's instructions to leave things as they were. I do understand how he feels, but he's an adult and that's his problem to deal with; it shouldn't have meant keeping the truth from Esme all these years.

'I've never been so embarrassed, Nancy,' I reply. 'And you're being very lovely about it, but Hugh ruined your evening, there's no escaping that.'

Nancy tuts. 'He didn't ruin it,' she says. 'He made it memorable certainly, but it was already that, and no one could spoil all the loveliness that had gone before. The opening was still everything I hoped it would be.'

'I'm just grateful that Esme and Theo weren't around to witness it. That would have been awful. Imagine how she would have felt? And Theo too.'

Nancy steps out of her heels and sighs with relief at being back on level ground. 'It wouldn't have been an ideal way to find out about you and Sam but, in my experience, with stuff like that there really isn't a right time. And if you wait for the perfect moment, it will never come. Sorry,' she adds quickly, 'that wasn't a criticism.'

'No, I know. But you're right. I do need to tell Esme. I know Sam has gone back home now but the longer I leave it, the harder it's going to get.' And that's not all, I think glumly, feeling a little overawed by the task ahead of me.

Nancy holds her arms up so that I can ease the jacket from her shoulders and remove it. 'Well, Sam will be at Saturday's shindig so maybe sometime before then might be good, if you can manage it.'

'Oh? I hadn't realised he'd be there. I wouldn't have thought it was his kind of thing.'

Nancy grins. 'What, a room full of empowered women? You may well be right.' She wrinkles her nose and I get the feeling she's weighing up whether to say something or not. 'Actually, he's coming to support me… Saturday is going to be a little… bigger… than I'd first anticipated.'

'How come?' I ask, as I fold up the jacket carefully and lay it on the table. 'Have you got some bigwig reporters coming in to cover the story?'

'No, nothing like that… Just…' She comes to a halt. 'I tell you what. How about I keep it as a surprise?' She laughs. 'I'm such a tease.'

'Yes, you are,' I say, holding out my hand for the trousers that Nancy is still wearing. 'I'm looking forward to it though. I can't wait to see you in your tux, you're going to look amazing. And I promise not to bring Hugh. A room full of empowered women is definitely *not* his kind of thing.'

She gives me a sympathetic look. 'Under the circumstances, that might be for the best.'

I nod. I'm no more looking forward to seeing a repeat performance between Sam and Hugh than she is. And Hugh still doesn't know I've told Sam about Esme. A sudden shiver ripples down my spine. I really don't want to think about what his reaction is going to be.

Nancy is still looking at me, an amused look on her face, and then she undoes the button and zip on her trousers and slips out of them in one smooth movement, handing them over with a cheeky grin.

'What?' I ask.

'You'll be able to meet the new love of my life on Saturday too,' she says, pulling her own top back on.

I wait until her head is free from it. 'Nancy Carmichael. You dark horse, you. Why didn't you say? Oh, what's he like? Tall, dark and handsome?'

She waggles a finger at me. 'Nuh-uh. No details,' she says. 'I want it to be a surprise, so I'll save all that until you meet.'

She yanks her jeans back on, glancing at the clock as she does so. 'Oh God, is that the time? I'd better run.' She leans forward to kiss me. 'Thank you *so* much, Alys. I can't believe that you've actually made me a tuxedo. It's going to look incredible.'

'I think it will. And you're happy to have all the crystals and whatnot, as we discussed?'

'Oh, yes! The more the merrier. I want to *sparkle*.' Her eyes light up and she flashes me a huge smile. 'Oh, I nearly forgot.' She fishes in the pocket of her jeans, pulling out a scrap of paper. 'This is for you. It's Sam's number.'

I stare at the slip in her hand. A row of eleven numbers, neatly written, so innocuous and yet so dangerous.

'I figured you might have need of it sometime. You know, just in case…'

She's already walking towards the door, where she stops to blow me a kiss. 'Speak soon,' she says. 'And Alys… talk to Esme.'

I stare at the empty space Nancy has left in my kitchen, wondering why on earth I can't be more like her. She doesn't let obstacles stand in her way, and it's obvious she's had just as many things to contend with. She's had a long-term relationship break down for one. But even though she's confided in me before that she'd had a few things to resolve, it's obvious just by looking at her that she's done exactly that. And now she looks fabulous.

I look down at my baggy top and shapeless linen trousers. I'm not saying I want to wear things that are tighter, but I could at least wear something that fits. So I bought a nice dress, so what? It was one drop in a huge ocean of opportunities missed. The slip of paper with Sam's number on it is still clutched in my hand and I lay it thoughtfully on the table. An opportunity missed? Or one yet to explore? I wonder…

I find my phone under a pile of letters on the side and pick it up decisively. If I don't do this now I'll start work on Nancy's jacket and kid myself I'm too busy to stop.

The call is answered just when I think it's going to cut to answerphone.

'Alys, hi… Is everything all right?'

'Hi, Tash, yes fine. Listen, I'm sorry to ring you while you're working, but I wondered if you're still running those aqua fit classes at the leisure centre?'

'Yeah, tonight… Hang on a sec.' She breaks off and I hear her say something in the background. 'Sorry… Yes, on tonight at seven thirty. Every Monday. Or there's one on a Friday afternoon for the over-sixties if you're interested.' I hear the smile in her voice.

'That might be more appropriate given how unfit I am. But could I just come along tonight if I wanted to? I don't have to have pre-booked or anything?'

'No, just turn up. Don't tell me you're actually going to take my advice, Alys? See, my nagging does pay off. But do come, they're great sessions, you'll really enjoy it. And you'll feel amazing afterwards, I promise.'

I look at Nancy's jacket. 'Right. I'll be there, seven thirty.'

I end the call and pick up Sam's number from the table, folding the slip of paper in half and stashing it in my pocket. Because I've realised what Sam's number is. It's a reminder of how I used to be. The curly-haired girl who thought she had the world at her feet.

*

It's still reasonably early when I get in, only a little after nine. I think Tash would have liked to have gone for a drink after the class and it was tempting, the evening is still warm and mellow, but although we chatted a little about my visit to see Becky at the National Trust, I told her I needed to get home. There are things that Hugh and I need to discuss and although I would have loved to confide in her, it wouldn't be right. She's family, and just a little too close for comfort right now. I need to sort out things with Hugh first. He's been particularly quiet since our conversation the other day and I'm under no impression that it's going to be easy. But I have to try. Every day that passes sends my guilt levels even higher.

But the kitchen is empty when I enter the house, and my call of greeting is met with silence. My note is still on the side where I left it, along with the dinner I'd made sure I prepared for Hugh before I left. It was in the fridge and all he'd had to do was reheat it. But now it's been abandoned in the warm kitchen, uncovered and spoiled. It makes me far crosser than it ought to, but it's as if it's been left there to make a point and I'm suddenly tired of my husband's moods.

A quick tour of the house confirms that he isn't home and, returning to the kitchen, I dump the untouched food in the bin. He hasn't had the decency to let me know where he is, but I can guess. His stomach will have got the better of him and, as his car is still in the drive and the local pub only five minutes' walk away, no doubt he's sitting in the beer garden tucking into steak and chips. That's all I need. The possibility of a sensible conversation is slipping further and further away from me.

I throw my swimming costume and towel into the washing machine and make myself some toast before sitting down to carry on with the embellishment of Nancy's tuxedo. It's nearer half past ten by the time I hear Hugh rattling the back door.

Whether he imagined I'd be in bed by the time he returned I don't know, but he looks surprised to see me as he lurches a little unsteadily into the kitchen.

'I didn't expect you to be home yet,' he says, his face glistening with perspiration. It's still a warm evening.

I get up and fill the kettle with water, setting it to boil. 'Didn't you? Oh, I think I said in my note I'd be home between nine and half past.'

Hugh opens his mouth to speak and then closes it again. His tie is still around his neck, at half mast, and he pulls it off, dropping it on the side by the cooker. 'Where have you been?' he asks, narrowing his eyes at the mess on the table.

'Hugh, did you even read my note?'

'I read it, yeah.'

I keep my voice light. 'Okay, so you know I've been out with Tash then.'

'That's what it said, certainly.'

I ignore him. 'Would you like a coffee?' I ask. 'Or tea? Perhaps it's a bit late for coffee.'

He takes a couple of steps towards me. 'What I'd like is an explanation. Of where you've been this evening. Or would you like me to guess?'

I had hoped that Hugh's steak and chips had been accompanied by a long, cool drink of Coke or something similar, but it would seem I was wrong. I wonder just how many pints he's had.

'Tash was working tonight,' adds Hugh. 'I checked.'

Anger begins to unfurl within me. How dare he? It's bad enough that he could even think I'm guilty of what he's implying, but now he's involved my brother-in-law too, and Tash when she finds out. Which she will.

'I know Tash was working tonight, Hugh, because that's where I've been, to one of her aqua fit classes at the leisure centre. It started at seven thirty, and ran for an hour. I got changed afterwards, and then helped carry her equipment out to the car. We chatted for a little while and then I drove the fifteen-minute journey home. I got back here about ten past nine, which you would know if you'd been here.'

I throw a teabag into a mug and pour boiling water on it. 'And do you know what's really sad, Hugh? That I didn't want to tell you what I was doing tonight because I knew you'd make fun of me. Or tell me why you didn't think I should bother going.'

'Well I don't, you look fine to me.'

'But what about me, Hugh? What about how I feel? I don't feel fine. I feel frumpy and flabby, and just once it would be really nice if you could support me in trying to improve myself rather than mock me for it.'

'Which is all very convenient, isn't it? Given that your desire for self-improvement seems to have coincided with Sam's return to the scene.'

'Oh, for God's sake, Hugh.' I prod his tea viciously, fishing out the bag and dropping it in the sink. It makes me even madder that all the while he's accusing me of spending a wild evening with Sam, what am *I* doing? Making him a bloody cup of tea. 'You know, maybe all this *has* coincided with seeing Sam again, but perhaps it's just because it's reminded me what I was like when I was younger. When I had hopes and dreams instead of settling for the faded version of myself I don't even recognise.'

'Oh, I see, and that's my fault too, is it?'

'Yes, maybe it is! When have you ever supported any idea I had? Any thought about anything. You always have the better idea, even down to what I wear for goodness' sake. Everything in my life is a compromise, Hugh, everything. In fact, some of it isn't even a compromise, I just put up with what you want because I get fed up of arguing, of trying to make my opinion heard, knowing that you're just going to bat it to one side. But I'm unhappy, Hugh. I'm forty-eight years of age and I have no control over my life and no idea where it's going. And all you can see is me doing the wrong thing again. Has it never occurred to you that I might be doing all this for you too? For us.'

Hugh doesn't look convinced, but he is at least listening.

'It can't be a good thing having one person in our marriage unhappy, can it? And whilst it might not happen straight away, we'll have an empty nest soon, and so maybe we should use this opportunity to plan how we want the rest of our lives to be instead of just complacently allowing them to roll along.' I pause for a moment, marshalling my thoughts. 'I didn't want to tell you this before because I wasn't certain it would come to anything, but I've applied for another job.'

Hugh narrows his eyes. 'I see, and you've been successful, have you? Is that it?'

'Not exactly, no.' I briefly explain about the conservation work. 'So you see, although it's voluntary to start with, in a few months' time there's every possibility that I'll be earning again and—' I come to a halt. It's been on the tip of my tongue to mention my redundancy money, the fact that I know everything that Hugh has been keeping from me. But his belligerent expression confirms that telling him tonight would be disastrous. 'It's something I really want to do,' I finish instead. 'It was all I ever wanted to do, actually, you know that. And now for the life of me I can't think why I didn't.'

'There seem to be rather a lot of things you're doing without telling me just lately, Alys.'

There's such a supercilious look on his face that I want to slap him. But I can't say a single word. He's a fine one to talk, but how can I throw his comment back in his face without incriminating myself? I haven't exactly been truthful. In fact, I'm as bad as he is right now.

'So are you going to tell me where you've really been tonight?'

Hugh's words cut across my thoughts, his snide expression goading me. Too late I realise that he's had a lot more to drink than I first thought.

'I told you, I've been to one of Tash's fitness classes,' I reply. 'You can ring and ask her if you want.'

'And what good would that do? She'll only tell me what I want to hear.'

My thoughts are hurling themselves around my brain. I'm desperately trying to think of something to defuse the situation and then it comes to me.

'Look, I've even got my costume here,' I say, crossing to the utility room and taking my wet things out of the washing machine. 'I might hang them on the line. They can stay out overnight, it won't hurt.'

I'm desperate to put some space between us so that Hugh can calm down. In a flash I'm through the conservatory and out into the garden, where I take my time to peg out my costume and towel. It's late now, the garden illuminated only by the lights of the house, and I gulp in the still warm air, scented with the stocks that fill the border under the conservatory window. If I can just get Hugh to believe what I'm saying now it will all be okay. Stay calm and don't react to his accusations with anything other than logic. He can have a cup of tea and sleep off the alcohol and tomorrow I can think more clearly about what I'm going to do. My conscience might be laden with guilt but I remind myself that, whatever he thinks, I am not having an affair. I brighten my expression and close the conservatory doors behind me, relocking them. There are footsteps behind me as I fiddle with the side of the door which always sticks.

'So you see, like I said, the pool is the only place I've been tonight. I certainly haven't been out with Sam and I promise I'm not having an affair with him. Why would I want to, when I love you?'

I give the key one final jiggle, feeling it slide around, and then I turn, a smile ready on my face.

Silhouetted in the doorway to the kitchen is Esme. 'What's going on, Mum?'

I can feel my face draining of colour. There's no way she wouldn't have heard what I said, and I can see from her expression that she has.

'Esme, crikey, is that the time? Have you had a good evening, love? Busy though, I bet.'

But she ignores me.

'What's going on?' she says again. 'Who were you talking about?'

I glance anxiously past her to Hugh who is leaning nonchalantly against the work surface, one leg draped casually over the other at the ankle. His expression is almost amused – *you got yourself into this mess,* it says, *you get yourself out of it.* He isn't going to help me at all. I look back at Esme, my mouth open.

'Oh, just someone we know… Someone at work.' I nod at Hugh, willing him to agree. Maybe Esme didn't hear exactly what I said. Maybe if we're just vague…

'No, you weren't,' she says, looking first at me and then at Hugh. 'You said the name Sam… Who did you mean?'

I can see she's trying to work it out. Running the name through her head, checking the possibilities. But there's only one person she knows called Sam. Her eyes widen.

'Yes, good question, isn't it?' says Hugh, in response.

She looks back at me. 'Sam, as in Theo's dad?' she asks.

'Esme, listen… Wait a minute…' I put out a hand towards her. 'It isn't what it sounds like. Your dad and I were just…' But I break off. I can't tell her we were arguing, it'll make things seem even worse. I'm caught between the two of them. What on earth can I say?

Esme takes a step backward, a look of horror crossing her face. 'Oh my God,' she says, slowly. 'It is, it's Theo's dad… And you're having an affair?'

'No! Esme, I'm not, I promise you. It's nothing like that.'

But she's shaking her head. 'You are,' she says. 'It all makes sense now. Your hair, the new dress…' Her hand is over her mouth. 'But you don't even know him. Christ, it's only been what, three weeks?'

Hugh lets out a snort of derision.

I stare at him, my own horror mounting. My head is screaming, *Hugh don't do this. Please don't do this.*

Hugh opens his mouth.

*Not in front of Esme.*

*Not now.*

*Please.*

'Oh, she knows him all right,' he says. 'She's known him for years. And what a happy coincidence this has turned out to be. You get your dream job. And your mother gets her dream man back again. After all these years.'

Esme's face begins to crumple. 'I don't know what you mean, Dad. Mum, what's going on?' She's close to tears.

'It's okay, sweetheart. I promise you. I'll explain… But let's just…' I need to get her out of the kitchen. Away from Hugh. I have no idea what he's going to say next and I can't let her find out like this. It's too cruel. 'Let's just go upstairs, Esme, I can explain.'

Hugh uncrosses his legs, and stands upright, holding onto the counter tops for balance. 'I'm sorry to have to tell you, Esme, but your mother and Sam were once married.' He gives me a triumphant look, which rapidly turns to puzzlement as Esme's breath shudders into a sob.

And with one final heartbreaking look, she flees the kitchen.

For a second it feels as if there's a vacuum in the room, sucking everything inside of it. I can't breathe. There's no air, no nothing. Hugh deflates like a slowly leaking balloon, suddenly and finally struck by the enormity of what he's done.

I cross the distance between us until I'm only inches away from him. 'You bastard,' I say. 'You stupid, *stupid* bastard.'

# CHAPTER NINETEEN

I can hear Esme crying through her bedroom door, the sound of her tears like a physical pain. She knows I wouldn't normally enter without her permission, but she also knows that today I'll override that rule in a heartbeat and so she's slumped on the floor in front of the door just like she used to do when she was a teenager, and my plaintive entreaties to open it go unanswered. The chunk of wood between us may as well be forty-foot high and fifty-foot wide. I can't get to her and it's breaking my heart.

'Esme, please. Just let me talk to you. I know on the face of it this sounds awful, but it isn't, not really. Esme…?'

But there's no reply. However much I try, whatever I say. She's just like her dad in that regard, so stubborn. I sag against the door. What am I thinking? She's like Hugh, she's not like her dad at all… Or maybe she is, I don't know. I don't know anything any more.

I slide downwards until I'm sitting on the floor too, my back up against the door. Perhaps I should be grateful that Hugh didn't spill the whole can of beans, but the little voice in my head is telling me that's only because he can't deal with her knowing he's not her real father and it's probably right. But where do I go from here? And when did all this become solely my responsibility? Shouldn't Hugh be by my side, and I his? Shouldn't we be facing these challenges together? Talking to Esme and supporting her as a couple, helping her to understand that whatever may have happened in the past it doesn't have to change her future.

Hugh has been Esme's father in every sense of the word from the minute she was born and no one, least of all me, would ever suggest that change. Even though I can see that having Sam as an extra dad could be a good thing for Esme, she could learn so much from it, I'd never suggest it. But I also know that discussing things rationally, as Esme's parents, is never going to happen. It's gone too far for that. I close my eyes. In an ideal world perhaps but not in my world, because my relationship with Esme is one thing, but where does this leave my relationship with Hugh? When he has kept so much hidden from me over the years and yet accuses me of having an affair. When he has set himself up as the victim instead and pointed the finger of blame at me. And I think I know the answer.

Esme is quiet now but still I sit here. My sadness has rooted me to the spot, silent tears tracking down my cheeks. I never wanted any of this to happen. I just wanted to be me. To feel alive again, to wake up the life that felt as if it was sleeping. Is that so very wrong? And maybe Sam *was* the catalyst for all this, but I can't magic him back into the bottle like the genie he seems to be. He's here and no amount of straightening my hair and carrying on like I did before is ever going to change that.

The door gives slightly behind me and I know that Esme has got up from the floor. I brace myself for its opening because she knows I'm here – she'll have felt it too – and, sure enough, her cracked voice whispers from behind me.

'Mum...?'

I get to my feet and then we're standing there, looking at one another across the threshold of the door. Her face is stained with tears and she looks more vulnerable than I ever remember seeing her before, but it gives me hope. It's only by being vulnerable that we reach out. I hold out my arms and she slips wordlessly inside, her head against my chest. My hair tangles with hers as I lean forward. My Esme. My girl.

Eventually she pulls away, looking up at me with eyes that are surprisingly full of empathy. Or maybe it's not such a surprise. In that regard she *is* just like her father.

'Will you tell me?' she asks.

I nod. 'Now?'

But she shakes her head. 'No, tomorrow. I'm too tired, Mum. I won't be able to take it all in.'

I lay a hand across her cheek, my thumb gently caressing the top of her cheekbone. 'And I promise you there's nothing to worry about,' I say. 'Everything is going to be okay.'

What else can I tell her?

Hugh is still downstairs when I return, sitting at the kitchen table nursing his cup of tea. His head hangs low over his mug and, despite my earlier anger, I hate to see him like this. I'm very aware of how much is at stake for him. I sit down quietly on the seat opposite him.

'And I suppose you want to talk some more, do you? I can see you're having trouble containing yourself.'

I hadn't expected anything less. Hugh's default stance is always defensive. I hold his challenging look for a moment. 'I'd rather we weren't in a position where we were having to "talk" at all,' I say, mildly. 'But as it happens I do think a discussion about this evening would be useful, as well as one or two other things.'

He scowls. 'What one or two other things? What else am I supposed to have done?'

But I bite my tongue. One thing at a time.

'Would you like another cup of tea first?' I ask. 'I'm going to make myself one.'

'Might as well,' he replies sullenly, pushing his mug towards me.

'Come on then,' he says, as soon as I've placed his mug down beside him. 'Let's hear what you've got to say.'

His attitude is infuriating. 'You first,' I say. 'I'd love to know on what level you think it's okay to firstly accuse me of having an affair, and secondly to blurt out to Esme that Sam and I were married. Although I suppose I should be grateful you didn't go the whole hog and…' I lower my voice, very aware that Esme is in the house. 'Do you not realise how sensitive an issue this is for her?'

A look of pain crosses his face and I'm not sure whether it's anguish at the things he said or from having had too much to drink.

'We need to talk to her, Hugh, both of us together, calmly and rationally, but before we do that, you and I need to do the same. And then we need to tell her everything.'

Hugh's head shoots up, his eyes wide. 'No,' he says. Definite. Not to be argued with.

'Don't you think she has a right to know?' I ask, getting up to close the kitchen door. 'Especially now. She's going to think it weird enough that I used to be married to Sam, but imagine how she'll feel if she finds out later that she's actually his daughter and we haven't told her.' I can't make my expression any more plaintive than it already is. 'It isn't how I wanted it to happen, but I can't see how we can keep this from her now.'

Hugh gets to his feet, striding across the room and coming to rest by the sink. He places both hands on the counter top and stares out into the dark garden. 'Kick a man when he's down, why don't you?'

'See, Hugh? This is exactly what I mean. It's not about kicking a man when he's down, it's about making you realise that you have a responsibility for this too. You're turning this into something that's my fault and it isn't. I didn't want things to be this way, remember? I've always disagreed about keeping the truth from both Esme and Sam, but that was easier when there was no chance that they would ever meet. But they have met, and this isn't fair to either of them.'

I soften my voice. 'Look, I understand how you feel, but you're not going to lose Esme. Your name is on her birth certificate and you and you alone have been her father her entire life. I think you need to have a little more faith in her than that. She isn't going to turn her back on you, she loves you.'

'And what if you're wrong?' says Hugh, turning to me, his eyes beginning to redden. 'She's my little girl, Alys. I can't lose her.'

I move over to him, laying a hand on his arm. 'You won't. But can't you see how wrong it is not to tell her? She's already confused. Having her dad all but accuse her mum of having an affair wasn't the nicest thing to hear. And not just with anyone either, but to a man she already knows, as her boss' ex-husband. But she's got a good head on her shoulders. She's kind and compassionate and mature enough to deal with this now. And she will. Once she has the bigger picture. I'm not saying it will be easy, but I think you're doing her a grave disservice if you keep this from her because of how you think she'll feel about you. She'd be insulted that you didn't trust her and if you're scared you're going to lose her, this is a guaranteed way to ensure it.'

Hugh's face contorts. 'Sam is not her father,' he says, bitterly. 'He never has been, and I can't stand the thought of him having anything to do with her. He doesn't deserve someone like her.'

'Hugh,' I say gently. 'You don't know Sam, not any more. And how do you know what kind of a father he'd be to Esme when you've never given him the chance to find out?'

'No, and I don't want to either.'

I sigh. I hadn't expected Hugh to agree with me, but he must have thought about this over the years, and it's his blanket refusal to even consider it that irritates me.

'Neither would I given the choice. Do you really think I want all this upset? To turn Esme's world upside down? But I'm trying to do the right thing, Hugh. Sam is not some faceless nobody that Esme will never meet, he's intrinsically involved in the business she works for. We can't go on letting them think they have one sort of relationship when, in fact, it's completely different. It's immoral apart from anything else. I'm sorry, but you have to consider what's right for Esme. She's an adult now and she should be able to make her own decisions.'

'That's easy for you to say when it's not you that risks losing her.'

'I know…' I pause for a second, holding Hugh's anguished look. 'But I honestly don't think you will. And it isn't just Esme that this affects, is it? It affects Sam too, and his family. I haven't known her for long, but Nancy is lovely; warm and compassionate. In fact, she already feels like family, and those are Esme's words, not mine. It will be just as big a shock to her, but even though she's now divorced from Sam, I know she'll do all she can to help support Esme through this. Instead of viewing it as something negative, why don't you think on it as Esme potentially gaining an extended family. Nothing could be better for her, given her position.'

He stares at me in disgust. 'Well, if you think that's what will happen, then you're incredibly naive.'

'Maybe I am. But it is one possible outcome for all of this, however improbable.'

Hugh fiddles with the handle of a mug that's been left by the sink. His eyes are downcast and I have no idea what he's thinking, but the silence between us is growing longer and longer.

'You've got all this worked out, haven't you?' he says eventually.

'Is that what you think?' I reply. 'I haven't got any of this worked out, Hugh. I'm simply trying to discuss it with you so that we can come to a joint agreement over the right way to move forward. I have thought about it endlessly over the years, of course I have. Haven't you? But thinking about it hypothetically is very different from actually being faced with it and having to decide what to do.'

Hugh considers my words, his expression unyielding. 'I have thought about it, yes,' he says. 'And my decision is still the same as it was twenty-four years ago. I took you and Esme in then because I believed that I was the best person to love and care for you both. And that belief hasn't changed.' Hugh's jaw is set in the same rigid way it always is when he's about to share his decision. 'I don't want Sam to have anything to do with Esme, and I certainly don't want him to have anything to do with you. Let him go home and then the rest of us can get on with our lives without him. Just as we always have done.'

'And you really think that's the answer, do you?' I reply. 'Just ignore it and it will all go away.' I'm not about to tell Hugh that Sam has already gone, or that he knows about Esme. Hugh's steadfast refusal to face up to things is infuriating. 'You don't think you need to say anything else?' I wouldn't normally push Hugh like this, but I'm not backing down, not this time.

He doesn't reply.

'So what are you going to say to Esme then? What are *we* going to say to her? I think at the very least you owe her an apology. And me for that matter.'

'Fine,' he says, eyes flashing. 'I'll apologise to Esme in the morning. And I'll leave you to explain about your marriage to Sam…' He breaks off, dropping his gaze. 'I'm sure you'll do a much better job than I will.'

It's as much of an admission that he's behaved badly as I'm going to get, but it also speaks to the fact that he wouldn't have anything nice to say about Sam, and I'm reminded that we still haven't discussed his comments from the other evening. I pick up my mug and swallow a couple of mouthfuls of tea. How did everything get so complicated? And how can one man make it so? I wrinkle my nose, wondering where to start.

'Hugh, why are you and Sam at such loggerheads with one another?' I ask. 'Apart from the fact that you've accused me of having an affair, you don't have a good word to say about him, or *to* him for that matter. Yet, as far as I'm aware, you were friends.

You even came to our wedding, but when Sam had his accident all that seemed to change… In fact, thinking about it, I find it really odd that when over twenty years have gone by, during which time you haven't seen him at all, the first thing you say to him is not "How are you?" or some comment about what an amazing recovery he's made, but a warning to stay away from me…'

My thoughts are coming faster now. 'When I put this together with a comment Sam made about not wanting to rekindle your friendship and you saying that I was the thing that came between you, then I don't much like the picture I'm seeing.'

Hugh studies my face, his mouth set in a hard line. 'I hate what he did to you, that's all.'

'No… there's more to it than that. You shouldn't hate him for what he did to me, because if we hadn't split up you and I would never have been. He should hate you maybe, but not the other way around.'

Hugh is desperately trying to find the words to contradict me, but he can't. He knows my memory of our conversation is accurate. His eyes narrow.

'I don't know what's got into you lately,' he says. 'But anyone would think you've forgotten what happened, Alys. When Sam left you high and dry, I gave you a job, a home. I've given you my life and now it seems as if you might be questioning that. As if you might have preferred the alternative… I should have a long hard think about what that would have been like if I were you.'

I swallow, hard, feeling tension tighten the muscles in my chest.

'I would have thought you'd be grateful, for everything I've given you,' continues Hugh. 'Not just materially, but in helping shape you into the person you are today. Knocked off all those nasty spiky edges for one.'

'And what if I liked my spiky edges, Hugh?' I retort. 'At least I had a personality then; an opinion, my own thoughts. What am I now? Some homogenised idea of a woman, your idea of a woman;

bland, compliant, unquestioning… Having to turn to you for everything and, worse, not even realising that this was the case.'

*Mistaking care for control…*

I take another deep breath. 'I've given you a lifetime of grateful, Hugh. I am grateful, but when did our marriage become so one-sided? What about what I've brought to the mix?'

He's silent, and I know he's not going to answer me.

'What about the dreams I gave up, Hugh? I know when Esme was little picking up my career again would have been difficult. But she hasn't been little for a very long time. And this isn't the first occasion I've mentioned it either. But each time I have, there's always been a very valid reason why it wasn't a good time, or why it was better I stayed at Harringtons. Someone less trusting than me might have wondered whether you preferred it that way, just so you could keep an eye on me.'

'Oh, don't be so ridiculous,' he splutters. 'You enjoyed it at Harringtons. God, you've even started moaning because I fixed it so that you're not there any more—' He stops abruptly, swallowing as he realises what he's just said.

I raise my eyebrows. 'Don't look so worried, Hugh, I'd already worked out that's what happened. And you're right, I didn't like it to start with. But only because I knew there had to be a reason for it, other than supposedly giving me what I've always wanted.'

For the first time I can see a flicker of unease begin to stir in Hugh's eyes.

'You see, I never really thought about it before. How as manager at Harringtons your salary together with mine should have been enough to cover our mortgage and living expenses quite easily. And yet we never seem to have any spare cash, do we? Money for Esme to go and do her diploma was a problem, money for cars, holidays, all the normal things that folks spend their money on. It never occurred to me to wonder why that was, and I'm quite disgusted with myself at how complacent

I've been. But now I know the truth of our financial situation, it makes perfect sense.'

I'm trying so hard to be strong, but I can feel my resolve weakening. If I let myself become upset I'll never be able to say the things I need to. Hugh's head has dropped, one hand cupping his forehead.

'Why didn't you tell me?' I ask. 'I'm your wife for God's sake, Hugh. We're supposed to share stuff like this… But do you know what's almost worse? Not the fact that you can get us into debt to the tune of eighty thousand pounds and not tell me, but that now it makes me wonder what else you might have done.'

Hugh's head jerks up. 'I haven't done anything,' he insists. 'So I made some bad investments… it happens. Investments that were supposed to transform our lives, not blight them,' he says bitterly. 'And I made them in good faith, Alys. You can't blame me for that.'

I look at him sadly. 'I don't blame you for that,' I say. 'I'm furious with you, but more than anything I'm hurt because you didn't believe in me enough to share those things with me. We should have discussed you taking out the investments in the first place but then, when things went wrong, we certainly should have. I could have helped. At the very least shared some of the burden.'

'It wasn't that, I didn't want to upset you.'

'Hugh, this was twelve years ago. And you've been systematically lying to me since. It's gone way beyond not wanting to upset me. How do you think I feel now?'

He holds my look for a second before glancing away.

'Ah… I see, so I was never supposed to find out. I get it. And of course the last thirty thousand pounds we owe should have been conveniently covered by my lump-sum redundancy payment. Well that explains why the money didn't go straight into my account like it ought to have done. What were you going to tell me, Hugh? I'm interested to know how you thought you were going to explain that one away.'

He shrugs. 'I'd have thought of something.'

It infuriates me that even now he isn't going to apologise. But my anger is quickly turning to sorrow. I can feel it building. I swallow hard, focusing on a spot on the wall. 'Well, I've taken steps to ensure that whatever is decided over the use of the money, it will be a decision we take together. It should never have been any other way.'

His eyes swivel to mine. 'What have you done?' he demands.

'Moved the money into my own account.'

It's as if the very room itself is holding its breath. I've never done anything like this before and my courage is almost gone. I have to remind myself what it is I'm fighting for. Hugh is angrier than I've ever seen him, but even now he still thinks he can have his way.

'And just in case you were wondering,' I add. 'It's in a new account. One you don't have the details to, so there'll be no moving it back either, not without my say-so. Nearly twenty-six years I worked at Harringtons. Turned up every day and worked my socks off trying to make the department the best it could be. So that money is mine, Hugh, I earned every penny of it. And I intend to have a say in what it's used for.'

His eyes lock on mine and I see the moment the arrogance dies, the moment when he realises that his plan isn't going to go the way he wanted it to. He suddenly slumps, and I see fear in his eyes now too. It makes me feel more sad than ever.

'But what about the debt, Alys? It has to be paid and now you're not working at all and—' He puts a hand to his face. 'Oh God.'

'Yes, it seems like you might need to discuss this with me after all, Hugh. Perhaps we need to finally start talking so that we can decide what to do. Plus, of course, if you remember, I may well be back in employment in a few months' time.'

'Yes… of course that is good news. So we can still use your redundancy money to settle the mortgage and—'

'No.'

His face turns suddenly scarlet. 'What do you mean, no?'

I don't know what to say. On the face of it, using my redundancy money to pay off the last of the mortgage would make sound financial sense, but there's a little voice at the back of my head that's refusing to cooperate. It's telling me that it has sound advice of its own and it's very insistent. Keep it in case you need it, it's saying. Otherwise you'll have nothing. And despite my best intentions, I'm listening to it. After all, I moved the money into an account of my own, didn't I?

'What I was going to say was that I'm sure if we make some economies we can carry on paying the mortgage until I'm earning again. It just seems such a shame to squander this lump sum now that we have it. We could use it for all sorts of things.'

'Like what?'

'I don't know, Hugh. I haven't really thought about it yet.'

He nods, his eyes raking my face for any trace that I might not be telling the truth. 'But, in any case, you've put the money where I can't get hold of it.' He gives me a tight smile. 'And you accused me of keeping things from you. New job, new dress, new bank account…'

'Hugh, you remortgaged our house and didn't tell me, twelve years ago… You engineered things so I was made redundant… Both rather more important things than applying for a job, or buying a new dress, don't you think?'

He leans in towards me. 'Yes, but I told you that everything I've done has been for a good reason. For us, to try to make our lives better. And I never lied to you… I may have kept certain things from you in order to protect you, but you're just as bad, you've been keeping secrets too.'

A wave of shame washes over me. He's right. And there's a very fine line between keeping secrets and telling lies. But which of those am I guilty of? I told Sam about Esme without Hugh's knowledge and I haven't exactly been truthful about meeting him.

I've kept the truth from Esme for all these years, against my better judgement, and now I can feel the lies I'm going to have to tell building and building, their pressure threatening to swamp me. Yet all I ever wanted was to do the right thing. I should tell Hugh, but I can't. If I do it will all be over. I take in a deep breath, trying to calm myself. To think about what words I'm going to say.

'Then what do we do?' I ask.

But Hugh has no answer. And finally he can see what it is he's done. And what the future might hold. 'What are *you* going to do?' he asks, quietly, defeated, awaiting his fate.

'Nothing, for the moment,' I reply. 'I'm having a hard time adjusting to the fact that my marriage isn't what I thought it was. That my husband isn't the man I thought he was either. I'm hurt more than anything. Hurt and disillusioned. We've been married for twenty-three years, Hugh. But if we want that to continue, we have to make some changes, *we* have to change. I don't want the rest of our marriage to be the same.'

I let out the breath I seem to be holding and, taking another, feel it fill my lungs. 'So, things will have to be different. As far as the debt goes, we have options. We could sell this place. We don't need a house this big, especially now that Esme is sorted; she'll be thinking about having her own place at some point. And everything else… we'll just have to take a day at a time.' Because I'm as much to blame as he is. 'But we'll do it together, through talking, through sharing, and being honest with one another.'

Hugh doesn't answer but there's the smallest of nods. He must hate this – that I seem to be calling the shots – but I didn't want this either.

All I wanted was what I'd fooled myself into thinking we had: a partnership.

# CHAPTER TWENTY

By the time I've showered and dressed, Esme is already downstairs, albeit still in her PJs. She's nestled into the armchair that sits in the corner of the kitchen, legs crossed on the seat, phone in one hand and a bowl of cereal cradled in her lap. The sight of her blue fluffy slipper-socks tugs at my heart. They're such a staple part of her lounging wardrobe that seeing her in them is so familiar and yet there's nothing normal about this situation at all. I've changed that. I've set into motion a chain of events which are now freewheeling out of control and I'm not sure what it will take to bring them to a halt.

'Morning, love. I didn't think you'd be awake yet,' I say.

She looks up from her phone, pulling a face. 'I couldn't sleep,' she says, giving me a weak smile. 'Too many things on my mind.'

I nod, not knowing where to start. How to even begin this conversation. Perhaps if I—

'Tell me about Sam,' she blurts out. 'Why don't I know about him?'

This is so hard for her but I'm woefully unprepared for hearing his name.

I take a seat at the table, my mouth dry. 'May I ask you a question first?' I say. 'But it's not a trick one, answer whatever you honestly feel.'

There's a wariness in her eyes but she gives her consent, spooning in another mouthful of cereal.

'What do you think of him? Sam, I mean…'

She stops chewing for a couple of seconds and then carries on, her eyes never leaving my face until she's swallowed the remains. 'I don't see what that has to do with anything.'

'No… no, of course not. Sorry, I shouldn't have asked you.' I take a deep breath, just as Esme lets out a sigh.

'Are you having an affair with him, Mum? Because if you are then—'

'No! I'm not… Esme, I swear to you, it's nothing like that.'

She dips her head and her shoulders sag even lower. 'Then what, Mum?' she says, looking at me again and I can see that she's close to tears. 'Because this is really hard to take in, you know. I came home last night to find you and Dad arguing, him accusing you of having an affair, and then I find out that you and Sam were actually married before. So Dad must think something is going on. And why didn't I know anything about this?'

'Esme, I'm just as upset about all of this as you, believe me. What happened last night shouldn't have, plain and simple. And I'm furious that it means we're having a conversation like this, instead of the one I wanted, which was very different. But I promise I'm not lying to you. I never have and I'm not about to start now. So I will explain, properly, *if* you'll let me…'

A tear slips out and rolls down Esme's cheek.

'Oh, sweetheart…' I'm by her side in an instant, kneeling on the floor, reaching for her hands. It's an awkward mixture of need and want all muddled up by the positions we're both in but, after a few seconds, Esme pulls away and plonks her bowl of cereal onto the table beside her. She uncurls her legs and leans forward so that we can hug. It's still an uncomfortable position for both of us, but it's a start, and I'm conscious that Esme still needs to keep a little space between us.

'I'm sorry, Mum.'

I push her hair away from her face. 'Don't,' I say. 'You don't need to be sorry.' I look at her tired face, overcome with emotion and anxiety. 'Oh, Esme, how did all this get to be so complicated? It should never have been this way...' I hold her look for a few seconds more and then adjust my position so that I'm sitting on the floor facing her, my own legs crossed in front of me. 'Shall I tell you?' I say. 'Start at the beginning?'

She nods as I settle myself, trying to find a more comfortable position. I still don't know how to tell her all this, I've let her down so badly. I promised her I wouldn't lie to her, but how many years have I been doing this, keeping secrets from her? Even now... Am I really ready to tell her everything? More importantly, is she ready to hear it? I close my eyes for a second and draw in a breath.

'I was very young when I first met Sam. Except he wasn't called Sam then, I knew him as Tom. Thomas Samuel Walker to be exact. I'd just started my first job, fresh from university, and the last thing I was expecting was to fall in love—'

'Wait... so he was called Tom? He changed his name?' She seems to find that fascinating. 'Why would he do that?'

'Because he wanted a fresh start. To put the accident and everything he went through afterwards behind him and start again. It was an incredibly difficult time, but it explains why I didn't know who he was, Esme; the name Sam Walker meant nothing to me. And until I met him I had no idea that the man who was behind The Green Room was the same man I married all those years ago.'

Esme nods, thinking. 'So you weren't with him then, when he changed his name?'

'No...' I trail off, my thoughts threatening to overwhelm me. I clear my throat. 'Maybe we should backtrack a little,' I say, trying to get my emotions under control. 'As I said, I met Sam just after I finished my studies. I was looking for a job to tide me over and a friend of mine recommended me to your dad. He was managing a department at Harringtons. Not here though, at their Cambridge branch. I got the job and so that's where I met him and on my first day working there, I met Sam too. He and your dad were also friends, you see, and—' I stop as she holds up a hand, but then she frowns.

'No, sorry, go on.'

'That's kind of it,' I reply. 'We fell in love, got married and—'

'I don't want the detail,' she says. 'This is just too weird, that you were actually married to Theo's dad.' She stares at me incredulously. 'I can't get my head round it.'

'I know. But, really, in itself there's nothing odd about it. It's only because you know Theo and Nancy that it seems strange. Plenty of other people have second marriages, your uncle for one…'

'Yes, I know. But Aunty Louise died, Mum, that's hardly the same.'

'Isn't it? Does it matter why the marriage broke up? When Uncle Ed married Tash we still had to get used to a new person in our lives, but now we wouldn't want him to be without her.'

'Yes… I guess.'

I watch her face carefully, but she seems to accept what I'm saying.

'So what happened then, why didn't you stay together?'

I look out the window, staring at the garden outside. 'Because of the accident,' I say simply. 'Because Sam couldn't bear for me to be around and so he ended things.'

Esme frowns. 'I don't understand,' she says. 'So you were already married when it happened?'

I nod, trying to push away the memories crowding my head. 'It was the single worst night of my life,' I reply. 'New Year's Eve. Sam had been working and was involved in a car accident on the way home. He—'

'Was drunk?'

I stare at her. 'No… Nothing like that. No one knows for certain what caused the accident. Sam was hit by a lorry, but the driver of it couldn't remember what happened either. The police think someone ran a red light but Sam hadn't been drinking, even though a few of them had stayed on after the restaurant closed to see in the New Year. He never drank when he was driving…' I break off as a sudden thought distracts me.

'Sorry… I…' I drag myself back to the present. 'You've seen for yourself what the result of the accident was. Sam wasn't even expected to live, let alone walk again. I didn't care. I was just glad he was still alive… Except that, as he began to get better, he decided that looking after an invalid wasn't the life he wanted for me and so he ended our relationship. He refused to see me, and then he moved away… There was nothing I could do, I tried but…' I trail off, giving Esme a weak smile. 'Anyway, I never saw him again, at least not until the day I bumped into him at Scarlett's party.'

Esme has been listening quietly, her face growing progressively more still. It is now full of empathy. 'But that's awful,' she says. 'What did you do?'

I shrug. 'Nothing much I could do except get on with things,' I reply. 'Fortunately, not that long after… your dad… well he got an offer of promotion, a manager's job at Harringtons, here in Norwich, and so he offered me a job too. It would be a new start at least and we'd always been friends so it seemed… sensible. Actually, I jumped at the chance, Esme, I didn't really think about it too hard. I thought what I needed was the chance to get away from all the memories and although it was very hard at first, our friendship gradually became something else, as these things do, and we fell in love. I think you know the rest.'

Esme uncrosses her legs, wriggling back in her chair. She stares down at her lap for a moment, deep in thought before looking back at me.

'Sam must have loved you very much,' she says.

I look at her quizzically, pulse quickening.

'Because he let you go,' she clarifies. 'Everybody knows that – if you love someone you let them go. If they come back to you then they were always yours. If they don't, then they never were.'

'Except that Sam didn't want me to return, Esme. In fact, he took great pains to ensure that I never did.'

'So you think he changed his name because he didn't want you to find him?'

'Possibly, but I think—'

'To protect you?'

I swallow. 'Esme, I think you might be over-romanticising this a little. Because clearly *all* Sam did was send me away, he didn't let me go and he certainly had no intention of me finding my way back.'

'Except that you did.' She stares at me, her mouth a round 'O' of surprise as she realises what she's just said.

My face is betraying me. A slow heat is creeping up my neck, flooding onto my cheeks. Because Sam and I always joked that we were meant to be together, that it was fated and that whatever happened, nothing could ever change that.

'And I thought you said that Dad and Sam were friends? And yet… Presumably he knows who Sam is now as well so…' She pauses, quickly adding up two plus two. 'Why does he think you're having an affair?' Her eyes widen. 'Oh my God, you are…'

I hold up my hands. 'No, no, I'm not. Esme, I swear to you. You have to believe me, I would never do anything like that.' I'm going to have to tell her, but I can't bear for her to think badly of me. 'What's happened is that I've seen Sam on a couple of occasions, but… *but,*' I stress, 'it was entirely innocent, just two people catching up on twenty-odd years of life in between then and now. We were both shell-shocked seeing one another after all this time and we could hardly just ignore it, there's a lot to talk about. But when I told your dad he jumped to conclusions and, well...'

'So you do love Dad?'

This is killing me. How can I possibly tell her how I really feel? Especially when I don't even know myself.

'Yes, sweetheart, of course I do.' I pause a moment. 'I'm angry with him right now – furious, actually – for upsetting you last night, let alone for what he said to me, but we've had a good marriage.'

She thinks for a moment, taking in what I've said. She's spent a lifetime living with us. Aside from the years while she was studying, she's been under our roof, as close to us as anyone could be. I guess now is the moment I find out whether I managed to paper over the cracks well enough, to fool her the way I've been fooling myself.

'But Sam was your first love.'

'Yes he was.' My hand is resting on the carpet and I splay my fingers idly, feeling the pile move between them, back and forth, back and forth. 'And Esme, I won't pretend that I didn't love him a great deal, I did. I was heartbroken when our marriage ended and continued to be so for a long while after. But life moves on, and a lot of years have gone by since then.' *Even though it feels as if it was yesterday.*

'Okay,' she says eventually, weighing up whether what I've said makes sense to her. 'But that still doesn't explain why Dad was accusing you of seeing him.'

'No, I know. And I'm just as confused about that as you are. But that's down to your dad and me to sort out. He has very... fixed... ideas sometimes, and I suspect this is just one of those times. I've been trying to do things a little differently over the last few weeks as well and your dad doesn't always respond well to change.'

'But you *are* different, Mum, anyone who knows you can see that. I mean, your hair for starters, you never used to leave it curly.'

'You said you liked it.'

'I do. It's just so different, seeing it that way all the time. It's just not the you I know.'

And I suddenly see how vulnerable she is.

'I'm still your mum, Esme, and I always will be. But that's not all I am. If I'm doing things differently it's because I want to. Because I've reached a point in my life where things are changing, and all I'm doing is responding to them. You're working now, your education is behind you. You're on your way, Esme, and you don't need me to hold your hand any more. I'm not working at Harringtons either, and that was a big part of my life, for a very long time. So it's making me think about things, that's all.'

'Nothing to do with Sam?'

I smile. 'Actually, I think it has a lot to do with Sam, but not in the way you're fearful of. I think meeting him again has simply reminded me of my younger self, about the dreams I had, the kind of person I wanted to be. And I'm not saying I'm unhappy about the way things are now. It's just that I can also see that now is the right time to make a few changes. And I'm simply enjoying exploring the possibilities.'

She nods, and then smiles suddenly. 'Jeez, Mum, *classic* midlife crisis…' She stretches out her legs and yawns, and I can sense she feels that the conversation is coming to an end.

What on earth do I do now? Do I let her just go? I return her smile, rolling my eyes. 'You're probably right.'

'I still think it's weird though,' she adds. 'About Sam. I mean, what are the chances of any of this happening? I like him though,' she adds. 'To answer your earlier question. Theo thinks he's a bit of a prat sometimes but I think that's just a father and son thing myself. They're so alike, but Theo just can't see it.'

She pauses. 'And it sounds awful, but I've never really met anyone like Sam before – you know, with so many scars and stuff. It freaked me out to start with. I wasn't really prepared for what he would look like, but once you stop thinking about it you realise how nice he is. He makes me laugh and he does this thing where he… I don't really know how to explain it, but when I tell him something, even when it's to do with the business and he'll have heard it umpteen times before, he looks at you like you've just discovered sliced bread. Does that make sense?'

More than you realise, I think, sadly, as I nod.

She's looking at me carefully and I know what's coming next. 'Does Nancy know, and Theo?'

'I've told Nancy,' I reply. 'I had to. Not because I didn't want to tell you, but because as soon as I saw Sam I realised that it might cause difficulties for you. The last thing I wanted was for there to be any bad feeling between any of us. Nancy was incredibly understanding, which given her own relationship with Sam was particularly—'

'Well yes, she would be, wouldn't she? I mean she—' Esme breaks off abruptly. 'It's okay, never mind. Sorry, go on, Mum.'

'All I was going to say is that Nancy was lovely about the whole thing and she understood perfectly why I was concerned about you. She also agreed with me that there was no real reason for it to be a problem unless we made it one. That with Sam due to go home there would be a very small number of occasions when you would see him and—'

Esme frowns, interrupting. 'But he sees Theo all the time, so there's every possibility that I'll see Sam too. I mean, Theo and I are friends and we…' She breaks off as her phone pings, a smile creeping over her face as she reads the message that has flashed up.

'Talk of the devil,' she says, a broad grin now on her face. She waves her phone. 'Theo keeps getting sent more and more photos of the opening night and he passes them on. Either that or he recounts conversations he's had with his mum. Honestly, he's still so excited about it, he's even worse than I am. I just about manage to calm down and then he sends me something else.'

'You get on well, don't you?' I say, watching her reaction.

'Who? Me and Theo?' She pauses as if to think for a moment. 'Yeah, we do, we just sort of clicked.' A smile begins to play around her face. 'Actually, Mum, it's weird, I feel like we've known one another for years. Does that sound silly?'

I'm glad I'm sitting down as a wave of dizziness hits me, leaving me reeling. There's a horrible fluttery feeling in my chest as if something is trying to get out, and I have to wait several seconds before I can tell if my heart is even still beating. I stare at the floor, reminding myself to breathe.

Esme's still talking and I have to drag my attention back to her, but I've missed what she was saying.

'Are you and Theo dating?' I blurt out. I have to know.

Esme blushes, her eyes wide. 'No! We're just really good friends, you know, but…'

Esme has never been able to hide anything from me. 'You'd like there to be more?'

She doesn't answer straight away, and with every tiny moment of time that passes her answer becomes even more clear. She sighs and screws up her face. 'I dunno, Mum. I mean, it's probably not a good idea, is it?'

I've always cherished my relationship with Esme, grateful that as she's grown older she's still remained open and honest with me. And I'd do anything for that not to change. I never wanted to break her heart.

I open my mouth, forcing out the words. 'Esme, there's something you need to know about Theo…'

'What? I know he doesn't have a girlfriend because he told me. Oh…' She stops. 'Well, I suppose he would, wouldn't he?'

I look at her sadly, at the curious smile she still wears. 'No, it's nothing like that.' I draw in a breath. 'Esme, when Sam had his accident it was a truly horrible time… things were all over the place and I… I wasn't well. And I wasn't thinking about anything much, only Sam, and him getting better. Everything else was on hold and…'

I can see her expression changing, the puzzlement in her eyes. She's wondering why I'm telling her this. Why I'm talking about Sam when I'd mentioned Theo's name.

'And so it wasn't until after, when I'd moved, that I even began to think about how I was feeling and…'

Her back is stiffening. She's beginning to work it out.

She sits forward. 'No…' she whispers.

'I'm so sorry… Esme… I never wanted to keep this from you. But I was already pregnant. Sam never knew, he—'

'Shut up!' Esme lurches to her feet, nearly falling over me in her haste to run. 'Just shut up!'

'Esme, wait!' I scramble to get up, clutching at her as she passes me. But I'm too late.

She's gone and the sound of her door slamming above my head shakes any last hope I had from my heart.

# CHAPTER TWENTY-ONE

I'd forgotten what it was like. That feeling of being caught in the middle of a storm, its fury shaking everything to its very foundation. You don't know when it's going to end or what the trail of devastation will be when it does. And it's just how I felt when you were in hospital.

I would tense every time a car went past, or if there was the slightest noise from outside, a fresh wave of adrenaline setting my pulse racing and my stomach lurching in shock. It was the waiting that did it, creating a hyper-alert state that there was no respite from. Every phone call could bring news, every car might bring a visitor. Anything and everything had the power to transform how I was feeling, to send my spirits soaring with hope that things would be okay, or send them plummeting with news of more setbacks, more difficulties to be faced. And it's just the same now.

Esme left the house two hours ago and, despite sending texts and leaving messages, I've heard nothing from her. I know she'll be okay, she won't have done anything stupid, and by now she will have arrived to begin her shift at The Green Room, but I feel helpless, adrift in the pain she must be feeling that I can do nothing to alleviate. She's a grown adult and yet I still feel like the worst mother on the planet. You shouldn't cause your children pain, should you? Tear their world in two? And I have no idea how to make things better.

I think about calling Tash, confiding in her, but what would I say? It would feel like breaking a confidence; letting someone else know about Sam when Esme has only just found out. Besides, even though I know that Tash would keep it to herself if I asked her to, these things have a habit of getting out and I don't like the thought of the rest of the family knowing. Especially not Angela with her judgemental comments; I don't think I could cope. And imagine how much harder this would be for Esme.

The afternoon stretches ahead of me in a seemingly never-ending number of hours to fill, and I'm grateful that Nancy's tuxedo is giving me something to occupy my time. Every crystal and sequin I sew on has to be carefully placed so that the distribution of them is even, and with each one I complete I'm having to stop and consider where the next should go.

So with Nancy already on my mind, it's no real surprise when there's a knock on the door in the middle of the afternoon and I open it to find her standing there. She takes one look at me and marches into the hallway with her arms outstretched.

Her hug is fierce and tight and just for a few seconds I can believe everything might actually be okay. She draws away from me, a hand placed on each of my arms so that she can hold me at a distance, scrutinising my face. Her gaze is difficult to withstand but I'm grateful for it because it's a no-nonsense face. A face that says, *tell me all about it and we'll sort this.*

She draws me into the kitchen, where she immediately walks to the window and stares out into the garden.

'You know, this is such a lovely room, isn't it? It struck me the first time I was here, but this is exactly the kind of space I'd like. Somewhere flooded with light, cosy but practical, and yet not one of those minimalist modern kitchens where you'd be afraid of putting down a teaspoon.'

Despite myself, I laugh. 'I think that might mean I need to tidy up a bit,' I say, looking around at the detritus left behind by lives in motion.

'Not at all,' comes Nancy's quick reply. 'This is lovely just as it is. You have a very good eye.' She gives me a sudden bright smile. 'Actually, would you do me a favour?' she asks.

'If I can…'

'Then give me a couple of hours of your time. I probably shouldn't even be doing this, but a house has just come up on the market that could be exactly the thing I'm looking for. But I know from the agent that there's been quite a bit of interest in it already and I don't want to miss out. Would you come and have a look at it with me? I'd love to have your opinion.'

Nancy is looking at me with such an expectant air of excitement that I'm finding it hard to refuse. 'If you really think I can help, yes, of course. When's the viewing?'

Her response is to pull out her car keys from her pocket and dangle them in front of me, grinning. 'Now?' she replies. 'Or rather, if we leave now, it will be perfect timing.'

I look around the room, at my sewing strewn across the table, at my dirty mug on the side. And I have no idea whether I've even brushed my hair or put on any lipstick.

'Where are we even going?' I ask, collecting my handbag from the cupboard under the stairs, enjoying the fact that I don't even care.

'The seaside,' declares Nancy, triumphantly. 'Apart from anything, a healthy dollop of ozone will do you the world of good.'

I stare after her as she walks back out into the hallway, following in a daze. I don't even look back as I pull the door closed behind me.

Moments later we're bombing along in Nancy's bright-red sports car, expertly cutting through the traffic in town. She keeps up a constant stream of inconsequential chatter until we're out onto the coast road where the traffic is thinner and the sky suddenly wide. She gives a heartfelt sigh.

'Ah, that's better, isn't it?' she says. 'The sun and the open road… nothing like it. I feel more relaxed already.'

I look at her sideways, amused by her behaviour. It's been very clear to me since the moment she arrived at our house that Nancy is well aware of both the state I'm in, and the cause of it. She might not know all the details, but she knows enough, and yet, apart from the comment about the seaside air, she hasn't made any mention of it. She turns slightly, catching my look.

'All in good time,' she says, turning back to look at the road, and I'm left under no illusion as to what she's referring.

I sit back and let the scenery slide past me.

'So tell me about this house then,' I say. 'What's it like?'

'The last piece of the jigsaw hopefully,' she replies, throwing me a mysterious glance. 'Other than that, it's not overly big, and it's old, but I don't know much more. I have a contact at the estate agency but they told me to ignore the details and just look at it with an open mind,' she explains.

'Odd,' I comment.

'Not really,' she replies. 'They know me quite well.'

She smiles and once again I'm left feeling as if there's something in Nancy's words which goes far beyond what she's actually saying.

The rest of the journey is almost silent, but I don't mind. It's companionable instead of awkward and I'm actually quite enjoying being out and about, a change from my usual routine. Strangely, things don't seem so oppressive away from the house. And I suspect that this has been Nancy's intention all along.

Fifteen minutes later as we glimpse the sea, Nancy pulls off the road and follows a much smaller lane inland for a mile or so. Shortly after, the sight of two gateposts signifies that we've arrived at our destination. The entrance is tight but Nancy navigates it skilfully, and passes through onto a driveway which sweeps away to our right. At the end is a small flint-stone cottage, nestled among the trees which surround it. I give her a cautious look because at first glance it seems far too small for anything she would require.

She fishes in the pocket of the car door and pulls out a set of keys, holding them aloft. 'Shall we go and have a look?'

I look at the cheeky expression on her face. 'Nancy, just how well do you know this estate agent?' I ask.

'Oh, quite well,' she says airily and climbs from the car.

As we approach I realise that the drive has actually brought us to the rear of one side of the cottage and, skirting around to the front, I can see that it's actually much bigger than it looks. I'm shading my eyes from the sun, trying to sort out the jumble of windows and doors, when a flash of something catches my eye. I walk forward together with Nancy onto a lawned area bordered by tall shrubs, and it's there that I realise the silvery spark I saw is actually the glint of sunlight on water. Spread below us, in a sweeping semicircle, is the sea, fringed by a perfect strip of sand.

'Oh, yes!' Nancy almost punches the air. 'I was told to expect the unexpected, and wow… Just look at that!'

I spin around, trying to orientate myself, but still not quite able to work out how the sea can now be so close in front of us. I'm speechless.

Nancy gives a gleeful shriek and sets off towards the house, leaving me trailing in her wake.

And the sea view is not the only thing that's surprising about the house. We're ten minutes into our tour of the ground floor when Nancy pulls open another door, probably expecting to find more reception rooms. What lies ahead, however, is a short corridor with a window either side, and beyond that another kitchen. She looks quizzically at me before suddenly stopping dead. She races through the kitchen to the room on the other side.

'It's two,' she shouts. 'Alys, come and look. It's two cottages… joined together… Oh my God, this is *perfect*!'

\*

'So, come on,' says Nancy a little while later. 'Honestly, what did you think?'

We're sitting on a bench at the end of the garden, looking out to the sparkling blue bay in the distance. Nancy is beaming from ear to ear and it's very clear to see how she feels.

'Do you need to ask?' I reply. 'Although… do you really need two cottages? They're both beautiful but how will you join them together? It doesn't look like it would be that easy.'

But Nancy smiles. 'It's very simple,' she replies. 'Because I'm not going to.'

I give her a quizzical look. 'But why?'

She puts a finger to the side of her nose in response. 'Never mind that for a minute,' she says. 'What about the cottages themselves, what did you think to those?'

I don't even need to think about it. I'd live here in a second. 'Beautiful,' I reply. 'Light, airy, but incredibly homely too. If I could I'd put my slippers on right now and curl up with a book in the chair by the window. And those fireplaces…'

Nancy nods. 'They *were* lovely, weren't they?'

She looks so incredibly happy that I reach out my hand to give hers a squeeze.

'Yes, I think this will do very nicely, very nicely indeed…' She turns to me. 'Now all I have to do is convince your daughter not to leave.'

My mouth drops open. The conversation has turned so quickly and in the excitement I'd actually forgotten about this morning's events. 'Esme?'

'Hmm. Didn't I say? She handed her notice in this morning.' Nancy squeezes my hand in return. 'She doesn't mean it, of course. She was upset, anyone could see that. No, not thinking straight at all. So when I knew I was coming here, I hopped in the car to fetch you. I thought a different environment might make it easier for you to tell me what's happened. Much more so than at home.'

To my embarrassment I burst into tears; Nancy's thoughtful concern breaking down the dam holding my emotions in check. And so, with the sea breeze on our faces and the sun warming our skin, I tell Nancy everything.

She's silent for a few moments, not angry, or upset, but quietly thoughtful. And her voice when she finally speaks is full of warmth and compassion.

'I should have known who she was, of course, the moment I met her. Perhaps I did… deep down. There was something about her, but at the time I just didn't see it for what it was. Esme has this way of looking at you as if there's no one else in the room. As if what you have to say is the most interesting or exciting thing she's ever heard. And there's only one other person I know who does that.'

'Sam,' I say.

She nods. 'Does he know?'

'I told him the day before he went home. I didn't know what to do but I thought he had a right to know. I'm not asking anything of him, Nancy, but I couldn't let him and Esme continue to meet whilst still being unaware of their true relationship. The longer that went on, the worse it would get.'

'That makes sense,' Nancy replies. 'It all does actually.' She pauses. 'In fact, it was Sam who urged me to come and look at this place,' she adds. 'The last little piece of the jigsaw puzzle. And now I know why he was so keen that I should. He would never divulge a confidence to me, but I knew there'd be a reason for his eagerness. And I honestly can't think of a better one.'

She smiles at my puzzled look. 'The move to Norfolk was important for all of us, for me most of all, but buying this place could really cement our fresh start. It's somewhere for me to begin afresh, with someone new, building a home of our own, but the second cottage could provide Theo with a place of his own too. Somewhere he can stretch his independent legs, but not too far away from Mum. Of course we could also use it to put up guests…'

She breaks off to give me a meaningful look. 'Like Sam, for example. If he wanted to get to know someone a little better, then it would be the perfect way to do it.'

And suddenly I see what she's been getting at all along. A new life for her family, separate from Sam on the one hand but still allowing them to share all the good things they still have in common. And now perhaps including Esme too. Suddenly my dream of how things could be between us all moves a little bit closer.

'I think that's amazing… That you can be so… sensible, and rational. Caring…' I give a wry smile. 'I'm not used to that response. I thought you'd be upset, or angry at the very least.'

Now it's Nancy's turn to look confused. 'Why would I be any of those things?' she says. 'Esme belongs to a time before me and Sam, and I've nothing to fear from her, just everything to gain. I told you before that Sam and I had a good marriage, and we did… and then we didn't, but now we have a good friendship and I'm happier than I've ever been. So is he, actually.' She smiles wistfully. 'And he always wanted a daughter…'

I swallow, torn by the memories her words bring back, dreams of what might have been. For Sam too, all shattered…

'But you have Theo.'

Her face takes on a look of fond maternal pride. 'We do. And we wouldn't have changed that for the world.' She stares out to sea, still smiling, before turning and looking back at the house behind us. 'If you don't mind me asking, Alys, what are you going to do?'

And there it is, the question that I've been trying to avoid thinking about all day. 'I really have no idea,' I reply, sighing. 'But in a way what happens next isn't for me to decide at all. It's for Esme to choose whether she wants to have a relationship with Sam or not. Either way, I think he'll abide by her wishes.'

'Oh, I agree,' replies Nancy. 'Sam must be shocked – this new revelation goes hand in hand with everything he still feels about his accident, don't forget, and that's going to make it harder for him to process. But the fact that he wanted me to come and look at this house is already a good indication of where his head is at. I'm pretty certain that he would love to get to know Esme, but if she didn't want that… He'd be sad, but understanding, I think.'

I nod. 'And I want to thank you for everything you've done to support Esme too. Handing in her notice this morning was a knee-jerk reaction to how scary this new situation is for her, but once she can see a way forward, she'll think again, I know she will.'

Nancy smiles. 'I've already told her that I won't accept her resignation today. I could see how upset she was so let's see what the next week brings. If she still wants to leave then… But I don't think it will come to that. Things will ease, I'm sure of it. For you and Hugh also.'

'I hope so. I've found out some things about him that I really don't like and I certainly don't appreciate the way he's behaved just lately, but… I have to accept the blame for some of that. I've changed over recent weeks, I don't exactly know why, but I feel it, I can't pretend that I don't.' I give a rueful smile. 'I don't think Hugh can quite figure out who he's married to any more.'

Nancy pulls a sympathetic face and squeezes my arm. 'Don't use the word blame,' she says, gently. 'That makes it sound as if you've done something wrong. And if the changes you feel within yourself feel right, then you certainly haven't done anything wrong, quite the opposite. I've been where you are, Alys. I recognise some of the signs… There were things within me that I'd buried deep for years refusing to acknowledge them. But sometimes they start shouting so loudly you have to admit they're there. And that's not necessarily a bad thing. Change in a marriage can be good, and sometimes long overdue. And the best we can hope for is that our partners want to join us on that journey, that they're just as excited by it as we are. But sadly that isn't the case for everyone. Some see it as a threat, or they simply don't understand that it's an opportunity for them to change for the better too.'

'And for you, Sam was one of those people,' I say, recognising the sadness with which I say it. Was I hoping for better from him?

'No, actually he wasn't,' replies Nancy. 'It's just that in my case where I'm going, Sam can't follow.'

I frown. 'Sorry, I don't understand what you mean.'

But Nancy just smiles. 'You will,' she says.

# CHAPTER TWENTY-TWO

There's an email waiting for me when I get back. It's from Becky at the National Trust informing me that my application to volunteer has been given the green light. I can start whenever is convenient. She suggests that I give her a call in the morning to discuss what hours I might like to do and then take it from there. The thought fills me with hope. It definitely feels like this is the right thing to do.

I sit back down at the table where I left Nancy's tuxedo earlier and roll one of the crystal beads between my fingers. I'd shown my progress to Nancy when she'd dropped me home again and she was delighted with what she saw. I'm pleased with it too, but it would have been awful if she hadn't liked it. She's so excited about this weekend and I marvel that despite everything going on in her world, she still manages to give all her energy over to whatever she's involved in and her attitude spurs me into action.

Telling Esme about Sam has been a good thing, I remind myself. It's taken us one step closer to the end of the tunnel and surely soon we'll be able to see a glimmer of light at the other end. All we have to do is keep heading forward and be positive about the changes in our lives. Embrace the opportunity that we now have to make things different... better. I know that Esme is hurting now, but she's resilient, and I trust her to come to the right conclusions.

My problems with Hugh aren't insurmountable either. We've been together for twenty-three years for heaven's sake, and that has to account for something. It's true he hasn't handled our financial situation well and he certainly should have discussed it with me all those years ago, but if I accept that he did it to make our lives better then I really can't blame him because his investments didn't turn out the way he wanted. Things could have gone the other way and would I even have cared that he hadn't told me if that were the case? I smile to myself. A little positive reframing is what you need, Alys.

Hugh doesn't normally get home until around seven and so I still have an hour or so left before I need to make a start on cooking dinner. Something really special, I think – one of Hugh's favourites, plus a dessert. He has such a sweet tooth. And so, with thoughts of how I can more sensitively recount what's happened today running through my head, I crack on with the embellishments on Nancy's tuxedo.

It's quite possible that Hugh has been having a think about our situation too. He comes through the door with a smile on his face for a change and, not only that, but he's bought a bunch of flowers for me. It doesn't matter that they look like he got them from the garage where he usually stops for petrol, it's the thought that counts.

I'd hastily shoved a bottle of white wine in the freezer about half an hour ago and, as I take it out, offering to pour him a drink, he comes up behind me and lowers his head to my neck.

'That is a lovely thought,' he murmurs. 'But I think I'd better give the booze a miss this evening. I don't think it does me much good.'

It isn't exactly an apology, but I'll take it. I turn around and kiss his forehead. 'A cup of tea then? Or some lemonade?'

His eyes light up. 'Homemade?'

But I have to shake my head. ''Fraid not,' I reply. 'But I do have some lemons,' I add as his face drops again. 'I can squeeze in some fresh juice if you like?'

He thinks for a moment. 'Yes, perhaps that will make it taste better. Go on then, I'll have a lemonade.' He turns away, lifting the lid from one of the pans on the cooker. 'Is that stroganoff?' he asks, dipping his finger into the sauce. 'Made with proper mustard?' He smiles. 'I shall look forward to that.'

I smile too, moving away to collect a lemon from the fruit bowl. It was a good choice, I think, glad that I'd remembered to add the Dijon at the last minute. I'm wondering when either of us is going to mention Esme though. After all, Hugh will be well aware that I'll have spoken to her today, but perhaps I should let him broach the subject.

'Actually,' says Hugh from behind me. 'I might just go and have a shower before dinner's ready. It's been very hot again in the office today. But you could always bring my drink up to me…' He holds my look for a second and it's clear what he's really asking.

'Oh,' I reply, a little flustered now. 'Um…' I'm really not in the mood, but I need to be giving here too, I remind myself. Things will never improve without both of us making an effort. I do a quick mental rejig of my timings. I haven't put the rice on to cook yet, so all is not lost. And if I turn off the stroganoff and cover it, it should be okay to reheat while I pan-fry the steaks. They don't take long after all…

I smile. 'Yes,' I say, as firmly as I can. 'I'll do that.'


The sauce has split a little by the time I get back to it, but I just about manage to recover it. Hugh doesn't say anything anyway and tucks into it with gusto, occasionally looking up and smiling, catching my eye. He still doesn't seem in any hurry to discuss yesterday's events and, much as I don't want to spoil the mood, I'm desperately trying to think of a way to broach the subject. Just as I'm about to mention casually that I've spoken to Esme,

Hugh lays down his knife and fork and pours himself some more water from the jug on the table.

'You know, I've been thinking about this redundancy money of ours,' he says.

'Oh yes,' I say lightly.

'And I can see how you might have got the wrong idea about it,' he continues. 'And I guess that's simply because you don't understand our finances like I do. Perhaps if I'd taken the time to explain the benefits of having our mortgage paid off now, you wouldn't have even considered using the money for anything else.' He pauses to give me a bright smile. 'So I've had a bit of a think and I reckon you should have some of that money for yourself, as a treat, to buy whatever you want with it, something really frivolous if you like. In fact, you don't even have to tell me what it is. How's that?'

Hugh is looking so pleased with himself I really have no idea what to say. The redundancy money is one of the things we should be discussing, but surely it's not the most pressing matter. I'd much rather we were talking about Esme, and how she's feeling. I nod, trying to look grateful.

'Good, then I'm glad that's settled. I checked the figures again today too, so what do you say to five hundred pounds?'

I stare down at the food on my plate, at the congealing sauce, and feel suddenly sick. I can't believe that Hugh thinks the discussion about our finances is over. That he can consider that giving me five hundred pounds of my own money is a grand gesture, when what it feels like is second prize in a raffle. It's still a lot of money, it isn't that which is bothering me, more that he can be so dismissive. This isn't a discussion at all, it's Hugh coming to his own conclusions and then telling me what he's decided. Again.

I inhale as calmly as I can, pushing down everything else I'm feeling. I take a sip of my water to compose myself and mask my expression, which I'm sure is betraying me. Then I plaster a smile on my face.

'Thank you, Hugh. I don't know what to say—'

'Well, fair's fair,' he says. 'It's only right that you should have some of it.'

*Shut up, Hugh. Shut up…* My head's beginning to feel like it might explode.

'I wondered if we might talk about Esme,' I say. 'Only I spoke to her, as you suggested.'

Hugh raises his eyebrows. 'I see… So she knows about your marriage to Sam?'

I nod.

'And you explained that it's all very firmly in the past and that, despite his connection with The Green Room, there's no need for *you* to see him again.' He takes another drink, casually turning his glass round and round once it's back on the table. 'No doubt you were also able to reassure her that he's no threat to her…'

*Threat? Why would Sam possibly be a threat?*

'Well, I…' I break off, anger beginning to surge. 'She was very upset, Hugh. It wasn't that easy, she—'

He looks up.

'Well, she… She's handed her notice in,' I say, stalling for time. I know I need to tell him the truth, but I just can't find the words.

'I beg your pardon. Why on earth has she done that?' He sits back in his chair. 'Oh, for goodness' sake! After the run-around she's given us over this job, how much of a dream come true it's been… now she goes and jacks it in at the first hint of any difficulty.'

'I don't think it's that, Hugh, she—'

'And so she's not going to be earning either, is she?' He rubs a finger across the crease in his brow. 'And I imagine she'll just assume that we'll support her again.'

'I don't suppose she thinks anything of the sort! In fact, I doubt it's even occurred to her; she has rather more important things on her mind.' I lower my voice, allowing some of my anger to show. 'But, in any case, I wouldn't have thought there'd be any question over supporting her temporarily if she needs us to. She's our *daughter*.'

Hugh clears his throat, looking a little sheepish. 'Yes, of course. I rather meant… never mind.' He shakes his head.

'Besides,' I continue, 'she won't actually be leaving her job at The Green Room because Nancy thinks far too much of her to let her just walk away. Esme was very upset, that's all, she wasn't really thinking straight; Nancy knows that.' I press my fingers into my palms. 'But there's something else, Hugh,' I say quietly. 'Something that's only just come to my attention.'

A flicker of irritation shows in his eyes. 'Go on,' he says.

'I hadn't noticed anything untoward before, but it's just something Esme said this morning – about Theo. It made me realise how close they've become. I thought they were simply friends, work colleagues, you know.'

Hugh leans towards me, his elbows on the table. 'Alys, what are you telling me?'

I can't hold it back any longer. 'I've told her,' I blurt out. 'She knows about Sam… all of it.'

He looks down at his plate and for a horrible moment I think he's going to hurl it across the room, but then he sticks his face even closer to mine. 'I'm sorry, Alys, but for a moment there I thought you said you'd told Esme that she has a cripple for a father.' His eyes are hard, grey steel.

'Yes, I told her, Hugh.' I fling the words at him, lifting my chin at his flushed face, standing my ground. 'But don't you *ever* call Sam a cripple again!' White-hot anger prowls around the base of my throat. 'I had to tell her, Hugh, what else was I supposed to do? Think about it… about her and Theo… We can't let them have a relationship for God's sake, they're half-brother and -sister!'

'Yes, I can work out the family connection, thank you.' He swallows, licking his lips slowly. He's on the edge of letting go of his anger and I automatically lean back in my seat, glad that the table still separates us. His eyes search my face, assessing what he sees, measuring it against some internal scale he's using to condemn me. 'You know, I'm not sure what you're more upset about; the fact that you've just ruined Esme's life or the fact that I've called your boyfriend a cripple.'

The force of his words hits me so hard he might as well have slapped me. I don't want to think about what he's just said, but is it true? Is that what's making me so angry? I shake my head, trying to clear the questions from my mind. Why am I even doubting myself? I know I've done the right thing. I look away, trying to grab the thought in my head, the one that will help to convince me I had no other course of action. And then I see it, the quick flash of a supercilious smile that flickers on Hugh's face. A mistake that I was never meant to see.

'You know something, Hugh, I'm not sure what *you're* most upset about, the fact that you're not Esme's father, or the fact Sam is.' I carry on before he has a chance to interrupt. 'Today, yet again, I've tried to do what I believe is right. I've always thought that Esme should be allowed to know who her biological father is. Not because I expected her to go dashing after him, renouncing you in the process, but because I believed it was right that she should. But I've also always known how difficult this would be for you, the man who has loved and cared for her her whole life, and who is terrified of losing her. Except that in the end I had no choice but to tell Esme – when I learned about Theo this morning, I had to respond. However, I made it clear that she was born out of love, and has been raised in love, and she understands that very clearly; she knows how much you love her. So it's a pity that *you* don't seem to trust her enough to know that. I wanted to discuss this with you calmly and rationally, knowing how it would make you feel, wanting to make it as easy on you as possible because I love you too. But you know, Hugh, you're making it almost impossible for me to do that.' I look up at him sadly. 'So I really don't know what to do now.'

Hugh opens his mouth, but for once nothing comes out.

'And yes, it does upset me that you called Sam a cripple. Because even after everything he's been through, he is still a warm, witty and wonderful man. His *body* is damaged and he lives with the problems that causes every single day of his life, but *he* is far from being crippled. What hurts me the most, however, is that this was never a competition, Hugh. It was never about who I loved. At least it wasn't until you made it one.

'You've never been able to accept that I loved Sam and you did your very best to turn him into a monster, but what you've never understood is that I could love you both. I see Sam's love reflected on the face of our daughter every single day. How could I possibly push him away when I love her so much? And I see your love, in the home we built together, in the pride I feel when I see Esme attaining her dreams. These last few weeks haven't been about my choosing between you, Hugh, they've been about wanting you both in my life for very different reasons. You just couldn't believe in me enough to let me. I wish I knew why you hate him so much.'

'Because he never should have had you in the first place,' he fires back. 'You were supposed to fall for *me*, not him. *I* got you that job at Harringtons, flashed the cash around, took you out, looked after you at work. But you met him once and that was that. Lured by his history degree and love of bloody poetry. So what if he can recite all of Shakespeare's sonnets? It doesn't make him a better person.'

I stare at him, incredulous.

'You were *jealous* of him? No, it's worse, you *still* are... I don't believe it, Hugh. For goodness' sake, aren't you forgetting that I *did* fall for you? We fell in love, we got married. We've been married for twenty-three years.'

He sticks out his chin. 'I was always second best,' he pouts. 'Even after I made sure I came first. And what am I supposed to think? With him back on the scene and you behaving like someone I don't even know, having coffee with that weird woman…'

'Nancy's not weird. It's probably escaped your notice but she's one of the few friends I've had over the years, one of the nicest friends I've had.'

'You've had plenty of friends.'

'I had people from work I went out with, Hugh, that's not the same thing at all.' I shake my head. 'That's beside the point anyway, it doesn't change the fact that—' I stop suddenly. 'What do you mean, *after I made sure…?*'

Hugh's eyes flick away. And something cold begins to stir at the base of my spine. 'No, you damn well answer me this time, Hugh. Why did you say that?'

'I don't know, it wasn't for any particular reason. It's just one of those things… And I *was* second best. You always loved him more than me.'

'I loved him, Hugh, that's all. I was married to him. Like you might have loved other women before me. Different, and nothing to do with you and me. But then my marriage with Sam was over and you and I…' I look at his face, the slightly turned away angle of his head, the eyes that won't quite meet mine. 'That isn't just something you say…' I can feel pressure building behind my eyes, an almost overwhelming desire to shake him, to finally know the truth of what's been eating at me all this time. 'What did you do? Tell me!'

Hugh holds my look for just a second but it's enough for me to see the truth; the guilt… the *triumph*. I stand up, my chair scraping across the floor. 'Dear God, tell me you didn't cause Sam's accident…'

A split-second pause, but it's enough.

'You should see the look on your face,' says Hugh. 'Don't be so melodramatic. I told him a few home truths, that's all. That he wasn't good enough for you. That he didn't come from the right background, and that he was never going to amount to much. I mean, working in a restaurant...'

'You arrogant pig!' I spit. 'Can you not see the irony, when he's done far better for himself than you ever have? And he's done it in spite of everything else he's had to contend with.'

'You can mock me, Alys, but at the end of the day he obviously saw the sense of my words because look what he did – left you high and dry at the first sign of trouble. I guess he had plenty of time to think about things while he was in hospital.'

'You bastard!' And I'm not letting this go. 'So just when exactly did you have this "conversation", Hugh?' My eyes are burning into his.

'Okay! I'll tell you. I was at the restaurant, on New Year's Eve. I'd had too much to drink, all right? Laid it on a bit thick. But he had it coming, rubbing it in about how you and he were looking forward to the coming year, all the things you were going to do...'

'Yes, and starting a family was one of them! Except little did I know I was already pregnant, only by a week... Our little Esme, a tiny bundle of cells...' I hold his look. 'And you robbed her of her father...' He can see it in my eyes, I don't even have to tell him.

'No!' shouts Hugh. 'I forbid you. You are not going to tell Sam.'

'I already have,' I reply. And then I walk away.

# CHAPTER TWENTY-THREE

The very next thing I do is move my night things into the spare room. I can't bear the thought of Hugh even being in the same space as me, let alone the same bed. The idea that he might have been responsible for Sam's accident, however indirectly, is filling my head. It was the one thing I could never fully understand about what happened – Sam was such a careful driver and yet something on the drive home that night had made him lose his concentration. And now I know exactly what it was: Hugh's bitter and spite-filled words. The thought brings with it the images that had haunted me for so long afterwards: Sam's car a mass of tangled metal, the sight of him in the hospital when I first saw him, on the edge of death, blood everywhere. And the look on his face when he had told me he didn't want to see me again.

It's all coming back to me, wave after wave of those awful memories, the things I'd been unable to get out of my head. It had made me sick when I thought about the terror that Sam must have felt, the pain, the awful screeching and crunching sounds the last he heard before flames licked at his skin, white-hot… Had I been the last thing he thought of before his injuries claimed him?

And then afterwards he had lain in the hospital, unable to see any future for himself, thinking about what Hugh had said, convincing himself, whatever he might have thought before the accident, that Hugh was right, he really was no good, and never would be. And so he had pushed me away. He had never given me the chance to fight for him, to show him that my love was big enough, that it could withstand whatever life would throw at us. And I will never forgive Hugh for that. He became my knight in shining armour and I let him, loved him for it. But it was a love built on deceit and jealousy. How could I have been so blind?

I sit on the edge of the bed, arms around my knees, literally trying to hold myself together as I let the tears come again. All the feelings I'd tried so hard to banish, to cut from my life, now as fresh as the day they were first created.

At some point Hugh must have come up to bed as the house is in darkness when I creep from the room hours later. There's no light showing from under our bedroom door and I tiptoe down the stairs, like a stranger in my own home. I have no wish to talk to him, now, or at any point in the near future. And I have no idea what to do.

I'm surprised to see that it's only just gone midnight as I enter the kitchen, the soft glow of a full moon shining through the window. I collect a glass of water, intending to take it back upstairs when I notice that Hugh has left the conservatory doors open. The air inside is still warm, silvery and calming and so, instead of locking the doors, I take my drink and make for my favourite chair.

'Mum?'

The voice comes from behind me, soft and full of love. Esme is curled in the other chair, still in her chef's whites, but hair loose from its bun, flowing over her shoulders. She gets to her feet.

'Sweetheart… Are you okay?'

Her face glows in the dim light, tentatively smiling. 'Are you?' she whispers.

I hold out my hand. 'I asked first,' I say, pulling her towards the two-seater at the other end of the room. I wait until she's settled before reaching out and tucking her hair back behind her ears. 'It's been quite a day, hasn't it?' I say.

'I didn't answer your calls, Mum, or your messages. I'm sorry.'

'I knew you were safe.'

'I was too upset… not at you, just…'

'Too much to take in. It's okay, Esme, I understand. Do you know that over the years I've thought about the moment when I would tell you so many times, but in my head it was always different, nicer. Like it is in the movies – soft light, gentle music playing in the background – not like real life at all.' I smile sadly. 'But I'm sorry you had to find out the way you did. I wanted your dad to be there too, Hugh, I mean… but…'

'It's okay, Mum. I'm okay. Not really okay… but for the moment.' She screws up her face. 'Does that make sense?'

'It does, it makes perfect sense. So you're feeling a little better?'

She considers her reply for a few seconds. 'I think what I'm feeling is less scared,' she says. 'I thought everything was going to change, but then I realised that it doesn't necessarily mean that. Maybe in the future, when I want it to, if I want it to… Actually, Nancy helped me to see that.' She gives a rueful smile. 'After all, she knows Sam better than anyone. And she said that it didn't mean that Dad doesn't love me, or that Sam automatically does. He doesn't even know me, not really.'

'All these things are true,' I reply. 'And I'm glad that you've been able to talk to someone. I'm even more pleased that it was Nancy,' I say. 'She's rather worried about you too.'

'She said,' answers Esme, nodding. 'And I'm not going to hand my notice in, don't worry.' She pauses a moment. 'Hang on, when did *you* speak to her?'

'This afternoon. I went to look at a house with her actually. Or houses… Rather a surprise, but it made sense. And we had a good chat too.'

'Ah… that would explain it,' she replies. 'Nancy didn't say but I had a feeling she knew the whole story even before I told it to her. She seemed really cool with everything though.'

'She was. I can't believe how amazingly understanding she's been about everything. Except that it seems she's had some issues to deal with in her own life, so maybe she understands that things are not always straightforward.'

'I think you've hit the nail on the head, Mum.' She tucks her legs up underneath her, leaning into my side. 'But what about you? How are you feeling? Have you spoken to Dad any more? Hugh, I mean…'

I wince. 'Oh, this is so difficult. Just one of the myriad things we're going to have to navigate. I don't even know what to call him… but Hugh's still your dad, and he always will be.'

'I know.' She squeezes my hand. 'So let's just call him Dad… Sam is… someone else.'

I nod, grateful for her response, in spite of how I'm feeling about Hugh. 'Esme, I won't lie to you, your dad has done and said some things that I need to have a good think about. They matter, you see. And I can't just ignore them.' I'm fighting so hard to keep my voice level, to stop my emotion from spilling over.

'I know you two haven't been good lately,' she replies. 'He's said some nasty things.' She lifts her head from my shoulder and looks at me closely. I know where the conversation's going.

'He did. He'd had too much to drink at the time, but all the beer did was amplify what's been in his head anyway. And most of it seems to have been about Sam. Totally unfounded, of course, but still…'

'Not nice?'

'No. And the fact of the matter is that, irrespective of whatever happened in the past, I have met Sam again and that's something that both he and I are going to have to deal with. Just as you are.'

Esme snuggles up against my shoulder. 'I can't help thinking that all this is my fault. None of it would have happened if I hadn't gone to work for The Green Room.'

I grab her hand. 'Esme, that's not true. They might not have happened *now*… but all those events in your past still existed, you didn't cause them.'

'I kind of did.'

'What, by being born? Oh, and you had some control over that, did you?'

She lifts her head and gives me a look that is pure Sam and I feel the tug of it deep inside.

'Actually, I can't think of a better time for you *to* find out. Yes, it's been a shock for all of us, but much better finding out when you have people around you who can support you with it. Besides, I could have bumped into Sam at any time. I have a feeling the truth would have come out eventually, and I know it's not a particularly popular view of the world, but I often wonder what role fate has to play in our lives.'

Esme plucks at a piece of fluff stuck to her trousers. 'That's the oddest thing,' she says. 'Remember how I told you that Nancy reminded me of you. I think it might even have been after my very first day with them; that she just felt as if she'd be like a second mum to me. And Theo…' She gives a rueful sigh. 'Now that I think about it I can see that our relationship has always been more like brother and sister… relaxed, you know, comfortable…'

'Oh, Esme…'

'No, it's okay,' she says, turning to me. 'It honestly is. It's much better this way. If I'd have fallen in love with him, we'd probably have broken up at some point and then what would I have done? It would have made it impossible to carry on working with him and, sorry, but I'm not going to give up doing what I've set my heart on just because of a man. No, I'm really glad we're just very good friends.'

I close my eyes. Isn't that exactly what I did? Gave up my career because of what Hugh wanted, mistook friendship and gratitude for love? And despite the situation I can't help but smile. My Esme, still just making her way in the world but who manages to be far wiser than both her parents.

She looks at my expression. 'God, Mum, just because you're friends with someone of the opposite sex, it doesn't mean you're about to jump into bed with them.'

I do laugh then. 'Oh, Esme… if only your father could hear you say that.' But it's an empty wish, I remind myself. It wouldn't change anything.

She nods, her face full of sympathy. 'Will you and Sam…' She trails off, uncertain how to finish.

'No, I don't think we can see each other,' I fill in for her. 'It's complicated. I really did love Sam, maybe I still love him, but we're not together any more, Esme, we haven't been for a very long time.' And yet I can remember it as if it were yesterday. 'And I'm with your dad now. I can't just give up on twenty-three years of marriage at the first sign of trouble…'

I stop, Hugh's words from the night before coming back to me. Wasn't that just what he accused Sam of doing? Except that Sam didn't give up, he was made to.

I try to brighten my expression. 'Besides, there's so many other people to think about. You and Theo, Nancy… You all have a relationship with Sam that it would be quite wrong to alter.'

Esme is quiet for a moment and I can only imagine the thoughts racing around her head. 'So, what happens now?' she asks.

I rub her arm. 'That's a difficult one,' I say, slowly. 'And I'm afraid I don't have all the answers. All I do know is that between you and Sam, whatever comes next is up to you both. I've certainly made no promises and there's no expectation either. No timescale. So you must take all the time you need to come to a decision that's right for you, whatever that is.' I slide my hand down her arm and entwine my fingers in hers.

'And what about you, Mum?'

I take a deep breath. 'Don't you go worrying about me, I'll be fine. And I'm not about to rush into anything. But, like you, any decisions I do make will be because they're the right ones for me. Because—'

'You matter too,' she murmurs, squeezing my fingers back.

'We all do,' I reply. 'Every single one of us. That's what makes it so hard.'

# CHAPTER TWENTY-FOUR

It's the morning of Nancy's talk, and I don't know who's the more nervous, me or her. It must be her, surely? After all, she's got to stand up in front of a whole crowd of people and deliver a speech to them. All I'm worried about is that her tuxedo will somehow fall apart, or that she'll split her trousers. And of course the fact that Sam will be here.

I've never been to an event like this before, and to say I feel out of my depth doesn't even come close to describing my emotions. What I want to do is run. There is confidence oozing out of every pore of the women around me and perversely it's having the opposite effect on me. If I could shrink and make myself small and unobtrusive, I'd do it in a heartbeat. I've attended one or two residential training courses over the years with Harringtons and on every single occasion had to steel myself to even turn up. Enjoyment was not something I even considered. They were a trial to be got through, nothing more, and the excitement I can see on the faces around me would seem to belong to a different breed of women entirely.

I've never found the lure of the limelight appealing, never craved the attention that success might bring. And, from what I know of Nancy, that's not what motivates her either. And yet she's up there, on the podium, about to give a speech to the hundred or so women who are here. And I'm finding it hard just being a part of the audience as Nancy's guest. Maybe that's why conservation appeals to me – a line of work that entails being closeted away with relics for hours on end. It's quiet and studious and, if you do your job well, the end result is practically invisible.

The conference is being held in a large hotel just outside the city centre. With its red-bricked exterior, mullioned windows, pointed gables and flanks of tall chimneys, it looks like something out of a fairy tale. The room we're sitting in is large and airy with a high ceiling and gilded cornices and panelling. I've spent the last ten minutes looking at the chandeliers alone.

This motivational session has been scheduled just before lunch on the first day, designed to give a rallying cry to all the delegates who are here. From this they'll go on to a networking buffet lunch before the weekend sessions begin in earnest. It's absolutely terrifying. And the pressure on Nancy to deliver must be enormous.

Esme and Theo are seated beside me and, as I look around the rest of the audience, I spot two figures making their way along the edge of the seats. It's Sam's gait I notice first, as distinctive as a fingerprint. He's doing what he always does, being unobtrusive, slipping in at the last minute when everyone's attention is elsewhere and then sitting on the fringes. And I'm reminded yet again who made him so.

As I watch, I realise that the figure following behind is not merely another latecomer, but someone who has clearly arrived with Sam. She's taller than he is and extraordinarily pretty and slender, with tumbling brown hair halfway down her back. Beside me, Esme gives my hand a quick squeeze. Has she noticed my involuntary intake of breath?

'Okay, Mum?' she whispers.

I nod, distracted. I've just spotted Sam's hand on the woman's arm. A solicitous touch, but a familiar one, and, as I watch, she says something to him. His head dips towards hers. They're inches apart. And then she laughs, glossy hair tumbling over one shoulder.

He looks at her as she pulls away, not a glance, but something longer, deeper and more meaningful. I can't bear to watch any more and I turn back to Esme, squeezing her hand in reply. I know that seeing Sam again is hard on her too, but I hadn't banked on how it would make *me* feel. Why didn't I realise that Sam would likely have a new partner too? I'm not sure how I'm ever going to get through any of this.

I fix my eyes straight ahead to where Nancy is giving her notes one final read through before she has to start speaking. She looks amazing. The tuxedo fits her like a glove. The fabric is soft enough to accentuate her curves, and with her white hair and diminutive figure, it sparkles gently under the lights. If she had a wand in her hand I wouldn't think it odd.

As I check the time the light focused on the podium brightens and an expectant excitement ripples through the audience. Nancy takes a step forward, the spotlighting catching the sequins and crystals of her jacket, magnifying them ten-fold. She looks like a shining star. *Oh, Nancy, that's clever...*

An awed hush falls.

'Hello,' she says simply. 'I'm Nancy. And I'd like to tell you the story of my life.'

Ten minutes later she has every person in the room under her spell.

It isn't that what she's saying is remarkably different from what many people have said before. It's a story of the highs and lows of starting up a business, of running that business and, when it becomes successful, the demands that places upon you. Except that Nancy's delivery is so honest, so self-deprecating and shot through with her bubbly humour that she transforms an ordinary story into something that speaks to every person's life in the room. Where Nancy has been, we've been too. What she's felt, so have we, and it unites the audience. Heads are nodding all around me. Faces are smiling in recognition of what she's saying.

But then Nancy stops speaking and stands quietly for a moment. The seconds roll past and still she's silent. I'm beginning to wonder if something's wrong, if perhaps she's feeling unwell, when she suddenly steps forward again, coming out from behind the podium to stand in front of it, where she adopts a far more relaxed pose.

'Now I've told you all about me and what I do, does anyone want to know the truth?' she asks, lifting up her head and tilting it as if she's listening. A little frisson of something approaching fear shivers through me. What on earth is she going to say?

But then she laughs, throwing up her hands. 'Oh, that got you, didn't it?' she says, turning this way and that, setting off little fireworks of light from her jacket. She waits until the noise from the audience dies down.

'But seriously though, that is a really good question. What is the truth? And is my truth even the same as yours? Because while everything I've just told you is one hundred per cent accurate, it's just my view of it; someone else could have an entirely different one. So I wanted to ask you how you see me… standing up here, talking to you about running a successful restaurant. Would you see me as confident? Ambitious? Hard-working? Talented even…?'

She grins, bowing slightly as if to accept a compliment graciously. 'And if you think any of those things apply, what would you think if I actually told you who I am?' She pauses for a moment. 'The answer to that question, of course, is that I'm exactly the same as you… I *am* the woman who is terrified of making a fool of herself, scared she won't know where the toilets are, feeling foolish when everyone else seems to be able to find them but her. I am the woman who's scared she's wearing the wrong thing… scared that she's a vegetarian and there'll be nothing to eat… scared that she's too tall, too short, too fat, too skinny, too loud, too quiet, too confident, not confident enough…'

There's a ripple of amused laughter running around the room.

'You want more…? I'm worried that my roots are showing, that my lipstick doesn't really match my outfit, that the spot on my forehead is standing out like Belisha beacon, that…' She holds up her arms. 'You see, what I'm getting at is that I am literally every person who's ever walked the planet. Yet there have been times in my life when I really thought this wasn't good enough and that to be successful I had to be someone else. But then in a moment of lucidity I asked myself, what if none of these things mattered? What if I could stand in a room and not think these things? What if I could live my life free from the shackles of all these endless questions and judgements, and instead simply accept them? Wouldn't that be the biggest empowerment of them all?'

I can see heads nodding all around me, excitement growing. You could hear a pin drop.

'And in turn that got me thinking about the roles I've played in my life. About how many of them were real and how many were pretend – fake projections of myself that I held in front of me like a shield – either because I felt I needed to, or because I felt that others expected it of me. But given the choice… would I hold it there at all? Because what I realised then is that not only was it a shield but a barrier too, blocking from sight everything that lay beyond. And until I had lowered that shield there would be no moving past it, and I really, really wanted to discover what was on the other side. And importantly, who I could be without it.

'But taking down that shield was scary, after all it had been there a long time. But gradually, as I lowered it bit by bit, I accepted that what I had originally thought of as a weakness – my vulnerability – was actually my biggest strength. It allowed me to be truly open with myself and other people and discover who I was, and who I am. And, of course, once I knew that, then everything else became so much easier.' She pauses, her eyes roving the audience, another smile lighting up her face.

'So to summarise, I guess I just want you all to know that you can run a successful business, whoever you are, and whatever you believe in… as long as that thing you believe in is yourself. So don't let anyone tell you you have to *be* a certain way, or *do* a certain thing. Don't let people tell you that you can't run a business because you are a wife and a mother, run them *because* you're a wife and a mother.'

She points to each of her fingers in turn as if ticking off items on a list. 'Just know who you are – know what you want to do – love yourself for being and wanting those things – and use that knowledge to drive all your interactions, your relationships, and everything you undertake. Because it's only when you are one hundred per cent true to yourself that you can really put your energy behind things, unencumbered from constraint. And that's how you nail it.' She drops her hands. 'I hope in the course of this weekend you can all find a little time to ask yourselves those same questions… and maybe find the answers too.'

A spontaneous round of applause breaks out, but Nancy isn't finished yet. She holds up her hand, waiting a few more moments.

'And just one last thing… Believe me, it *is* okay to be the person who's terrified they won't find the loo and end up walking around looking lost. So, if that does ever happen to you, just find the person who does know – you never can tell what might happen. For me, it was the start of a beautiful friendship.' She looks across then, staring straight over at Sam, as she dips her head to acknowledge the tumultuous burst of clapping.

There's almost too much to take in. I have no idea what to think, what to say even. Nancy could well have written that speech just for me, and I'm sure everyone else in the room feels the same way. And yet that last part was obviously directed at Sam, but why now? In fact, I don't even want to think about it. I turn to Esme, her mouth slack in open astonishment.

'Wow,' she says. 'Just… wow.'

She slumps back in her chair, trying to assimilate everything she's just heard and, as she does so, it gives me a clear line of sight to where Sam and his girlfriend are sitting. I hadn't intended to look in their direction, but now that I am what I'm seeing is not what I'd expected at all. The woman beside Sam is on her feet, clapping as if her life depended on it, her hands held high, almost level with her face. Beside her Sam claps too, but not towards Nancy, towards his companion instead as if he's applauding something she's done. And then I see it, the direction of the woman's eyes, looking not at Sam, but locked instead on someone else's gaze. I follow the line of it. To Nancy.

An elbow nudges me gently in the arm and I see Esme grinning at me, before glancing back to where I had been looking. 'Do you get it now, Mum?' she says.

And I do. The move up here, the opening of the new restaurant, Sam… their break-up. Suddenly, it all makes sense. And relief floods through me.

\*

'Oh my God, you were just brilliant!' I squeal, throwing my arms around Nancy when we're finally able to get to her. 'And you look amazing.'

She hugs me back, pulling away as she laughs to give us a twirl. 'Don't I just? Someone made me this gorgeous suit…' She holds out her arms to hug Theo and Esme in turn and then she stops, looking beyond them, at the two people making their way towards us.

I knew it would happen of course. That at some point during the day Sam and I would meet again, it's one of the things I've been most nervous about. Whether Esme knew he'd be here I don't know but, as I flick a glance at her, I can see that she's still smiling, looking just as relaxed and happy as she has all day. Even so, I feel for her. This isn't easy for her either and I should have thought about it, checked with Nancy at the very least. I don't even know whether Sam is aware that I've told Esme about him yet and I can't begin to imagine how she must be feeling.

But, as I take a step backward to accommodate the two people joining us, I see Nancy catch Sam's eye and give a slight nod, and yet again I'm reminded just how special these two people are. I needn't have worried at all. Sam leans forward to kiss Nancy and then simply stands back and waits. It's Esme who moves to him, placing a hand lightly on each shoulder, mindful of his balance, and then kissing him on the cheek.

'Hi Sam,' she says. And it's as simple as that. The first meeting is over. I know it's only the start of whatever comes next for both of them, but it is a start and I'm inordinately proud of Esme. For her understanding, her maturity and her compassion.

I'm so busy thinking about Esme, however, that as Sam steps towards me, I realise I'm as equally unprepared for meeting him as she is. The slow smile that I loved so much spreads over his face until it reaches his eyes, setting alight the gold flecks within them. He moves to kiss me but then, just at the last moment, he turns his cheek so that it rests against mine and it's somehow far more intimate a gesture. I can feel his warm breath on my ear, the slight scratch from his stubble and the arm not holding his stick sliding around my waist, his fingers spread wide.

'Thank you,' he whispers, and I feel the soft pressure from his lips, only a split second but the imprint of them burns into my skin. And the thought of him sheer takes my breath away.

It feels as if everyone will have noticed what just happened – the intensity of emotion, rising around us like smoke – but, as I pull away, I realise of course that no one has. No one except Sam and me.

'Alys?' The sound of my name startles me and I look up to see the woman who arrived with Sam now standing by Nancy's side. 'Can I introduce you to someone very special,' she says. 'This is Ruth.'

It seems the most natural thing in the world to hug her too and as we move apart I can see that she's perfectly relaxed. She's been a part of this family for a while, I realise.

'It's so lovely to finally meet you, Alys,' she says. 'I've heard so much about you that it seems a little unfair we haven't met until now. But I've been away for several weeks and it just wasn't possible.' She grins at Nancy. 'Are you ever going to stop telling people that we met because you couldn't find the loo? I never quite know how to introduce myself!'

Nancy beams at me. 'Ruth's an estate agent,' she says, giving me a meaningful look.

'Of course…' I reply, laughing, suddenly understanding how Nancy had managed to obtain the keys for the cottages we viewed. 'That makes perfect sense.'

'Although she's also a valuer and auctioneer, so you two are going to get along like a house on fire. She loves anything with a bit of history to it as well.'

'Which might explain why she fell for Nancy in the first place,' adds Sam, grinning.

And I look at him, laughing and embracing his wife's new relationship, fully and without any ill-feeling or bitterness. It makes me see just how wonderful a man he really is. The difference between him and Hugh stands out in stark relief, and I know there's no way that Hugh would be here supporting me in this way if the shoe were on the other foot. It's an incredibly sad thought. Not for me, but for Hugh, who always wanted to be the best, who thought he could be the best, but who, in the end, just couldn't quite find it within himself. I really hope that one day he does.

'Come on,' says Nancy. 'Let's go and get something to eat. I'm dying to see what the catering is like here.' She winks. 'I've heard it's quite good.'

Lunch isn't a drawn-out affair. The delegates are on a schedule, and so after only half an hour or so people are beginning to move, heading for the next part of their conference. I can't help but wonder how many of them, if any, have noticed how momentous today has been. It feels as if there should be fireworks exploding, or dramatic music playing at the very least. But who knows, maybe I won't be the only one who looks back on this unremarkable Saturday in the middle of August and remembers it as the day when their life changed.

Theo and Esme will head back to the restaurant soon; their working day is just beginning, and for Nancy too, I guess. As for Sam, I have no idea what he'll be doing next, or where he'll be going, and I know I have no right to ask.

The room has almost emptied and I can see that the staff are anxious to get the lunch things cleared away. I get to my feet, saying my goodbyes and fishing in my handbag for my car keys. I'm almost at the door when I feel a touch on my arm. I turn to find Nancy and Ruth behind me.

'Thank you for coming today, Alys,' says Nancy. 'And for this absolutely amazing suit. It's been just perfect.'

I look over her shoulder to where Theo and Esme are standing, getting back into work mode, ready for the afternoon and evening ahead. With them is Sam, chatting easily, all three of them laughing and smiling.

'I wouldn't have missed it for the world,' I say. 'And you're right. It has been perfect.' I give both her and Ruth an impulsive hug. 'And it's been so lovely meeting you too,' I add, meaning every word. If Nancy has anything to do with it, I know I've just found another friend.

Nancy looks at me then. 'What are you going to do?' she asks.

I take in a deep breath. 'Well, I have a massive pile of ironing, the bathroom to clean and tea to make.'

'That wasn't what I meant,' she chastises gently.

'No, I know… And for the moment I'm not sure what I'm going to do, but the future is mine to make. There are going to be some hard things to face, some tough decisions to be made, but I also have hope that things will turn out the right way. One day at a time, that's all I can do.'

Nancy looks at me, a soft smile on her face. 'You have to be yourself, Alys,' she says. 'It's the place where everything starts, and if you're lucky where everything ends too.' And then she turns back toward Ruth. 'Live your life, Alys. Be extraordinary.'

# CHAPTER TWENTY-FIVE

Hugh never did ask me about Nancy's talk. When he'd got home from work that evening, I'd politely enquired if he'd had a good day, and he'd answered my question briefly and that was all. Throughout the whole of that evening and the next day, he'd steadfastly refused to talk about anything which made mention of Nancy's name, or Sam's for that matter. It was as if they didn't even exist. He'd spoken briefly to Esme before she'd left for work on Sunday but the rest of the time he'd appeared just as he always had, albeit slightly quieter than usual. The only indication that anything untoward had happened was his slight hesitation as he replied to any question asked of him. It was the only thing that allowed me to see he was thinking about recent events at all.

And now I'm only twenty minutes' drive away from my first day at the conservation centre and I don't know how I feel. My phone flashed with a message from Tash this morning. *You go, girl*, is all it said, and it made me smile; it's exactly the sort of thing Tash would say. But she's right, I have to make the very best of this opportunity. And, in fact, despite my nerves and trepidation over what the day will hold, I'm actually relieved that I will have something else to occupy my thoughts for a while. Something that isn't Sam.

I can't get over the enormous sense of relief I felt on finding out that Ruth was, in fact, Nancy's partner and not Sam's, and Nancy's final words to me had reverberated around my head the entire weekend. *Live your life*, she had said… and of course what she'd meant was that I should live mine and no one else's. And it made me wonder just whose I had been living all these years. It's become the question I'm finding the hardest to answer – if I'd have known then what I know now, how would my life have turned out? Would it even be any different?

Because the simple fact of the matter is that Sam did send me away, for whatever reason, and however much I loved him, he made that decision, taking away my choice with it. And the person I became as a result, the one I've been desperate to change these past few weeks… I've been blaming Hugh for that, but how much of it was actually down to Sam?

I glance in the rear-view mirror as I drive, catching sight of myself as I do so. It's time to own up, Alys. Time to admit that the only person who has ever been responsible for the person I became is me. And if I want to live my life, and be extraordinary in the only way I know how, then the future is down to me.

It's a thought that occupies me for the rest of my journey, into the car park, out of my car and right up to the studio. It's only when I raise my hand to knock on the door that I think about what I'm actually here to do and feel a moment's terror at what lies ahead. But it's fleeting; Becky's smiling face seconds later convinces me everything is going to be okay, that and the warm and welcoming smell I remember from so long ago. It's wool and fabric, a slight mustiness of age, but it's a reminder of how I used to feel walking into the studio at uni: that I was home, and safe.

I'm surprised when, what seems like only a short while later, Lucy tentatively suggests that I might like to have a break and go for some lunch. I've been sitting with her for the past hour, quietly watching her infinite patience and skill as she continues working on the carpet I saw weeks ago at their open day. Both she and Becky have talked me through the aims and scope of their latest restoration project as well as showing me another much smaller project they are working on in tandem. It's a wall hanging that will require careful cleaning and a few patch repairs, and it's on this that I will begin to practise the procedures that once came so naturally to me.

The morning has flown but I'm tired as I walk back out to my car. I'm not used to concentrating for such a long period of time and it's been years since I've had to take in so much new information. Even being a volunteer requires paperwork, it seems, and a full introduction to health and safety policies and procedures but, most importantly, we've discussed my hours and I'm now committed to three full days a week here. Becky's desperation for some help was immediately evident and any thoughts I had of easing myself in gently soon flew out of the window.

The summer is making a valiant effort to linger for a few last weeks and, collecting my handbag from the boot of my car, I fully intend to sit in the sun to make the most of it as I eat my lunch. I can now get a small discount from the National Trust tea room next door and, although I won't usually be able to afford to eat here, on this, the first day of a new adventure, a treat seems perfectly reasonable.

The car door slamming behind me doesn't even register until I become aware of steps approaching in my direction, crunching on the gravel underfoot. And I can see his reflection in the side window as I relock the car. I must admit he's the last person I expected to see.

'Hugh,' I say, turning round quickly. 'Is everything all right?' I glance at my watch – Esme would have already gone to work by this time and it's Hugh's day off.

He frowns gently. 'I didn't know I couldn't get into this place,' he says. 'I've been sitting in the car for the last hour.'

I turn back to look at the door to the studio. 'No, it's not open to the public… Sorry.' There's a sign that states this very clearly, advising visitors to telephone the head conservationist for an appointment. 'But I didn't know you were coming.'

Hugh still looks a little put out but he brightens his expression as I search his face for any sign as to why he's here. 'No, I… Perhaps I should have let you know.' He pauses. 'Although I didn't actually know I *was* coming… not this morning anyway. I just thought I ought to come and see where you were, and how you were doing, that kind of thing. Not because I'm keeping tabs on you,' he adds quickly. 'Just because I thought I should take an interest in what you're doing.' He looks around him. 'Alys, is there somewhere we can go to talk? Just for a few minutes.'

It's strange enough seeing Hugh here, let alone hearing that he wants to talk to me, but I nod, motioning forward. 'I was just about to go to the tea room for some lunch,' I reply. 'It's next door.'

He nods, all at once looking a little anxious. His lips are moving slightly as if he's rehearsing what he wants to say. 'Have you had a good morning?' he asks.

'I have. I was terrified I wouldn't know anything, but it's surprising how much I do remember.'

Hugh regards me for a moment. 'You should have done this years ago, shouldn't you?'

Now we've moved out of the shady car park and into the sun I can see his forehead is glistening with tiny beads of sweat. 'Possibly,' I say cautiously. 'But everything has its time, Hugh; maybe this is simply the right time for me.'

He looks down at his hands. 'And have we had ours, Alys?'

I stop dead, feet crunching on the small stones beneath them. I never thought I'd hear Hugh say something like this. It's always been me who started difficult conversations.

'Let's go and get a coffee,' I say evenly. 'We can talk properly then.' It's not a question I'm prepared to answer standing here. But this is so unlike Hugh I'm wondering if something has happened to make him behave this way.

I lead him along the path to the small stone and flint building that houses the tea room. It's busy – there's a steady hum of conversation inside and the clinking of cutlery and plates – but most folks seem to be already seated and the queue is small. In no time we're on our way back outside with a cup of coffee each and a large Chelsea bun for me. I'm feeling the need for a sweet treat more than ever.

Minutes later we're sitting on a bench tucked in the corner of the tea-room garden. The sun is warm, bouncing off the brick behind us, and bees buzz the planters of flowers surrounding the building. It's a lovely setting but more importantly it's quiet, and there's less chance we'll be overheard. It would be lovely to just sit and soak up the atmosphere but Hugh's question is looming larger by the minute and I'm desperately trying to think of a way to answer him when he expels a long sigh.

'I did a terrible thing,' he says. 'I ruined a life… two lives, three possibly…' He hangs his head and, despite the possible truth in what he's saying, my heart goes out to him. Facing the truth is never easy.

I let his words sit between us as I peel off a layer of the Chelsea bun from the outside and offer it to him. He shakes his head, so I take a bite, chewing as I think how to reply.

'You said some terrible things,' I say. 'But whether you ruined a life… that's a different matter. No one can prove that you directly caused Sam's accident, although I suspect that driving home in the frame of mind he must have been in… well, I don't need to spell it out.' I look across at him, holding his gaze. 'Maybe it's enough that you think you did.'

His jaw clenches. 'It is… Alys, believe me, it is.'

I soften my expression. '*But*, you also did a very good thing. You took me in when I had nothing. And when we found out I was pregnant, you accepted it. You loved Esme as if she were your own, and you've raised her and looked after her ever since. And I'm not stupid, Hugh. You were young, madly jealous of my relationship with Sam, and love built on that basis isn't necessarily real love, but I think you've proved over the years that it was, especially with Esme. I know how much you love her, Hugh, just as I know you love me.'

He nods fervently, but he's not going to ask me whether I love him. 'Do you love Sam?' he asks instead.

'I love the Sam I knew back then,' I reply, licking my lips to get the sugar from them. 'Nothing will ever take that away. But I don't know him now. Time changes us all, and if I got to know him better, who knows… I might not even like him.'

I pause, trying to work out how to say what I need to. Things have gone too far to be anything less than honest. No more secrets. No more lies. 'But I'd be lying if I didn't say I was in love with the idea of us, Hugh. And I'm sorry, but what that means for you and me… I don't know.'

I sigh. 'I never imagined that Sam would ever come back into my life. I dreamed about it, in that over-romanticised way where everything is perfect, but I do also know that real life isn't like that. The trouble is that now he *is* back in my life I can't just ignore that fact either. And what I'm having most trouble deciding is whether what I'm feeling is real or just my fantasy. Does that make sense?'

Hugh nods sadly. 'Thank you,' he says. 'That was honest at least.'

'I don't think we can afford to be anything less, do you?' But it's a rhetorical question. Hugh has finally worked this out. 'What made you come here today?' I ask. 'Now, I mean, when you could have waited until I got home.'

He pulls a face, sheepish and apologetic at the same time. 'It was something Esme said,' he admits. 'And I thought that if I didn't come and say something now, I probably never would. By the time you get home this evening I'd have talked myself out of it, I'm very good at that… as well you know.'

He holds out his hand and I automatically pass him a piece of my bun. It's such a familiar routine that the poignancy of it hits me head on. The weight of all that's at stake here.

He chews thoughtfully. 'But Esme was right,' he continues after a moment. 'We had a bit of a… chat, before she went to work. And she told me how she would always think of me as her dad, no matter what happens between her and Sam.' He nods several times in succession. 'Which, yes, is exactly what you said, I know, but hearing it from her, it made a difference. She told me I needed to trust her, to have faith in her, just like you did. And what happened is that I stopped seeing her as my little girl and instead as the person she's grown up to be: strong, independent and incredibly wise.'

He looks across at me and I smile back. I can picture the exact expression on Esme's face as she imparted her wisdom.

'She made me realise something, Alys. Something I'm rather ashamed to admit. Because you see I don't think I've ever had faith in anyone, not really. I denied it when you accused me of it, but you were absolutely right. I've never even believed in myself and I think that's where it all began to go wrong. Sam was a much better person than I could ever be. At least that's what I thought. And whether that was true or not, I never bothered to find out, least of all try to improve myself. So instead I got the stupid idea in my head that if I couldn't be as good as Sam, then perhaps if he weren't there at all, things would finally begin to go my way. So I made it happen. And I saved you, and I saved Esme. Me, not Sam, but me, and all that gratitude felt good. I'd finally done something I could be proud of. I mean, I must have, you kept telling me that.' He lowers his head.

'But I made sure that you were eternally grateful, Alys. By having no control over your life, everything you had was because I had given it to you, what else were you to be, but grateful? And I'm ashamed to say I liked it that way. That's why I behaved the way I did when you suddenly started to make your own decisions, be your own person again. It was like you'd cut off my air supply, that constant flow of gratitude I'd had for so many years dwindling away when you realised that you no longer needed to… what was it you said? To pass everything through my filter. Pathetic, isn't it?'

'Hugh, it wasn't as bad as that, I…' But I trail off, because I know that he's right. In essence, that's exactly what had happened.

He picks up his coffee cup from where he'd placed it on the ground and takes a long drink, before lowering it to his lap, still looking straight ahead. 'What's going to happen to us?' he asks.

'I don't know,' I answer truthfully. 'There are so many things we need to deal with. I need to learn to trust you again, to forgive you. And I need to make sure that Esme is okay. Her relationship with Sam will develop, I'm sure of that, and it's going to mean that he may be around a bit more, and you're going to have to deal with that and support her just as much as I am. So I don't know how this ends, Hugh, I really don't. But I'm learning who I am now, and what I need to be happy. And now you need to do the same, wherever it might lead you. There's no magic solution and no crystal ball either, but we can try, all of us, that's all we can do. Facing the truth is never easy. But living a lie is worse.'

Hugh's eyes are on me as I say my final words and I can see that he accepts what I'm saying. It isn't just me that's been living a lie.

'I should really get back,' I say, draining the rest of my coffee.

'Yes, yes, of course,' says Hugh, getting to his feet. He holds out his hand for my mug. 'Can't have you being late, not on your first day.'

I take a step forward. 'Thank you for coming though, Hugh…' I trail off, not really knowing what else to say. This awkwardness with one another, not knowing quite how to behave, it isn't something we've had to navigate before. 'And we can talk some more if you like, when I get home.'

Hugh nods and I can see from his face that, although it's probably the last things he wants to do, he will. This time he will.

'I wondered whether… well, seeing as you will have been out all day, and you'll be tired, whether you might like to go out somewhere – for dinner, I mean? Not anywhere extravagant, but just, you know…'

I smile. 'Yes… I think I'd like that.' I motion to the cups in his hands. 'Would you mind taking those back inside?' I ask, quickly glancing at my watch. I don't know what to do, what to say, how to part. Will he expect me to kiss him?

I point towards the studio, taking a couple of steps. 'I should…'

'Yes,' he says, but he makes no move towards me, simply stands, smiling, the mugs held in front of him.

A slight breeze ruffles my hair as I turn away, blowing a curly tendril over my shoulder. The sunlight makes it dance, threads of the brightest copper.

I turn back.

'Bye, Hugh.'

# CHAPTER TWENTY-SIX

*Five months later*

I'm beginning to think that Nancy must have got it wrong, but she was adamant that all I had to do was wait. Except that, even with my thickest coat on, it's perishing. It's January now and a vicious wind is blowing across the exposed harbour wall. I've been here half an hour already and my spirits have plummeted as low as the temperature. I glance at my watch again, not wanting to give up but realising with every passing moment how foolish this is. I should never have come.

I wind my scarf even tighter around my neck and stare back out to sea. It might be beautiful in the summer, bright blue with scudding clouds chased by the breeze, the horizon hazy in the distance, but today it's grey and forbidding. I get to my feet, the backs of my legs frozen from the hard stone ledge on which I've been sitting, and walk slowly to the end of the harbour wall. The very tip of it is surrounded by a railing, the other side of which is a sharp drop to the sea below, and only metres away the other arm of the wall curves its way around the bay, keeping safe all that lies within it. A huge pile of wooden posts has been stacked here, their ends capped with metal turned orange with rust. I've gone only a few steps beyond them, however, when I see what I've missed all along. Hidden from view is a lone figure sitting on the end of the lowermost planks. My nerves, which have kept a low-level fluttering in my stomach all morning, suddenly roar into life and your name barely makes it out of my throat.

'Sam?'

You're writing something, thick fingerless gloves hampering the progress of your pen across the page of the notebook you're balancing on your lap. You look up and it's just like I've pictured for all these weeks; a slow smile lighting up your face, turning your eyes to liquid gold.

'Hello, Alys.' You say it as if you've been expecting me and my throat tightens even further.

All my carefully rehearsed lines fly out of my head and I stand there feeling foolish, and very conscious that my nose must be bright red from the cold.

'Nancy said I'd find you here,' I say. 'She said that you walk this way every day.'

'Did she now?' he replies, an amused expression on his face. 'Well, she's right, it's my morning exercise routine. I haul my arse up here and then eat a croissant and drink a coffee through chattering teeth while filling my head with the metaphysical.' He smiles again, lifting his notebook slightly. 'Some of it even makes it down on paper.'

'You always said you would write one day.'

He gives me a quizzical look. 'I did, didn't I? Well, I figured now was a good time to do so.' He pauses for a moment. 'My reward for making it this far through life.'

I nod. 'Aren't you cold?'

Sam pops his pen in a pocket before closing his notebook and hoisting himself to his feet. 'Mind over matter,' he replies. 'As with a lot of things. But you look freezing.' He indicates the harbour. 'Let's walk,' he adds. 'And you can tell me how you come to be standing on a quayside at the farthest tip of the country. When did you even get here?'

'I drove down yesterday. I'm staying in an Airbnb place tucked off the road by the harbour. Just room for me and the cat… You know, the proverbial one.'

A warm smile settles over his face. 'Ah yes, the one you swing, of course…' He stops a moment to adjust the grip on his stick. 'And you drove all the way down here? In the middle of January, when nothing is open and the weather is just desperate.'

He's wondering why I'm here but I'm not quite ready to answer that question yet. 'Have you spoken to Nancy?' I ask instead.

He makes a show of thinking. 'A few days ago, why? Should I have?'

I shake my head. 'No, it's just that… she mentioned you were thinking of retiring, selling your share of the business and settling down?'

His eyes are on my face now, searching for clues. 'Did she now?' He starts to walk again, his rolling gait pulling him away from me and then back like a boat bobbing on the tide. 'Put like that it makes me feel rather old, but I've talked about it recently, yes. In fact, I've been doing quite a lot of thinking just lately. And this little corner of the country has always been a good place to think. I'm not as involved in The Green Room as I once was, but it still demands a lot of my time and energy and, while I used to think it was that which kept me going, now I'm not so sure.'

'Oh?'

'Well for starters I'm finding the travelling something of a strain so it would make sense for me to stay in one location. But that's not London, I don't want to live there any more. Plus, I have other things I'd like to do with my life, things which are a lot less stressful than running a business.'

He pulls a face. 'I'm not getting any younger, Alys, none of us are, but this old body of mine's a bit battered and if I don't start taking better care of it, I'm not sure how long it's going to last me. The way I'm living – long drives, hours sat in front of a computer, rubbish food because I haven't got the time or energy to cook properly – none of this is helping, so something has got to give. And I think the business may well be it.'

'I see,' I say softly, trying to ignore the way my heart is sinking. 'Well, that makes sense. And the sea air must be good here, I would imagine. Plenty of places to walk too.'

Sam doesn't reply, just smiles, and we take a few more steps before he suddenly stops. 'Where did you say you were staying?' he asks.

'I didn't exactly. But it's called Sailway, on Fore Street. Do you know it?'

He nods and then grins. 'I should do. I live two doors down… White Cottage. It's, um… white, would you believe?'

I roll my eyes. 'I walked past it this morning on my way down here. If I'd have known you were there I wouldn't have bothered freezing my butt off.'

'Yes, I'm surprised Nancy didn't mention it.'

'Hmm, so am I,' I say darkly, knowing full well why Nancy had suggested I meet Sam on the quayside. But when she dreamed up her foolproof romantic reunion she didn't factor in the near minus temperatures.

'How about I make you a hot chocolate?' he says. 'In return for your commitment.'

'One of your special ones?'

Sam gives me a peculiar look. 'Is there any other kind?' he says.

We carry on down the quayside, pausing a moment to let a young boy and his father pass by. The lad has tight hold of a kite and Sam raises a hand in greeting.

'Morning, William,' he says, smiling. 'Make sure you hold on tight to that today, there's a fair wind blowing.' The boy smiles shyly in return but he nods and I'm reminded that this is where Sam has made his home, where he *is* at home.

Minutes later we're at his front door and I hold his notebook while he fiddles with his gloves and keys. Eventually the door swings open and a wave of the most delicious heat rolls out.

'Oh…' We've walked straight into the living room where a log burner is dancing with flame.

'Nice, isn't it?' He indicates one of two squishy pale-blue sofas. 'Park yourself there and I'll get some milk on.'

I do as I'm told. The heat is wonderful but it isn't what made me start as I entered the room. The room is almost identical to the tiny cottage I shared with Sam when we first got married. Except we didn't have a log burner, it was an open fire, with a cast-iron grate that drew beautifully. It was one of the reasons we bought the cottage in the first place. And I can remember it as if it were yesterday.

I close my eyes and lean back against the cushions. I should never have come. This isn't my house, it's Sam's. The place he's made his home, his life, and one which is over four hundred miles away from mine. I was silly to think that there was even the remotest possibility… I thrust the thought from my head as Sam reappears in the doorway.

'Have a look at this while you're waiting,' he says. 'And let me know what you think.'

He hands me the piece of paper he's holding. It's from an estate agent. The same agency that Ruth owns. I stare at the sheet in my hands, at the warm red-brick cottage with traditional flint panels.

'The village is pronounced Stew-key,' comes the voice from the kitchen. 'Not Stiff-key as you might expect.'

I can't help but smile. 'What is it with you and places that aren't pronounced the way they're spelled?'

Sam's face reappears around the doorway. 'Oh yeah… I hadn't thought of that. What do you think anyway?'

I scan the details, flipping the sheet and studying the full-colour photos. 'Beautiful…' It's stunning actually; a three-bedroom detached cottage with a landscaped garden on three sides and oozing charm. But I don't really want to say any more because I'm not yet sure what I'm holding in my hands. So instead I lay it on the coffee table in front of me and unwind my scarf, taking off my coat and draping both over the back of the sofa. And then I sit, staring at the flames in the log burner until Sam reappears carrying a mug.

'Are you not having one?' I ask.

He puts the mug down on the table, a gentle smile creasing his face, and I wince at his back as he retreats. Of course he's having a drink, except that he can't carry two while his other hand is holding his stick.

'Sorry, Sam,' I say just as soon as he reappears. 'I wasn't thinking… I'm not…'

But he holds up his hand. 'No apologies,' he says. 'I know you're not used to this.' And his eyes lock on mine. 'Yet.'

He takes a seat beside me, not close, but enough to set the air vibrating between us. 'So… the cottage in Stiffkey, do you like it?'

'It would be hard not to,' I reply. There's another question I need to ask but I'm afraid to, the answer might not be one I want to hear. But then again, there's a reason I drove for seven hours to get here. 'What's it for? A holiday home?'

'No, not really,' he replies, leaning forward to pick up the details. 'But I'm glad you like it because I had an offer accepted on it yesterday. And it's only an hour away from Norwich. Half an hour from Blickling Hall.'

I swallow. 'Is it?'

Sam grins. 'Yes, it is…'

It's beginning to feel very warm in here.

'But I thought… when Nancy said you were looking to retire and settle down, I thought she meant, well I…'

'You thought she meant here, in Mousehole?' He shakes his head in amusement. 'I love it here, but it's not somewhere I could retire to – too many bloody hills for starters, the old legs would never cope.' He places the paper back down. 'But this, this is somewhere I can settle. For all sorts of reasons, not least of all because curiously I'm finding myself drawn to the wide open spaces of Norfolk…' He grins. 'But it's a good job you came when you did. One day later and we would have missed one another.'

I catch the look in his eye. 'That's beginning to be something of a habit.'

'Isn't it?' he replies. 'Makes you wonder…'

I can feel a warm glow blooming on my cheeks. 'It does…' I trail off, giving him a curious look. 'Although, where were you off to this time?

'Norfolk,' he replies. 'I have a few things to do. People to see…'

'Oh…'

He smiles. 'So now are you going to tell me why you drove for seven hours just to be here? And before you answer that, Alys, can I just say that if it wasn't to see me I shall be deeply disappointed.' Sam drops his head, suddenly fascinated by something on the floor. And I realise that this is as hard on him as it is on me.

I'm just wondering what to say when he suddenly looks up again. 'I know about Hugh,' he says.

And I realise I already have my answer. 'Well then you do know why I'm here,' I reply. It's been two months now since Hugh and I split up. 'There's a very long story, but the short version is that, in the end, things between us just didn't work out. We tried, and I almost thought we might make it, but with Esme finally beginning to live the life she wanted, the ties that bound Hugh and I together just weren't there any more. And in the end we found we had nothing much in common. In fact, all we did have were the differences between us. It was Hugh who suggested we part, actually.'

I smile wistfully. 'He said that for once in his life he was going to do the decent thing. In fact, what he said, very eloquently for him, was that I wasn't a glass treasure he could keep locked inside a box. And that by doing so all these years, he'd never seen the best of me either. He'd never seen me shine.'

I'd expected Sam to smile, or laugh, passing off Hugh's comment with a caustic remark, but he doesn't. Instead he purses his lips together and I instinctively know what he's thinking.

'I know what he did, Sam,' I add. 'I know what he said to you. You mustn't blame yourself for what happened.'

There is the ghost of a smile. 'He told me I wasn't good enough for you,' he replies, a slight tremor in his voice. 'And when it came down to it, he was right, wasn't he? I never fought for you, Alys. And I should have. What your life became, all of it, that was down to me, I—'

'No! You had enough of a battle on your hands, Sam. You didn't need another one. And no one is to blame for the way my life turned out – not you and not Hugh either. I have to take responsibility for my own decisions too. If *I* couldn't stand up for who I am, then I certainly shouldn't have expected other people to.' I pause. 'And I had Esme too, don't forget… It wasn't all bad.'

There's a softness to Sam's face as he turns to look at me, the light from the fire giving his face a golden glow. 'We have Esme,' he replies, almost a whisper. Or a wish…

I reach out my hand. 'We do,' I say. 'We always will.'

Sam glances down at the piece of paper still on the coffee table. 'I heard about your job too,' he adds, clearing his throat. 'Congratulations.'

I nod. 'Thank you. I start on the first of February, although in truth there won't really be any change to what I'm doing now. Except that I'll get paid of course. That always helps.'

He nods, weighing up this new information. 'But what will you do? About the house?'

'We'll sell it,' I reply. 'It's the obvious thing to do. A new start for both of us.'

'I'm sorry,' says Sam.

'Don't be. It isn't the house that will make me happy. It's not about material things, is it? It never has been.'

'No,' says Sam, quietly. He stares into the fire and, as I watch, a small smile turns the corners of his mouth. 'I was just thinking,' he continues, knowing that I'm looking at him. 'About the little boy with the kite, about what Hugh said.'

I give him a puzzled look.

'Do you know that William goes down to the quay nearly every day, whether the wind is blowing or not. He takes his kite and if he's lucky he'll get to play out its string and watch it fly. It doesn't always happen of course, but he simply waits for when it does, and then… then you should see his face, Alys. It's full of wonder, of admiration, of awe… from something as simple as watching a kite fly. And that's how I always felt when I was with you. Oh, the joy I got in watching you fly. But all the while I knew that there was still this thread between us, almost invisible at times, and that when the wind wasn't full, or its energy was spent, I would be the one you would return to… always.'

I stare at him, at the face that looks so very different from the one I first knew, but underneath it all, the same man I fell in love with. So different from Hugh who only ever wanted to keep me locked within a box so that he, and only he, could be the one to take me out, to give me my freedom. Whereas Sam, Sam wanted me to go wherever the wind took me, wherever my ribbons shone brightest and fluttered the hardest, and all he ever asked of me was that he could be there to watch me as I did so.

I inch my fingers along the settee until they're just brushing his. 'Do you know one of the most wonderful things about Norfolk is that it has these big wide open skies… it's perfect for flying kites.'

# A LETTER FROM EMMA

Hello, and thank you so much for choosing to read *The Wife's Choice*. I hope you enjoyed reading this story as much as I enjoyed writing it. If you'd like to stay updated on what's coming next, please do sign up to my newsletter here and you'll be the first to know!

*www.bookouture.com/emma-davies*

At Bookouture, writers fall into two broad groups (names invented by ourselves I should add) – those who write for The Dark Side and those who sit on The Sparkly Step. Since joining Bookouture, I've always been a firm Sparkly, but my previous novel, *My Husband's Lie*, saw a return to perhaps a much earlier style of writing for me, but one which took me very firmly off The Sparkly Step. I've always touched upon the darker side of life in all my books, but with *The Wife's Choice* I've again really explored the emotional dilemmas which we all face from time to time. It's not The Dark Side however, I hope you agree, and only a teeny bit Sparkly so I think I've landed somewhere in the middle with this one. I've really enjoyed being here, however, so I think I might stay for a while...

Of course none of this would have happened without the support of my wonderful editor, Jessie Botterill, who has been so encouraging and supportive of this slightly different style. Huge thanks to her and everyone at Bookouture for making this possible, but also to you, lovely readers, for choosing to read my books. You really do make everything worthwhile.

Having folks take the time to get in touch really does make my day, and if you'd like to contact me then I'd love to hear from you. The easiest way to do this is by finding me on Twitter and Facebook, or you could also pop by my website where you can read about my love of Pringles among other things...

I hope to see you again very soon and, in the meantime, if you've enjoyed reading *The Wife's Choice*, I would really appreciate a few minutes of your time to leave a review or post on social media. Every single review makes a massive difference and is very much appreciated!

Until next time,
Love, Emma xx

 @EmDaviesAuthor

 emmadaviesauthor

 www.emmadaviesauthor.com

Printed in Great Britain
by Amazon